The Three Midshipmen

by

W.H.G. Kingston

Double 9
BOOKS

The Three Midshipmen
by W.H.G. Kingston

Copyright © 2024

All Rights reserved.

ISBN: 978-93-64285-18-6

Published by

DOUBLE 9 BOOKS

2/13-B, Ansari Road
Daryaganj, New Delhi – 110002
info@double9books.com
www.double9books.com
Tel. 011-40042856

This book is under public domain

ABOUT THE AUTHOR

William Henry Giles Kingston (1814-1880) was an influential English writer, best known for his adventure novels targeted at young readers. His works, particularly those with nautical themes, have captivated audiences with tales of heroism, exploration, and moral integrity. Debut: Kingston's literary journey began with the publication of "The Circassian Chief" in 1844. Genre: He specialized in seafaring adventure stories that were highly popular in the Victorian era. Output: Prolific in his writing, Kingston authored over 130 books, many focusing on nautical adventures and aimed at young readers. "Peter the Whaler" (1851): One of Kingston's early successes, detailing the adventures of a young whaler.

"The Three Midshipmen" (1873): Part of a series chronicling the exploits of British naval officers.

"The Three Admirals" (1891): Continuation of the naval adventure series, showcasing themes of bravery and exploration. Impact on Children's Literature: Kingston's adventure stories have had a lasting impact on children's literature, particularly in the adventure genre. Kingston's contributions to literature have made him a celebrated author, particularly known for his ability to inspire and entertain with stories of exploration and heroism. His works remain a testament to the adventurous spirit of the 19th century and continue to be enjoyed by readers around the world. Enduring Popularity: His tales of the high seas and distant lands continue to be appreciated for their timeless appeal and adventurous spirit. Kingston's contributions to literature have made him a celebrated author, particularly known for his ability to inspire and entertain with stories of exploration and heroism. His works remain a testament to the adventurous spirit of the 19th century and continue to be enjoyed by readers around the world.

CONTENTS

Chapter One
Early Days

Ours was a capital school, though it was not a public one. It was not far from London, so that a coach could carry us down there in little more than an hour from the *White Horse Cellar*, Piccadilly. On the top of the posts, at each side of the gates, were two eagles; fine large birds I thought them. They looked out on a green, fringed with tall elms, beyond which was our cricket-field. A very magnificent red-brick old house rose behind the eagles, full of windows belonging to our sleeping-rooms. The playground was at the back of the house, with a grand old tulip tree in the centre, a tectum for rainy weather on one side, and the large school room on the other. Beyond was a good-sized garden, full of apple and pear trees, but, as we very seldom went into it, I do not remember its appearance. Perhaps, were I to see the place again, I might find its dimensions somewhat altered. The master was a first-rate schoolmaster. What his attainments were, I cannot say; but he understood managing boys admirably. He kept us all in very good order, had us fairly taught, fed us with wholesome, if not luxurious, food, and, though he used his cane freely, treated us justly. We held him in awe, and yet we liked him.

It was after the summer holidays, when I had just got back, I heard that three new boys had come. In the afternoon they all appeared in the playground. They were strangers to each other as well as to us, but their similarity of fate drew them together. One was a slightly made, dark, and somewhat delicate-looking boy; another was a sturdy little fellow, with a round, ruddy countenance, and a jovial, good-natured expression in it, yet he did not look as if he would stand any nonsense; the third was rather smaller than the other two, a pleasant-looking fellow, and though his eyes were red with crying, he seemed to be cutting some joke which made his companions laugh. He had come all the way from Ireland, we heard, and his elder brother had that morning left him and gone back home, and that made him unhappy just then. He at once got the name of Paddy in the school. He did not mind it. His real name was Terence Adair, so sometimes he was called Paddy Adair.

"I say, you fellow, what's your name?" asked a biggish boy of the stoutest of the three new-comers.

"Jack Rogers," was the answer, given in a quiet tone.

"I don't believe it," replied the big boy, who was known as Bully Pigeon; "it's such a rum name."

"I'll make you believe it, and remember it too," exclaimed the new-comer, eyeing the other from head to foot, and walking firmly up to him, with his lips closed, while he moved his head slowly from side to side. "I tell you my name is Jack Rogers—Now!"

The bully did not say a word. He looked as if he would have liked to have hit, but Paddy Adair had followed his new friend, and was evidently about to join in the fray if it was once begun; so the big boy thought better of it. He would gain no credit for attacking a little fellow the first day of his coming. There were many witnesses of the scene, and Jack was unanimously pronounced to be a plucky littlE chap. Pigeon, defeated in one direction, turned his attention to the first-named boy, who had scarcely moved since he entered the playground, but kept looking round with his large black eyes on the scene before him, which was evidently strange to his sight.

"What are you called, I should like to know?" he asked in a rude tone.

"Alick Murray," was the answer, in a quiet, gentlemanly voice.

"Then you come from Scotland, I suppose?" said the bully.

"Yes, I do," replied the former.

"Oh! I wonder your mamma would let you go away from her," observed the big boy, with a sneer.

"My mamma is just dead," answered Murray, in a mild tone, a tear springing to his eye.

"Shame! shame!" shouted the voices of several boys who had come up; among them that of Jack Rogers was the loudest.

"I didn't mean to say anything to hurt him," said the bully, sneaking away. "I'll pay you off for this some day," he muttered as he passed Jack.

Jack looked after him and laughed.

"He'll have two to fight if he tries it, mind that," said Adair to his new friend.

Jack thanked him, but said that he should soon be able to tackle him, if he could not just now. He would try at all events.

"That's it," cried Terence enthusiastically. "That's just what I like. If you are knocked down you can but get up again and try once more."

"So my papa says," observed Jack. "He's a first-rate father, let me tell you. He never would let any of us give in except to himself. He used to throw us into a pond, and tell us to swim, and unless we had actually been drowning, nothing would have made him help us; so we all very soon learned, and now there isn't a chap of my size I wouldn't swim against. We live down in Northamptonshire. My papa has a place there. We are all very jolly. There are a number of us, sisters and brothers. You must come down and see them some holidays. You'll like them, I know. There's no nonsense about them."

Terence said he should like it very much, if he did not go back to Ireland. He had three brothers and a sister, but they were all older than himself. His papa was the Honourable Mr Adair, and he had an uncle, Lord Derrynane. He did not know whether they were rich or not. They lived in a big house, and had a number of servants, and people were constantly coming and going; so he supposed they were. The truth was, as I heard afterwards, they were living a great deal too fast, and Terence had nothing left as his share of his father's property, except, as he said, his debts. That, however, was no fault of his.

"I say," observed Jack, "don't let us leave that poor fellow alone any longer. He seems very low-spirited about his mother. It's natural, you know; though I don't like to see a fellow blubbering just because he has hurt himself, or lost a peg-top, or anything of that sort."

So they went up to Alick Murray, and began talking to him, and Terence said something funny and made him laugh.

"I wonder what games they have here?" asked Jack.

"Coach-and-horses," said a biggish fellow, who had just entered the playground with some long strips of leather over his arm and a whip in his hand. "Now, if you three fellows will just be harnessed, you'll make a very good unicorn."

They all looked at each other, and as the big boy spoke in a good-natured tone, they agreed to do as he wished. Jack and Alick were harnessed together; Terence insisted on going as unicorn.

"I say, though," cried Jack, looking back; "what are you called? I always like to know the name of the driver."

"Ben Trotter when I'm not called Master Benjamin Trotter," was the answer.

"Not a bad name for a coachman," observed Jack, beginning to prance and kick about. He got a cut with the whip in return for his remark. Terence reared and neighed, and kicked about furiously all the time, like a high-mettled steed who wanted to be off; and at last, Trotter having got the ribbons adjusted to his satisfaction, away they all went round the playground at a great rate, looking with great disdain on those boys who had only got string for harness. Thus were the three new-comers first yoked in fellowship. They were very much together ever afterwards, though they also had their own especial friends. Murray and Rogers were the most constant to each other. Murray was a studious, gentle boy. He had more talent than Jack; that is to say, he did his lessons a great deal better, and never got into any scrapes. Jack never picked a quarrel, but he now and then got into one, and was apt in his lessons to give a false quantity, and sometimes a translation of his Caesar which put him down to the bottom of the class. Murray was always ready and able to help him, but Jack was not a fellow who would consent to trust to the help of another. When he really tried, he could always do his work, and very creditably too. Adair, unlike his friends, was nearly always getting into trouble. He would not think enough about consequences. Once he and others had been letting off fireworks of their own manufacture in a remote corner of the playground. Notice was given that an usher was coming. They threw away their combustibles, and fled. Terence, however, had a piece of lighted touch-paper, which, in his hurry, he shoved into his pocket. It was already full of a similar preparation. He was caught and hauled away into the schoolroom to receive condign punishment. He tried to look very innocent, and requested to know why he was dragged along so unceremoniously. Paddy, under no circumstances, ever lost his politeness. Unhappily for him just as he reached the door the proofs of his guilt became apparent. Streams of smoke and sparks burst out of his pockets, and the master had to pull out the burning paper to prevent him from being seriously injured. As to his lessons he very frequently was at the top of his class, but he never could manage to keep there many days together. For some neglect or other, he soon again lost his place. Still he was a general favourite. Even the masters could not help liking him. The three new boys were put into one room. They slept there for several halves. On one occasion Terence had kept away a good deal from Jack and Murray, and associated more than was his custom with several of the less nice boys. Among them was Pigeon, the bullying fellow. I happened to be awake one night, when, by the pale moonlight which streamed in at the windows, I saw Paddy Adair sit up in his bed and look about him. Pigeon and another biggish fellow did the same. They signed to each other, and slipping on their clothes, crept with their shoes in their hands out of the room. I could not go to sleep, wondering what had become of them. Jack Rogers slept near me. He likewise had seen what had occurred. They were absent about half an hour. They returned as noiselessly as they had gone out, and crept into bed again, of course thinking that no one had observed them. No sooner was the door closed than there was a strong smell of apples in the room, and presently "crunch! crunch! crunch!" was heard.

"Those fellows have been stealing old Rowley's apples, now," thought Jack; "and that donkey Paddy Adair has, I'd bet, been heading the party."

He felt as if he were a spy by not letting them know that he was awake, so he sat up and said, "Hillo! you fellows, what have you been about?"

"Is that you awake, Jack?" answered Adair. "Never mind, we've had great fun. Have an apple, will you?"

"No, thank you," said Jack, "I'd rather not;" laying considerable emphasis on the last words.

"He doesn't deserve one as he hadn't the pluck to go and get them," said a voice from under the bedclothes.

"Who says that?" exclaimed Jack, sitting up in bed.

"Why, I say you would have been afraid to go and do what we have done," answered Bully Pigeon, summoning up more courage than was his wont.

"Afraid!" exclaimed Jack, springing out of bed and slipping on his trousers. "Afraid of what? Afraid of stealing? Afraid of telling a lie I am; but I'm not afraid of *you, you thief,* I can tell you."

Even Bully Pigeon could not stand this. Unless he would be jeered at and called sneak ever afterwards by all the little boys in the school, he felt that he must retaliate. He jumped up and sprang at Jack, aiming a blow, which, if the latter had not slipped aside, would have knocked him over. Jack, notwithstanding this, sprang back, and put himself on his defence, not only warding off the next blow Pigeon struck, but planting another between his eyes, which brought fire into them with a vengeance.

This enraged the bully, who came thundering down on Jack with all his might, and would have wellnigh crushed him, but Pigeon found a new assailant in the field whom he did not expect—one of his own party. It was Paddy Adair.

"I can't stand that, and I won't," he exclaimed, aiming a blow at Pigeon's head which sent him backwards; while Alick Murray, who had likewise jumped up, appeared on the other side of him.

"We are thieves, I tell you; we've been stealing old Rowley's apples, and Jack Rogers is right," cried Terence.

"A very true remark, boys," said a deep voice which all recognised full well. The door opened, and old Rowley himself, habited in his dressing-gown, with a candle in one hand and a birch in the other, appeared at the entrance, followed by good kind Mrs Jones, the housekeeper. Every one scuttled away to their beds as fast as they could go, except Alick Murray and Terence. Murray was the first Rowley laid hands on, and, putting down his candle on the mantelpiece, he was about to make use of his birch. Murray disdained to utter a word which might inculpate others, and I knew he would have received a flogging without complaint, but Terence cried out, "No, no, it wasn't him—I was one of them—flog me if you like."

"Well, get into bed," answered Rowley, in a voice which did not sound as if he was very angry. "You two have the spoils upon you, however;" saying this, he went to the beds of Bully Pigeon and the other big fellow, and gave them as sound a flogging as they ever had in their lives, while Mrs Jones retired to a little distance, though I believe she always came in the hopes of softening the vigour of the master's arm. He went round to the other rooms, and treated the rest of the culprits in the same way, and we had reason to suspect that he had watched the whole party as they returned from their marauding expedition. All the culprits were sent to Coventry the next day for a week, except Terence, who had however led the expedition, though he did not plan it. "I have great respect for the person who is not afraid to call a thief a thief, or a lie by its right name," said Rowley not long afterwards, looking significantly at Terence.

Time sped on, we were getting up in the school, new boys were coming and old ones were going away, when the first night after our return from the Christmas holidays, we all lay awake talking of our adventures.

"This is my last half," said Jack; "I've made up my mind to be a sailor, and my father says I may; and an admiral, a friend of ours, has promised to get me a ship; and so it's all settled, and I'm going."

"Are you, old fellow? how capital!" exclaimed Terence. "I've been asked if I would go to sea, and I said yes; for there's nothing else I want to do that I know of, but I little thought you would be going too. Well, that is good, and clenches the matter."

"I am very glad to hear it," cried Murray; "it is what I have been longing to do for years past, almost since I could read. The only profession I felt that I should ever like was the navy, but I never saw a chance till these holidays of being able to go into it. I believe it is settled; I shall know shortly, I hope."

"What, are we all three going? how capital! What fun we will have," cried Jack. "Of course they'll let you. Oh, hang it, you must go with us." Murray seldom talked much of what he wished to do, or expressed his feelings, except perhaps to a trusted friend like Jack, but of the three companions he had probably the strongest will, and when he had set his mind on an object, no one could exert himself more resolutely to accomplish it. He wrote and wrote to his friends, expressing his wish in as strong terms as he could, giving many excellent reasons for having formed it. Before many weeks had passed, Murray received a letter. The contents would have made Jack and Terence throw up their caps and shout, had they under similar circumstances received it. He felt a choking sensation, and the tears sprang to his eyes. All his long-cherished hopes were about to be accomplished. He had the promise from the First Lord of the Admiralty of an appointment speedily to a ship. The half came to an end, the school broke up, and the boys separated with all animosities and quarrels sunk in oblivion; and in the belief that they should meet each other again soon, if not at school, somewhere or other. Jack went home, and was then sent, by the advice of his naval friend, to an academy at Portsmouth, where young gentlemen were prepared for the navy. Jack wanted to become a real sailor, so he set to work manfully to stow away all the navigation he could pick up. He soon also made himself known and respected among his companions, much in the same way that he had done at his old school. At last he heard that he was appointed to a ship, but that he was to go home before joining to take leave. He was first to go to Selby the tailor, to get measured for his outfit.

"You'll like to have your uniform at once, sir," observed Mr Selby; "most young gentlemen do." Jack thought it would be very nice, as his best clothes were already shabby; so in an incredibly short space of time he found himself exactly fitted in his naval habiliments with a dirk by his side, and a gold-lace cap. He did not like to wear them in the street, "lest he should appear conspicuous," he observed to a schoolfellow, so he did not put them on till he was ready to start in the morning by the coach up to London. He had got leave to go down to Eagle House to visit his former master and old schoolfellows, and how grand he looked as he walked up and down the playground, handling his dirk. Even Pigeon felt a great respect for him, and looked on him with somewhat an eye of envy, and thought he should like to go into the navy. Had he gone, he would have had to learn many a lesson, or would very soon have been kicked out of it again. Jack dined at the master's table at one end of the long dining-room, and good Mrs Jones looked at him very proudly, for she had always thought him one of her best boys; and many an eye gazed wistfully at his anchor buttons and dirk and smiling jovial countenance, as he laughed and chatted with wonderful ease with old Rowley, as if he was not a bit afraid of him; and some idle fellows envied him his emancipation from Virgil and Horace, and other classical authors, for whom they had so little affection themselves. Then he had to jump up and hurry off to catch the coach, in order to reach the mail, which was to carry him down that night to Northamptonshire. Jack could obtain no certain information about Murray and Adair, but old Rowley told him he understood they had already been sent to sea. Jack spent three very jolly days at home. He had a big trunk filled with all sorts of things which he was to stow away in his chest. Then the moment came for parting—the family were not much addicted to crying, not that they did not love each other very much. Jack's little sister Lucy cried the most. He promised to write to her, and she promised to write to him and tell him about everybody and everything, and the horses and dogs, and something very like a tear came into his eyes, and a difficulty of speaking to which he was not accustomed, as he gave her his last kiss. Just then, Admiral Triton, Jack's naval friend, drove up to the door, and by a mighty effort all traces of his feelings were banished—not that the Admiral would have thought the worse of him a bit on account of them. The Admiral was of the old school. He had one leg, the other being supplied by what looked remarkably like a mop-stick. His appearance was somewhat rough, especially when he went out in rainy weather, and his countenance was not a little battered, but his heart was as tender and almost as simple as Jack's or even Lucy's for that matter. He had insisted on taking Jack to Portsmouth and seeing him on board. "It will be an advantage to the youngster perhaps, and, besides, it will freshen me up a bit myself," he observed to Jack's father; "so say no more about it, neighbour Rogers."

On their arrival at Portsmouth they went to the *George*, and the Admiral then took Jack to try on the rest of his kit.

"And I say, Mr Selby," observed the Admiral, "just shake the reefs out of the youngster's clothes at once, will you; why you would stop his growth if you were to swaddle him up in that way."

"Certainly, Admiral; but young gentlemen nowadays fancy well-fitting trousers," observed the tailor.

"And tight-pinching shoes, which will give them corns, and prevent them stepping out like men," observed the Admiral; "but though they are silly, wiser people should not humour them."

Leaving Jack with the tailor, who was really a very trustworthy man, Admiral Triton stumped down to the well-known Point, to have a look about him, as he said. While he was standing there, with his hands in his old pea-coat pocket, gazing out on the harbour, and thinking of bygone days and many an event of his youth connected with that place, a man-of-war's boat ran in among the wherries, and a youngster sprang out of her, a small portmanteau being afterwards handed to him.

"Hillo, my man! if you're inclined to gain a shilling, just carry this up to the *George* for me, will you?" exclaimed the midshipman, addressing the rough-looking, one-legged seaman he saw before him. The Admiral was so tickled with the notion, that without saying a word he touched his hat, and taking the portmanteau, stumped off with it, followed by the owner. Two waiters were standing at the door of the *George*. When they saw the Admiral they hurried forward.

"Pray, Admiral, let me help you in with that thing," they exclaimed eagerly. At the same moment up came Jack. He burst into a jovial fit of laughter. There before him stood Terence Adair, in midshipman's uniform, the very picture of dismay.

"Oh, sir, I beg your pardon, I did not know you were an Admiral!" he exclaimed. Just then he caught the eye of Jack, who had gone up to the Admiral. Paddy's countenance brightened a little. "How lucky!" he added. "Do apologise for me, Jack."

"Well, well, but I say, youngster, you are not going to do me out of my shilling; just hand me that, at all events," said the Admiral, laughing. "Another time save your money, and carry your shirt-collars yourself."

Terence, fumbling in his pocket, produced the coin, which the Admiral bestowed on an old blind man who was passing at the moment. Jack and Terence shook hands heartily. A look from the first assured the other that he need not have the slightest fear of the consequences of his mistake.

"What ship do you belong to, youngster?" asked the Admiral.

"The *Racer*, sir," said Terence; "she's a fine frigate—there's not another like her in the service." The Admiral looked approvingly when he heard the remark.

"Why, she's my ship," exclaimed Jack, "though I haven't joined yet."

"Yours, Jack! how capital!" cried Terence in a tone of delight; "well, that is fortunate." The Admiral seemed much amused at the meeting of the two friends. Terence had come on shore to see his relative Lord Derrynane, whom Admiral Triton knew; and they all dined together, and the next day the Admiral accompanied the two lads on board their ship, which had just gone out to Spithead. She was a thirty-six gun frigate, and worthy of all the encomiums Terence had lavishly bestowed on her at dinner. The Admiral stumped all over her, and examined all the new inventions, and went into the midshipmen's berth, which was a very natty one; and he sat down and talked of old times during the war, and told a good story or two, and made himself perfectly at home, and introduced Jack "as a fellow who would speak for himself by and by;" and when he went away he was voted a regular trump, and no small share of his lustre fell on Jack. The Admiral and Jack went on deck. The former was in no hurry to leave the ship. He took a great interest in all that was going forward. They walked the deck for some time. The Admiral stopped, and said with more seriousness than was his wont: "Jack, I have given you several pieces of advice which you have taken well from an old sailor who has lost his leg in the service of his country, and has been pretty well riddled and knocked about besides. I must give you another, the most important of all—never forget that you are a Christian, and never be ashamed of confessing it. Your Bible tells you what that means. You've got one in your chest. Read it often, and learn from it. Nail your colours to the mast, and fight under them. You'll thus keep your spiritual enemies at bay, as I hope you will those of your country." Jack grasped the Admiral's hand to show that he understood him, but for the life of him he could not have found words to express what he wanted to say. They had stopped, and were looking over the ship's side. Jack espied a boat pulling up under the frigate's quarter, with a midshipman's chest and a midshipman in her.

"What, more youngsters!" growled out an old mate; "we've our complement, and more than enough already." Jack's heart gave a jump of pleasure. He thought that he recognised Murray. It was a curious coincidence, if such was the case, that the three schoolfellows should meet. The boat came alongside, the chest was hoisted up in spite of the old mate's growls, the midshipman followed, and in another minute Jack Terence and Alick were shaking hands, and laughing heartily at their happy encounter. Murray said that he had not come to join the *Racer* permanently, but that he had been ordered a passage to the Mediterranean, where the sloop of war to which he had been appointed was stationed. The Admiral told Murray that he knew his father, and that he was glad a son of his had chosen the navy as a profession. He then heartily shook hands with the three lads; and when he went on shore all the midshipmen of the ship manned the side ropes to show their respect to the fine old sailor, and gave him three cheers as he pulled away. Jack confessed that, somehow or other, he felt more inclined to pipe his eye on that occasion than on any of his other leave-takings. Two days after this the *Racer*, bound for the Mediterranean, was running out at the Needles, whose jagged peaks and high white cliffs rose in picturesque beauty on the left hand. The wind was fair, the sky blue, and the water smooth, and the three midshipmen looked forward with delight to the numerous adventures they expected to encounter.

Chapter Two
In the Mediterranean

The gallant frigate, which bore the three midshipmen and their fortunes, was soon plunging into a heavy sea, caused by a strong breeze from the westward, which she encountered as she stood across the Bay of Biscay. "There we lay all the day, in the Bay of Biscay, oh!" sang Paddy Adair, as he, with other young gentlemen, sat in the berth after dinner; but, as he sang, there was a tremulousness in his voice ominous of a troubled soul within, while the "Oh!" came out with a peculiar emphasis which brought down upon him the laughter of the other youngsters, who, having been rather longer at sea, had become accustomed to such joltings and tumblings about. Jack meantime, who had just come below from his watch on deck, was attacking, with a ferocity which made it appear as if he was contending with some bitter enemy, instead of a plentiful dinner, the boiled beef and biscuit the boy had lately placed on the table. When spoken to, he scarcely looked up, but continued cramming mouthful after mouthful down his throat, while his eyes rolled round and round; and more than once he gazed at the door, contemplating evidently how he could most quickly make his escape on deck. Alick Murray meantime leaned back at the end of the berth, with a book in his hand, under the impression that he was reading; but his head ached; his dinner had been untasted, and, though his eyes may have seen the letters, they conveyed no impression to his brain. The rest of the members of the mess were variously employed. Some were writing up their logs; others doing their day's work; a few reading, and some were discussing subjects, if not very erudite, at all events, apparently highly amusing to themselves, from the peals of laughter they occasionally elicited. Two youngsters were having a quiet little fight in the corner, pummelling each other's heads to their hearts' content, till brought to order by a couple of books aimed scientifically across the berth by old Hemming, the senior mate of the mess, who, from constant practice, was very perfect in that mode of projecting missiles. There were several other passed mates in the berth, and two assistant-surgeons—one of them old enough to be the father of any of the youngsters—and a second master and a master's assistant, and the captain and purser's clerks, and three or four other midshipmen of various ages.

All of them did not belong to the frigate, but some were supernumeraries going out to other ships on the station. The fathers of some present were of high rank, and they had been accustomed to all the luxuries wealth can give, while others were the sons of poor men, officers in the army and navy, who had little beyond their pay on which to depend. Altogether they formed a very heterogeneous mass, and a strict system of discipline was required to keep them in order. Captain Lascelles, who commanded the *Racer*, was an officer and a gentleman in the true sense of the word, and he wished that all the officers under his command should deserve the same character. Those belonging to the gun-room were mostly men of this description, but one or two scarcely came up to it. Of these one was the lieutenant of marines. He formed an exception to the general character won by that noble corp—for a braver and more gallant set of men are nowhere to be found. Lieutenant Spry was not a favourite either with his superiors or with those below him. The midshipmen especially disliked him, and he seemed to have a decided antipathy to them.

To return to the midshipmen's berth: Jack Rogers continued to bolt his beef, Alick to fancy that he was reading, and Adair to try and sing, when, in spite of his courage, nature, or rather the *tumblification* of the ship, triumphed;—springing over the table, he rushed up the hatchway towards the nearest port on the upper deck. Now, as it happened, Lieutenant Spry was with uneasy steps endeavouring to take his constitutional walk along the deck at that moment, and Paddy, not seeing him, ran with his head directly against the lower button of the marine officer's waistcoat, whereon the seasick midshipman found his ears pinched, and received a shower of no very refined epithets. Poor Terence, who, essentially the gentleman, would not have retorted if he could, was able only to ejaculate, "Beg pardon, sir!" when the usual result of seasickness followed, to the no small disfigurement of the marine's white trousers. The enraged officer, on this, thundered down invectives on poor Paddy's head, and finished off in a most un-officer-like way by kicking him down the hatchway from whence he had just emerged. Adair returned crestfallen and miserable, brooding over the injury and insults he had received. There could have been no doubt that a formal complaint made to the captain would have brought down a severe reprimand on the head of the marine officer, but the idea of making a complaint never crossed the imagination of the midshipman. Paddy, however, told his story to his companions, and even Murray agreed that Mr Spry had merited punishment. They eagerly discussed the subject—all the midshipmen had been insulted in the person of Adair, and it was not long before a bright idea was elicited from among them. On board the ship, belonging to the men, was a large monkey, whom they called Quirk, a very tame and sagacious animal, who had a peculiar aptitude for learning any trick which any person had perseverance enough to teach him. "He'd know more nor any of the ship's boys if it weren't for his tail," the men used to remark after the performance of one of his clever tricks.

"Capital!" exclaimed Jack, forgetting all about his seasickness and clapping his hands with delight when the idea which had been brought forth was propounded; "he'll do in it first-rate style—ha, ha, ha!" and a merry peal of laughter ran through the berth.

The gale blew over, and the sea once more was bright and blue, as the frigate made her way towards the Rock of Gibraltar. For several days the three midshipmen were wonderfully quiet below; sometimes they were forward, and sometimes they sat together at the farther end of their own berth. They had needles and thread and scissors under weigh, and bits of red cloth and leather, and indeed all sorts of outfitters' materials, the employment on which seemed to afford them infinite satisfaction. Mr Spry, as in fancied dignity he paced the quarter-deck, of course did not remark the constant absence of so insignificant a person as a midshipman from it; and the recollection that he had behaved not altogether in a becoming way to Adair did not probably cross his mind. Now the lieutenant had a peculiarly pompous air, and the habit, whenever he wished to blow his nose, of drawing his white cambric pocket-handkerchief from his breast pocket with what he thought peculiar dignity, and of flourishing it in his hand after each operation in a fine theatrical style. He had read in some advertising circular that the use of a fine cambric handkerchief always marks the gentleman; so he considered that if he purchased a set, no one would afterwards venture to doubt his claim to that character. All day long, Jack, or Alick, or Paddy, sometimes singly and sometimes all together, were forward in the company of no less important a character than Quirk, the monkey. It is extraordinary how perseveringly they devoted themselves to him. Had they employed the same time in teaching some of their fellow-creatures, the ship's boys, they might have imparted a considerable amount of useful knowledge, notwithstanding what the men said on the subject. At last they considered that the time had arrived for bringing their labours to a triumphant result.

One fine calm morning the marines had been called out to drill. For some reason Lieutenant Spry did not at once make his appearance, but a representative came forward instead in the person of Master Quirk, who sprang aft to the spot which should have been occupied by the lieutenant, dressed in full fig, with red coat and belt and hat, and a sword by his side, while his breast pocket was well stuffed out with a huge piece of white cotton. "Attention!" cried out some one on deck. The men unconsciously obeyed, and instantly Quirk drew out his handkerchief, and, spluttering with a loud noise, flourished it vehemently in the air. On this, even the self-possession of the marines gave way; and instead of being angry, they burst into uncontrollable fits of laughter, which were joined in by all the spectators, who were crowding aft to see the fun.

At that moment Mr Spry rushed on deck, using his handkerchief exactly as Quirk had been doing. When the whole scene burst on him, his fury knew no bounds. He rushed to his station at the head of his men, which the monkey seemed in no way disposed to vacate, nor did he till his quick eye caught sight of the toe of the officer approaching him, when, with a loud chuckling "Quacko! quacko! quacko!" he leaped nimbly up the ringing.

It was some time before order was restored; and even while his drill was going on, a merry peal of laughter reached the ears of the fuming lieutenant from different parts of the deck, in which he felt certain he could recognise the voices of Adair and his two friends. The moment the drill was over, instead of acting like a wise man, and passing the matter over as an occurrence in no way intended to annoy him, he went aft and made a formal complaint to Captain Lascelles. As every man who chooses to encourage a toady can have one, so even had Lieutenant Spry, in the person of one of his men, who had watched the proceedings of the midshipmen, and now came forward as a witness against them. All three were summoned to the cabin, and they could not, of course, deny the charge. The captain had considerable difficulty in keeping his countenance, as Paddy, acting as spokesman of the party, pleaded their cause. He did not mend it when he confessed that the trick had been played in consequence of the way the lieutenant had treated him.

"It is mean, and unchristian, and altogether wrong, to harbour revenge, young gentlemen," said the captain. "I cannot now take cognisance of Mr Spry's conduct on the occasion to which you allude; and I conclude that he will be satisfied if you apologise to him. As the conduct of which you have been guilty was public, so also must be your punishment. Go up, each of you, to one of the mast-heads, and remain there till I call you down. Adair, do you go to the mizen-mast; Rogers, take the mainmast; and Murray, the foremast. I have settled that matter, I hope, to your satisfaction, Mr Spry," observed the captain, with a freezing manner, which somewhat damped the dignity of the lieutenant.

Up the rigging went the three midshipmen, each of them obtaining possession of a handful of biscuit and a piece of beef to stay their hunger, as they had a prospect of losing their dinners unless the captain relented sooner than could be expected. There they all sat on their lofty perches, occasionally making telegraphic signals to each other, and not particularly unhappy with their punishment.

The captain and gun-room officers were taking their for noon quarter-deck walk, and nearly everybody on board was on deck, when a loud chattering was heard, and who should be seen mounting the mizen rigging but Quirk, still habited in his red coat, with his hat fixed firmly on his head, intent, most clearly, on mischief. No sooner did he get alongside Adair, than, pulling out his handkerchief, he flourished it vehemently in his face; and then, as if satisfied with the performance of his lesson, he slid down the mizen topmast stay, and in an instant after was up again close to Jack, before whom he performed the same ceremony. Paddy and Jack almost fell from their perches with laughter, especially when Quirk sprang forward along another stay, and paid a similar visit to Murray. Everybody on deck was looking on, and all abaft were amused, with the exception of Lieutenant Spry, who was in a towering rage, vowing that he would demand a court-martial, and get the midshipmen, or the monkey, or himself—nobody knew exactly which—dismissed the ship. The lieutenant shouted out to somebody to catch the monkey, but as he did not name any one in particular, no one went, and he had the pleasure of observing his own peculiarity exhibited backwards and forwards, from mast-head to mast-head, several times in succession. A joke must have an end; and the captain, seeing that the best way of bringing this to a conclusion (it being somewhat subversive of discipline) was to call the midshipmen down, they were allowed to return once more on deck, while Quirk's new red coat and accoutrements were seized and hove overboard, to appease the rage of the marine officer. However, Quirk, having been carefully instructed, lost no opportunity of exhibiting his talents; and whenever the marines were drawn up, or the seamen were at divisions, if he happened to be loose, he invariably appeared in front of them flourishing a piece of canvas, or a bit of paper, or anything he could lay paws on to represent a pocket-handkerchief.

At length that classic sea, whose shores have been the scene of the most interesting events of the world's history—that sea which leads to Italy, to Greece, to the Holy Land, to Egypt, with its wondrous Nile and grand old mysterious ruins—the Mediterranean, was sighted; and the frigate dropped her anchor below the high rock of Gibraltar, also celebrated, somewhat in later times, for the way in which it was captured by Sir George Rooke, and has been kept ever since by the obstinate English. The midshipmen had just time to run through the galleries perforated in the rock, to climb to its highest peak, and to get a look at the frolicsome monkeys which dwell in undisturbed liberty on its south-eastern side, before the ship again sailed. They heard that the *Firefly*, the sloop of war to which Murray was appointed, had gone to Greece, so they had the prospect of remaining some time longer together. At Malta the *Racer* remained only a few days, when she was ordered off to the Ionian Islands.

The first place at which she brought up was in the harbour of Corfu. It is a lovely spot. The picturesque hills of the island are seen on one side, and the lofty mountains of Albania on the other, of the strait which divides it from the mainland. Here Murray was separated from his two old schoolfellows. The *Firefly* came in, and he had to join her. The three midshipmen had made good use of their time, and had picked up a fair amount of seamanship. They had now some practice in boating, an amusement which the captain always encouraged; for, as he observed, almost as many lives were lost from ignorance of how to manage a boat properly, as in any other way. This sort of work Jack and Adair especially liked. The frigate had put to sea to visit some of the neighbouring islands, and had more than once returned into port; when one forenoon Captain Lascelles summoned Hemming into the cabin.

"I have a despatch to send to Janina, Mr Hemming," said he. "You will take the cutter and two of the midshipmen with you—Adair and Rogers. Send them back as soon as you land. You will take horses and travel across the country, and the frigate will call for you in the course of a few days."

"Ay, ay, sir!" answered Hemming, who never spoke a work more than was necessary in the presence of his superiors.

Jack and Paddy were delighted when they found that they were to go on the expedition; for, though old Hemming kept somewhat a taut hand over them, they had a just regard for his good qualities. They secretly also resolved to indemnify themselves on their return passage by having as much fun as they could. The cutter was a fine boat; and as they had a fair breeze they made rapid progress towards their destination. They sat very demurely, one on either side of old Hemming, eating their bread and cheese, and taking the half wineglassful of grog, which he handed to them each time that he helped himself to a full tumbler.

"That is quite enough for such little chaps as you," said he. "If you were to begin now, and to take two or three tumblersful as I do, by the time you are my age, you would have drunk fifty hogsheads of rum, and I don't know how many tons of water."

Perhaps Hemming's calculations were not exactly correct, but the advice was, at all events, good. He took care that it should be followed by leaving them only half a bottle of rum for their return—putting the remainder of the bottles into the saddle-bags he had brought for his journey. Jack and Terence watched him trotting off on a Greek Rosinante with the said well-filled saddle-bags behind him, a thick stick in his hand, and a brace of ship's pistols in his holsters, till he was out of sight.

"Terence," said Jack, "we ought to return to the boat, and get under weigh."

"Yes; but I vote we do something in the catering line first," was the answer.

So they found their way to the market, where by dint of signs and a few words of *lingua franca*, they laid in a store of fruit and fowls, and fish and vegetables of various sorts, with two or three bottles of what they understood was first-rate Samian wine. With this provision for the inner man they returned to the boat, and made sail for Corfu. The wind was light, and they made but slow progress. However, they were very happy, and in no hurry to get back to the ship. It happened that they had been lately reading James's *Naval History*, and Paddy especially had been much struck by some of the exploits performed by single boat's crews.

"Jack," said he, "I don't think we ought to go back to the ship without doing something."

"We are doing a good deal," answered Jack, who was very matter of fact. "We are eating a jolly good dinner." He held up the leg of a chicken. "This is the last of a fowl I've had to my share."

"Ay, but I mean something to be talked about—something glorious," answered Paddy. "Let's take a prize."

"A prize! Where is one to be found?" asked Jack, in no way disinclined to do something.

"Oh! we'll fall in with her before long," replied Paddy. "One of these Greek chaps. They are all pirates, you know, and would cut our throats if they dared."

Paddy was jumping rather too fast at conclusions; but Jack, who also thought it would be a very fine thing to take a prize, although some doubts crossed his mind as to the propriety of so doing, did not attempt to dissuade him from his intentions. It never occurred to the young aspirants for naval renown that they should have made the men get out their oars and pull, as there was a perfect calm. The boat floated quietly on all night. Soon after daylight they espied a long, low, lateen-rigged craft stealing along close in with the land—her white canvas dimly seen through the morning mist.

"That shall be our prize," exclaimed Paddy, standing up in the stern-sheets; whereon he made the crew a speech, and talked a great deal about honour, glory, and renown, and treading in the steps of the old heroes of Great Britain, and prize-money, and several other themes. The last-mentioned his auditors understood somewhat better than the first. It was all the same to them whether England was at war or not with the nation to which the craft in view belonged. Their officers must know all about the matter, so there was no dissentient voice; and now, getting out their oars fast enough, they pulled away with a hearty cheer towards the craft in sight. The vessel was undoubtedly a Greek. Her crew probably could not conceive why they were chased. The wind was too light to enable them to make much way with their sails; and though they had oars, they were unable to urge on their craft fast enough to escape the English boat. From the gestures of their pursuers the Greeks saw that they were about to be attacked, and as the cutter ran alongside they attempted to defend themselves; but although the seamen had only the boat's stretchers, and Paddy and Jack alone had pistols, which fortunately would not go off, the Greeks very speedily gave way and tumbled down below.

"What are we to do now?" asked Jack, who, having joined the ship later, was under Adair's command.

"Carry our prize in triumph into Corfu," answered Paddy, taking a turn with a dignified air on the deck. "I should like, to see what that prig Spry will say to us now."

As the Greeks could not speak a word of English, nor the English a word of Greek, no explanations could be made. The Greeks shrugged their shoulders, and having been accustomed to be knocked about a good deal by the Turks, and to untoward events in general, took things very philosophically. A breeze sprang up, and with the cutter in tow, the midshipmen shaped a course, as well as they could calculate, for Corfu. The Greek crew were far more numerous than the English; so Jack advised that a guard should be set over them lest they might attempt to retake the vessel—an occurrence, he had read, which had often happened when proper precautions were neglected.

"I hope it's all right," observed Jack, "but what we have done seems somewhat funny."

"Who fears?" answered Paddy. "What else have we to do but to fight our enemies?"

As Jack had not a ready answer to this question, the subject dropped. Their attention was soon occupied by seeing a vessel standing up the channel, so directly to cross their course.

"She's the *Firefly*," exclaimed Jack; "is she not, Thomson?" he asked of the boatswain of the boat.

"No doubt about it, sir," was the answer; and in a lower voice, "And now, my wigs, won't the youngsters catch it!"

When the sloop of war drew near, she fired a gun as a signal to the Greek vessel to heave-to. As the midshipmen knew what that meant, they at once obeyed, and in a short time a boat was seen pulling towards them; a lieutenant and a midshipman were in her. The latter was no other than Alick Murray. They cordially greeted him; and Terence had begun to boast of their achievement when the lieutenant, Mr Gale, exclaimed, "What does all this mean, youngsters? What have you been about?"

Terence tried to explain, but everything he said only made matters worse. Happily, Mr Gale was a very kind, judicious man, and soon comprehended that the midshipmen had acted through ignorance and thoughtlessness.

"Had you reached Corfu with your so-called prize, you might have been brought into serious trouble," he remarked. "As no great harm has hitherto taken place, perhaps we may induce the Greek master and his crew not to make any complaint. I will see what can be done."

"Oh, yes, sir," exclaimed Alick Murray; "if we can bribe him off I shall be glad to pay any sum you think necessary. Fortunately, I have the means at my disposal;" and he put a purse into Mr Gale's hand. "Don't say a word about it, my dear fellows," he added, as Terence and Jack were expostulating with him for spending so much money on their account. "As we have done the harm, we must stand the blame, you know," they said.

Mr Gale had long been accustomed to the Greeks, and spoke their language fluently; and having first frightened the master by proving to him that his detention was his own fault, because he had not explained that he was an honest trader, in order to show the good feeling of the English, he promised forthwith to liberate him. The Greek was profuse in his thanks, especially when the lieutenant, to exhibit the magnanimity of his captors, presented him with a bottle of rum and a few piastres.

Perfectly satisfied with this turn in the state of affairs, the Greeks were voluble in their expression of gratitude, and waving their hands, pressed them to their hearts, as the two boats pulled away for the corvette. Captain Hartland, her commander, soon after they came on board, gave the two midshipmen a severe lecture for their behaviour, and telling them to make the best of their way back to Corfu, advised them not to boast too loudly of their exploit. Alick, who was decidedly a favourite, had, they found in the meantime, contrived to plead their cause. They followed Captain

Hartland's advice, but they felt very crestfallen and sheepish for some days after they got back to their own ship. The story, however, leaked out in time, and Terence and Jack had, of course, to stand a good deal of quizzing on the subject. At last, a Paddy's Prize became a cant saying on board, when anybody had taken anything to which he had no right.

Several months passed away—the winter came on. The *Racer* met with a severe gale, in which she was partially dismasted, and received so much damage that she had to put into Valetta harbour to repair. She found the *Firefly* there, and as Captain Hartland had the character of being very attentive to the instruction of his midshipmen in seamanship, Captain Lascelles got him to take Terence and Jack with him for a cruise while the frigate was refitting. Nothing loath, they transferred themselves, with their chests, on board the corvette, and once more the three schoolfellows were together. They found the life on board the corvette very different to that of the frigate. Their hands were constantly in the tar-bucket and paint-pot. They were for ever employed in knotting and splicing, and in rigging and unrigging a model ship, which had been made on purpose to instruct them. All the midshipmen of the brig were compelled to man the mizen-mast, and to take it completely under their charge. This system very much increased the knowledge of the practical details of seamanship, which it is important every officer should know. A good officer is thoroughly acquainted in the most minute particular with everything men are required to know, and a great deal more. This remark refers not only to the Navy, but to the Army, and to every other calling in life. The *Firefly* was a very happy ship; for though no one was allowed to be idle, the captain was kind and just, and took care that each person should do his duty; so that the work to be done was equally divided among all hands.

On quitting Malta she sailed for the eastward, and was for some time kept cruising among the Ionian Islands, and on the coast of Greece, carrying despatches from place to place. The wind had been from the northward, and the ship had been kept somewhat close in with the Greek coast, to shorten the distance to be run from one spot to another, when one of those severe gales, which in the winter season in the Mediterranean sometimes spring up suddenly, came on to blow. The corvette was caught on a lee shore and embayed. It was night. All hands were called. The fury of the gale increased. Sail was taken off the ship, but still it was necessary to carry far more than would have been set under other circumstances, that she might, if possible, beat out of the bay. She was pressed down till the hammock-nettings were almost under water. Still her masts stood, but no one could predict how long they could bear the terrific strain put upon them. Darker and darker grew the night; the vivid flashes of lightning very now and then revealing the countenances of the officers and crew, as they strained their eyes in their endeavours to discover through the darkness how far off was the much-dreaded shore. The three midshipmen stood together, holding on to the weather bulwarks with some of the gun-room officers. Others were at their stations in different parts of the ship. The lightning showed that the cheeks of the oldest were pale. They full well knew the terrific danger in which the ship was placed. The captain stood calm and collected, conning the ship, and ready to take advantage of any shift of wind which might enable her to get a point off the shore. No one moved—no one spoke—the howling of the gale and the dashing of the waters were the only sounds heard. Suddenly all were aroused into activity by the deep full tones of the captain's voice. "About ship!" "Down with the helm!" "Helm's a-lee!" "Maintopsail haul!" "Haul-of-all!" were the orders given in slow succession. Round came the ship in noble style, but it was soon clear that she had gained nothing by the change. Her course did not point more off shore on her present tack than it had done on the former one. No land could be seen, but men were stationed in the chains with the lead to give notice of their approach to it. It was soon evident that the ship was drifting nearer and nearer to the shore, the rocky and dangerous character of which every one on board full well knew, yet each was prepared to struggle to the last to do his duty, whatever might befall them.

"What's going to happen?" asked Paddy. "People don't seem to like this fun."

"We shall have to swim for it, I suspect," remarked Jack.

"We must be prepared for the worst," observed Alick Murray. "Rogers, Adair, has it ever struck you that we maybe summoned at any moment to stand in the presence of the Judge of all men? What shall we have to say for ourselves? The thought should not make us cowards, but we should not drive it away—I know that."

While Murray was speaking there was a terrific report. The foresail was blown out of the bolt-ropes. At the same moment a more than usually bright flash of lightning, which darted across the whole northern sky, revealed the frowning rocks of the coast under their lee. "Prepare to anchor ship!" cried the captain. It was a last resource. The remaining canvas was furled. The best bower was let go; the topmasts were struck; and it was hoped that the ship might hold on till the gale abated. No one went below. This work performed, all hands returned to their stations. Once more the gale came down on them with increased fury. The ship plunged into the foaming seas which rolled up around her. The best bower parted. Another anchor was let go, and the full length of the cable veered out. An hour more passed by in anxious suspense; death, in its most ferocious aspect, threatening all on board. The cable parted. The sheet anchor was let go, and alone now kept the brig from destruction. Still the gale did not abate. The night wore on. The officers forward reported that the ship was dragging the anchor—her last hope of safety.

"It must be done," said the captain with a sigh, to the first lieutenant. "Order the carpenter to cut away the foremast."

The carpenter and his crew were prepared for what they had suspected was inevitable. Their axes gleamed as the lightning flashed vividly around them. The crew stood by to cut away the rigging with axes and knives. Down came the mast with crash to port, and floated quickly by towards the shore. The next few minutes were passed with intense anxiety by every one on board.

"Does she hold on, Mr Gale?" the captain asked of the first lieutenant.

"She still drags, sir," was the ominous reply.

"The other masts must go," cried the captain.

The order was quickly executed. The mainmast fell to starboard, followed by the mizen-mast, and the late gallant-looking ship floated a dismantled hulk amid the foaming waves. But the sacrifice was in vain; scarcely had the masts gone than the last cable parted, and the gallant ship drifted onwards towards the threatening shore. Still Captain Hartland was not a man to yield while a possibility remained of saving his ship and the lives of those entrusted to him. The corvette carried aft two heavy guns for throwing shells. Some spare hempen cables were got up from below, and made fast to them; when hove overboard they checked her way. Daylight at length came, and revealed her terrific position. High cliffs, and dark, rugged, wild rocks, over which the sea broke in masses of foam, appeared on every side. Pale and anxious the crew stood at their stations. The wind roared, the cold was bitter. A startling terror-inspiring cry was heard. "The last cable has parted!" The three midshipmen shook hands; they believed that they were soon to be separated, never to meet again in this world. On— on, with heavy plunges, amid the foaming waters, the doomed ship hurried to meet her fate.

Chapter Three
Amongst the Greeks

Onward drove the sloop of war with the three midshipmen on board to certain destruction. "Heave the guns overboard!" cried Captain Hartland, on the discovery that the last cable had parted. Severe indeed was the pang it caused him to give the order. As the ship rolled, first the starboard, and then the guns on the other side, were cut loose and allowed to run through the ports. With sullen plunges they disappeared in the foaming seas.

"There go all our teeth," cried Paddy Adair, who even at that awful moment could not refrain from a joke. Even Murray smiled.

"I wish that I were like you, Paddy," said Jack; "I couldn't have said that sort of thing just now."

"Well, but I'm sure that I can't help feeling as if every tooth in my mouth had been hauled out with a huge wrench," observed Adair. "There! there goes the last."

"We must lighten the ship aft as much as possible, Mr Gale, and make sail on the stump of the foremast, so as to force her up on the beach," observed the captain. "If we can find the beach," he added in a lower voice.

These orders were promptly obeyed. Every man worked with a will. There was no hurry, no confusion, though all were engaged in the most active exertion. No one seemed to be conscious, while thus at work, that in a few short minutes their fate might be sealed. Meantime, sail being set forward, while the ship headed on towards the shore, Captain Hartland and the master were engaged in looking out, in the hopes of discovering some sandy beach between the rocks, on which they might run the ship. Still they scarcely expected to find what they were seeking for; yet no one on board would have guessed from their looks what very slight hopes they entertained of success. The work was done; the ship hurried through the raging surf. Still the most perfect discipline prevailed; not a man quitted his station. Here and there a few might be seen loosing their shoe-ties, or getting ready to cast off their flushing coats; but no other sign was observable that an awful struggle for life and death was about to commence.

"Where are we driving to, Jack?" asked Adair; "I cannot make out through all this spray."

"I thought I caught a glimpse of a white patch not much bigger than my hand when we were at the top of the last sea," answered Rogers. "I hope it may be sand."

"Starboard, starboard!" shouted the captain. Three hands were at the helm. The spokes flew quickly round. A little sandy bay appeared; it seemed under the ship's bowsprit; then she was enveloped in a thick cloud of foam; the terrific roar of the surf became deafening. On flew the corvette; a concussion which sent all who had not a secure hold flat on the deck was felt, and the seas came rolling up with tremendous force, heaving her broadside to the beach, and about twenty fathoms from it. Still they did not at first break completely over her; a rock, inside of which she had been judiciously steered, somewhat broke their force.

"We are ashore—we are ashore!" was the cry, but still every man waited for the captain's orders. He stood calm and collected, with his officers round him. His glass was in his hand; he was constantly looking through it watching the shore.

"Some people are collecting on the heights, and will soon be down on the beach," he exclaimed. "Hold on till they come, my lads, and we may be able to send a line on shore." This exhortation was not unnecessary, for the seas rolling in constantly struck the vessel with such terrific force, that it appeared she could not possibly hold together, while two or three men, who had incautiously relaxed their hold, were washed overboard and drowned. A beaker or small cask was in the meantime got ready with a line secured to it. The most important object was to form a communication with the shore. It was evident that if a hawser could once be carried between the ship and the beach, the crew might be dragged along it and be saved. As soon as the people began to collect on the beach, the cask with the line attached to it was hove overboard. All watched its progress with intense anxiety, for all felt that no time was to be lost in getting the hawser on shore. The cask neared the shore, then the wave rolled on, but again coming thundering down the beach, carried it back almost as far as the ship. Again and again the attempt was made, and each time the cask, almost getting within the grasp of the people on shore, was hurled back once more out of their reach.

"I think, sir, I could manage to put the jolly-boat on shore, if you will allow me," said Mr Wenham, the second lieutenant, addressing the captain.

"The risk is very great, Wenham," said the captain, shaking him by the hand; "but go if you think fit."

"Volunteers for the jolly-boat!" sang out the second lieutenant. Several men sprang forward; he selected four. The boat was launched into the raging sea, and they leaped into her, carrying a line. With a cheer from their shipmates they shoved off. Rapidly the boat approached the beach, borne onward with a huge wave. Intense was the anxiety of all who watched her. She reached the spot where the sea curled backward in a mass of raging foam. Down it came upon her. A cry was heard uttered by the Greeks on shore, as well as by the seamen on board. Over went the boat, and all her hapless crew were engulfed. Rolled over and over among the seaweed and masses of the tangled rigging and pieces of the wreck, they struggled in vain to gain the shore. One after the other they were swept out to sea and lost. It was evident that none of the other boats would serve to carry the line on shore. Again the experiment was tried with a cask, but failed.

"I say, Murray—Adair," exclaimed Jack, earnestly, "do you know, I think that I could do it. I was always a first-rate swimmer, you know, for my size. I'll ask the captain's leave to try."

"No one in the berth is better able to do it than you are," replied both his companions.

"Oh Jack, I wish that I could go with you," cried Murray, as he wrung his hand.

"So do I," added Adair; "but I know that I could never swim through that surf."

No time was to be lost, so Jack Rogers worked his way up to Captain Hartland, and offered to swim on shore with the line. The captain looked very much astonished, and replied that he thought the risk was too great.

"Do let me try, sir," urged Jack. "I'm like a fish in the water, I am indeed, sir; and if I don't reach the beach I can but be hauled back again, you know. I've a notion that I could swim through all that foam. I've done something like it before now."

"You are a brave fellow, Rogers," exclaimed Captain Hartland; "I will not prevent you." Jack, delighted, began to throw off his clothes, which he handed to Adair and Murray, to prepare for his swim.

"Mr Gale, tend the line carefully, and haul him in if he seems distressed," said the captain to the first lieutenant. Jack had a belt secured round his body, so that it could not slip off or cut him, and he had the line made fast to it. Watching his opportunity as a wave rolled in, he boldly sprang out on the top of it, and was borne onwards towards the shore with little or no exertion to himself. He wisely reserved all his strength for the last struggle at the end of the trip. Every one watched him with intense interest. Not a word was spoken, but a hundred hands were eagerly held out to him from the shore, to show him the welcome he would receive on landing. Some of the strongest men among the Greeks joined hands and formed a line into the sea, that the outer man might clutch the bold young swimmer if he could get within his reach. Meantime a boat's oar and some line had been cast on shore. Some of the Greeks, more thoughtful than the rest, had secured the oar to the line, and stood ready to let it float out as Jack approached. He saw the aid prepared, and made towards it. He waited outside the place where the sea which took him in broke into foam, and then, when another sea rolled in, exerting all his strength he dashed forward; but in spite of all his efforts, the undertow was carrying him out again; still he bravely struggled on. He saw the men on shore holding out their hands to him; could he but make head for a distance of two or three more fathoms he would succeed. Another sea rolled in. "Hurrah, hurrah!" resounded from all sides; "he has grasped the oar." He was almost exhausted, still he clutched it with all his might. Cautiously they drew him onward. He could not have held on many moments longer, but the men who had formed the chain into the water seized him by the collar, and he and the end of the line he had so gallantly conveyed through the raging surf were carried up in safety on the beach. Murray and Adair had watched his progress with an interest such as none but true old friends can feel. Tears of gratitude sprang into Murray's eyes, and his heart bounded with joy as he saw that Jack was in safety. Adair did not feel less satisfaction, but he expressed it differently, by joining heartily in the shout given by the rest of the ship's company. A hawser was immediately attached to the line, by which it was drawn on shore, and one end being made fast round the stump of the foremast over the topgallant forecastle, the other was secured round the rocks. A traveller with a line and slings being now fitted to the hawser, the men were told off to be conveyed on shore, the boys and those of lowest rating, being, as is customary, sent first. The traveller being hauled backwards and forwards, one after the other the men were conveyed to the beach. The operation, however, was a slow one, and not without danger, as part of the hawser was completely at times submerged by the breakers. Meantime the sea had made a breach over the afterpart of the ship, carrying away portions of the bulwarks. A piece of the planking, as it washed by, struck Adair on the leg, and knocking him down, the sea would have swept him overboard had not Murray seized him by the arm, when Mr Gale coming to his assistance they carried him forward. He was too much hurt to move, and they were afraid his leg was broken. Murray sat with him on the deck, holding on by a ring-bolt and supporting him in his lap. Notwithstanding the accident, they both of them had held fast to Jack's clothes. What was their surprise not ten minutes afterwards to see Jack himself make his appearance on board.

"Why, Rogers!—why have you come back, my dear lad?" exclaimed Captain Hartland.

"To look after my clothes, sir," answered Jack; "and besides, sir, I didn't like to be going on shore out of my turn; none of the officers have gone yet." The captain must have been puzzled what reply to make to this reason, for he said nothing. Night was now coming on; still many people remained on board.

"Come, bear a hand, my hearties; let us be getting on shore out of this," cried some of those left on board to their shipmates. All who had gone before had been landed safely, but it was necessary to be very careful during the transit in keeping a tight hold of the slings, especially in passing through the surf. One man, a fine young topman, grasped hold of the traveller, and with a wave of his hat gave the sign to haul away. He went on well for a few seconds, apparently thinking it a good joke, till a roller overtook him. In an instant the poor fellow was torn from his hold, and the raging waters rushing down again carried him far away beyond human help.

"Now, Murray, it is your turn," said Mr Gale; "we will see by and by how we can get Adair on shore."

"No, sir, thank you," said Murray calmly; "I would rather stay by Adair. If he cannot be landed now, he will require some one to look after him."

"Go, Alick, go," said Adair faintly. "Don't mind me."

"Come, Rogers, you must be off then," exclaimed the first lieutenant, in a hurried tone. "See, the men are waiting to haul you on shore."

"Please, sir, Paddy Adair is an old schoolfellow of mine, and now he is a messmate; and while he is in that state and unable to help himself I cannot desert him, indeed I cannot, sir," said Jack very quietly. "I'm very hardy; the cold and wet won't hurt me. I'd much rather Murray went."

"No; I agreed to stay first," said Murray; "I cannot go."

"Then we'll both stay," said Jack. "That's settled, sir, isn't it?"

Mr Gale had not seen exactly how the seaman had been lost; and believing that there was nearly as much risk in making the passage in the dark as in staying, agreed to allow the youngsters to do as they wished, resolving at the same time to remain by them himself. The captain had gone forward; and before he was aware of it, believing that everybody had left the ship, he was hurried by those in charge of the hawser into the slings.

"We are coming sharp after you, sir," they exclaimed, anxious to secure the life of their captain.

Such acts of devotion are too common in the navy, where the men have officers they esteem, to be thought much of by them.

The three midshipmen, meantime, remained together, sheltered as much as possible by the topgallant forecastle, but still the sea was continually breaking over them. The night was very dark, and the wind bitterly cold; the lightning too at times flashed vividly, revealing the horrors with which they were surrounded. Mr Gale had seen the last of the people off, they thinking that he was going to follow; but two other unfortunate men demanded his care. One was a marine, whose arm had been broken; the other the assistant-surgeon. The latter, never strong, had become exhausted with the exertions he had gone through; and, when urged to go on shore, he had declared his inability to venture on the rope. He felt, poor fellow, that if he did, he should be washed off and drowned. It was sad to hear the groans of the poor marine, as he lay secured to the deck near them. Jack felt that he could have borne the trial much better, had he and his friends been alone on the wreck. The surgeon made no complaint, beyond the utterance now and then of a faint moan. The horrors of death were encircling him around. Fortunately Mr Gale had secured a flask of brandy, a few drops of which he occasionally administered to the sufferers. He also succeeded in fishing out from forward some of the men's clothing, which he distributed among the party; and then, having done all that a man could do, he sat himself down, almost overcome, to wait till the morning, when he might hope to get the survivors on shore. Adair's leg gave him excruciating pain. Rogers sat on one side of him, Murray on the other, supporting him in their arms, and endeavouring, by every means they could think of, to alleviate his suffering, by gently rubbing his legs, frequently changing his position, and tightly grasping his hands.

"Thank you, Alick; thank you, Jack," said he faintly; "I'm better. I'd not die this time, if it were not so bitter, bitter cold; but I wish you two fellows were safe on shore. I should never forgive myself if any harm was to come to you."

"Oh, nonsense, Adair, don't think about us. We are all very well, and shall be very well, no fear," was the answer; but Jack spoke in a voice very different to his usual tone. The exertions he had gone through had been almost too much even for his well-knit frame; a sort of stupor was stealing over him, and his senses began to wander. Murray discovered his condition with great alarm. He called to him to arouse himself.

"Oh, Jack, don't give way," he exclaimed. "If you fall asleep, the cold may overpower you."

Mr Gale, hearing Murray's exclamation, gave Jack a few drops of brandy, which revived him. Murray gladly took a few drops. At the moment of trial he was not found wanting. In spite of his more delicate frame, he bore up as well as the strongest. Thus the night drew slowly on. How earnestly did all on the wreck long for the blessed light of day. Three of them had the consciousness that they had remained both from a high sense of duty and from the call of friendship, and this undoubtedly contributed to support them. They too well knew in whose right arm they had to trust to save them. Jack had not forgotten the lessons he had received at home, nor the counsel given him by Admiral Triton. But Jack on no subject was much of a talker; he was a *doer*, however, which is more important. The nearer a matter was to his heart, the less he allowed it to come out on his tongue, except at the proper moment. By some of his shipmates, who did not understand him, he was considered rather a close fellow. The same might be said of Murray, even in a greater degree. Few indeed guessed, when they saw his slight frame and delicate features, how much he would both dare and do. The power of passive endurance of all three was most fully tried during that awful night. None of them flinched. Murray alone, however, never allowed himself for a moment to lose his consciousness. The rain and sleet came down with pitiless force; the bleak wind howled round them, the sea beat over them, the ceaseless breakers roared in their ears all the night through. Murray felt as if it would never come to an end. Every moment too the ship seemed as if she was about to break up, when he knew that death must be the lot of all remaining on board. How thankfully he saw the first faint gleam of dawn breaking in the east, to him a sign, as he afterwards said, that the moment of their preservation was at hand. He shook Jack, and pointed it out to him.

"All right, old fellow," answered Jack; "I'm ready for a swim." But Rogers did not know what he was saying, for he nodded off again. Adair was with difficulty aroused to consciousness. He was utterly unable to help himself or to move. Had he been left alone he must have perished. Murray called loudly on Mr Gale. He sprang up; though, when he moved, he found his limbs very stiff. They went to examine into the state of their other companions. Both the poor fellows were dead. The survivors felt that they had still greater reason for gratitude that they had been spared while others had been taken.

When daylight increased sufficiently to enable them to discover objects on shore, they found Captain Hartland and several of the men, with a number of the Greeks, assembled on the beach to help them. Another pair of slings on a second traveller was now fitted, and Adair being placed in it, Mr Gale accompanied him on shore, helping him along through the surf. Murray and Jack followed, several of the men, with ropes round their waists, rushing out into the surf to help them, for no men more than sailors know how to appreciate the act of devotion the two lads had that night performed. The captain met them as they came dripping out of the surf, and shook them heartily by the hand. He was one of those doing men who do not expend many words in expressing their feelings. The words he did speak were very gratifying to the young midshipmen. He would not allow them, however, to remain on the beach, but had them all carried up to the nearest house, and put to bed, when the doctor soon arrived to attend to poor Adair's leg. The house where they were lodged was of some size. It belonged to a Greek nobleman, who was absent at the time of their arrival, but an old woman, a sort of housekeeper, and her two daughters had charge of it, and took very good care of them. Their attendants did not come very near the classic models they had read about at school, but they were good-natured and kind, and evidently anxious to please them. The three midshipmen did their best to talk Greek, but though they summoned up all the choicest phrases they had learned at school, they signally failed at first in making themselves understood. At last they bethought them of putting all their previous knowledge of the Hellenic tongue out of the question, and of pointing to things and asking their names. Frequently they found a great similarity between the modern and ancient Greek, which assisted them very much in recollecting the names of the things they learned. They thus in their turn rather surprised the natives by the rapidity with which they acquired their language.

"I used to think it a great bore to have to learn Greek when I was coming to sea," observed Jack; "but now I find that there is use for it even here, besides helping one on wonderfully with one's own language."

The midshipmen were not left alone all this time to the care of their Greek friends. The doctor and their shipmates used now and then to look in on them. They found that an attempt was being made to get the ship off, and of course all hands were engaged in the work. Jack wanted to get up and help, but the doctor would not let him, thinking he would be much better employed in helping Murray to look after Adair. They all heard, however, with great interest of the progress of the undertaking. But one night it came on to blow again harder than ever; a tremendous sea rolled in, and the poor sloop was irretrievably bilged, and in a few days broke up altogether. The three midshipmen were very sorry for this, but they got over the loss of the ship with philosophical resignation, as other midshipmen have under like circumstances done before them; and with the rest of their shipmates amused themselves very well in shooting snipe and red-legged partridges, in wandering about, in trying to talk Greek, and in doing nothing, till a brig of war arrived and carried them all back to Malta. Captain Hartland and his officers were tried for the loss of his sloop, and honourably acquitted; and Adair and Rogers rejoined the *Racer*, to which, to their great satisfaction, a short time afterwards Murray was appointed. The *Racer*, after a cruise to the westward, came back, and was ordered to proceed to the Greek Islands to assist in repressing piracy, an occupation to which the descendants of the heroes whose deeds were sung by Homer of old have of late years been somewhat addicted.

"I wonder whether you will take another prize, Paddy," said Murray with a quiet smile, in which he frequently indulged; but Jack and Terence begged that the subject might not be alluded to.

The *Racer*, before long, fell in with an English merchant brig having a flag of distress flying. The man-of-war hove-to, and the brig sent a boat on board. The poor master who came in her was in a sad plight.

"I have been tricked, robbed, and cruelly treated, sir on the high seas!" he exclaimed, as he appeared on the quarter-deck.

"What has happened? Tell me your story, and I will see what can be done for you," answered Captain Lascelles.

"Why, sir, I was bound out of Liverpool with a cargo of manufactured goods for Smyrna, when yesterday, as I was standing on my course with a light wind, I fell in with a polacre brig with a signal of distress flying. I hove-to, when her boat came alongside me with a dozen cut-throat looking fellows in her, in red caps, and one very fine gentleman with pistols in his belt, and a sword by his side. He was very polite, and said that he was hard up for several things, but would only trouble me for some biscuit and water. I was very glad to get off so cheap, for I guessed what sort of a calling his was, so I gave him as much as he wanted. He spoke a *lingua franca*, which he found I understood. He said that he had known very unjust complaints being made by merchantmen against his poor countrymen, and that, if I would be so obliging, he would be very thankful if I would give him a certificate that he had treated me and my people kindly, and had only taken a little bread and water. Of course I was very willing, and thought him the mildest and best-mannered of pirates; so I gave it to him at once. Immediately he got it he put it in his pocket, and, turning to his people, told them to knock down every one of my men who made any resistance, and clapping a pistol to my head ordered me to hand out all my cash. Meantime the polacre ran alongside, thirty or forty cut-throat fellows jumped on board, and very quickly transferred the cargo of the *Pretty Polly* on board their vessel. When they had completely gutted my brig, the pirate captain made me a polite bow, and thanking me for the certificate, which, he said, he had no doubt would be useful to him, wished me good-day, and returned on board his vessel, leaving all my people with their hands lashed behind them. His followers had amused themselves by painting my poor fellows' faces, and otherwise ill-treating them. One had a tar-brush jammed into his mouth, another a towel stuffed down his throat; and my mate they had almost beaten to death because he had ventured to show fight."

"Which way did the polacre stand after she left you?" asked Captain Lascelles.

"To the eastward, sir."

"You would know her again?"

"That I should, among a hundred like craft."

"Can you come with us?"

"No, sir, but I can let my mate go," answered the master to Captain Lascelles' last query; "he knows every bale of the cargo too, and he'll not forget our friend or his craft."

The mate of the merchantman, Mr Dobbin, came on board, and the frigate continued her course. From the account given of him, Captain Lascelles had little doubt that the pirate was the very man he was in search of, and whose stronghold he had been directed to attack. Among the numerous isles of Greece there are several of small size, with but little room on their summits for cultivation, which have for ages past, from their inaccessible character, afforded a secure retreat to the somewhat piratically disposed inhabitants. The *Racer* was now in search of one of these respectable little strongholds of piracy.

"Will the Greeks show fight, I wonder?" said Jack. "I should like just to have a sniff of gunpowder."

"It may blacken your face more than you expect, youngster," answered old Hemming, who sat at the end of the berth; "however, we have not yet found out where the fellows are hid."

"I hear that the captain has discovered their retreat, and that, if the breeze holds, we are likely to be not far off them this very evening," said Murray, who had just come below. "It is said we are to attack them in the boats."

"Hurrah! that will be fun!" exclaimed Adair. "I suppose the captain will let some of us go."

"Be sure of that, youngsters; the expedition would never succeed without you," said old Hemming in a sarcastic tone.

Murray's information proved to be right. The frigate stood on for an hour after dark, and then dropped her anchors in a bay to leeward of a rocky island, at no great distance from the one to be attacked. Captain Lascelles' object was to take the pirates by surprise. The boats had, therefore, a long way to pull. They were to proceed in two divisions. One was to land a body of bluejackets and marines, so as to attack the fort in the rear; the other was to approach it on the sea side, and to endeavour to scale the heights. The second lieutenant and old Hemming had charge of the two divisions; they had each a midshipman with them, and a mate and a midshipman went into each of the other boats. Adair was with the land party. The division to which Jack and Murray belonged was to attack the fort in front. The men gave a suppressed cheer as they shoved off, and then away they pulled as eagerly as if they were going on a party of pleasure. They had a long pull; but many a joke was cut, and many a suppressed laugh was indulged in, till they got so near the spot that silence was imposed on every one. Hemming's party landed at the back of the island. They were to lie concealed as near as they could get to the fort, till the other division threw up a rocket as a signal that they were attacking, and were discovered by the enemy. Jack and Murray were in boats close together. The night was very dark. They could just see that high, rugged, black cliffs towered up above them, and that they were entering a little cove or harbour, through a narrow entrance which put them in mind of a huge mouse-trap. The boats had muffled oars; not a sound was heard; but had any one been on the lookout, the phosphorescent flashes as the blades touched the water would have betrayed them. The boats reached some black slippery rocks. The crews, led by their officers, leaped out, leaving two boat-keepers in each; and, holding their cutlasses in their teeth, away they scrambled up the steep and rugged cliffs.

Chapter Four
Alas, poor Paddy!

The night was very dark: Jack and Murray and their companions, in perfect silence, climbed up the rugged precipice which formed the outworks of the island fortress. They knocked their knees and cut their shins against the sharp points of the rocks, and scratched their hands and faces with the thorny plants which grew out of the crevices; but, undeterred by these obstacles, they boldly scrambled on till they saw some figures moving above them, and a shower of stones came rattling down on their heads.

"Powder is scarce among the pirates, I suppose, that they treat us in this way," remarked Jack, as he was nearly knocked over by a stone striking his shoulder.

"Yes; these Greek heroes are defending their stronghold as the Tyrolese defended their Alpine homes," answered Murray; "but come along, we shall soon have them at close quarters."

"Hurrah! the enemy have found us out. Fire the rocket down there below!" shouted the lieutenant in command. The order was quickly conveyed to the boat, and up flew a rocket with a loud hiss through the darkness, its bright stream of light forming a beautiful curve over the fortress. All necessity for silence was now over, the men shouted and cheered and cut many a joke at each other's mishaps as they clambered on up the height, some of them slipping half the way down again, as, indifferent to danger, they too carelessly attempted to scale unscalable rocks. Still the whole body, by no small exertion, foot by foot, worked their upward way till they reached the summit. What was next going to happen? The enemy, it was evident, had a due respect for British courage, for they had fled from the ramparts and undoubtedly had taken up a stronger position in the interior of the fortress. Perhaps they had formed a mine ready to spring, and the idea that such might be the case created a few very uncomfortable sensations in the breasts of some of the assailants. To feel the ground shaking under the feet during an earthquake is far from agreeable, but it is a mere pleasant excitement compared to the feelings a person experiences, when he knows that at any moment he may be lifted off his legs and blown up into the sky in company with some dozen wagon-loads of stones and earth, and bricks and mortar, and beams and rubbish of all descriptions. I do not know that Jack allowed such an idea to trouble him much, and if Murray thought about the matter it did not make him hang back at all events; for on he and all the rest pushed to meet the enemy. Had they made any calculations on the subject, they would have found that it is better to move quickly across dangerous ground just as it is to skate rapidly over thin ice. The shouts and cheers of the seamen, it appeared, had struck terror into the hearts of the pirates, for they did not come forth from their places of concealment. The storming-party passed by some low huts, but no one was within, and then they came to an open space. Just then, through the gloom, they caught sight of a band emerging from behind some buildings opposite, and advancing boldly to defend the place. They themselves, apparently being hidden by the dark shade of the huts, were not seen. So, waiting a little, out they rushed, clearing the open space at full speed to meet the pirates. Pistols were flashing, cutlasses were clashing in an instant of time, and all parties were engaged to their hearts' content in a desperate struggle. Jack descried a young pirate, as his size showed him to be, on the right of the party, and they at once, as if by mutual consent, singled each other out, and were instantly hot at work like the rest, slashing away with their cutlasses most desperately. "Yield, you young pirate, yield!" sang out Jack, finding that he could gain no advantage over his opponent.

"Pirate! I'm no more pirate than you are," was the reply, in a voice which Jack instantly recognised as that of Paddy Adair, whose skull he had been endeavouring so hard to split.

"Oh! Paddy, is that you?" cried Jack. "Well, I'm so glad that I didn't hurt you. But I say, old fellow, if you are not a pirate, where are the rascals? Let's go and find them out."

"Hillo! what's all this about?" sang out Mr Thorn. "Why, Hemming, is that you? I thought you were pirates."

"I paid you the same compliment, sir," answered the old mate, with a slight touch of irony in his tone, for Mr Thorn had just shot off the rim of his cap. "You very nearly spoilt my beauty by mistake."

"I am very sorry for that, Hemming," answered the lieutenant coolly; "but I wonder where the fellows have got to. We must rout them out."

Fortunately, the most serious injury inflicted was to Hemming's cap, and, as Paddy afterwards declared (not very correctly, as they had found no one to conquer), the victorious party hurried off in search of fresh enemies. They soon came to the door of a large building; it was bolted and barred. "The pirates are inside here, my lads, there can be no doubt of it," shouted

Mr Thorn. They soon found a spar, a brig's topmast. The heel made a capital battering-ram, and with a cheery "Yeo, ho, ho!" the seamen gave many a heavy blow against the oaken door. It cracked and cracked and groaned, and at length, with a loud bang, burst open. "Stand by, my lads, to cut down the fellows as they rush out," cried Lieutenant Thorn; but as the pirates did not come out, the sailors, following their officers, cutlass in hand, rushed in. They found themselves in a large hall; they looked about for the ferocious pirates armed to the teeth, and resolved with the last drop of their blood to defend their hearths and homes. Loud shrieks and cries, however, assailed the ears of the seamen, and by the glare of a brazier of burning coals in the middle of the apartment they beheld three old women. Their appearance was not attractive; they were very thin and parchment-like, and dark; but they might have been very good old bodies for all that. They had, distaff in hand, been sitting, spinning, and talking over affairs in general, if not those of their neighbours, when they had been aroused by the unwelcome sounds of the battering-ram. While the door resisted its efforts they had prudently kept quiet, but when it gave way, they expressed their very natural fears by the sounds which had reached the seamen's ears. As the storming-party advanced, they shrieked louder and louder, but did not run away, because apparently there was no where to run to.

"Don't be frightened, missis," exclaimed Hemming, taking one of them by the arm. "Tell us where the men are, whose heads we have come to break. We won't hurt you."

The old ladies, however, made no reply to this assurance; but only screamed on, probably because they did not understand English. As no one of the party spoke a word of Greek, there was little chance of any information being obtained from the ancient dames. Perhaps they had an object in screaming, to cover the retreat of their friends; so thought Lieutenant Thorn, because if the pirates were not in the fort, who else could have pitched down the stones on their heads as they scrambled up? Certainly not the three old women; that would have been a disgrace. They would not have had time even to have hobbled away and retreated to the place where they were found. Many of the men declared vehemently that they had seen the heads of the pirates, long-bearded fellows, looking over the ramparts, and that they could not be, even then, very far off. Accordingly, leaving Murray with a couple of sailors to look after the three old women, the two parties of seamen, under their respective officers, once more divided to go in search of the outlaws.

"I say, Jack, don't you take me for a pirate again, if you please," said Terence, as they separated. They wandered about in all directions, putting their noses into huts, and their cutlasses into heaps of straw and litter of all sorts; but the whole place seemed deserted. They found nothing. Perhaps this was because they had no torch, and the night was very dark. Already a few faint streaks of daylight were appearing in the sky, when, as Terence was standing near Hemming, a trampling of feet was heard, and loud shouts in the distance.

"Hurrah! here come the Greeks, they have been routed out at last," cried Paddy. They could just make out a body of men stooping down, they thought, and hurrying towards them, not seeing that their enemies were ready to intercept them.

"Cut them down, if they don't yield themselves prisoners," sang out Hemming, leading on his men. Paddy sprang on boldly, in his eagerness to meet the foe, and instantly afterwards was knocked head over heels by one of his opponents. He felt as if he had been run through by a bayonet or a pike, or something of that sort, though he could not make out exactly where he had been wounded. There was a terrific shouting in the rear of the enemy, and he had no difficulty in recognising the voices of his shipmates, especially those of Jack and Murray. The shouts came nearer and nearer. He picked himself up to see what had become of the enemy, but they were nowhere to be found. Instead of them, a flock of goats, chased by Mr Thorn's party, and frightened by their shouts, were butting away with heroic valour at anybody and everybody who came in their way, while daylight revealed the laughing countenances of his friends, who had seen his overthrow and the enemy which caused it. Paddy did not much mind, however. He rubbed himself over, and finding that he had no bones broken, or any puncture in his body, burst into a loud laugh.

"I shouldn't be surprised but that those are the very fellows with the long beards we saw standing at the top of the ramparts, and whom everybody took for pirates," he exclaimed. "As they turned round to scamper away, they kicked the stones down over us. We are all in one box, that's a comfort. No one can laugh at the other." Thus Adair very adroitly turned the laugh from himself. Every one acknowledged the probable correctness of his surmises, but still Mr Thorn thought it right to continue his search for the outlaws. No information could be obtained from their fair captives, as Paddy called them. There could be little doubt that there must have been very lately a number of men in the fort, for it could not be supposed that three old women would be left as the regular garrison of a pretty strong fortification. They were still continuing their search, when daylight revealed to them a couple of boats under all sail, standing away to the northward, and by the course they were steering looking as if they must but a short time before have left the island. Mr Thorn ordering Hemming to take charge of the place, leaving him Rogers and a few more men, hurried down the height, to go in pursuit of the flying enemy.

"Remember the captain's orders were, that we were to attack and make prisoners of the men alone, but that goods of every description and all private property is to be strictly respected."

"Ay, ay, sir," answered Hemming, meaning that he understood the orders received.

Hunting about they discovered a very steep winding path down to the harbour. By it Mr Thorn and his followers descended to their boats, and away they went in hot pursuit of the pirates. The wind was light, but as they could both pull as well as sail, they made tolerable way after the chase. Meantime the party in charge of the fort became very hungry, and as they had left their provisions in the boats, it was necessary to send for them. Adair accordingly, with a couple of men, was despatched on this duty. He had no great difficulty in finding his way, as he could see from one end of the island to the other, and he soon reached the top of the cliff, below which the boats had been left; he looked over the edge of the cliff, but he could discover no boats. He hallooed to the boat-keepers, but there was no answer.

"They must be asleep, Mr Adair," observed one of the men.

"So I might think if I saw any boats," answered Terence. "But the boats are not there, I am sure."

To ascertain the fact, however, more certainly, they descended to the beach. No boats were to be seen. They looked behind the points of rock on either side, but no boats were visible. They shouted at the top of their voices, but the only sound in reply was the shriek of some sea-fowl, startled from their resting-places in the cliffs.

"Have we got to the right spot, do you think?" suggested Terence, hope springing up in his breast that they had made a mistake.

"No doubt about it, sir," was the answer; "I remember climbing up through this very gap; there are the marks of our feet plain enough."

"And the marks of a good many other feet too," observed Terence, examining the ground. "I am very much afraid that the boats have been run away with by the pirates; but what can have become of our poor shipmates, I cannot think."

His men agreed with him in the opinion that the pirates must have made off with the boats; and, after searching about in every direction for the poor fellows who had been left in charge of them, they returned to the fort with the unsatisfactory news. All hands had, in the meantime, grown ravenously hungry. The old women could not, or would not, give them any food. At all events, they turned a deaf ear to all their hints and signs that it would be acceptable. Some very black dry bread was discovered, and also some fowls, but no eggs were to be seen; and fowls, Mr Hemming was afraid, would be looked upon as private property. What was to be done? The provisions from the boats would soon arrive, and then they might lawfully satisfy their appetites. I forgot to say that Mr Dobbin, the mate of the merchantman which had been plundered, had come to try and identify the stolen property. While storming the fort, he had been as active as any one, and showed that had there been work to be done he was the fellow to do it. To employ the time till they could get some breakfast, Hemming determined to commence a systematic search for the stolen property. They hunted and hunted about with great zeal, examining every hut and every heap of rubbish.

"I wonder, after all, if this is the place the pirates are accustomed to hide in," observed Jack. "It would be a sell if we had made a mistake altogether."

"What could have put that into your head, Rogers?" exclaimed Hemming, feeling rather queer. "Oh, no! there's no doubt about it."

Still, as he got more and more hungry, and searched still farther in vain, his spirits began to sink to zero, and he could lot help believing that Jack might be right. Just then here was a shout from some of the party. They were standing before a dilapidated hut, the door of which they had broken open. Presently the mate of the merchantman appeared dragging out a bale of goods.

"Hurrah! we have not searched for nothing!" he exclaimed. "There seems to be a good bit of the ship's cargo in here."

A number of valuable bales of cotton and cloth, and some silk, were hauled forth, all of which the mate identified as having formed part of the cargo of his ship. Still there was a very large part of the missing property not forthcoming. Nothing else was found for some time, till one of the men, of an inquisitive turn of mind, happened to poke his head into one of the pigsties, where, in the farthest corner, his eye fell on several bales piled up one above the other to the roof. The clue to the sort of place in which the well-known ingenuity of the Greeks had taught them to conceal their booty once being discovered, a considerable amount more was brought to light. Still much was missing. Just then Adair and his men were seen returning.

"Hurrah I now we'll have breakfast," cried Jack, who declared that he could eat a porcupine or a crocodile, outside and all, he was so hungry. What was his dismay, and that of all the party, when they found that no food was forthcoming, and that the boats were not to be found. Just then their hunger was most pressing, and they left the subject of what had become of the boats for after consideration. The brown bread by itself was very uninviting. Jack looked at a fat pig in the sty with the eye of an ogre.

"Is it possible that the pirates could have stuffed some of the silks and laces inside that huge porker, Hemming?" asked Jack, "I've heard of some Flanders mares coming across the Channel stuffed up to the mouth with lace," observed Adair.

"If it were possible, I think we should be right to search that pig," said Hemming, looking very hard at the unconscious object under discussion, who went grunting on, asking somewhat loudly for food.

"There's no doubt about it," cried the mate of the merchantman. "She'll make prime pork chops too."

The men had been meantime collecting sticks and lighting a fire: perhaps they shrewdly guessed how the discussion might end.

"Here, butcher, you'll understand how to cut that pig up better than any of us, so as to see what is in her inside," said Hemming. In a very short time the fat pig was converted into pork, and some prime chops were frizzling and hissing away before the fire. No laces or satins were found inside, but instead some very delicious pig's fry, which, under the circumstances, was perhaps more acceptable, especially as the laces would, I think, have been spoilt had they been stuffed down the pig's throat. The old women made a great lamentation when they saw their pig being killed, but they were pacified by having some of the chops presented to them, and then they produced some salt, and some better bread, and some lemons, and plates, and knives, and forks, which latter were of silver. Their female hearts evidently softened when they found that no harm was done to them, and that killing the pig was a case of necessity; and though they were not communicative, simply from want of language to express themselves, they chattered away to each other most vehemently. They spread a table in the hall where they had been first seen, and seemed to wish to do their best to serve their uninvited guests. The seamen made very merry over their feast of pig, though they were rather in want of something to wash it down. Poor fellows! they had neither tea nor coffee. At length the old ladies produced a jar of arrack—very vile stuff it was, but the seamen would have drunk it without stint had Mr Hemming allowed them. He, however, interposed, and insisted on serving out only a little at a time to a few of the men. The effect was such as to make him jump up and kick over the jar, by which all the liquor was spilt, very much to the disappointment of those who had not had any.

"I don't mean to say that these respectable old ladies put anything into the spirits, but somebody did, and you would have been very sorry for yourselves if you had taken much of it," he observed, as he reseated himself.

This little incident rather astonished the old ladies, but not understanding what was said, they took it to be the effect of pure accident, and continued as attentive as before.

"When the boats come back, you shall have your grog, my lads," said Hemming; "in the meantime, if any of you are thirsty, there's a well of cool water. The pirates will scarcely have thought of poisoning that."

By the time the feast was concluded, very little of the pig remained; the seamen declared that they had never eaten better pork in their lives. The rest of the day was spent in searching for stolen property, though only a few bales of merchandise were discovered, stowed away here and there, in the oddest places imaginable. Meantime Hemming and Jack began to be somewhat anxious about Mr Thorn and the boats. Evening was coming on, and they ought long before to have returned. In vain the old mate and the midshipman scanned the horizon. Not a sail was to be seen approaching the island. Two or three vessels only passed far away in the offing. Many other rocky isles were rising out of the ocean like blue mounds, some of them faint and misty from the distance they were off. Towards one of them the boats had directed their course. It was well-known that many of them were, and had been for ages, the haunts of pirates.

"I say, Hemming, suppose Mr Thorn has been entrapped by some of those piratical fellows out there; what will become of them, I wonder?" said Jack.

"We shall have to go and hunt them out," was the answer. "The pirates will scarcely venture to hurt them."

The evening drew on and darkness returned, and still no boats made their appearance. Mr Hemming, who was really a very good officer, especially when in command, and when he felt the responsibility of his position, had a strict watch kept all night, for he thought it probable that some of the pirates might be hid in the island, and, when they found how few were left in charge of the fort, might attempt a surprise to recover the booty. The night, however, passed away quietly, and in the morning Jack was despatched in the cutter to carry information of what had occurred to the frigate. Jack had a long pull, for the wind was contrary. He kept his eyes about him all the way, looking into every nook and corner, for he could not tell in which a pirate-boat might have taken shelter, and he thought it more than likely that one might suddenly pounce out and try to capture him. None appeared. This, however, did not make him less cautious for the future. One of the many pieces of advice given him by Admiral Triton was never to despise an enemy, and always to take every precaution against surprise. A soldier or sailor in war time should always sleep with one eye open, and his arms in his hands, the Admiral used to say, speaking somewhat metaphorically. The foolhardy folly which had made many officers neglect proper precautions, has caused the destruction of many brave men, as well as the failure of many important enterprises. At last Jack reached the frigate. Captain Lascelles was very much vexed at hearing of the loss of the boats. He instantly ordered the *Racer* to be got under weigh to go in search of them. It was very intricate navigation among those isles and islets and rocks, especially at night, but the wind was fair, and there was a moon to shed her pale light over the ocean. The lead was kept constantly going, and hands were stationed aloft as lookouts. The *Racer* had got just off the island of which Hemming was left in charge, when a lookout forward announced a boat on the starboard bow. The boat was pulling towards them, and the frigate being hove-to, she came alongside, and Alick Murray appeared on board. He reported that they had overtaken the pirates who were in possession of the boats close to a rocky island, and were on the point of capturing them when half a dozen boats started out and completely turned the fortunes of the day. On this, Mr Thorn, seeing that they must inevitably be overpowered, ordered him to endeavour to make his escape, and to give notice of what had occurred. This, though pursued, he had been able to do. Jack having reported the starving state of the garrison, a boat was sent with provisions and men to ascertain also how Hemming and his party were getting on. She returned in half a hour with a favourable report, bringing off Mr Dobbin, the mate of the merchantman, and the frigate then continued her course for the second piratical stronghold. She did not come off it till near noon the next day, and then had to sail twice round it before a landing-place could be discovered. Some little anxiety was felt for the fate of Mr Thorn and his men, for the pirates were not supposed to be gentlemen who stood on ceremony as to the treatment of their prisoners.

"If they dare to injure our people, the Greeks well know that we would sweep every one of them off their rock into the sea," said Captain Lascelles. "Clemency on such an occasion is cruelty to others."

Scarcely had the frigate hove-to off what appeared to be a little harbour, than a boat with a white flag was seen coming out of it. In ten minutes a splendidly dressed Greek came up the side armed with a handsomely chased sword and pistols, and a red cap set jauntily on one side.

"Can any one speak Italian?" he asked, in a soft tone, in that beautiful language.

"Yes, I can," answered Captain Lascelles.

"Then, sir, I have to make great complaints of ill-treatment from your people," replied the Greek; and he made out a long story to the effect that he, a quiet, respectable landowner, whose sole aim was to cultivate in peace a few acres of land descended to him from a long line of illustrious ancestors, that he had been insulted, attacked by an aimed force, suspected of robbery, of which he was incapable; that some of his poor peasants, in their horror and alarm, finding some boats, had jumped into them and induced their crews to assist in pulling them to a neighbouring island, hoping there to be safe; that they had been pursued, and that then, and not till then, had they been compelled to resort to some gentle force for their own protection. While the Greek was speaking, Mr Dobbin came up behind him, and made signs that he was the very man who had plundered their brig.

"Why, sir, the master of an English merchantman complains that you ill-treated his people and robbed his vessel."

"*O Signori, impossibile*; that I should be guilty of such an act!" and the Greek smiled sweetly and put his hand on his heart.

For a moment he was, however, a little taken aback when Mr Dobbin, stepping forward and confronting him, said, "Do you know me?"

"*Ah si, adesso me ricordo!* Ah yes, now I recollect," said the Greek, with a bland smile. "But you shall judge, sir, how unjustly I am accused. I did lately take charge of a brig for a friend. I was suffering from want of water and bread. See the deceitfulness of the world; I asked it humbly, they gave it willingly, and at the same time this certificate," and he produced the paper signed by the master of the brig. The impudence of the Greek almost overcame the captain's composure.

"Notwithstanding that paper, I must detain you," he observed.

"What! Detain an independent chieftain, who comes on board your ship under the sacred protection of a flag of truce, a thing unheard of by all civilised nations," exclaimed the Greek in a tone of indignation and astonishment; "no, no, you will not do that."

The Greek was right; Captain Lascelles would not do a wrong even to obtain an undoubted right. The Greek knew that he had outwitted us. The result was that he undertook to send the boats and their crews on board the frigate unharmed, on condition that the island was not attacked by an armed force. To these terms Captain Lascelles was obliged to consent. Mr Thorn and Murray soon came back, very well, but very much vexed at what had occurred. The island was afterwards searched, but nothing was found, and the *Racer*, having taken on board all the recovered booty, conveyed it to Corfu, where the merchantman was waiting to receive it. After a month or so, when the frigate got back to Malta, Captain Lascelles found that the independent Greek chieftain had lodged a complaint to the effect that his cattle and poultry had been wantonly destroyed. On inquiry, the matter resolved itself into the slaughter of the pig. It came out that Jack and Adair had proposed the crime. The Admiral at the time thought it better to take no notice of the affair. However, he soon after invited the two midshipmen to dine with him, and both of them found themselves served with rather a large helping of roast pork.

"You are fond of pig, young gentlemen, are you not?" said the Admiral, with a laugh in his eye.

"Yes, sir, very, especially when I have to kill one in the line of duty, and am ravenously hungry into the bargain," answered Paddy, with all the simplicity of an Irishman. The Admiral laughed, and as he was fond of a joke, and knew both Lord Derrynane and Admiral Triton, he often asked the two youngsters for the sake of passing it off and telling the story about the pig and the pirates.

Soon after this Jack and Terence met with a severe trial. For the first time since they came to sea they were separated, and Adair was appointed to a ten-gun brig, the *Onyx*. Happily that class of vessels no longer exists in the navy. They obtained the unattractive title of sea-coffins, from the number of them which had been lost with all hands. They carried a heavy weight of metal on deck, had but little beam, but were rigged with taut masts and very square yards. Still these circumstances did not trouble Adair half as much as parting from Jack and Murray.

The frigate and the brig were sent to cruise in different directions, and for several months did not meet.

"A brig of war is in sight," said Jack, entering the captain's cabin, sent by the officer of the watch; "she has made her number the *Onyx*."

"Signalise her to heave-to when she nears us," said Captain Lascelles. "I will be on deck presently." In a short time another signal was run up. It was to invite the captain and officers of the brig to dine on board the frigate. It was very readily accepted, and in a short time the tall frigate and her little companion might have been seen quietly floating near each other, their sails scarcely filled by the light breeze, and their rigging and hulls reflected vividly in the calm water. The midshipmen had a great deal to talk about, and numerous adventures to describe more interesting to themselves than to anybody else. They had a very merry party also in the midshipmen's berth, and all were sorry to find that it was time for the officers of the brig to return on board. When Captain Lascelles and his party came on deck he cast his eye round the horizon.

"I do not like the look of the sky out there," he remarked, pointing with his hand to the eastward. "Captain Sims, I must advise you to get on board as soon as possible and shorten sail, or your brig will be caught in a squall before you are ready." Captain Sims was not a man fond of rapid movement, but on this occasion he saw that no time was to be lost.

"Good-bye, Paddy," said Jack; "take care of yourself aboard the little hooker there, and we'll have many a jovial day together before long."

"Good-bye, Rogers; good-bye, Murray; good-bye, old fellows," answered Terence.

"The brig is a jolly little craft, in spite of what they call her."

"What's that?" asked Murray.

"The sea-coffin," answered Terence, as they shoved off. The two boats which had brought the captain and his officers made the best of their way to the brig. They were soon close to her. The white cloud had meantime been growing larger and larger, and yet there was scarcely a breath of wind. Many on board the frigate did not believe even that a squall was brewing. Suddenly the clouds, as if impelled by some mighty impulse, came rushing on, not in a direct line, but with a circular motion, towards the spot where lay the two ships of war.

"All hands shorten sail," cried the first lieutenant. "Man the fore and main clew-garnets, spanker brails—topsail-halyards—clew up—haul down, let fly of all." These and sundry other orders followed in rapid succession. The squall, seeming to gain rapidity as it advanced, struck the frigate before it was expected. Jack and Murray had hurried with others to their stations aloft, and were endeavouring as rapidly as they could to get those orders they received executed, but the exertions of all were insufficient to take the canvas off the ship in time. Over heeled the frigate on her beam end, the water rushing in at her lee ports—some of the sails were split to ribbons, sheets and halyards were flying loose, and a scene of confusion prevailed such as she had never before been in. The whole surface of the ocean was a mass of white foam, surrounded by which the ship lay an almost helpless wreck. The helm was put up but she would not answer it.

"We shall have to cut away the mizen-mast," observed the captain. "But we'll try and make head sail on her first." This was done. A suppressed shout of satisfaction showed that she felt its power, and away she flew like a sea-bird before the squall, the darkness of night coming on to bide all surrounding objects from their view. Then, and not till then, had any one time to turn a glance towards the *Onyx*. Not a glimpse of her was to be seen. Jack and Murray had watched the boats get alongside, and they were on the point of being hoisted in when the squall struck the frigate. Both of them had a sad apprehension that they had seen the masts of the brig bending down before the squall, but so great at the moment was the uproar and confusion that it appeared more like the vision of a dream than a reality. The instant the squall blew over, the frigate beat back towards the spot where, as far as it could be calculated, the brig had last been seen. Had she bore up she must have been passed. In vain every eye on board was engaged in looking out for her. All night long the frigate tacked backwards and forwards. Not a trace of her could be discovered. Daylight returned; the sun arose; his glorious beams played joyfully over the blue surface of the ocean just rippled by a summer's breeze, but it was too evident that all those they sought and the gay little craft they manned lay engulfed beneath its treacherous bosom.

"There's one of us gone," said Jack, as he bent his head down over the table of the berth to hide his face. "Poor Paddy!"

Murray said nothing, but his countenance was very sad.

Chapter Five
Roasting the Bully

The midshipmen were aroused by the cry of "All hands shorten sail!" The boatswain's whistle had not ceased sounding along the decks before Jack and Murray were on their way aloft, the first to the fore, the other to the maintop, where they were stationed. A heavy squall had struck the frigate, and she was heeling over with her main-deck ports almost in the water. Up they flew with the topmen to their respective stations, while the officer of the watch was shouting through his speaking-trumpet. "Let go topgallant-halyards. Clew up, haul down." Then came, "Let fly topsail-halyards. Clew up. Round in the weather braces." Down came the yards on the caps. The sails were now bulging out and shaking in the wind. Out flew the active topmen to the yard-arms. Jack, as he had often before done, ran out to get hold of the weather earing. He was hauling away on it while the men hauled the reef over to him. He had already taken two outer turns with it, when, as he leaned back, he felt himself suddenly thrown from his hold. In vain he tried to clutch the earing; it slipped through his fingers. Headlong he came down, striking the leech of the sail. Mechanically he clutched at that. Probably it broke his fall. In another moment he was among the foaming waters, with the ship flying fast away from him. Murray had meantime been watching to see which mast would have its sails first reefed, and as he looked forward he saw Jack fall from aloft. He guessed that he must have struck his head when falling, and that he would be senseless when he reached the water. In a moment his jacket and shoes were off, and down he slid like lightning by the topmast weather backstay, and, leaping into the water, swam towards the spot where Jack had fallen. Captain Lascelles had seen the accident. He was on the poop. Stepping back, he himself let go the life-buoy, noting exactly the spot where the accident had occurred. But not an order did he give. Perfectly cool, he stood waiting till the sails were reefed. Murray meantime caught sight of Jack, who lay senseless on the water, to the surface of which he had just risen, after having once gone down from the force with which he had fallen into the sea. Murray dreaded lest he should again see him sink. He exerted all his strength to get up to him. The life-buoy was not far off. Had there been time he would have first towed it up to Jack, but he was afraid if he did that he would in the meantime sink. Murray swam bravely on. The foam, as the wind swept it off the surface of the sea, dashed wildly in his face, but he kept his eye fixed steadily on Jack's head, that should he go down again, he might know exactly where to dive after him. Murray, under Jack's instruction, had been constantly practising swimming, and he now very nearly equalled his master in the art. His courage was as high, and what he wanted in muscular strength he made up by his undaunted spirit. He longed to know what had become of the frigate, but he would not turn his head to look. His first object was to get hold of Jack, and to keep his face out of the water, that, when animation returned, he might not be suffocated. With steady strokes he swam on, admirably retaining his presence of mind. Every stroke was measured. There was no hurry, no bustle, with Murray; he knew that such would only bring worse speed. What an excellent example did he set of the way to attain an important object! Calmly eyeing it, and though clearly comprehending all the difficulties and dangers which surrounded him, with unswerving courage pushing towards his point. "Keep up! keep up, Jack!" he sang out, but Jack did not hear him. The seas, every moment increasing, came roaring towards him, while the foam dashed over his head. He surmounted them all. "I am here. Jack! I am here!" he repeated, as he grasped Jack by the collar and turned him over on his back, so that his face might be uppermost. A faint moan was all the reply Rogers gave. It was satisfactory, as it assured Murray that he was alive. Now he looked round anxiously for the life-buoy. It had drifted away before the gale. But then he also had the wind in his favour, and he did not despair of overtaking it. With one hand supporting his shipmate, and with the other striking out, he swam steadily on as before towards the life-buoy. Evening was coming on. Darkness he knew would soon overspread the sea. He knew that. He knew the difficulty there might be in finding him and his companion. A far more practical swimmer than he might have despaired, but he did not. Murray did not trust to his own right arm to save him. He looked to help from above. He knew if it was right it would be afforded him. If not, he was prepared to meet his fate.

Meantime away flew the frigate. The moment the sails were reefed, the captain issued the orders he had been anxious to give. "About ship," "helm's a-lee." Never did the crew more strenuously exert themselves to box round the yards. They knew who was overboard, and the two midshipmen were favourites with all hands: Murray for the calm, gentlemanly, officer-like way in which he spoke to the men, and for the thorough knowledge of his duty he always displayed; Jack for his dash and bravery, and good spirits and humour with which he carried out any work allotted to him. They now saw that neither was Murray wanting in dash and courage. As the frigate was standing back towards the spot where the accident had occurred, preparations were made for lowering a boat. There was no hurry or confusion in this case. Her proper crew were called away. The second lieutenant took charge of her. Some people called Captain Lascelles a very strict officer. It is true he never overlooked a breach of discipline or carelessness of duty. He used to say that a breach of discipline, however trifling, if allowed to pass, was like a small leak, which, if permitted to continue, will go on increasing till the ship founders. Thus, among other good arrangements, every boat on board was kept in readiness to be lowered at a moment's notice, and everybody knew exactly what to do when a boat was to be lowered.

Captain Lascelles did not allow his feelings to appear; but he was intensely anxious about the fate of his two midshipmen. He would have given all the worldly wealth of which he was possessed to be assured that they would be saved. The thick clouds brought up by the gale increased the gathering gloom. Neither they nor the life-buoy could be seen. He had carefully noted the exact course on which the frigate had run since they went overboard, so that he was able to calculate how to keep her, so as to fetch back to the same spot. There were also many sharp eyes on the lookout forward, endeavouring with all their might to discover the lost ones. In those southern latitudes darkness comes on with a rapidity unknown in lands blessed by a long twilight. Thus, before the frigate got up to the spot where the accident had occurred, the night had come down completely on the world of waters.

"I am afraid that the poor lads must be lost," said the second to the first lieutenant. "We ought to hear them or see something of them by this time."

"Don't say that, Thorn," answered the first lieutenant. "Rogers is the midshipman who took the fine on shore when the *Firefly* was wrecked; and Murray, though so quiet, is a very gallant fellow. They will do all that can be done to save themselves. I should indeed be deeply grieved if they were lost."

There was a good deal of sea at the time running, but not enough to make the lowering of a boat a matter of danger if carefully performed.

"Well heave the ship to, and lower a couple of boats to go in search of the lads," observed the captain.

The first lieutenant issued the necessary orders, and the ship was brought up to the wind and hove-to. Mr Thorn eagerly went to lower one of the boats. Hemming took charge of the other. Their respective crews sprang into them. The falls were properly tended and unhooked at the right moment, and, getting clear of the ship, they lay ready to pull in whatever direction might be indicated. Here was the difficulty.

"Silence fore and aft," sang out the captain. "Does any one hear them?"

In an instant there was a dead silence. No one would have supposed that many hundred human beings were at that moment alive and awake on board the ship. Every one listened intently, but no sound was borne to their ears. Even Captain Lascelles began to give up all hope.

"The poor widowed mother, how will she bear it?" he muttered; "and that honest country gentleman—it will be sad news I shall have to send him of his son."

Scarcely had the captain thus given expression to his feelings, when a bright light burst forth amid the darkness some way to leeward. A shout spontaneously arose from all on board. "They must have got hold of the life-buoy, they must have got hold of the life-buoy," was the cry. "Hurrah! hurrah!" The two boats dashed away, with eager strokes, in the direction of the light.

Meantime Murray had towed Jack steadily on towards the buoy. He began to feel very weary though, and sometimes he thought that his strength would fail him. He looked at the buoy; it seemed a very long way off. He felt at last that he should never be able to reach it. "I'll not give in while life remains," he said to himself. Just then his hand struck against something. He grasped it. It was a large piece of Spanish cork-wood. He shoved it under Jack's back, and rested his own left arm on it. He immediately found an immense advantage from the support it afforded. "Who sent that piece of cork-wood to my aid?" he thought; "it did not come by chance." The assurance that he was not deserted gave him additional confidence. Jack also gave further signs of returning animation.

"Where am I?" he at length asked, in a tone of voice which showed that his senses were still confused.

"In the middle of the Mediterranean; but there's a life-buoy close at hand, and when we get hold of it we shall be all to rights," answered Murray.

"What! is that you, Alick?" asked jack. "I remember now feeling that I was going overboard; but how came you here? Has the ship gone down?"

"No, no; all right; she'll be here to pick us up directly, I hope."

"Then you jumped overboard to save me!" exclaimed Jack. "Just like you, Alick; I knew you would do it."

Jack lay perfectly still all the time he was talking. It did not seem to occur to him that he could swim as well as his companion.

"Here we are!" cried Murray; "Heaven be praised—I was afraid that I should scarcely be able to make out the life-buoy, it is getting so dark."

He placed Jack's hand on one of the beckets, and took another himself, and together they climbed up, and sat on the life-buoy. Murray drew the piece of cork up alongside, observing, "I do not like to desert the friend which has been of so much service in our utmost need, and to kick it away without an acknowledgment."

Jack laughed. He had now completely come to his senses. "I'm very much obliged to you, Friend Cork," said he. "I know, Murray, what you are going to say; I am, indeed, thankful to Heaven for having thus far preserved me, and to you too, my dear fellow. But, I say, can you make out the ship?"

"Not a shred of her. I scarcely know in what quarter to look for her."

"Well, then, all we shall have to do is to hang on here till daylight. The weather is warm, so we shall not come to much harm if the wind goes down again, and I am very certain the captain will come and look for us."

"It may be a question whether he can find us, though," said Murray. "By-the-bye, I do not think that the buoy was fired. If we can find the trigger we will let it off, and that will quickly show our whereabouts."

"A bright idea," answered jack. "Hurrah! I've found it. Now blaze away, old boy." Jack pulled the trigger as he spoke, and immediately an intensely bright bluish light burst forth above their heads, exhibiting their countenances to each other, with their hair streaming, lank and long, over their faces, giving them at the same time a very cadaverous and unearthly appearance. Jack, in spite of their critical position, burst into a fit of laughter. "Certainly, we do look as unlike two natty quarter-deck midshipmen as could well be," he exclaimed. "Never mind, we have not many spectators."

Jack and Murray's coolness arose from the perfect confidence they felt that they would not be deserted while the slightest hope remained of their being found; and now that they had set off the port-fire they were almost as happy as if they were already safe on board. They had not much longer to wait. Presently a hail reached them; they shouted in return, and soon afterwards they saw a couple of boats emerging from the darkness. One took them on board—the other towed the life-buoy; and in half an hour more their wet clothes were off them, and they were being stowed away between the blankets in the sick-bay, each of them sipping a pretty strong glass of brandy and water. Of course, when the excitement was over, a very considerable reaction took place, and several days passed before they were allowed to return to their duty. Captain Lascelles then sent for Jack, and inquired how he came to tumble overboard? Jack had to confess that in his zeal he had gone beyond his duty, and that, instead of remaining at his station in the top, he had been attempting to do work which ought to have been performed by one of the topmen.

"You were wrong, as you will see, Rogers," remarked Captain Lascelles. "Remember that there is a strict line of duty, and that going beyond, as you call it, may be quite as injurious to the service as neglecting any portion of it. Your business was to see that the men were properly reefing the topsail. By going out on the yard-arm you could not do this, and were thus neglecting your duty—not going beyond it. I have no intention of punishing you, on condition that you will recollect what I have said."

Jack promised that he would, and thanked the captain for his lecture. Murray got, as he deserved, a great deal of credit for his gallantry; and he was not a little delighted to receive the gold medal, some time afterwards, from the Humane Society. Soon after this occurrence, the frigate was sent to Gibraltar. She there took on board several passengers for Malta. One was a bear, which was sent as a present to the captain of a line-of-battle ship on the station, from some consul in Africa, who knew that he was fond of pets; another was a young gentleman going to travel in the East. The captain had given him a passage, as he was a relation of some brother officer who could not take him himself. He had been offered, and accepted, a berth in the gun-room. Neither Jack nor Murray had seen him, nor had they heard his name before they sailed. The next morning, after they had lost sight of the rock, when they went on deck, who should they see walking up and down, with an air of no little consequence, and having a pair of lilac kid gloves on his hands, but Bully Pigeon. Jack and Murray forgot all his bad qualities, and only thought of him as an old schoolfellow. So they went up to him, and cordially put out their hands.

"Why, Pigeon, how are you, old fellow? Who'd have thought of seeing you here?" exclaimed Jack.

Pigeon drew himself up. "You must have made a mistake; I—I don't remember you," he answered.

"Oh! but we do you, very well, at Eagle House. I'm Jack Rogers, here's Murray. We two came together. You didn't leave, either, before us," said Jack. "Oh! you must remember all about it."

"Ah! now I think I do," replied Pigeon, extending the tips of his fingers. "There was another fellow went to sea at the same time. Paddy something— Oh! ye-es, I remember."

"Ah! Paddy Adair, you mean. Poor fellow, he was lost in the *Onyx*," answered Jack, in a sad tone.

"Oh! I remember—he was always a harum-scarum vagabond," said Pigeon, in a sneering way.

"He was as true a fellow as ever stepped!" exclaimed Jack indignantly. "If he were here, Pigeon, you would not speak so of him." The bully, as usual, was silenced. It was not Jack's way to cut anybody, but neither he nor Murray felt inclined to have any intimate conversation with their old schoolfellow. Still they could not help asking him about the school, and the various changes which had taken place since they left.

"Well, I'm glad it prospers," exclaimed Jack. "It was a first-rate, jolly good school; there was no humbug about it. I spent many happy days there."

Murray echoed these sentiments. Pigeon of course sneered, and observed that, "though there were a good many noblemen, and sons of gentlemen, there were a number of sons of merchants and city people."

"Ah! that is just what there should be," said Jack. "It is the very thing that keeps England so well together. When the gentle born you speak of find that the sons of city men are as gentlemanly, as clever, and as honourable as themselves, and can play cricket or leapfrog, or anything of that sort, perhaps better than they do, they learn to respect them, and treat them as their equals ever afterwards. That is one of the very things that made our school so good. We used to think of fellows not for what they were but for what they did—except, perhaps, a few miserable sneaks, who 'carnied' up to a fellow because he had a handle to his name."

Pigeon did not respond to this sentiment, because he had been noted far doing the very thing that Jack reprobated.

Jack could not help describing Pigeon in the berth, and the general opinion was that he deserved to be well roasted while he remained on board—in other words, that he should be made the common butt, at which the shafts of their wits should be aimed.

They had plenty of opportunities of shooting the said shafts, for Pigeon exhibited an almost incredible amount of simplicity in all things connected with the sea. I do not mean to say, for one moment, that they were right in playing off their jokes on Pigeon. I have an especial dislike to practical jokes; and those I have generally seen carried out have been decidedly wrong, and very senseless and stupid, without a particle of wit.

They had not been long at sea when one night Pigeon was encountered walking the deck, and every now and then stopping and looking eagerly over the side.

"What do you see there?" asked Jack. "Anything out of the common way?"

"All those sparkles, what can they be?" exclaimed Pigeon, pointing to the flashes of phosphorescent light which played among the foam dashed off from the sides, and which were seen in the wake of the vessel.

Hemming came by at the moment. He had taken an especial dislike to the bully. "Those sparkles! don't you know what they are? I thought everybody did," he observed, in a tone of contempt. "Well, there's a Russian fleet just gone up through the Straits, and every man, woman, and child aboard them smokes, from the admiral to the admiral's baby, and those are the ashes out of their pipes and off the ends of their cigars. Why, that's nothing to what you sometimes see. If we were close in their wake, there would be light enough for us to see to steer by."

"Law, you don't say so!" exclaimed Pigeon. "I should have thought the water would have put them out."

"Not down in these latitudes. It's too warm for that," answered Hemming gravely.

Pigeon was seen, when he went into the gun-room, entering the remark in his notebook.

A few days after this Pigeon was walking the deck in solitary grandeur, when, as he passed the marine-sentry at the gangway, of course no notice was taken of him. Now he had observed that, on certain occasions, the sentry presented arms to the officers. This he had taken into his head was in consequence, not of their rank, but of their being gentlemen. He therefore thought that the same respect ought to be shown to him. Instead of complaining to the officers or to the captain, when he would have been well laughed at, he thought fit to take the law into his own hands, and, walking up to the sentry, soundly rated him for his want of respect.

"And who bees you?" asked the sentry, cocking his eye—he was a wag in his way; "do you belong to the horse-marines, sir?"

"No, I do not; I am Mr Theophilus Pigeon, and you must treat me properly, or I shall report you."

"I thought as how you had drunk many a pint of Pigeon's milk when you was a baby," observed the marine, with perfect gravity.

Pigeon's measure had already been very accurately taken on board by the crew.

"Fellow, you are an impertinent scoundrel," exclaimed Pigeon. "What's your name?"

"Mum's the word," answered the marine, with perfect gravity.

"Ah! you think I am not up to you, do you?" cried Pigeon, glancing at the marine's musket. "I see it where you forgot that it was, ha! ha!"

It was some time before Pigeon could find the first lieutenant to make his report. In the meantime the sentries had been changed.

"I am sorry, Mr Pigeon, that you should have received any impertinence from any of the people on board," said the first lieutenant kindly. "Can you describe the man!"

"Why, he had a red coat and white belt," etcetera, etcetera.

"I am afraid that won't help us," said the first lieutenant, laughing.

"Ah! he thought himself very clever; but I know his name, I saw it on his musket. It was Tower!" exclaimed Pigeon triumphantly.

A general laugh followed this announcement, for Tower is the name engraved on all Government arms issued from the stores in that ancient fortress of London.

He used to find his way into the midshipmen's berth and to make himself quite at home, occupying the space which, as Hemming observed, a better man might fill. Various devices were made to get clear of him. One of the officers had a horn with which he now and then startled the silence of the decks—a practice, by-the-bye, rather subversive of discipline. One day, while Pigeon was in the berth, the horn was heard to sound.

"What's that?" he asked.

"Hurrah! the mail coach come in from Sicily," exclaimed Jack, starting up and rushing out. "Come along, it's a sight worth seeing. You'll have letters by it to a certainty, Pigeon."

Away rushed Pigeon up on deck, while Jack, amid the laughter of the rest of the occupants, returned to the berth. The captain and several of the gun-room officers were on deck, when Pigeon made his hasty appearance, and hurried eagerly to the side.

"What is the matter, Mr Pigeon?" asked Captain Lascelles.

"The mail from Sicily! the mail from Sicily!" ejaculated Pigeon. "Has it gone? Am I too late to see it?"

Even the captain could not help joining in the laugh which was raised against the once dictatorial bully of little boys at school.

"Oh, you have not missed it," said Mr Thorn. "Go down to the berth again, and say that we will call you when it heaves in sight."

More mystified than ever, Pigeon returned to the berth, when he was welcomed with shouts still more vehement than those which had received him on deck. The place he had left was occupied, and no one offered to make room for him, or asked him to sit down—a pretty strong proof that he was not wanted. Such is the deserved fate of school bullies when they get into the world, and have their measures properly taken. Still the midshipmen had not done with him. Quirk, the monkey, had remained, on his good behaviour, part and parcel of the crew. For the sake of the men, with whom he was a decided favourite, any slight misdemeanours which they could not contrive to hide were generally overlooked. Quirk occasionally paid a visit to the midshipmen's berth, where he sat up at table cracking nuts, "evidently under the impression," as Jack observed, "that he is one of us." Quirk had soon struck up a friendship with the bear, who was a very tame beast, and could play almost as many antics as he could, only in a more sedate way. Wherever Quirk went, Bruin would endeavour to follow; and one day, while the midshipmen were at dinner, the latter, led by the monkey, was seen approaching the berth. Nuts and biscuits were held out. They were easily tempted in. Room was made for them, and they were regaled to their hearts' content on all the delicacies of the season which the men could produce.

"We'll have them again, and we'll have a friend to meet them," exclaimed Jack.

"A bright idea!"

"Who?" was asked.

"Pigeon," said Jack; and so it was settled.

That afternoon Mr Pigeon received a note written on pink scented paper, to the following effect:—

"The gentlemen of the midshipmen's berth request the pleasure of Mr Pigeon's company at dinner, to meet two distinguished foreigners, in every way worthy of his acquaintance and friendship."

Pigeon asked the gun-room officers whether he ought to accept the invitation.

"Certainly, it will be an insult if you don't," was the answer.

They might possibly have suspected that a joke was brewing, but they said nothing. The dinner-hour on the next day arrived. The berth was kept as dark as possible, and when Pigeon presented himself at the door he was ushered in in due form, and with unusual politeness handed to the upper end of the berth.

"Dinner!" cried the caterer. "Bear a hand, boy."

The midshipman's boy, who had been standing against the door, grinning from ear to ear, had to decamp.

"Before the soup comes, Mr Pigeon, let me introduce our other guests— Señor Don Bruno, who is on your right side, and Monsieur de Querkerie, whom you will find on your left. Manners makes the man, and as their manners are unexceptionable, I hope that you will consider them as men, and treat them, as men should men, with due civility."

The screens by the side of the berth were at this instant withdrawn, when Pigeon beheld a bear sitting on one side of him, and a monkey on the other, both dressed with huge shirt-collars, large ties, and broad ribbons across their breasts. Astonishment, rage, and fear struggled within for the mastery.

"Don't be alarmed at their looks, my dear sir," said Hemming. "There are no better behaved gentlemen on board. Allow me to help you to soup. Rogers, you take care of Monsieur de Querkerie; Thompson, see to Don Bruno."

This was a necessary caution, for the monkey gave signs that he was about to thrust his paw into Pigeon's plate, which act would have belied the assertion just made in his favour, and would certainly not have been pleasant to the human guest. Bruin, who had a handful of hard biscuit before him to munch, was behaving himself very well. Hemming kept serving out the soup with the greatest gravity amid roars of laughter, not a little increased by Pigeon's perplexed countenance. What to do he could not decide. He felt that a joke was being played off on him, but he was too much afraid to resent it, or show his indignation, and therefore he did the very best thing he could have done under the circumstances, he went on eating his soup without speaking. All might have ended well had not Quirk, not understanding fully the proprieties of the dinner-table, darted out his paw and seized a lump of potato from the soup-plate. Pigeon could not stand this, but shoving the denied plate from him, he made a dash with his spoon at Quirk's face, almost knocking some of his teeth down his throat. The monkey retaliated, and not without Jack's utmost exertions could quiet be restored; I will not say peace or harmony, because that was out of the question.

"I beg pardon, Mr Pigeon, we thought you might like the companionship of our foreign guests, as you are supposed to have some qualities in common," said Hemming, in a grave tone. "But as you do not appear to admire their society, pray remove to the other side of the berth, where you will be more at your ease."

Pigeon was glad enough of an excuse to get away, but he was puzzled to settle whether it was safer to pass the bear or the monkey. At length he decided to get behind the former. At that moment Bruin took it into his head to lift up his huge back, and catching poor Pigeon between the legs, he sent him right into the middle of the table, with his head into the soup-dish, while Quirk, delighted at the opportunity, caught hold of his heels, and getting a kick, sprang in revenge on the part of his body most exposed to attack, which he bit till the wretched victim roared with pain, and Jack had by main force hauled him off. Hemming and Murray, with others, as soon as their laughter would allow them, dragged Pigeon off the table, apologising with tears in their eyes for the mishap which had occurred. Pigeon's first impulse was to roar out for a basin and towel to wash off the soup from his face; and when his features were made clean, though earnestly pressed to come back, nothing could persuade him to take his seat till Bruin and Quirk were removed from the berth. In truth the mess were not sorry to get rid of them, for to more than one sense they were somewhat unpleasant companions. All things considered, it was voted that Pigeon had really behaved very well, and the lesson he had received did him a great deal of good, and while he remained on board he seemed to think very much less of himself. I cannot defend the conduct of Hemming or Jack, or any one concerned in the affair, but my belief is, that had Pigeon not spoken disparagingly of Adair, whose memory Jack and Murray so fondly cherished, the trick would not have been played. Malta was visited, so were the Ionian Islands, and the frigate clove through the waters of the Levant.

"A sail in sight to leeward, sir," said Jack, entering the cabin, cap in hand, one afternoon, while the captain was at dinner.

"What does she look like?" asked Captain Lascelles, applying his table-napkin to his mouth, and finishing his glass of wine as a man does when he has to move in a hurry, while he fumbles in his waistcoat-pocket for his toothpick case.

"The first lieutenant thinks her a heavy frigate, or a line-of-battle ship," answered Jack, "and she is not English."

In a moment the captain was on deck, and taking an earnest look at the stranger through his telescope. At that period all captains of English men-of-war had received orders to be very circumspect with regard to their conduct towards French ships, for there was no doubt that France was seeking cause by which she might pick a quarrel with England. The *Racer* had now been cruising for some time, and Captain Lascelles could not tell whether the stranger in sight might or might not prove an enemy with whom he might speedily be engaged in deadly strife. The wind was from the north, and the

African coast, a thin blue line, was rising to sight in the horizon. The helm was instantly put up, and all sail made in chase.

"Hurrah!" exclaimed Jack, rushing into the berth, and throwing up his cap; "there's a chance of a brush this time and no mistake. The gun-room officers say that the French are certain to be at war with us by this time. They are going to help Mehemet Ali, so if the stranger is not a Frenchman, she is pretty certain to be an Egyptian, and either one or the other will do."

The information was received in the berth with general satisfaction. Only one person heard it with dismay. That was Pigeon. He turned very pale.

"What shall I do? Where shall I go?" he exclaimed. "I didn't come here to fight. Couldn't I be put on shore?"

"No, but you can keep below and help the doctor, where you may be of use and out of harm's way, if we don't go down, or blow up during the action," said Murray, with no little disdain in the tone of his voice.

"Oh! oh!" groaned Pigeon. "Go down, or blow up! Oh, dear!"

Chapter Six
Paddy Adair, Hurrah!

The beautiful frigate looked like a vast cloud of snowy whiteness, as, with studding-sails alow and aloft, she swept proudly along over the blue waters of the Mediterranean in chase of the stranger. The latter had been standing to the eastward; but seeing herself pursued, she also altered her course, and ran off before the wind towards the land. Night was coming on, and it was very important to get up with her, near enough to ascertain her character, to prevent her escaping, should such be her design, in the dark. Every one was on deck or in the tops, looking out at the stranger, and those considered themselves fortunate who could command the use of a spyglass. One person—bully Pigeon—was below, and he sat quaking on a chest in the orlop deck, where he had been told that he would be least likely to have his head shot away.

"I am a non-combatant, you know. It would be very wrong in me to expose my life," he observed with a trembling lip. "If I was one of you, of course I would do my duty as bravely as anybody; but as I am a civilian, and am come aboard for my health, I think it is my duty to take care of myself."

"Oh! of course," was the reply; "so precious a person should run no risk of losing his valuable life."

"Oh, I wish poor Adair were with us," exclaimed Jack. "He did so wish to see a real fight; and to have to go out of the world without having been in one was very trying." Jack spoke just as his feelings for the moment prompted him, without much consideration, I suspect.

"Do you know, Rogers, that since we escaped in so wonderful a way from drowning, I have more than once thought that perhaps some of the people of the *Onyx* may have been saved," observed Murray. "I do not say that I have any great hopes on the subject, but still I cannot help thinking that it is possible."

"I'm afraid not, though; we should have heard of them before now," replied Jack. "But if anybody escaped, I would rather it were Paddy Adair than any one else."

Their conversation was cut short by that rolling sound of a drum which makes the heart of every true man-of-war's man leap with joy. It followed the captain's order to the first lieutenant, "Beat to quarters." What magic was there in the sound of those words! In an instant every one, from the first lieutenant to the smallest powder-monkey, was in full activity. Bulkheads were knocked away, firescreens were put up, the gallery fire was extinguished, the magazines were opened, powder and shot were handed up, the small-arms were served out, the men buckled on their cutlasses, and stuck their pistols in their belts.

Although Captain Lascelles fully believed that he should gain the victory, he was too good an officer and too wise a man not to take every possible means to secure it. It was soon evident that the *Racer* was coming up hand-over-hand with the chase, and before long it was clearly made out that she was, at least, a fifty-gun ship. She showed no colours, and as to her nationality opinions were divided. Some thought she was French; but then in opposition to this conjecture, it was asserted that a French fifty-gun ship was not likely to run away from a frigate, whereas a Turk or an Egyptian was very likely indeed to do so. The officers on board them were generally very inefficient, while a total want of discipline prevailed.

"That craft ahead must have a very bad conscience, or she would not be in such a hurry to get out of our way," observed Jack; "she's a Turk, or I am a Dutchman."

"So the captain thinks, which is fortunate, or you might have to turn into a Dutchman, or else break your word," observed Murray.

"I wish that he were a Frenchman. I should so like to have a tussle with him," said Jack. "Let people talk as they will about liberty, equality, and fraternity, I agree with my father, that the French never will like the English till they have taught us to eat frogs, and have thrashed us on a second field of Waterloo, and I hope that time may never come."

"I hope not either," said Murray. "But I have no wish to go to war with France or Frenchmen. If they are bad friends, they are worse enemies, and not to be despised, depend on that; no people could have fought better than they did during the last war."

"That is the reason I should like to fight them again," exclaimed Jack. "What is the use of fighting with people who can't fight?"

Murray laughed at Jack's style of reasoning. He had not arrived at the conclusion which an older man might have reached, that fighting under any circumstances is a dreadful business, and that the person who gives the cause for the fight does a very wicked thing, utterly hateful in the sight of God. Never let that truth be forgotten.

Darkness was now rapidly coming on. The stranger could just be seen looming through it. Captain Lascelles felt pretty confident, however, that he should come up with her before she could make her escape. Night at last settled completely down over the ocean; still she could be seen, though very indistinctly. On the two ships flew before the breeze. At length the master, who had been examining the chart in his cabin, came up to the captain.

"We are drawing in very near to the coast, sir," said he. "It will be safer to keep the lead going."

"But where the ship ahead can float so can we," observed Captain Lascelles.

"She may manage to run in between reefs on which we may strike. Never let us trust to the leading of an enemy, sir," was the answer.

"You are right, master, you are right!" exclaimed Captain Lascelles, in a tone of warm approval. "Send a hand with the lead into each of the chains. We'll run no risk of casting the ship away."

Soon the voices of the leadsmen were heard through the still silence of night, as the gallant frigate clove her way through the calm waters.

"By the deep nine," sang out one on the starboard side.

"By the mark seven," was soon afterwards heard from the man in the port chains.

"Quarter less six," was the next shouted out.

"We are shoaling our water rapidly," observed Captain Lascelles to the first lieutenant. "Stand by to go about."

All eyes had been fixed on the dark mass ahead. Onward it seemed to glide through the darkness. Every one felt certain that their eyes did not deceive them. There still appeared, they all believed, the sails of the stranger, a huge towering pinnacle reaching to the sky. Yet so near the ground were they that it was dangerous for the frigate, though of course drawing much less water, to stand on.

"Was she a ship of mortal fabric?" some of the more superstitious among the seamen began to ask.

As they looked, the tall pyramid seemed to rock, and then suddenly to dissolve into the air. A sound, at the same time, came from the southward, as if of breakers dashing on a rocky shore.

"Hands about ship," shouted the captain, with startling energy.

The cry was repeated by the first lieutenant, and quick almost as the answer of an electric message, the boatswain's whistle uttered the well-known call along the decks. Round came the ship, and when the eyes of those on board were turned to the south, not an indication could be discovered of the ship which had thus far led them in the chase.

"We'll keep her off and on during the night," said the captain to the first lieutenant.

"At daylight we will stand in, and see what has become of her. There is little doubt, however, that she has gone on shore. I trust, as there is not much sea on, that the people will contrive to save themselves."

At this time the Sultan of Turkey was running a great risk of losing the greater part if not the whole of his dominions. Mehemet Ali was one of the most remarkable men who have appeared in the East during this century. Although of the lowest origin and unable to read, having become a soldier, he raised himself by his talents and intrigues to the highest rank in the Turkish army. Being sent to Egypt, he deposed the ruler of that province, and became pacha in his stead. He even showed that he allowed no sentimental scruples to prevent him from accomplishing any object on which he had set his heart. Believing that the Mamelukes might be as troublesome to him as they had often proved to the Sultan, he invited 500 of them to a feast, and then had all of them murdered with the exception of one, who escaped by leaping his horse over a high wall. The idea was simple and very oriental. He might have made them his friends, but he thought that might be too difficult a task, so he chose the other alternative. Now Mehemet Ali thought that it would be much pleasanter to be an independent sovereign than a tributary to the Porte, so he threw off the Turkish yoke. Then he thought that he might as well rule over Syria also, and he accordingly marched his army there and took possession of the country. His ambition increased with his conquests, and at last he resolved, if he could, to mount the throne of the caliphs. He was backed up in all his proceedings by the French, who knew that if he succeeded they might easily take possession of Egypt on some excuse or other; while the Russians were well pleased to let him play his game, because they knew that the Sultan might call them in to his assistance, and thus they might get hold of Constantinople. The Egyptian army in Syria was commanded by Ibrahim Pacha, the adopted son of Mehemet Ali. He advanced his victorious standard to within a short distance of Constantinople; but then, instead of pushing on and occupying the city, he delayed till the Russians had reached the shores of the Bosphorus. He in consequence thought it wiser to enter into a treaty by which he secured the Pachalic of Syria and Adana as well as that of Egypt for himself and his father. At first the tribes inhabiting Syria welcomed him as their deliverer, but they soon found that they had not changed rulers for the better, and that he fleeced them as much as had the pachas appointed by the Sultan. They therefore entreated the Sultan to take them under his protection. He accordingly sent an army to their relief. It was now that England and Austria thought it time to interfere. Neither of them wished the Egyptians to succeed, because the Russians would have had an excuse for interfering. The Russians did not want anybody but themselves to interfere, but when the English, Austrians, and Prussians came forward, they were compelled to put a finger into the pie, to counteract the efforts of the French. The French would gladly have aided the Egyptians for the sake of gaining a footing in the country, but as they were not ready for war they thought it wiser to refrain from all open acts of hostility. The Turkish army advancing sustained a defeat from the Egyptians, while their fleet, which had been sent to the Dardanelles, sailed for Alexandria, and joined that of Mehemet Ali.

The four powers accordingly entered into an agreement to make him withdraw his army from Syria, and offering him the ultimatum of the hereditary sovereignty of Egypt and the possession during his life of Saint Jean d'Acre. If he refused, he was to have only the government of Egypt, and the four powers were to compel him by force to accept this arrangement. The sturdy old pacha, however, backed by France, resolved to hold out. A British squadron was therefore sent to blockade the ports of Egypt and Syria, with a few Austrian and Turkish ships, Russia undertaking not to take possession of Constantinople. The French had not been consulted in the matter, and had they felt themselves sufficiently strong, there is little doubt that they would have supported Mehemet Ali, at the expense of a war with England. Thus much was at the time known to Captain Lascelles. Much circumspection was therefore required, for it was difficult to understand who were friends and who foes. The French commanders might have received secret orders to attack the English after a certain day; the Egyptians might at any moment do so, if they felt themselves strong enough to be assured of victory; while it was more than probable that any Turkish ships might have gone over to the Egyptians, and have thus become enemies. Few of the officers turned in that night; they were all anxious to ascertain who the stranger was, and what could possibly have become of him. Captain Lascelles took the frigate in as close as he could venture, and though each time every eye on board was turned eagerly towards the shore, not a sign of a ship could be discovered. At length daylight dawned, and a white sandy shore was seen, with bare dark rocky heights rising behind it. "There she is! there she is!" broke from many voices as all the glasses on board were directed towards the shore. There lay stranded the huge black hull of a ship, her masts gone by the board, and her rigging hanging down in confused masses on either side, while the white surf dashed up around her. What had become of the people it was impossible at that distance to say. Captain Lascelles, who was on deck, ordered the ship to be hove-to.

"I wonder what is next to be done," said Jack to Murray; "I hope if the boats are ordered away you and I will have to go in them." Very soon the order was given. "Barge and first and second cutters away!" Jack and Alick belonged to the two latter. They hurried to get them ready. The crews were armed, and a three-pounder was placed in the bow of each boat. Mr Thorn had charge of the expedition. It was not expected that there would be any fighting, but as a precautionary measure it was necessary to be armed. No one now supposed that the stranger was French. There could be little doubt she was either Turkish or Egyptian, but why she had run on shore it was difficult to say. The idea was that she had been purposely lost. In high glee at the thoughts of an adventure, the party shoved off from the frigate. Mr Thorn was directed to ascertain the character of the ship, and to render assistance if it was required. A light breeze from the westward enabled them to stand in under sail towards the shore. As they drew towards the wreck, they looked anxiously to ascertain her condition. She was on shore about a quarter of a mile from the beach. All the masts were gone, some of the guns had been hove overboard, others had their muzzles still appearing through the ports. Many of the crew were on board, but a considerable number had made their escape to the shore, their red caps and petticoat trousers showing that they were either Turks or Egyptians. As the boats got close up to the ship, the people on board began to gesticulate furiously, and it seemed with no very friendly intentions. Of this they gave proof, for they got some smaller guns on the quarter-deck slewed round, and began firing away at the boats. Fortunately their gunnery was very bad, or they might have cut them to pieces. On seeing this, Mr Thorn made a white pocket-handkerchief fast to a boat-hook, and waved it towards them, but the barbarians seemed to hold a flag of truce in very little respect, as they continued firing as before. Just then, Rogers and Murray observed a young officer; he seemed to rush up from below, and furiously attack the men with his sword, driving them from the gun. He then leaped upon the taffrail and waved his hand to them and shouted, but they were too far off to hear his voice.

"Murray, Murray, who do you think that is?" shouted Jack.

"I know who it is like," answered Murray. "It is like—"

Just at that moment a terrific roar was heard. The entire vast mass of the wreck seemed to be lifted up bodily into the air. Up, up it went. Lurid flames and dense volumes of smoke burst forth, and then down came the huge mass shattered into a thousand fragments; beams, and guns, and planks, and human bodies, and the various contents of the ship all mingled together. A cry of horror escaped from the boats' crews when they saw what had occurred.

"Pull for your lives, my lads," shouted Mr Thorn. "Give way now."

The men, recovering from their amazement, required no second order, but pulled away as hard as they could from the burning wreck. Happily they were no nearer, for in an instant afterwards down came burning fragments of the wreck, covering the sea far and wide, the terrific shower almost swamping the boats. Although several pieces struck them, no one was materially injured. The whole occurrence occupied not a minute of time. The ship, however, continued burning furiously, and the guns in the forepart of her, which appeared not to have been blown up, as the flames reached them went rapidly off, one after other, sending their shot whizzing away on either side.

"Some of the poor fellows may have escaped with their lives, and may be struggling in the water. Can't we go back and try to pick them up?" said Jack to Hemming, who commanded his boat.

"A right notion—that we ought, Rogers," answered Hemming, who was too high-minded even to refuse to take a suggestion offered by a junior. Hemming made the proposal to Mr Thorn, and back dashed the boats, not a man in them recollecting even for a moment that the people they were now so eager to save, had but a few minutes before been most unwarrantably firing away at them. Jack too had a strange feeling that he knew the appearance of the young officer who had interposed in their favour, but still it was too vague to allow him to ground any strong hopes on it. Murray had, however, conceived the same idea. With what eagerness they pulled about looking out for their struggling fellow-creatures! First they hauled on board a stout Turk, who did not appear to be much the worse for his flight and ducking, except that he was, not unnaturally, in a dreadful fright. If he had conceived the idea that he had already entered Paradise, the big-whiskered jolly tars, instead of the houris he might have expected to welcome him, must quickly have shown him his mistake. He looked up with a stare of astonishment as he was placed at the bottom of the boat. Another poor fellow had had his leg almost blown off, but still he clung on to a piece of plank. Hemming quickly formed a tourniquet with a handkerchief to stop the bleeding, while a savage-looking fellow was being hauled in, who even then cast a scowl of defiance and hatred at his preservers.

"You might as well have said thank you, instead of looking so glum, old boy," observed one of the men as he placed him alongside his companions.

"There's a young Turk hanging on to a spar away there, and waving to us," cried Jack, putting the boat's head in the direction he indicated. "Give way, my lads."

Murray's boat was pulling in the same direction. Jack got up first to the young Turk, as he called him, and almost tumbled headlong into the water in helping him on board.

"It is, it is," he shouted; "it is himself! I thought so."

"Who? who?" asked Murray eagerly.

"Paddy Adair?" cried Jack, almost bursting into tears. "It's Paddy himself."

"Paddy Adair, hurrah! hurrah!" was echoed from all the boats.

"Paddy, my dear boy, where have you come from?" asked Hemming, with unwonted gentleness in his tone. Jack had got Terence's hand, and would not let it go.

"The last place I came from was the poop of that Turkish ship which is burning away there; then I went up into the air, I believe; and lastly, you have hauled me out of the water; the remainder of my adventures would take some time to tell, so you had better try and pick up any more of my shipmates who may still be alive. There were a good lot of us altogether turned into sky-rockets."

Paddy had not forgotten his habit of joking. The boats altogether picked up some fifteen or twenty Turks, whom they landed on the beach, with the exception of those who had been injured, whom in mercy they conveyed on board the frigate. A considerable number had been drowned from leaping off the forecastle when the ship was in flames, and being unable to swim. Altogether a very large number of the crew must have been lost.

"But, Paddy," said Jack, looking earnestly up in Adair's face, while he still held his hand, "you haven't really turned into a Turk, have you?"

"Give me a boiled leg of pork, and some pease pudding, and prove me," answered Terence, laughing. "No, indeed; these wide nether garments and this red cap are the chief Turkish things about me, and the latter I thus gladly cast from me, and as soon as I can get a pair to supply their place, I'll gladly throw the others after the cap." Paddy as he spoke hove the fez into the sea with a look of intense satisfaction. "If you knew what I have gone through, you would not be surprised at my pleasure of getting rid of everything to remind me of it," he observed.

The boats made the best of their way out to the frigate, to report what had occurred.

"What have you been about? what has happened?" were the questions eagerly asked, as they got alongside and handed up the wounded Turks.

"Why, we have been and found Paddy Adair," shouted Jack, unable any longer to restrain his feelings.

The eager faces of several midshipmen were seen at the gangway, looking out to ascertain the fact by ocular demonstration.

"It's quite true, Paddy Adair is found, Paddy Adair is found," exclaimed a dozen voices in joyful tones. The words were taken up, and echoed along the deck, "Paddy Adair is found; hurrah for Paddy Adair!" Especially vociferous were his own messmates, who were delighted to get him back again, and happy at the same time to have an excuse for using their lungs. The boats were hoisted up, and Paddy, having changed his wet Turkish costume for a dry midshipman's uniform, was sent for into the cabin to give an account of his adventures to Captain Lascelles. He, however, reserved a still more detailed account to give to his messmates in full conclave assembled in the midshipmen's berth. The only person on board who had not heard of Adair's arrival was Pigeon. He had laid down after breakfast on a sofa in the first lieutenant's cabin, and gone fast asleep. About luncheon-time he awoke, and rubbing his eyes sat up, and feeling hungry after all the excitement and fright he had gone through, arose and went into the gun-room. Finding no one there, he bethought him that he would go and honour the midshipmen with a visit, and talk of what he would have done if the ship had gone into action, and his services had actually been required. He was, somewhat to his surprise, welcomed with a cordiality to which he was not much accustomed. In a short time the conversation turned to the loss of the *Onyx*, and to the character of Paddy Adair. One said one thing of him, and one or two hazarded slightly disparaging observations. The bait took.

"Oh, he was, I remember, always a foolish dunder-headed Irishman," observed Pigeon; "I could thrash a dozen such fellows as he was. No one thought anything of him at school, I remember."

"Oh, bully Pigeon, oh, bully Pigeon, that you know right well wasn't the case," exclaimed Paddy, popping his head in at the door of the berth.

Pigeon looked up at hearing the voice, and turning very pale, while his countenance exhibited a look of intense horror, fell back in a fainting fit, which afforded an excellent excuse to several of the youngsters for throwing half a dozen tumblers of water over him. Some of the water was cold, and some was rather hot, but the effect was the same. He got a thorough ducking, and after spluttering not a little, and coughing as the water dashed into his mouth, he quickly recovered his senses. It was some little time, however, before he could be convinced that Paddy Adair in *propria persona* sat before him. Harmony was soon restored, and Paddy assured him that he did not intend to frighten him so much, and that he hoped he would forgive him. Never was a happier party assembled in the berth at dinner than on that occasion. Paddy's health was drunk, and he was warmly congratulated on his escape and return on board, even by the seniors of the mess.

"And now, Adair, let us hear all about it," said Hemming, when the cloth had been removed and the young gentlemen were discussing their walnuts and wine.

"Why, it is not a very long story," observed Paddy, "for do you see most of the events took place in a somewhat rapid way, my last skylark especially. However, you shall hear. We had just got on board the *Onyx*, and the commander had ordered the boats to be hoisted up, when, as the men were engaged in the operation, the squall struck her, and over she went in a moment—not a rope parted, nor a sail, I believe—just like a nine-pin knocked over by a ball. I was still in the captain's gig on the weather side. Feeling her going, or rather gone, I believe it was more from fright or instinct than from any exercise of my reasoning powers, I seized a couple of oars under my arms, slid overboard down her bottom, and struck out with all my might away from the sinking hull. I never struck out so hard in my life, for I felt that I was swimming for my life. I believe that I gave myself a shove off with the oars, which helped me rapidly to increase my distance from the brig. Suddenly I felt myself drawn back, and I thought that I was going to be sucked under water—so I was for a short time; but I held a tight grasp of the oars, and once more quickly rose to the surface. When I looked round there was not a sign of a brig. I shouted, no one answered. I could see no one floating alive on the spot where the trim craft had lately glided in all her pride and beauty. I was alone on the dark troubled sea. The foam dashed in my face, and the waves tumbled me about terribly, and I thought more than once that I should have to let go and sink with the rest. I felt very miserable and very sorry that so many fine fellows had lost their lives, for I was too certain that I alone had escaped, and then I began to think how grateful I ought to be that I had been so mercifully preserved. I can't talk about that; but I wish you fellows to know that I do not think or feel lightly on the subject, that is all. Night was rapidly coming on, my prospects were far from pleasant, and somewhat limited too, as I could only just make out the tumbling seas on either side of me. I felt pretty certain that the frigate would come back to look after the brig; but scarcely hoped that such a speck as I was would be seen. Still I determined to keep up my spirits, and to hang on to the oars as long as I could. Sometimes I put my legs up over them, and thus I both changed my position and floated very comfortably. Perhaps an hour had passed after the brig had gone down—it appeared as if several had elapsed—when I felt a sort of drowsiness come over me. Suddenly there appeared right over me a big dark object. I guessed that it was the bow of a vessel. I sang out with all my might. She was very nearly running me down. As she did not quite run over me, it was fortunate that she came so close. A rope was hanging over her side; I found my hands grasping it. It must literally have been towed over me; I clutched it with all my might, and found myself hauled up on the deck of a low latine-rigged craft running under her foresail before the squall. The crew had red caps on, and loose trousers, and talked a language I could not understand, so I concluded that they were Turks or Moors, or Egyptians; they were very good-natured though. They took me below and gave me some arrack, which was very nasty, and they took off my wet things, and rigged me out in one of their own suits. When I explained that my ship had gone down, they understood me perfectly. Next they made me eat some lumps of meat off a skewer, with some rice and biscuit, and then signified that I might lie down on a mat in the cabin and go to sleep. I did not awake till morning. I wanted to put on my own uniform again, but they would not give it to me, and I began to fear that they were going really to turn me into a Turk.

"For several days we sailed on. Where we were going to I could not make out, for they would never let me see their compass. At last we made the land somewhere on the coast of Syria, I am pretty certain; and, running in, we found a fifty-gun ship, brought up in a roadstead a couple of miles off the shore. The *Mistico* went alongside and stores of all sorts and provisions were hoisted up out of her, and then without my leave being asked I found myself transferred, like the rest of the bales of goods, to her deck. I had not had a particularly pleasant time of it among the very dirty crew of the *Mistico*, so I thought that I might have changed for the better. I was much obliged to them, however, for saving my life; so we parted very good friends, and when the little craft shoved off, I waved them an affectionate farewell. I soon found that I had not much improved my condition. The larger the ship, the greater was the amount of dirt and disorder. No one knew their duty, at all events no one did it. How they managed to exist a day without being blown up or foundering, I do not know. They were constantly smoking with the doors of the magazine open and ammunition scattered about, and night and day with every prospect of a squall, the lower deck ports were ever left open. I got hold of some of the officers, and tried to show them the danger they were running; so they rubbed their caps about their heads and opened their eyes and tried to look very wise, and followed my suggestions. But the next day things were as bad as ever. However, when they found out that I was up to a thing or two, they insisted on making me an officer. What rank I held I never could tell. I only knew that everybody obeyed me, and that none of the officers interfered with my commands. This complaisant conduct did not arise so much from respect for me, as that they might save themselves trouble. I never met with men who seemed to hate it so much, from the captain to the youngest powder-monkey. My great difficulty arose from no one understanding a word I said, nor could I understand anybody. Still, we got on very well under ordinary circumstances by signs. At last I happened to go forward and to utter a few words of English. One of the men forthwith pricked up his ears.

"'Beg pardon, sir, you'd find an interpreter convenient, I think,' he said, touching his cap.

"'What, are you not a Turk?' said I.

"'I am not and I am,' he answered; 'I have become a Turk.'

"'You are a renegade, in truth,' said I.

"'Your honour has hit it,' he replied.

"I am sorry to say he was an Irishman.

"'But I'm ready to serve a countryman, and I think I can help you at a pinch.'

"'I shall be much obliged to you,' I answered; and from that time forward Pat Hoolan became my interpreter and right-hand man.

"He was a great ragamuffin, and I did not trust him more than I could help; but he was very useful to me, and I believe faithfully interpreted the orders I issued through him. I learned also from him some of the politics of the ship. The captain was a great rascal according to our notions. He cheated the crew of their pay and their rations, and his government of the stores and provisions, and indeed anything on which he could lay his hands; while he had been tampered with by some of Mehemet Ali's emissaries, and was only waiting an opportunity to carry his ship into Alexandria. Such was the state of affairs when we put to sea. He had just before found out that his treachery had been discovered, and that another Turkish ship had been sent in pursuit of him. He tried to get to Alexandria but could not, so we knocked about running from our own shadow till you hove in sight. He then did what he had long resolved to do, ran the ship on shore. He and most of the officers and some of the men escaped in the boats, leaving me with the remainder to be blown up as a reward for my services. No thanks to them I escaped, and that's the end of my story."

Two days after this a brig of war hove in sight. She signalised "Important news," "The war has begun." The frigate made sail towards her. The two men-of-war, as they drew near each other, hove-to, and the commander of the brig came on board the frigate. It was soon known that the *Racer* was to join the squadron of Sir Robert Stopford. All sail was immediately made on both ships, and together they steered a course for the coast of Syria.

Chapter Seven
To save the Flag

"I say, Jack, can you tell me what all this row is about between us and these wide-breeched, red-capped niggers, the Egyptians?" asked Adair, as he stood by the side of Jack Rogers on the quarter-deck of the *Racer*, while the latter, with his spyglass under his arm, was doing duty as signal midshipman. The outlines of many a picturesque hill and white stone stronghold, famed in ancient and modern history, rose in the distance on the Syrian coast out of the blue glittering ocean.

"Why," replied Jack, "I'm not much of a politician, Paddy, but as far as I can make out, old Mehemet Ali wants to be Sultan of the Turks, and we won't let him; and so Charlie Napier told him that if he didn't draw in his horns within twenty days, we would blow his fortresses on this coast about the ears of his pachas. He, in return, told Charlie to go to Jericho, that he intended to keep what he'd got; and so now we're going to do what we promised. We shall have some fun, depend on it."

"Now I understand all the ins and outs of the matter," replied Paddy. "There's nothing like knowing what you are fighting about."

"There, up goes a signal from the flag-ship," cried Jack, putting his glass to his eye, and pointing it towards the *Princess Charlotte*, Sir Robert Stopford's flag-ship, which, with the *Powerful*, *Thunderer*, *Benbow*, and several other line-of-battle ships and frigates, sloops and steamers, joined by a Turkish squadron under Admiral Walker, and a few Austrian ships, was cruising off Beyrout.

"The signal for the captains of each ship to assemble on board the *Princess Charlotte*," cried Jack. "Hurrah! the fun's to begin."

The captains having visited the flag-ship, the squadron stood in, the larger portion taking up a position opposite the town, which they forthwith commenced bombarding, while the rest were employed in landing troops at different points to co-operate with the Turks, and to distract the attention of the Egyptians. Suliman Pacha, Governor of Beyrout, in spite of the shot and shell showered into his fortress, held out bravely and fired away in return as hard as he could. It was the first time the three midshipmen of the *Racer* had been under fire, but as she had not to take any very active part in the affair, they voted it very slow work.

"Is this what you call fighting?" said Jack. "It seems to me as if all the fun was on one side."

"Stay a bit, my boy," observed Hemming; "this is only just the beginning of the game. Before many days are over perhaps we shall be at something which will make you cry out the other way."

"At all events, we have silenced them; see, up goes a flag of truce on the old castle," exclaimed Jack.

Jack was right in his fact but wrong in his conclusions. A boat was instantly sent on shore to inquire the meaning of the white flag. She quickly returned to the flag-ship bringing the Indian mail, with a polite message from Suliman Pacha, assuring the admiral that he was not at war with individuals, and that he should feel a satisfaction in forwarding all letters to and from India. Sir Robert Stopford, himself so generous and polite, was the very man to appreciate such an act of courtesy: he therefore sent back the boat immediately with a case of wine, warmly thanking the pacha, and begging that he would accept it as a slight acknowledgment of his kindness. This little episode over, the belligerents began firing away at each other as hard as ever. The pacha showed that he was as brave as he was courteous, for in spite of all the cannonading he would not give in. A short drama was, however, enacted, which showed the midshipmen a little more of the realities of war. An Egyptian deserter came on board one of the ships, and gave notice that a train of gunpowder had been laid along a bridge leading to the eastern castle, in which was collected a large quantity of gunpowder, with the intention of blowing up into the sky any of the besiegers who might succeed in entering the place. The deserter offered to guide any party formed to cut off the train. Commander Worth, of the *Hastings*, undertook to accomplish the dangerous service; and numbers of officers and men volunteered to accompany him. Jack and Murray and Adair were among others eager to go. However, it was not likely that more than one midshipman from the frigate would be allowed to accompany the expedition. The morning of the day in which it was to take place, Murray had been sent with a message on board the *Hastings*. He came back with a flush on his cheek and a look of intense satisfaction on his countenance.

"Jack, Terence, my dear fellows, congratulate me. I'm to go. W—, who has known me for some time, has applied for me. He did so in most flattering terms. He said he wanted a midshipman who would be calm and collected whatever might occur, and yet one on whose courage and resolution he could perfectly rely, and he has selected me. It is that he has spoken of me in such flattering terms that has given me so much pleasure. I wish that you two fellows were going also."

"I wish we were," said Jack. "But I congratulate you, Alick; you'll do justice to W — 's choice. That I know right well."

"There will be more work to be done than when we attacked the pirate's stronghold the other day," observed Adair. "Well, I hope that my turn will come before long; I don't feel as if I had any right to wear starch in my shirt-collar till I've taken part in some real downright fighting."

Jack and Terence warmly shook Murray's hand, as he stepped into the boat which was to convey him on board the *Hastings*.

"I say, old fellow, don't now forget to come back to us safe and sound in life and limb," cried Terence, laughing; "remember the fright I gave you and Jack. Don't give him and me the same, and we'll take care that Pigeon does not malign your character in your absence."

Away went Murray. To say that he was in high glee would be to use a wrong term. There was a calm satisfaction and proud joy in his heart at the thought that the time had arrived when he might have an opportunity of distinguishing himself in the noble profession he had chosen, and to which he was so devotedly attached. Neither Rogers nor Adair would have felt as he did; and yet, though neither of them could be considered less brave than he was, yet in reality he was the bravest of all three, because his mind was so constituted that he clearly saw all the dangers to be encountered and knew every risk he was running. The expedition rendezvoused round the *Hastings*. The ships stood in as close as the depth of water would allow them, and then, opening their fire, the boats shoved off and pulled away for the bridge which led to the castle. As soon as they appeared a heavy fire of musketry was opened on them from the fortifications; but in the face of it the men clambered upon the bridge and, led by their gallant commander, rapidly pushed on across it. Jack and Terence eagerly watched the progress of the boats through their telescopes. Their chief sympathy was concentrated on that which contained Murray and his fortunes. They looked upon him as a dear brother, and, in spite of their apparent light-heartedness, they both felt the deepest anxiety for his safety. In a very short time the whole party were hid from sight by the thick smoke which surrounded them. Murray, with his brave companions, in spite of the leaden shower which came pattering around their heads, pushed on till they reached the spot where the train was laid. A few buckets of water, brought for the purpose, quickly cut off the train; then on they went to the gates of the castle. They were not long in blowing it open. In they rushed, putting the defenders to flight, who made their escape by an opposite gate, rejoicing in the belief that the infidel besiegers would soon be blown up sky high, and become the food of ghouls and vampires. They were sorely disappointed when they found that the castle did not blow up, and that the giaours had taken entire possession of it. The English leader saw that no time was to be lost. He and his men hunted about and soon came upon the casks of powder of which they were in search. "Now, my lads, heave them over the walls into the sea," he sang out, setting the example which the men were ready enough to follow. Cask after cask was stove and thrown into the sea till some sixty or seventy casks had been destroyed. Sentries had been placed to give notice of the approach of the enemy. Notice was given that they were returning in force. "Now, my lads," cried Captain W—, "we'll carry off some of these casks to pepper the fellows with their own powder." The idea just suited the taste of the seamen. Each man shouldered a cask, and, fearless of the consequences should a spark of fire get inside one of them, away they scampered through the gates and across the bridge with their booty. As soon as the enemy caught sight of them they again opened their fire. Several of the daring party were hit. The officers cheered them on. The fire was hotter than ever. One officer fell. He was a midshipman. The men rallied round him, and lifting him on their shoulders bore him on towards the boats. He did not breathe or give a sign of life. "Who is it? who is it?" was asked. They reached the boats and shoved off, for the Egyptians were gathering in force to attack them. Jack and Terence, perched on the hammock-nettings, were looking out for the return of the expedition. The frigate was close in, and the boats had to pass her on their way to their respective ships. One of the boats of the *Hastings* came first, the one in which Murray had embarked. A union jack was thrown over a part of the stern-sheets.

"Who have you there?" asked Jack, not able to restrain his anxiety.

"A midshipman, sir, who has been killed," was the answer.

"Oh, Terence, it must be Murray!" exclaimed Jack, almost falling off the hammock-nettings overboard. "And yet, no, it can't be; it must not be. Who is he, that midshipman?" shouted Jack; but the boat was already at some distance, and the people in her did not hear the question asked.

The report soon got about the decks that Murray was killed. Jack and Adair would have been gratified at hearing all the things said about him, and the grief expressed at his loss. Still, after giving vent to their grief for a time, they began to hope that possibly he might not have been killed, but only desperately wounded, and they resolved to ask leave to go on board the *Hastings* to ascertain the state of the case. As they were going aft for that purpose, a boat came alongside, and in a few seconds afterwards, who should appear on deck uninjured in limb, and in capital spirits, but Murray himself.

"Who are you? what are you? where do you come from?" exclaimed Terence, scarcely knowing what he said. "Why, Alick, to a certainty you are dead, are you not?"

"I hope not," answered Murray, laughing at the reception his two friends were giving him. "I have not been hit or hurt that I know of."

"All right," exclaimed Jack, springing forward and grasping his hand, which he wrung heartily. "I am so glad. It would have been too dreadful if you had been killed."

"Unhappily, one poor fellow of our party, a midshipman, L—, of the *Hastings*, was killed," observed Murray. "However, let us promise each other for the future, not to fancy that any accident has happened to those who are absent, unless we have very strong evidence of the same."

"Agreed! agreed!" the other two exclaimed. "Whatever anybody else may tell us, we'll all believe that we shall meet again somewhere or other, and be happy together."

It is extraordinary what an effect the notion the three midshipmen had taken up had on them. If Adair was away, though perhaps on some far-distant station, Jack frequently had to say that he did not know where he was to be found, but he always added, "I am certain that we shall meet again before long. What message shall I give him?" Murray said much the same thing of Jack or Adair, and they said the same of Murray. I cannot follow them through the various scenes of the war in Syria. While Sir Charles Napier, to his great delight, was acting the part of a general on shore, with some of his naval followers as his aides-de-camp, they were employed on board their ship, which, with the rest of the squadron, was engaged in sailing along the coast in cooperating with the army, and in blowing up and capturing one fortress after another of those which still held out for Mehemet Ali. Now and then both bluejackets and marines landed, and, much to their satisfaction, stormed the old pacha's strongholds, and literally fulfilled Charley Napier's promise of pulling the stones about the ears of his governors. On one occasion success did not attend the British arms, but, as Paddy Adair observed, "It's an ill wind which blows no one good," and he here had an opportunity which he had so long desired of distinguishing himself. The fortress was a very strong one, with a high thick-walled tower which looked fully capable of defying the battle and the breeze for a thousand years. The ship stood in with the intention of battering it down, but after firing away for an hour or more, little impression was made, and it was resolved to endeavour to take it by storm. Jack had to stay on board, greatly to his disgust, and he did say that he considered himself a most ill-used officer. Adair and Murray accompanied the body of seamen who, with the marines of the squadron, and some mountaineers who had been taken on board along the coast, were landed to form the storming-party. The ground between the castle and the sea was laid out in gardens. Here a body of the enemy was drawn up. The storming-party landed to the south of the town, covered by the fire of the ships, which also cleared the gardens of the enemy. The marines and bluejackets now pushed bravely on, but encountered a terrific fire from the troops within the forts. Murray and Adair were side by side, scrambling over walls and leaping ditches, and cutting through hedges of prickly pears in spite of the showers of shot which rattled round their heads.

"I say, Alick, poets talk of genial showers; I wonder what they would call the shower now rattling round us?" cried Adair, as he waved on his men.

"A leaden shower, I should think," said Alick.

"Not far wrong, my boy, but I'm afraid it will not make us grow, though," answered Adair. "But I say, the shot do pepper, though."

They did, indeed. Numbers of the marines and sailors were knocked over.

"There's another poor fellow down," cried Adair, stooping down to help up the man, but his aid was of no avail. A deep groan escaped from his bosom, his musket fell from his grasp, and he was dead. Adair with a sigh, for the marine had been his servant, let go his hand and sprang on. In vain the British and their allies fired away at every loophole and embrasure where a man's head or firelock was to be seen. The enemy rattled away as rapidly as ever, and no impression seemed to be made on the walls, while numbers of the storming-party were falling one after the other around. Now a poor fellow would spring up into the air shot through the head, and now would fall down with a groan, and rolling over, clutch convulsively at the earth; one would utter a sharp shriek as he fell; others, with the blood streaming from their limbs, would endeavour to scramble on till they sank with a cry of pain exhausted to the ground. The midshipmen now began to comprehend more clearly than they had ever before done the stern realities of warfare. They got within thirty yards of the walls when they found themselves in front of a crenelled outwork with a deep ditch before it. In vain the officers looked for some part of the castle wall which might prove practicable. Not a spot appeared accessible, and nothing but the ugly-looking muzzles of the enemy's muskets were visible through the loopholes. Most unwillingly was the command given to retire, and most unwillingly was it obeyed.

"I say, Murray, I don't like this—to have to turn my tail on those red-capped gentry," exclaimed Adair.

"We must obey orders, at all events," observed Murray. "Steady, my men, steady," he added, as some of the sailors were turning round to take a parting shot at the foe.

The marines were drawn off in beautiful order, and the whole party were soon out of the reach of shot. As they were pulling off, Murray and Adair remarked that a flag which had been planted in the garden, in front of the fort, was left flying.

"That will never do, the enemy will be getting it," cried Adair. "I say, Alick, let you and I go and see if we cannot pull it down, and carry it off."

"With all my heart," answered Murray. "Let us put back at once; we must ask Captain A—'s leave as we pass his boat. He will not refuse it, I am sure."

The crew of their boat were delighted at hearing what the midshipmen had resolved to do, and pulled back to the shore with a will.

As they passed Captain A—'s boat Adair sang out, "There's an English flag left flying on the shore there, sir; those red-capped fellows will boast that they took it from us if we let it stay. May we go and get it?"

The commander of the expedition saw that if it was to be done, no time was to be lost, as the risk to be run would increase by delay, or the Egyptians might see the flag, and sally out and take it.

"A brave idea; go and prosper, my lads," he answered promptly.

"Thank you, sir, thank you," answered Murray and Adair in one breath, while their crew bent with all their might to their oars.

"Oh, Alick," said Adair, "I do so wish that Rogers was with us. This is just the thing of all others he would have liked."

"I wish he was, indeed," answered Murray. "But I dare say something else will turn up before long in which he may be able to take a part."

The boat very soon reached the shore. All the crew wanted to go on the expedition, but the midshipmen would only consent to take one. They had their cutlasses by their sides, and pistols in their belts, but their arms were not likely to be of much use. The instant the boat's stem touched the beach, they sprang on shore; and, running along across the beach, scrambled over the first wall they encountered, and found themselves in the garden.

Scarcely were they there, when the sharp eyes of the enemy fell on them, and they were saluted with a hot fire of musketry.

"Skip about—dodge them—fly here—fly there; take care they don't hit you," sang out Paddy, suiting the action to the word. "The more we jump, the less chance we shall have of being hit."

The midshipmen's movements, as they hurried on, were not unlike those of Wills-of-the-Wisp.

The enemy could not conceive what they had come for, and probably supposed that they were madmen who had escaped on shore, and were coming to join them. For a short time the firing ceased. As the smoke cleared off, those on board the ships could see what was taking place, as well as could the enemy. Every glass was turned towards them. Jack among others recognised his friends, and saw what they were about. They were not wrong in supposing that he would long to be with them. He would have given a finger, or even a right arm, for the sake of being of their party.

On they went. They had another wall to get over. They climbed to the top of it. The enemy at last suspected what they were about, and came to the conclusion that if they were mad they had method in their madness, so they began once more furiously firing away at them. Eastern matchlocks are fortunately not like Enfield rifles; or their lives, if they had had nine, like cats, whom they so resembled in their activity, would not have been worth a moment's purchase. Murray and Adair raced on as merrily as if they had been playing a game of prisoner's base. They clambered up a wall, at the top of which the flag-staff had been placed. They waved it about their heads; and, giving a loud cheer, down they leaped to the ground, where their companion was ready to receive them. Happily they did so, for the next moment a thick shower of musket-balls came rattling across the spot they had left.

"Not hit, Alick?" asked Adair, as they scampered back as hard as their legs would carry them.

"No; I hope you are not," said Murray.

"Can't say for a certainty," answered Terence; "I feel a funny stinging sensation in my side as if something or other was the matter."

Whatever it was it did not impede his speed. At length it seemed to strike the Egyptians that though they could not manage to knock over the young giaours with their matchlocks they might with their scimitars; so a band of fierce-looking fellows with long moustachios, wonderfully wide breeches, and gleaming blades, sallied out of the fortress to endeavour to overtake them. The Egyptians ran very fast and felt very savage, but they might just as well have tried to catch three active tomcats. Dick Needham, their companion, was the first to perceive that the enemy was in pursuit of them.

"There's a lot on 'em a scampering after us, sir," he observed coolly.

"All right," answered Terence. "Their friends inside the fort, then, will be less likely to keep firing at us; and I should like to see the followers of the prophet, whether Turk or Egyptian, who can catch us in a fair race like this."

To do them justice, however, the enemy made good play over the ground. The outside garden wall was reached and leaped, and now the three adventurers had a fair run for it along the beach towards their boat with the red-capped gentlemen, as Adair called them, in hot pursuit. A long straggling branch of a tree had been thrown upon the beach. Adair did not observe it, and suddenly he found himself toppled over on his head. He thought that he had broken his leg.

"Take the flag and run, Alick," he exclaimed, throwing the flag-staff to Murray. "Never mind me, I'm too much, hurt to move."

"Not when I have a pair of legs to run off with you, sir," cried Dick Needham, lifting Paddy upon his shoulders, running off with him as if he had been a baby. "It was not for that, sir, that I comed here to look after you."

Paddy felt that it was not a moment to stand on his dignity, so he was very much obliged to Dick for carrying him. Murray took the flag, but would not leave him till he had seen him hoisted upon Dick's shoulders. Away they went then as before; but the Egyptians had gained considerably on them, and hallooed and shouted, and, worse than all, fired off their pistols with as good an aim as they could take, running as they were at full speed. Fortunately the bullets did not reach the fugitives; just then the latter caught sight of their boat, which they had left under shelter of a rock. The Egyptians did not see her, and so they ran on, which they otherwise would not have done. What was their surprise, then, to find themselves saluted with a round of grape-shot from a gun in her bows, and a volley of musketry, while a true British cheer reached their ears. Dick and Murray responded to it, and so did Paddy in a voice which showed that there was not much the matter with him, and all three very speedily tumbled into the boat, while the enemy turned tail and scampered back to the fort. The boat immediately shoved off to return to the frigate.

"What is the matter with you, Paddy?" asked Murray, as soon as they had taken their seats. "I hope you are not much hurt. Let me see."

"My knee bothers me a little, but my side is the worst," answered Adair. "And, as I am a gentleman, look here, the fellows have shot away the handle of my sword!"

Such was the case. Adair had indeed had a narrow escape; his coat was torn and his skin slightly grazed. An eighth of an inch on one side, and he would have received a very ugly, if not a mortal, wound. Happily he was very little hurt, and the cheers with which the boat was received, as she got alongside the frigate, made him forget entirely that anything was the matter with him.

"Oh! I am so jealous of you two fellows," exclaimed Jack, as they were all seated together in the berths. "You'll make me volunteer to lead a forlorn hope, or to do something terrifically heroic. However, the fun is not over yet; we shall have plenty more work to do before long."

The fun, as Jack called it, was not over. Sidon was soon afterwards attacked by a squadron under Sir Charles Napier, in his usual slap-dash gallant determined-to-conquer manner. The ships bombarded, then the Turks, marines, and bluejackets were landed, and stormed one castle after another, killing or putting to flight every one who opposed them. Jack, Murray, and Adair, to their great delight, were all on shore together. The cannonading had not, however, driven the Egyptians from their entrenchments, so the ships again opened their fire. Captain Austin, at the head of a Turkish battalion, had taken one castle, Captain Mansel, with great gallantry, led a body of marines into another, and then they fought their way into another castle which overlooked the town, not, however, without some loss. And now the commodore conceived that the time had come for storming the town itself, and, putting himself at the head of the troops, he led them on. The three midshipmen, with a body of seamen from the different ships, were with him. They broke into some strongly fortified barracks, and drove out the enemy, then they fought their way through the streets to the citadel. Several boats had brought their ensigns, Jack carried theirs at the end of a pole.

"Hurrah, now!" he sang out; "let us have our colours on the top of the wall before any one else." Terence and Murray echoed the sentiment; and, leading on some of their men, they endeavoured to reach the spot before a boat's crew of their Austrian allies, led on by a midshipman, as well as before other parties of British seamen. Never was there a better race. No one felt inclined to stop at obstacles, and everybody who attempted to oppose them was killed. The governor of the town was encountered. He was offered quarter, but he would not receive it, and before any officers could interfere two marines ran the brave old gentleman through the body, and he died like a true Turk as he was.

When the enemy saw that their chief was dead, and that there was no one to lead them, they wisely threw down their arms, resolved, like brave men, to live and fight another day for a more profitable cause.

Jack and his companions pushed on, and having now fewer enemies to encounter, made still greater progress. The higher part of the town was reached; with shouts and loud huzzas they scrambled up to the summit of the walls, and, planting the British banner, Sidon was proclaimed to have fallen into the power of the allies. Fortunately the commodore and his followers came upon a thousand men concealed in a vaulted barrack, who were prepared to rush out and cut them off, but who, instead, were very glad to lay down their arms, and in the end every one of the garrison, three thousand in number, was captured. Tyre, that ancient city, was next captured; so was Caiffa, Tortosa, and other places; and at last the fleet appeared before Acre, still one of the most important places on the Syrian coast. Here the midshipmen saw what real fighting was. Acre presents two sides to the sea, one facing south and the other west. In consequence of this it was necessary that the fleet should attack in two divisions. It was a grand sight to see the mighty line-of-battle ships and the fine steamers, armed with their engines of destruction, approaching in order the devoted town, and still more when they began thundering away from a thousand loud-mouthed guns, confusing the senses with their roars and filling the air with their smoke. Even Jack felt his spirits awed as hour after hour, without cessation, the mighty uproar continued, and houses were overthrown and strong stone walls were seen crumbling away before the reiterated shocks of the iron shower levelled at them. The enemy, too, were not idle, and shots and shell came whizzing about the ships, striking down here and there many a gallant seaman and marine.

"Well, Alick, what do you think of it?" asked Jack, as, in the course of their duty, the two friends were brought together.

"That we are in earnest in what we are about; though I wish I could feel the poor fellows we are slaughtering deserved their fate more than I think they do," answered Murray.

"I don't understand those niceties," observed Terence, who had just then come up. "Those fellows don't do what we tell them, so we've a perfect right to kill and destroy them as fast as we can; but, halloo, what's that?"

As Adair was speaking a terrific noise, ten times louder than the roar of all the guns of the squadron put together, was heard, and high up into the air were seen to ascend fragments of walls, and beams, and human bodies, succeeded by a dense smoke, out of which flames burst forth and raged furiously. The castle had blown up, or rather the grand magazine within it, and in a moment nearly two thousand persons were hurried into eternity. The firing ceased—the combatants held their breath, aghast at the dreadful catastrophe; but the Egyptians, undaunted, soon again recommenced the action, and the ships bombarded on as before till sunset, when the action was discontinued.

"What tough fellows those must be to hold out so long," said Jack. "I should have thought they would have had enough of it before this."

The governor had already come to the same conclusion, and during the night he and his followers evacuated the place, and in the morning some Turks and Austrians were sent on shore to take possession. The capture of Acre terminated the war in Syria, for many of the tribes which had been hesitating which side to choose, joined the Sultan's forces, and the army of Ibrahim Pacha dwindled from 75,000 to 20,000 men. Sir Charles Napier went to Alexandria, and Mehemet Ali, persuaded that the tide of war had turned against him, undertook to evacuate Syria, and to restore the Turkish fleet, as soon as the Sultan should send him a firman, granting him the hereditary government of Egypt. Everybody engaged in the Syrian war got a great deal of credit, and my three friends came in for a midshipman's share of the honours showered on the victors. Once more the *Racer* was ploughing the waters of the Mediterranean with her head to the westward. She had been her full time on the station, and it was the general expectation that she would speedily be ordered home.

"Hurrah for old England!" was the joyous cry on board, and no one enjoyed the thoughts of returning home more than did the three friends, and yet there was a lump of bitter in the bottom of the cup to spoil this pleasure. It was the thought that in all probability they would be soon separated, for how long they could not guess—perhaps years might pass away before they could again meet. They resolved, however, to stick together if they could, and, at all events, never to fail in letting each other know their whereabouts.

The *Racer* reached Portsmouth at last. There was a paying off dinner, given by the midshipmen to the gun-room officers, at the far-famed *Blue Posts*. Old Hemming presided, and a very good president he made. The first course was over when a stumping on the stairs was heard, and the waiter, opening the door, announced Admiral Triton. Jack sprang up and grasped his hand warmly.

"I have taken the liberty of an old seaman to look in on you, gentlemen, on this occasion, uninvited; for I saw you just as you were all brought together, and I was anxious to meet you again before you all separate, probably for ever," said the Admiral—who, as may be supposed, was most cordially welcomed—after waiting for some time till the speech-making had begun. "You have had, I am glad to find from my friend Rogers, a happy ship. Many of you will, I hope, some day be captains; and let me impress it on you that on you yourselves will then mainly depend whether your ships also are happy ships or the reverse. To make them so, you must command your tempers (you cannot begin too soon to practise the difficult task), you must endeavour to study and promote the true interests of all under you, and you must act justly towards all men. To do this I must not fail to remind you that you must pray for strength whence alone strength for all difficult tasks can be given."

The Admiral's speech in no way interrupted the hilarity of the evening, and he added much to it by several amusing anecdotes, at which no one laughed more heartily than he did. The next day he accompanied Jack to Northamptonshire. No one was ever more cordially welcomed in a happy home than was Jack. It need not be said that, for at least three days, everybody did their very utmost to spoil him, though after that time he was treated very much as he used to be before he became a midshipman.

Chapter Eight
Bound for Africa

One morning, towards the termination of breakfast, Jack Rogers was leaning back in his chair, with a bit of buttered toast in one hand and the *Times* in the other, on the contents of which he was making a running commentary, when he stopped short, put down his toast, took a hurried sip of his tea, and exclaimed, "So my old skipper has got a ship again, and they say is going out as commodore to the coast of Africa."

"Dear me!" observed Mrs Rogers, "I am afraid that Captain Lascelles will not like that; I should always have such a horror of that dreadful station."

"Oh, mother, don't pray entertain such a notion as that," said Jack, with no little emphasis. "There is in the first place plenty of work to be done there, which in these piping times of peace is a great consideration. Only think of the fun of capturing a slaver, and what is more, of getting an independent command; or at least that is of a prize, you know, and being away from one's ship for weeks together. And then there is cruising in open boats, and exploring rivers, and fights with pirates or slavers; perhaps a skirmish with the dependents of some nigger potentate, and fifty other sorts of adventures, not to speak of prize-money and all that sort of thing, you know. Oh, to my mind, the coast of Africa is one of the best stations in the world, in spite of what is said against it."

When Jack made this assertion, he had never been there. He talked on till he had worked himself up to a fit of enthusiasm, and almost made his family believe that the African station was not so bad a one after all. The truth was that when Captain Lascelles paid off the *Racer* he promised Jack that should he get another ship soon he would apply for him, and Jack therefore felt pretty certain that he should himself be very soon on station, and he of course was anxious to prevent his parents or sisters from feeling any undue anxiety on his account. He could not sit down or turn his mind to anything all day till he discovered a copy of the *Cruise of the Midge*, over the graphic pages of which he was observed to be intently poring; and then he went and routed out of the library one or two books descriptive of the west coast of Africa. At dinner he could talk of nothing else but the Gold Coast, and the Ivory Coast, and Congo, and other places in those regions.

"Why, Jack, we might suppose that you were contemplating going out there from the way you talk about those places," observed one of his brothers, who wanted to bring some other subject on the tapis.

"And so of course I am," exclaimed Jack. "I should like to stay at home among you all; but as I have chosen a profession, and there is not another like it, I hope to stick to it, and I intend always to look out where there is most work to be done, and to go there."

"My dear child," said his mother, "but not to the coast of Africa."

Then Jack went into all the arguments in its favour, which he flattered himself had made so favourable an impression at breakfast, but which he found had all been forgotten, while the original very natural prejudice against it had once more asserted a pre-eminence in the minds of his family.

The next morning Jack was unusually fidgety till the post came in, and there was a blank look on his countenance when the post-bag was opened and it produced no letter for him. Soon after breakfast, however, Admiral Triton's carriage drove up to the door, and out of it stepped the admiral himself. He quickly stumped into the drawing-room, and having made his salaams to the ladies, produced an official-looking document from his pocket. Jack had followed him eagerly into the room.

"Here, my boy," said he, "is a letter from my friend Lascelles, your old captain. He says—let me see what he says. Oh! here it is. 'I cannot find the address of Jack Rogers, so pray tell him to come down to Portsmouth at once and join the *Ranger*. I have just been appointed to her, to go out as commodore on the African station. Let his outfit be got ready accordingly. I have no doubt that he will find some opportunity of distinguishing himself; and as he has already served four years, there is a fair chance of his getting his promotion when he returns home.' The rest is private," observed the admiral, when he had concluded this somewhat laconic epistle. "And now, Jack, I congratulate you, my lad," he continued. "You have been quite long enough on shore to rub up your shore manners, and that is as long as a midshipman ought to remain at home. How soon shall you be ready?"

"In ten days or a fortnight I think that I could get his shirts and flannel waistcoats made, and his socks marked, and his—"

"I beg your pardon, my dear madam, but by that time the *Ranger* may be halfway across the Bay of Biscay. Ten or fourteen hours you should say. He must go and see his ship fitted out. He'll never be at home in her unless he does. Well, well, then the day after to-morrow I intend to go down with him. I enjoyed my last trip so much that I would not miss the opportunity of seeing him on board his new ship. I know what you would say, my dear madam, but a longer delay would be objectionable. Rogers will agree with me. There, it is settled, so let us say no more about the matter."

Thus Jack found himself, more speedily than he expected, about to go once more afloat. That afternoon, in company with two of his brothers and his sister Mary, he galloped round and paid his farewells to his friends in the neighbourhood; and then his chest was packed, the contents of which all the womankind in and out of the house, for a long way round, had been employed without cessation, night and day, in getting ready. So when the admiral, as he had done four years before, drove up to the door, he was perfectly ready to accompany him. Jack did his best to keep up the spirits of his mother and sister to the last, though just as he was going they gave way, and he himself was nearly upset. All the fighting he had seen had not hardened his heart. Away he and the admiral went down to Portsmouth. The next morning they were, soon after breakfast, on board the *Ranger*, then fitting out alongside a hulk. She was a six and thirty gun frigate, no great improvement on the *Racer*, but still a ship which an actively disposed officer might well be glad to get. Several of the officers had already joined, and the admiral made a few favourable remarks about Jack, which placed him at once in a favourable light in their eyes. Captain Lascelles, who was living on shore, welcomed him very kindly, and Jack was very well pleased with what he saw of his future companions. The third lieutenant of the frigate had not been appointed. However, three or four days after Jack had joined, who should make his appearance but old Hemming, who had, on the paying off of the *Racer*, got his somewhat tardy promotion. Jack did not know that he was promoted, and was not a little pleased to find that he was their third lieutenant. Jack had written to Adair and Murray directly he found that he was appointed to the *Ranger*, urging them to exert all their interest to get appointed to her likewise, but he had not yet heard from either of them. One was in Ireland, the other in Scotland. Hemming laughed when he told him what he had done.

"Their friends may take some trouble to get them on board a ship going to the Mediterranean, or to keep them on the Home station; but depend on it they will not bestir themselves to have them sent out to the Coast," he remarked.

Captain Lascelles' character was well-known, so he soon got his ship manned and ready for sea. Admiral Triton had gone over to the Isle of Wight, and now came off to Spithead to see the last of them. There was still room for another midshipman. They were expecting every day to sail, and Jack was in despair at not hearing from either of his friends, wondering what would have become of them, when a shore-boat was seen coming off to the ship, and Paddy Adair and his chest came up the side.

"Hurrah!" exclaimed Jack, as soon as he saw him; "that is jolly. But I say, old fellow, where is Murray? I wish that he was here too."

Adair could not tell, and they puzzled their brains in vain to account for his silence. The topsails were loosed, the capstan was manned, and to a merry tune the men were running round and heaving up the anchor, and as the fine old admiral was shaking hands with all he knew on board just before stepping into his boat, Jack could scarcely persuade himself that four years had passed over his head since, with the exception that Murray was not present as one of the *dramatis persona*, precisely the same scene had been enacted. The *Ranger* had a quick run to Sierra Leone, where her arrival was welcomed with very great delight by all on board the ship she came to relieve. The frigate at last cast anchor opposite Freetown, and Jack and Adair were allowed with several of the officers to go on shore.

They were surprised at finding so large and flourishing a town, with a population, although the greater number are black or coloured, so generally intelligent and well off. They saw churches, and colleges, and schools, and places of education of all sorts. They were told that many of the negroes liberated from slavers have become wealthy, and that the sons of men who landed on those shores twenty years ago ignorant savages, are now receiving a first-rate education, and studying Latin, Greek, and Hebrew, many of them diligently preparing for becoming ministers of the gospel. Freetown, built on rising ground, close to the sea, has a very picturesque appearance. Jack and Adair were also struck with the number of people who came into the town to trade, and with the signs of industry everywhere visible. However, they were not sorry to find themselves once more at sea, with a sharp lookout kept night and day for slavers. The officers were in general very different in appearance from those in the *Racer*, though they were all very good sort of fellows. The oddest looking was Dr McCan, the surgeon. He was a jovial-faced short man, and from having lived a life of ease on shore he had grown enormously fat. As he had also got into a very comfortable practice, he did not at all like coming to sea, but at the same time, as he was a true philosopher, instead of moaning and groaning, he tried to make himself as happy as under the circumstances he was able. The first lieutenant was a veteran of the old school, tall and thin, but as lithe and agile as he had been when he was twenty years younger. He was constantly employed, because every captain who knew him wanted him as his first lieutenant, and so, because he was so very good in that capacity, John Holt remained still a lieutenant. He did not complain beyond an occasional grumble; indeed those who knew him suspected that he rather preferred being looked on as one of the best first lieutenants instead of holding a higher rank, when he would have had to remain on shore and be forgotten. The second lieutenant and master were both rough and ready seamen, short, strongly-built men, with light hair, and large bushy whiskers and beard; they were wonderfully like each other. The purser was one of the most gentlemanly and best educated men in the ship. The marine officer was also a very excellent fellow, but he squinted awfully, which made him carry his head somewhat on one side; and his face was broad and strongly seamed with lines, which twisted in a way that made him look as if he was always laughing. He however did laugh very frequently, more especially at his own jokes, which, if not always original, were very amusing. In the midshipmen's berth there were several mates of long standing, who had come out on the station in the hopes of getting their promotion, while besides Rogers and Adair there were three other midshipmen, with their usual complement of other grades. The frigate lay long enough off Freetown to make every one rejoice to find themselves once more at sea. Lookouts were constantly aloft on the watch for slavers. They had not been at sea many days, when the exciting cry of "Sail ho!" was heard from the masthead. Several of the officers were soon seen going up the rigging with their spy-glasses slung over their shoulders to look out for the stranger. She was made out to be a ship dead to leeward. All sail was instantly made in chase—she might be a merchantman, or possibly a man-of-war; but that was not likely, and Captain Lascelles had received information that a large slave-ship was expected off the coast. It was not till nearly an hour had elapsed that the stranger bore up and made sail to escape. This left no doubt as to her character, and every one looked forward to the capture of an important prize. The frigate sailed remarkably well, but a stern chase is a long chase, and several hours more passed before the topsails of the stranger were seen above the horizon. Jack and Terence could scarcely tear themselves from the deck even to go below to dinner.

"I say, Paddy," observed the former, "I wonder whether you or I shall be sent away in her when we take her. Will Hemming go in command, or will one of the mates?—Lee or Weedon, perhaps."

"Let us catch our hare before we eat her," said Adair. "I tell you what I do wish; that we were in a smaller craft, and then you and I would have a chance of getting sent away together. Wouldn't that be fun?" Jack agreed that it would, but both of them began to look very blank when darkness closed in on them, and the chase was still several miles ahead. When the frigate first made out the chase she was standing to the eastward, and was about a hundred miles off Cape Palmas. She was then running towards the Bight of Biafra. Captain Lascelles kept the frigate on nearly the same course, edging slightly in towards the land, for he suspected that the ship was bound in for one of the harbours on the Gold or Slave-Coast, and would probably stand in towards the land during the night. Neither of the midshipmen turned in that night. The thought that they were about to take their first prize kept, indeed, many others out of their hammocks, and sharp eyes were on the watch for her in every direction during the night. In spite of their sharpness, however, not a sign of the chase could be discovered. Yet as she was not seen on either hand, the probabilities were that she was still ahead.

"Do you know, Terence, this reminds me of the time when we chased the Turkish frigate which had you on board off the Egyptian coast," said Jack. "I only hope that we may be more fortunate, and catch her before she gets on shore and blows up."

"I shall be glad if we can catch her on the water, or earth, or sky," answered Terence. "These slavers are slippery fellows, and it is no easy matter to get hold of them."

The night wore on. When the morning at length broke the mast-heads were crowded with visitors. They rubbed their eyes and their telescopes, and then looked through the latter, and rubbed and rubbed again; and then they pulled very long faces at each other, for the ship could nowhere be seen. Many of them remained aloft, still looking for her, but at last they came down and looked at each other, and voted themselves sold. However, they went to breakfast, and as they walked the deck after it they hoped that they might have better luck next time.

The men's dinner was just over, when once more everybody was put on the alert by hearing "Sail ho!" sung out from the mast-head.

"Where away?" asked Captain Lascelles, who was walking the deck at the time.

"Right ahead, sir," was the answer.

The captain himself went aloft. When he came down again he told Mr Holt that he believed she was the identical ship they had chased the previous day. The frigate rapidly got up with her.

"How jolly to think that we shall catch her after all," exclaimed Jack, as they got near enough to the chase to see halfway down her courses. "But what is the matter with her? She seems to have altered her course."

"She is becalmed, to be sure," answered Lieutenant Hemming, who heard the question. "Daddy Neptune has brought her up all standing, to place her as a punishment in our power. I only hope he will not make a mistake and becalm us till we get up to her."

In another hour or less the stranger was seen floating in the middle of a shining sheet of water of silvery hue. Still the frigate carried on the breeze. It was a question whether the stranger would get it, and perhaps make a fresh start, leaving her pursuer in the lurch. The excitement on board the frigate became greater than ever when the stranger was seen, for there was no longer any doubt about her character. Her taut masts, her square yards, the great hoist of her topsails, and her light cotton canvas, all showed her to be a slaver, probably combined with the occupation of a pirate. Gradually the wind decreased as the frigate neared her; when within about a couple of miles it fell a dead calm. Captain Lascelles gave a rapid glance round the horizon, and then ordered away the first and second cutters with a large whale-boat, and directed the second and third lieutenants and one of the mates to join them. Jack and Terence got leave to accompany Mr Hemming. It was very evident, from the appearance of the stranger, that she would give them some tough work before they took her. With loud cheers the expedition shoved off from the frigate's side and pulled away for the ship. The three boats contained altogether from five and thirty to forty hands. It was broad daylight. There would have been no use in disguising their intentions. If the slaver attempted to defend herself at all, they might well expect some desperate fighting, and from her appearance it could scarcely be expected that she would do otherwise. Hemming's boat, which pulled the fastest, got the lead. The men every now and then gave a cheer to animate each other. They rapidly neared the slaver, as the smooth shining water bubbled and hissed under the boats' bows. Oh, how hot it was, as the sun's rays came directly down on their heads; but no one thought of the heat, and they laughed and joked as if they were employed in some amusing occupation.

"I say, Paddy, I think we could do a beefsteak brown on these stern-sheets," observed Jack, putting his hand down by his side.

"That to be sure we might," answered Terence. "And here comes the pepper for them," he added, as the pirate sent a shower of round shot, grape, and canister flying around, and stirring up the water on every side, though fortunately no one was hit.

"Give it them in return, my lads," cried the second lieutenant; "marines, fire."

The marines were not slow in obeying the order, and as the seamen bent to their oars, they continued firing away as fast as they could load. The slaver's crew had evidently hopes of crippling their adversaries, for they kept up a brisk and well-directed fire; but, hot as it was, the gallant British tars were undaunted.

"That dark ship has, perhaps, four or five hundred poor wretches under hatches whom it is our business to set free," cried Lieutenant Hemming. "And then, my boys, if we do take her, what a lot of prize-money we shall get? Hurrah! hurrah!"

Hemming had been too long at sea not to know how to excite the spirit of seamen.

"We shall have some tough work, hurrah! hurrah! You'll knock over some of those pirates, depend on it."

Each officer excited his men by similar cries. Their only fear was that a breeze might spring up, and that the enemy might escape them. However, though they pulled hard, nearly half an hour passed from the time the first shot was fired till they got up to the ship.

"What an ugly set of cut-throats the fellows are," said Adair, pointing to the people who crowded the pirate's deck. "Let's be at them, Jack."

Jack was quite ready to respond to the proposal. The two other boats boarded on the starboard side, amid a hot fire of langrage of all sorts poured down upon them. Hemming pulled up on the port bow, sprang up the side, and soon fought his way upon deck. Jack and Adair were climbing in at one of the ports when the pirates fired the gun through it directly over their heads.

"Come on, Paddy, come on," Jack sang out; but Adair had been knocked over into the bottom of the boat.

Happily, however, he was only kilt, as the Irish say; so he clambered up again, and quickly followed his friend, accompanied by Dick Needham, who had joined the *Ranger*, and another seaman.

Fortunate it was for the midshipmen that they had so stout and true a seaman as Dick Needham as their companion; for they encountered a desperate resistance from the pirates, and were instantly engaged in furious hand-to-hand combats. Meantime, so surrounded were they by their enemies, that they could not tell what had become of the rest of their shipmates. More than once they were nearly driven back through the port by which they had entered. Jack saved Adair from an ugly cut on the head, and Adair in return saved Jack from being run through the body, by cutting down the pirate who was making the attempt to do it. Both of them, as well as Dick Needham, were nearly exhausted, and poor Tom Bowles, their companion, had received a wound which brought him to the deck, when Hemming's voice was heard above their heads, and he leaped down from the forecastle, off which he had driven the enemy. With loud cheers he led on his men; the pirates gave way before them. Then Lieutenant Collard and

Randall were seen fighting their way from aft. The pirates looked about them, and seeing enemies on every side, gave way, some leaping below, and some throwing themselves overboard. Fully a dozen pirates were killed, and a still greater number were wounded. Many did not even ask for quarter. Others threw themselves on their knees, as their captors followed them below, and entreated that their lives might be spared. The victory was not gained without loss. A marine and two seamen were killed and five were wounded, a large proportion out of the number composing the expedition. No sooner were the decks cleared than a terrific howl was heard from below. Mr Hemming rushed to the hold; just at that moment a whole host of negroes were seen emerging from it. He was barely in time to drive them back again.

"I know the rascally slavers' trick," he exclaimed; "they have been telling the poor wretches that we are going to murder them; and if they once had gained the deck, we should have had no little difficulty in preventing them from murdering us."

Then looking down the hold on the heaving mass of black humanity, he cried out, "Hear me, you piratical rascals; if you don't make those poor negro fellows understand that we are their friends, and have come to set them free, we'll hang every one of you at your own yard-arms before ten minutes." He knew that many of the crew understood English perfectly, indeed that some of them were English and Americans.

The pirates, finding that their plot was defeated, wisely came on deck, having explained to the slaves that no harm was going to happen to them. As they came up they were secured by the manacles which they had prepared for their unhappy captives. Some time was thus employed, and at length a breeze sprang up, and the frigate was seen bearing down upon them. The prisoners looked very blank when they found that they were to be transferred to her. The gallantry of every one engaged was warmly commended by Captain Lascelles. Hemming got the command of the prize, and to their great delight Jack and Terence were allowed to remain in her. The frigate and her prize then made sail together for Sierra Leone. They kept close in with the land in the hopes of picking up another prize. Before, however, they got round Cape Palmas they met with a strong westerly gale, which compelled them to bring up in a sheltered bay, which is to be found some way to the eastward of it. The scenery was not very interesting. Near them was a narrow neck of sand, with a few palm-trees on it, and a muddy lagoon on the other side. Still, men who have been long aboard are glad to find anything like firm ground on which to stretch their legs. Now the surgeon and the lieutenant of marines were constantly joking each other as to which of them possessed the greatest physical powers. If one boasted he had ridden fifty miles without stopping, the other had always gone ten miles farther. If one had leaped over a wide ditch, the other had leaped over one five feet wider, or if one said he had kept up a Scotch reel for an hour, the other had danced one for a quarter of an hour longer.

"I'll tell you what, doctor," explained Lieutenant Stokes; "I'll undertake to race you for a mile, each of us carrying another person on our backs."

"Done," cried Doctor McCan; "it shall come off at once. I'll take Adair as my jockey; you can take whom you like." Adair was the lightest midshipman on board, and the doctor thought that by getting him he had stolen a march on his military competitor.

"Agreed," answered Lieutenant Stokes, cocking his squinting eye in the most ludicrous way. "I'll take Rogers. He's a bit heavier than Adair, but I don't mind that. As you had the first choice of a rider, I must choose the ground. From the extreme end of that spit of land to the palm-trees near the neck is, I guess, about a mile." This was said while the frigate and her prize were brought up on their voyage to Sierra Leone. Doctor McCan looked at the white spit of sand, and thought what heavy work it would be running over it; but he felt that he was in honour bound to keep to the proposed terms. A party was soon made up to go on shore, and all hands looked forward to the fun they expected to enjoy from the exhibition. They had first to pull alongside the prize to call for Rogers and Adair. Hemming gave them leave to go, and they of course were nothing loath to accept the invitation. What Captain Lascelles would have thought of the matter I don't know. He might have considered that the exhibition of an officer of marines racing with a midshipman on his back was somewhat subversive of discipline. There was no surf on the shore, and the boats landed without difficulty. The ground was measured by the umpires. It was from the end of the point round the palm-trees and back again about a quarter of the distance to make up the mile. The doctor felt the sand with his feet. It was very fine and soft, and he began to repent of his proposal.

"Now, gentlemen, take up your burdens and be ready at the starting-post," said the master, who was chief umpire. They went to the ground, tossing up the midshipmen to make them sit comfortably on their backs.

"Now—one, two, three, and away you go!" cried the master.

Off they went, the marine officer prancing away with Jack in the pride of his strength, while the doctor ploughed his way steadily on through the sand, finding, even with Adair, that he had rather more flesh and blood to carry than was pleasant. Still Mr Stokes did not gain upon him. He too found that Rogers was no slight weight, though he was only a midshipman—as Jack said of himself, "All that is of me is good." For some time they were neck and neck. Hot enough they found it, for the sun was bright, the sand was soft, there was but little air, and what there was was in their backs. They were lightly clad, to be sure; but had they worn as little clothing as the most unsophisticated of negroes, they would have found it hot enough. They puffed, and they blew, and they strained, but still they persevered. At first neither Rogers nor Adair cared much about the matter, but they soon got as excited as the men who carried them, and eager for their respective steeds to win.

"I say, doctor," observed Adair, after they had gone about half the distance, "the sand inside of us there, along the lagoon, looks hard. It would not take us much out of our way if we were to go there, and you would then get along famously." Terence intended to give good counsel, and the doctor followed it. To his great delight he found the ground hard, and was getting on at a great rate. Jack urged Mr Stokes to take the same route.

"Stay a bit; all is not gold that glitters," was the answer. "That's treacherous sort of ground."

"But see, see how magnificently they get along," cried Jack, again wishing that he had a bridle to guide his refractory steed.

All this time the umpires and other spectators were keeping up merry shouts of laughter.

"There they go," shouted Jack; "they will be round the trees in no time."

Just as he spoke there was a loud hullabaloo from Terence, echoed by the doctor. Over they both went head first, but the doctor's heels did not follow, for they had stuck fast in the mud, into which poor Terence's head plunged with a loud thud. The doctor heroically endeavoured to pull him out, but his own legs only stuck deeper and deeper. As the marine officer came up and passed by them, he began capering about and neighing in triumph, while Jack barbarously inquired whether they would like to have a tow. At last Terence, covered with mud, black and most ill-odorous, scrambled out, and, by throwing to him the end of his handkerchief, contrived to haul out the doctor, who once more took him on his shoulders, and in sorry plight continued his course. Jack looked round and saw them coming just as Mr Stokes was about to round the palm-trees. He crowed loudly and waved his hand. It would have been wiser, however, if he had not begun to triumph so soon, for his steed's foot catching in a falling and half-hidden branch, over they both went, and were half buried and almost stifled in the soft hot sand. However, they picked themselves up; and, Jack, mounting, away they went towards the goal where their friends were ready to receive them. Just as they got up to it, down came the gallant marine once more, but Jack stuck to his back, and on all fours he crawled up to the winning-post. The poor doctor, with Terence, as Jack said, like a huge baboon clinging behind him, came in soon after; and the doctor declared that it was the last time, with or without a jockey, he would ever run a race on the shores of Africa or anywhere else. In the afternoon the blacks in parties were taken on shore under an armed escort to bathe and exercise themselves; and the next day, the wind shifting, the frigate and captured slaver again made sail for their destination.

"The frigate is signalising to us," said Jack one morning to Lieutenant Hemming, who had just come on deck. "She is going in chase of a sail to the southward. We are to continue our course for Sierra Leone."

In a couple of hours the frigate was out of sight. There appeared to be every promise of fine weather.

Hemming's chief concern was for the blacks, who were sickly. Several had already died, and not a day passed without four or five being added to the number. It was important, therefore, to make the passage as quickly as possible. For this object the commanding officer kept probably more sail on the ship than she would otherwise have carried.

Jack one afternoon had charge of the watch; all seemed satisfactory. As he was taking a turn on deck, he saw Dick Needham hurrying towards him and pointing to the sea to leeward. It was a mass of white foam. He shouted out, "All hands shorten sail!"

Hemming and Adair rushed out of the cabin. Hemming without speaking seized an axe, and began cutting away at the halyards; Adair and Jack followed his example. The crew flew into the rigging with their knives, but it was too late. The tornado was upon them; over went the ship; down, down she heeled. The seething water rushed in at her ports. Shrieks and cries arose from the unhappy negroes confined below. Jack and Needham's first impulse was to knock off the hatches, and a few blacks sprang on deck before the sea closed over their heads.

"The ship is sinking, the ship is sinking," was the cry fore and aft.

"Then a raft must be formed, my lads," sang out Lieutenant Hemming. "Never say die, while life remains."

Chapter Nine
Wreck of the San Fernando

The heart of the bravest man may well sink within him when he hears the cry uttered, in accents of despair, "The ship is sinking, the ship is sinking!" Rogers and Adair looked at each other, and thought that their last moments had really come. All the bright visions of the future which their young imaginations had conjured up, vanished in a moment. Well might they, for the ship lay hopelessly on her side, with more than half her deck under water. There arose from every side shrieks and cries of terror. There were the distorted countenances of the blacks, as they crowded up the hatchway, through which the sea was pouring in torrents, while their own men, intent on preserving their lives to the last, were clambering up the bulwarks or working their way forward, which was the part of the ship the highest out of the water. Hemming, followed by the two midshipmen with axes in hand, endeavoured to gain the same part of the ship. It was no easy task. The howling wind blew with terrific violence around them, and the seething ocean bubbled up, and sent its fierce waves dashing over their heads. "Oh, save me, save me!" cried Adair, as a sea struck him and washed him down the deck; but Hemming and Rogers caught the rope he had happily clutched and hauled him up again. At length they gained the forecastle, where most of their own crew had assembled and some few of the unfortunate blacks. They were the only survivors of the four or five hundred human beings who lately breathed the breath of life on board. Mr Hemming, looking round, saw that there was not a chance of the ship righting herself. He accordingly promptly issued orders for the formation of a raft. Such spars as were loose or could be got at, were hauled up on the forecastle. The topgallant masts and royals had been carried away, and fortunately still floated near; Jack saw them and got them hauled in. Hemming, meantime, was wrenching up the forecastle deck to assist in the formation of a raft. There was not a moment to lose, for it was evident that the ship was fast settling down. Fortunately a hammer and some nails were found forward.

"Here, my lads, lash the ends of these spars together, so as to form a square," cried Hemming, working energetically. "That will do; now this one diagonally—that will strengthen it; now these planks; nail them on as we best can on the top. That will do bravely; next lash these lighter spars above all, they will form a coaming, and prevent us from slipping off the raft." Thus he went on, by his activity and cheerful voice, keeping up the spirits of his men, and encouraging them to exertion.

"Mr Hemming," said Jack, "how are we to live without food? I must try and get some—who'll follow me?"

"I will, with all my heart," cried Dick Needham. Jack and he fastened ropes to their waists, and dashed aft towards the chief cabin, which was already under water. The tornado had passed away as suddenly as it began, so that the water was tolerably smooth, or they could not have attempted this daring feat.

"I know where a cask of biscuits was stowed. If we can get it out, it will be a great thing," cried Jack, preparing to dive into the cabin.

"I saw some beef in one of the starboard lockers," said Needham, accompanying him. Another good swimmer and diver followed them. All three remained under water so long, that those forward thought they were lost. Adair could not restrain himself, and was dashing aft, when Jack came to the surface puffing and blowing like a grampus. He had discovered the cask of biscuits, but no beef was to be found. What, however, was of great consequence, was a breaker of water which Needham found, and both were floated up to the raft forward. Two other attempts were made to get provisions, but in vain. All the rest of the party were engaged with all their might in increasing and strengthening the raft. Then the cry arose, "She is going down, she is going down!" Jack looked about him as he came to the surface out of the submerged cabin, and seeing that not a moment was to be lost, summoning his two followers, sprang forward. Adair, with outstretched hand, was ready to help him on to the raft as he felt the big ship sinking under his feet.

"Shove off, shove off, my lads!" sang out their commander. With spars and oars, the seamen forced the raft away from the foundering hull. Then, as the eddy formed by the huge mass going downwards through the water caught it, the helpless raft was whirled round and round, and then horrible seemed the fate in store for them. One side dipped into the sea, and all believed that it was going to be drawn down amid the vortex. The people held on tightly for their lives. Tossing violently, however, up it again came to the surface, and floated evenly on the water. Still their condition was melancholy in the extreme.

On counting numbers it was found that the fifteen men who formed the prize crew including officers, had escaped, with two Spaniards out of those who had been left on board to assist in working the ship, and twelve negroes. To supply all these people with food, there was only a cask of biscuits and about twelve gallons of water. How long they might have to remain exposed to scorching heat, fierce storms, or chilling fogs, it was impossible to say. Jack looked at Adair, and Adair looked at Jack, to read each other's feelings in their countenances. They felt for each other as brothers, and each trembled for the fate which might overtake his friend.

"How far do you make it out we are from the land?" asked Adair.

"Oh, not more than a hundred miles," answered Hemming. "That is nothing. The sea-breeze would drive us in there in the course of the day."

He did not say this because he thought it; he wanted to keep up the spirits of the people under his charge. Nor did he remind them that they were five or six hundred miles from Freetown, Sierra Leone, and a very considerable distance from Manovia in Liberia. A fore-topgallant studding-sail had been hauled on board the raft, and this set on a spar served them as a sail. As soon as the ship had disappeared, and everything floating out of her had been picked up, Hemming's first care was to arrange the people so as to trim the raft properly. He made them sit in rows back to back, with their faces to the sea. He, with Jack and Terence, sat in the centre by the mast on the cask of biscuits and the water. A spar, with a plank nailed to the outer end, served as a rudder, and two very inefficient oars were manufactured in the same way. For some hours after the tornado they were becalmed, and then a light air from the southward sprang up, which enabled them to steer towards the land. After some consideration, Hemming stood up and addressed the men. Jack and Adair admired the calm and collected, and, indeed, dignified way in which he spoke, so different to his manner when he was a mate. "My men," he said, "we are placed by Providence in a very dangerous position. We must trust to the help of the Almighty, not to our own arm to save us; still we must exert ourselves to the best of our power to take care of our lives; we must husband our resources, we must behave with the utmost order, we must be kind to each other, and we must keep up our spirits and hope for the best. If we pray to God, He will hear us, and if He sees fit, He will save us. Now, my lads, let us pray." On this the lieutenant offered up a sincere prayer for their preservation, and all who could understand him joined in it. Even the benighted blacks comprehended that he was performing some rite by which were to benefit. After it, Hemming again got up, "I told you, my lads, we must husband our resources. Till we see what progress we make, it will be wise to take only one biscuit a day. That will support life for some days, and if we take more our stock will soon be exhausted." The men replied cheerfully that they would limit themselves to any quantity he thought best. Poor fellows, they were to be sorely tried; the sun went down, and an easterly wind blew, and not only prevented them from approaching the coast, but again drove them slowly off it. When the sun rose the wind fell altogether, and they lay exposed to the full fury of its scorching rays. A thirst, which the small quantity of water served out in a teacup during the day could in no way assuage, now attacked them. Jack and Adair felt their spirits sinking lower than they had ever gone before. They could scarcely eat their small allowance of biscuit. They knew too that in another day the bottom of the cask would be reached. Still they tried to imitate Hemming in keeping up a cheerful countenance. Many of the people complained bitterly of their sufferings. The poor blacks said nothing, but three of them, almost at the same moment, sank back on the raft, and when those near them tried to lift them up, they were found to be dead. They were speedily lowered into the water.

"Adair, what is that?" asked Jack, as a dark fin was seen gliding round the raft.

"A shark," answered Adair. "See, there are two, three, four of them. We must have one of those fellows. They will eat us if we don't eat them, that is very certain. Here, Needham, have a running bowline ready to slip over the head of the first who comes near enough." The idea was taken up eagerly by the men; there being plenty of line on board, several of them sat ready with the bight of a rope in hand, hoping to catch one of those evil-disposed monsters of the deep. But death in the meantime was busy among their companions. One by one the blacks dropped off, till one only remained. He was a fine-looking, intelligent young man, of great muscular strength, and evidently superior to the rest in rank. He sat by himself, slowly eating crumb by crumb his share of biscuit, and gazing with steadfast eyes towards the land of his birth. Once more the wind got up, and sent the water washing over the frail raft, which worked fearfully, as if it would come to pieces.

"Never fear, my lads," said Hemming, "I know of no part which will give way. It will hold together, depend on that." In spite of all the working it did hold together. Hemming's face, though his words were always cheering, looked very grave. "Rogers, Adair, my friends," he said solemnly, "the water is expended, and there are no more biscuits—how shall I announce it to these poor fellows?" He thought a little. "Come now, lads," he cried out, "be smart about catching some fish; a change of food will do us all good."

No one asked for more biscuits or water; they knew it was all gone. Some gave way under the appalling thought. One of the Spaniards went raving mad, and threw himself into the sea, whence no one had strength to pull him out; the other fell back and died quietly.

"Some of our men won't hold out much longer," observed Jack to Hemming; "can we do nothing for them?"

"Nothing," answered Hemming solemnly. The cool air of the night seemed to revive them; but when the hot sun came out, and shone down on their unprotected heads, they died. Two more went raving mad. They chattered and sang, and then howled and shrieked. It was with difficulty they could be held down. One of them escaped from his companions, and threw himself into the sea. The other was prevented from following his example, but his strength gradually decreased till he also died. Scarcely was his body sent into the deep, than a fair wind sprang up, and the sail being hoisted, the raft went along at the rate of three or four miles an hour. No one had relaxed their efforts to catch a shark. A shout was given (not a loud one, for their voices were already hollow and weak), and several men were seen hauling in the head and shoulders of a large shark. How eager and anxious was the expression of their countenances, for they all dreaded lest their prize should escape them. Their strength too was scarcely adequate to the task. At last he was hauled up on the raft, but so violent were his struggles, that he nearly threw some of the people into the sea as they crawled up to him to despatch him with their axes. At last Jack, not knowing what mischief might be committed, sprang towards him, and aiming a blow at his tail, struck directly on it, and instantly he was quieted. Scarcely was the monster dead than the men's knives were cutting away at him. Some drank his blood, and others eagerly ate the yet almost quivering flesh. The officers, however ravenous they felt, got some thin slices, which they dried in the sun before eating. Food had thus been providentially sent them, but their sufferings from thirst soon became very painful. It was piteous to hear some of the poor fellows crying out for water when there was none to give them. Several more died from the grievous thirst they were suffering. Mr Hemming anxiously looked round the horizon. Not a sail was in sight in any direction. Hour after hour passed away. Their tongues became parched, and clove to the roofs of their mouths.

"This is dreadful," whispered Jack; "I don't think I can stand it much longer."

"I would give a guinea for a bottle of gingerbeer," exclaimed Terence.

"Oh, how delicious! don't talk of such a thing. I would give ten for a pint of the dirtiest ditch-water in which a duck ever waddled," said Jack; "however, we must try and not think about it."

Some hours passed slowly by after this, when Hemming's eye was seen to brighten up.

"Is there a sail in sight?" asked Jack and Adair, who were constantly watching his looks.

"No," he answered, "but there is a cloud in the horizon. It is a small one, but it rises slowly in the north-west, and I trust betokens rain. If it does not bring wind at the same time, our sufferings may be relieved."

How anxiously all on the raft, who had yet consciousness left, watched the progress of that little cloud, at first not bigger than a man's hand. How their hearts sank within them when they thought that it had stopped, or that its course was altered; but it had not stopped, though it advanced but slowly. Still it grew, and grew, and extended wider and wider on either hand, and grew darker and darker till it formed a black canopy over their heads; and then there was a pattering, hissing noise heard over the calm sea, and down came the rain in large drops thick and fast. The men lifted up their grateful faces to heaven to catch the refreshing liquid in their mouths as it fell, but Hemming lowered the sail, and, ordering the men to stretch it wide, caught the rain in it, and let it run off into the breaker till that was full. Then they filled the cask which had held the biscuits, and each man took off his shirt, and let it get wet through and through; and eagerly they sucked the sail, so that not a drop more than could be helped of the precious fluid should be lost. Then when they found that the rain continued, each man took a draught of the pure water from the cask, which they again filled up as before by means of the sail.

"Oh, Terence, how delicious!" exclaimed Jack, drawing a deep breath.

"Nectar," said Adair, draining a last drop in his cup. It was of a doubtful brown hue, and in reality tepid from falling on the not over clean and hot sail.

Jack and Terence learned the lesson, that the value of things can only be ascertained by being compared with others. That shower was the means sent by Providence to preserve the lives of many of those on the raft. Some were already too far gone to benefit by it. They opened their glassy eyes, and allowed their shipmates to pour the water down their parched throats; they seemed to revive for a short time, but soon again sank, and some even died while the water was trickling over their cracked lips. All this time the raft was constantly surrounded by sharks. The flesh of the first caught was almost exhausted, and though dried in the sun had become rather savoury.

"Come, my lads, we must have another of those fellows," cried Hemming, standing up, and supporting himself against the mast. "Can any of you heave the bight of a rope over one of them?"

"I'll try, sir," said Dick Needham, kneeling at the edge of the raft, for he had not strength to stand. How changed he was from the stout seaman he had appeared but a few days before. He made several trials in vain. Jack Shark always kept at too great a distance when the rope was thrown. At last one of the seamen took off his shoes, and, tucking up his trousers, stuck out his leg and moved it slowly backwards and forwards. The voracious shark saw the tempting bait, and made a dash at it. The seaman drew it in, and as the fish, disappointed of his prize, turned round whisking up his tail out of the water, Needham adroitly hove the rope over it. As the shark darted off Dick was very nearly drawn overboard, but the rope tightening brought up the shark; and as he turned round to ascertain what had got hold of his tail another rope was thrown over his head, and he was hauled, in spite of his plunges and struggles, on board. A few blows on the spine near the tail quickly finished him. He was soon cut up, some part of him was eaten fresh, and the rest was hung up to dry. The men would have thrown what they did not want overboard, but their commander reminded them that bad weather might come on, when they could not catch another, and that they should preserve a store for such an event. It was fortunate this forethought was shown, for that very night a strong breeze sprang up, and the frail raft was tossed up and down till there appeared every chance of its upsetting or being knocked to pieces. Happily more rain came down and refreshed them, and the clouds sheltered them from the scorching rays of the sun, or not one of them would have held out.

Sadly were their numbers reduced. Ten Englishmen and the young African chief only now remained alive. Some of them appeared almost at death's door, and they would have slipped from the raft had not their comrades held them on. Darkness again came down on the waters, and the wave-tossed raft drove onwards no one knew in what direction. The stars were hidden—they had no compass—nor, had they possessed one, was there a lantern by which to see it. Great were the horrors of that night and of two succeeding nights; still neither did the gallant Hemming nor his two younger companions allow their courage to desert them. They conversed as much as they could, they talked of their past lives, they even spoke of the future; nor did they forget to pray to Heaven for strength to support whatever might yet be in store for them. Still the wet and cold of the night, and the heat of the day, was telling fearfully on all of them.

"When do you think we shall reach the shore, sir?" asked Jack. "We have been driving for a long time towards it nicely."

"In two days if the wind holds," answered Hemming; "perhaps in less time we may sight it."

But the wind did not hold. Once more they knew that they were being blown off it. Their hearts sank. They wellnigh gave way to despair. Each of the officers took it in turns to stand up to keep a lookout for a sail or for land. Jack was standing on the top of the cask, holding on by the mast, when his eye fell on a white glittering object to the northward.

"Yes, it is! it is!" he exclaimed; "a sail! a sail! she must be standing this way." All but the weakest or most desponding turned their anxious eyes in the direction Jack indicated. The sight of some was already too dim to discern her, but others raised a feeble shout, and declared that she was standing close hauled towards them. How eagerly they watched her, till their anxiety became painful in the extreme. Some shouted, "We shall be saved, we shall be saved;" but others moaned out, "No, no, she'll not see us, she will pass us." Hemming stood up, watching the approaching vessel. He said nothing. He was not certain that she would near them. One hour of intense anxiety passed. There was very little wind. Another hour glided on.

"Yes, my lads, she is undoubtedly standing this way," cried Hemming. "But—" and he stopped. "She may be a slaver, and if so, I know not whether we should be better off than we now are."

"Surely, bad as they may be, they would not leave us," said Jack.

"Don't let us be too sure of that. There is nothing too bad for slavers to do," observed Hemming; "however, let us hope for the best."

The stranger approached. She had very square yards, very white canvas, and a black hull. If she was not a slaver, she looked very like one. Still, even if they had wished it, they could not have avoided her. On she came. Her course would have taken her somewhat wide of the raft. It was not seen apparently. Then suddenly her course was altered. Some one on board had made them out. The brig stood towards them. When she was scarcely more than half a mile off, it fell a dead calm. A boat was lowered.

"Those fellows pull in man-of-war's style," observed Hemming. "Grant she may be an English cruiser: but I fear not."

The almost dying seamen endeavoured to cheer, but their weak voices were scarcely heard over the waters. The boat dashed towards them. They could hear the officer in her speaking to his men. It was in Spanish.

"Then they are slavers, after all," cried Jack, with a sigh.

He had taken a great antipathy to slavers. To an Englishman no class of men are more hateful. The boat came alongside. The people in her regarded them with looks of commiseration. Well they might have done so; for more wretched-looking beings could scarcely have been seen. Two of them stepped on board the raft, to which they secured a rope, and began towing it towards the brig. Neither Hemming nor any of his companions could speak Spanish, so they asked no questions. They were soon alongside the brig, and were handed up on deck. They felt sure that they were going on board a slaver or perhaps a pirate; but what was their surprise to see several officers in uniform on deck, one of whom stepped forward and addressed them in very good English: "You are on board her most Catholic Majesty's brig the *San Fernando*. We will not ask you how you came into this plight. You shall be taken below, and all possible care shall be bestowed on you."

Hemming tried in vain to reply to this very kind and polite speech. He pointed to his mouth and signified that he could not speak. The necessity for exertion being over, he felt himself completely unnerved.

The officers were conveyed to the captain's cabin, the men to a sick-bay on deck; and the surgeon, if not very clever, was kind; and what they chiefly wanted was rest and food. Jack and Terence fell asleep, and slept twenty-four hours without waking: so they said. Several days passed, however, before they were able to sit up in their beds. At last they were able to crawl up on deck. It was wonderful then how soon they picked up their strength. Hemming took longer to come round. Dick Needham was about as soon as they were. Two poor fellows died on board, so that eight only of the prize crew ultimately remained alive. The brig, they found, had come out nominally in search of pirates, and was then bound across to Cuba. The captain was a very gentlemanly man; so were some of the officers, especially the first lieutenant, who spoke English well. One of the sub-lieutenants, or mates, also spoke a little English, so they got on capitally. The captain said he would not go back to Sierra Leone, but would land them at Fernando Po. The brig, they found, had touched, while they were in bed, at several places along the coast: and what with light winds and baffling winds her progress was much delayed.

"I wonder, Paddy, when we shall ever get on shore again," said Jack. "I should like to get back to the frigate, to let them know that we are not all lost; for I'm afraid that they will be writing home not to expect to see us again, and all that sort of thing; and then all our families will be going into mourning for us."

"I'm afraid mine would find it a hard matter just now to pay for the said black garments," said Adair. "They were in a bad way as to money matters when I left home. The famine and the fever killed the people, and rent did not come in; and to say the truth, I don't know that any of them will trouble their heads much about me."

"Oh! don't say that, Paddy," exclaimed Jack; "still I don't know. Sometimes I have wished that the dear ones at home would not be so unhappy when they hear that we are lost; and then again I should be very sorry if they did not love me, I own. I only hope that they may not hear of the loss of the prize."

When they were able to observe the state of things on board they discovered that the brig was in a very bad state of discipline. The crew were a worthless set of vagabonds, the scum of some Spanish port, pirates, slavers, and cut-throats of all descriptions. The officers tried to get obeyed but could not, and at last seemed to give it up as a bad job; some of them, indeed, were very little better than the men. The brig consequently was constantly getting into irons or being taken aback by careless steering, and it was only wonderful that she had got thus far on her voyage without a serious accident. The captain and first lieutenant, though pleasing in their manners, were evidently not much of seamen, and took their observations in a very careless way. Hemming, on questioning them, found that they had not been to sea for a long time, and, had they not been compelled, would not have come now. They seemed fully aware that things were not as they should be; but they shrugged their shoulders, and said that they could not help it. By this time Hemming, as well as the rest of the people, with the exception of two poor fellows, had almost recovered their strength. The weather had hitherto been fine, but it came on very thick one night, and began to blow hard; but the wind was fair, and the captain, who was in a hurry to get over his voyage, continued to carry on a press of sail. Lieutenant Hemming and the two midshipmen, who did not like the look of things, with the rest of the English, continued on deck.

"Are you certain that you know your exact position?" asked Hemming of the first lieutenant.

He was not indignant, but he laughed and said that the master was a good navigator, and that he must be right; Hemming had formed a different opinion. An hour passed. Suddenly, Jack and Adair, who were walking together, were startled by a cry from the lookout forward, which they guessed was, as it proved, "Breakers ahead." They, with Hemming, ran forward to ascertain the state of things, and there they made out through the darkness on the port bow amass of white breakers. No sooner did Hemming see them than he rushed aft to put the helm to port, while the officers on deck were giving different orders. When he got to the wheel he found that it had been put the wrong way, while the yards were being braced up first in one direction, then in another. The next instant the brig struck with a tremendous crash, throwing those on deck off their legs, and those below out of their berths. The following sea lifted the brig nearly her entire length more ahead, jamming her between two rocks, and a third came rushing on board, and made a clean sweep of everything on her decks. Jack and Adair and Needham were together.

"There are those two poor fellows below, sir. Don't let us forget them," said the latter.

"Certainly not," exclaimed Jack and Adair together. They dived below and brought them up, and then followed Hemming and the rest of their shipmates into the main rigging. The authority of the Spanish officers was now completely gone. Not an order was obeyed; indeed, every man seemed to be aware that he must look out for himself, and that there was no one on whom he could depend.

The first sea which came on board washed away several unfortunate wretches; their shrieks and cries for help were heard as they were dashed against the rocks, no one being able to render them the slightest assistance. The greater part of the crew began to collect in the rigging and the tops, and there they seemed to prepare themselves to spend the night. Indeed, dark as it was, it would have been difficult, even with strict discipline, for them to have concerted effectual measures to save themselves. The gale increased, and with it occasionally bright flashes of lightning darted from the black clouds. By their light, as they went zigzagging around them. Jack, whose eyes were the sharpest, thought he discerned close to them a rock, towards which he resolved, should the vessel go to pieces, to endeavour to make his way. He pointed it out to his companions.

"Stick by me, Paddy, you know; as I'm a good swimmer I may be able to lend you a hand," he sang out to his messmate, who knew full well that he could trust to his help.

Terrific, indeed, was that night. Few of those who long to follow a sea life, if they could see pictured out before them all the sufferings and hardships they may be called on to endure, would not hesitate before adopting it. The roar of the waves as they dashed over the rocks, the howling of the wind in the rigging, the groaning of the hull at each successive blow she received from the seas, mingled with the cries and shrieks of those who had remained on deck, or had fallen from the rigging and been washed overboard, together with the oaths and blasphemies of many of the survivors, mingled in one chaotic and terrific uproar, which stunned and bewildered the senses. Some hours thus passed. At last Hemming's voice was heard calling them quickly out of the rigging; without hesitation they obeyed him. The brig had heeled over on her side, and her decks were exposed to the full fury of the sea.

Scarcely had Jack and Terence descended than the mainmast with a crash went by the board, throwing off many who clung to it and crushing others.

"Follow me, my lads, and we'll try to get on the rock close aboard us," shouted Hemming, as he began to clamber, often covered by the seas which roared up over the ship, along the unstable mast, the extreme end of which just touched the wave-washed rock.

"Come along, Paddy, come along," cried Jack, as they also endeavoured to work their way in the direction taken by their commander.

Chapter Ten
Again United

The lightning flashed brightly, the sea, roaring loudly and wildly, dashed over them, seeming angry at being disappointed of its prey, as the two midshipmen climbed along the mast, till, reaching the very cap of the topmast, they found that it rested on a small rock. Here all the English were collected, including the sick men, who had been helped along the mast by their messmates. They soon found, however, that the sea broke over the greater portion of the rock, and that even the highest part was wet and slippery with the spray. It also was evident that the wreck considerably broke the fury of the seas, and that when she went to pieces the rock would be untenable. No one, however, felt inclined to fold his hands to rest. At length Hemming said that he thought he saw something dark on the opposite side of the rock, and that he observed when the sea washed up it came surging back as it does between two rocks, and that thus he hoped there might be a larger one farther on. They had contrived happily to get hold of the topgallant halyards. Unreeving them, Hemming fastened one end round his waist, and ordered the men to hold the other while he felt his way across the seeming gulf. Jack and Adair strained their eyes eagerly after him as he disappeared in the pitchy darkness among the roaring waters. On he went, they gradually paying out the rope. Suddenly it slackened, and with horror they felt that he was being carried off by the hungry waves. They were about to haul in the rope to try to save his life, when once more it straightened and he seemed to be proceeding as before. At last they felt that the end was being lifted up, and all the slack hauled in. They fancied also that they heard his voice shouting to them; but it came to the teeth of the wind, and they could not understand what was said.

"I will go over and learn what he wants," cried Jack, guessing that he wished them to join him.

Jack, as he spoke, seized the rope, and grasping it tightly worked his way on till he found himself surrounded by the foaming sea as it dashed through a passage which he saw evidently separated two rocks. More than once he was plunged over head and ears, but on he went wading among the rugged rocks, and every instant expecting to be carried off his legs. Often he had to stop to recover his breath. Once he was completely off his legs and had to float on his back, while he worked his way along by the rope. At length he reached the side of a large rock, and by the fact of the lichens growing out of its crevices he knew that he must be above the reach of the waves. In another minute he found himself alongside Mr Hemming, who congratulated him on getting safe across. They shouted to the other people to join them, but their voices were drowned by the noise of the tempest. At last Jack begged that he might go and hurry them over, and argued that as he was the slightest of the two, he should run less risk of being carried away. Jack seized the rope, and in spite of the waves which washed over him, by stopping every now and then and grasping it with all his might, he succeeded in returning to the spot where his shipmates were collected. Some of the Spanish officers and men were also on the rock, though others were on the forecastle of the brig, and a few still clung to the shattered poop. At that moment a tremendous sea knocked the poop to pieces and sent most of the wretches who clung to it to destruction, a few only reaching the rock.

"Come, Adair, now is your time to cross," cried out Jack. "Quick, quick."

Jack, seizing Terence's hand, guided him to the rope. Terence crossed without much difficulty, Dick Needham and the rest following with their sick comrades; Jack brought up the rear, but a sea caught him, and he had to hold on like grim death to save himself. Dick and another man had, just before they left the wreck, snatched up a couple of muskets. They had both once been cast away among savages when they had felt the want of arms to defend themselves. The first faint streaks of daylight were appearing in the sky when the Englishmen found themselves assembled on the top of the rock. No sooner did the Spaniards ascertain where they had got, than they made a rush to follow; their officers and men indiscriminately crowding over, shoving each other aside, and all trying to be first. The consequence was that numbers were washed away and drowned. Hemming's first care was to ascertain the condition of his own people. None were much hurt. The two sick men had been brought over in their blankets. These were spread out in the air, where they quickly dried, and the poor fellows were then wrapped up in them again and placed in the most sheltered spot on the top of the rock. In the meantime the afterpart of the brig had gone to pieces, and the foot of the rock was strewn with a vast number of things sent up by the waves. Among them, unfortunately, was a cask of spirits which had come out of the hold. The Spanish seamen quickly discovered it, and in spite of all their captain and officers could do, they insisted on broaching it. Often British seamen have done the same, but there have been numerous instances where, without uttering a word of complaint, a crew have seen casks of spirits started by their officers that they might not have the opportunity of getting drunk. At first the Spaniards were quiet enough, till they produced some leathern cups and rapidly passed the liquor round. The officers no longer attempted to exert any control, and some even sat down and drank with the men. How desolate was the scene on every side of the barren rock on which the Englishmen stood! Below them were groups of men, many of them already half drunk, sitting round the cask of liquor only just above the wash of the sea. The shore was strewn with fragments of the wreck, with casks, chests, furniture, sails and rigging, and with mangled bodies, many of whom might probably have been saved had their comrades exerted themselves. On the small rock a few wretches were still collected, the sea every instant breaking over them. Now one and now another would be washed away, while scarcely one made an attempt to save himself. The bow of the brig still held together. On it were collected some dozen men or more. Having hitherto found it a place of safety they seemed afraid to quit it, while on the sea around fragments of the wreck and broken spars were floating, a few poor fellows clinging to them and crying for help to those who could afford them none. A dull grey sky was overhead, and far as the eye could reach the ocean seemed a mass of white foam increasing the dreariness of the view, while in the far distance appeared a blue line so faint that many doubted whether or not it was the land. On the rock not a blade of grass nor a drop of water was to be found, so Hemming saw that it would be necessary to use every exertion to provide for his men. Accordingly he sent Jack and Adair with three of them to collect what things they could pick up at the foot of the rock. Fortunately they discovered four small breakers of water, and a couple of casks of salt meat with a bag of bread. These they dragged to the top of the rock, hoping to conceal them from the Spaniards. Unhappily the latter caught sight of the casks of water, and, fancying that they contained brandy, came hurrying up to get them into their power. In spite of all Jack and Adair could do, one was broached and the invaluable contents recklessly spilt on the ground. Still the Spaniards, unconvinced that the others only contained water, advanced with threatening gestures towards the English. Needham grasped his musket, Mr Hemming seized another, and made signs that if they approached nearer they would blow out the brains of a couple of them at all events. This made those in advance of the rest hesitate, for they did not remember that the muskets had been thoroughly wetted and could not go off. The Spanish officers generally sided with the English, and tried to explain that, as there was no water on the rock, all would be suffering from thirst, and that therefore the contents of the casks were more precious than any spirits.

"That may be the case, but then those hated Englishmen shall not boast that they prevented us from doing what we intended," exclaimed one of them, rushing to seize a cask.

Hemming waited till the fellow got within reach of his fist, and he then hit him such a blow on the chest that he sent him rolling back head over heels till he reached the edge of the rock, when down he went among a group of his comrades, who were sitting carousing together below. Each of the Englishmen singled out an opponent, and treated him much in the same way, all this time many of the Spanish officers standing by and not attempting to interfere. The Spanish seamen, finding that nothing was to be obtained but hard knocks, retreated to secure their share of the liquor. Often had Jack and Adair cast their eyes round the horizon in the hopes of discovering a sail by which they might escape from the rock, but none appeared. Meantime hunger was pressing; the head of one of the meat-casks was knocked off, and the biscuits were spread out to dry. In vain they tried to light a fire. There was plenty of driftwood, but it was too wet; so they had to eat the meat raw. Their appetites were thus quickly satisfied. At first the sky gave indications of an improvement in the weather, but by noon it came on to blow as hard as ever. They made all the signals they could devise to induce the people who still remained on the wreck to quit it, but they soon found by the wretches' frantic gestures and maniacal shouts that they also had got hold of a cask of spirits, and were in as bad a condition as their comrades. They were soon indeed seen snapping their fingers, and dancing about the decks as if they were in a place of perfect safety. One poor wretch slipped overboard, but his companions, instead of trying to help him, only laughed and shouted the louder, nor did they appear to comprehend that he was drowning before their eyes. A few remained on the small rock. Every now and then one would carelessly get within the influence of the seas, and several were thus swept away. The larger part of the crew who had been carousing at the foot of the big rock, soon began to dispute with each other; their voices grew higher and higher, their actions more vehement. Knives at last were drawn, and one lay a corpse by the side of his companions. This act of violence, instead of sobering the rest, induced another to take up the quarrel, and another and another joining, in a short time the greater portion were engaged in a deadly hand-to-hand struggle. The officers contented themselves with merely shouting and ordering them to desist, and of course their commands received no attention. In a few minutes several of the combatants lay weltering in their blood, and two of them, locked in a deadly embrace in each other's arms, fell off the rock into the sea, and a huge wave rolling in washed them both away. The gale was increasing, the wreck rocked to and fro, large portions were constantly being detached and hove against the rock. At length a sea heavier than any of the preceding ones came roaring in. It struck the wreck. High over it the foaming waters rushed, the spray from it almost blinding Hemming and his companions, far above it as they stood. A piercing shriek reached their ears, the squall passed by. They looked towards the spot where the brig had been. Not a particle was to be seen hanging together. Not one of those clinging to it escaped. This catastrophe appeared to have no effect on the other Spaniards. Even when a sea came and washed away several of those who had remained on the lower rock, the rest went on quarrelling and shouting and shrieking as before. Sometimes, without any apparent reason, a wretched man would throw himself off the rock, when he was soon swept out of sight by the retiring sea. Some rolled off helplessly drunk into the water, and were washed away. Hemming and his companions would have helped them had they been able, but their own countrymen would not allow the English to interfere, and they were compelled to desist. They felt, indeed, all the time, that those who held their own lives so cheap were not likely to pay any respect to theirs. While watching with painful interest the scenes which have been described, they observed a cask drifting towards the rock. The Spaniards saw it also. Adair, with Needham and three other men, hurried down to secure it. The Spaniards rushed to the spot at the same moment, and two of them, in their eagerness to obtain the coveted prize, for they of course believed it to contain spirits, fell headlong into a surging sea, which, sweeping out again, carried them both far away. Adair meantime got hold of the cask, and was in triumph bearing it up the rock, when the Spaniards surrounded him, and, though Dick and the other men fought most desperately, succeeded in carrying it off. The effect of the fresh supply of fire-water was most disastrous. The Spaniards became almost raving mad, and, excited to fury by the opposition they had encountered from the English, now drawing their knives, advanced once more in a body towards them. Some even of the Spanish officers joined them, others, however, stood surrounding their captain, but seemed inclined to take no part in the fray.

"Are you going to see us murdered before your eyes, gentlemen?" exclaimed Hemming with indignation. "If they murder us they will murder you, depend on that." The appeal had an effect, and, drawing their swords, the Spanish captain and his superior officers sided with the English. On rushed the infuriated Spaniards, uttering the fiercest oaths and threats of vengeance. Fortunately, besides the two muskets many of the English had knives, and all had provided themselves with boats' stretchers, or pieces of spars, which served the purpose of singlesticks. They were thus not ill prepared to meet their assailants. The shock came. Headed by Lieutenant Hemming they stood firm. One of the first victims was a young Spanish officer. He fell pierced to the heart by the knife of one of his countrymen. It showed the Spanish officers that their safety depended on that of the English. Again and again the infuriated wretches rushed at them; but were beaten off by the English quarter-staves. All this time the wind had been howling and the sea dashing fiercely against the rocks; indeed, the elements were in perfect accordance with the mad strife going forward on that isolated spot of earth. Night too came on to add to the horrors of the scene. Then the clouds opened and flashes of the most vivid lightning darting from the sky played like fiery serpents round the rock, while crashing peals of thunder rattled and roared around them. At first the seamen took no notice of the storm; then came a loud, thundering explosion, and two of their number lay blackened corpses on the ground. In an instant, seeing what had occurred, they fled with shrieks of dismay down the rock to the spot whence they had come. Amid wind and rain, the lightning flashing and the thunder roaring, the survivors passed that terrific night.

The day dawned at last. Hemming's first resolve was to try and conciliate the unfortunate wretches by offering them food. Their officers gladly agreed to the proposal. The sun came out, the driftwood dried, and at last a fire was kindled. The Spanish officers were far superior to the English in the art of cooking. They made hot cakes out of the wet biscuit, and in a short time had a number of nice-looking little bits of meat ran upon wooden skewers. Having satisfied their own hunger, they offered the food to the men below, who at first thought that they were mocking them; but when assured that the Englishmen were willing to forget what had passed, one by one came up with a sulky and doubting manner to take what was offered to them.

"I doubt those fellows even now," observed Adair; "the sooner we are away from them the better."

Hemming hearing this, observed that he proposed making a raft, and in spite of all they had undergone, venturing on it to the coast of Africa, which he was confident was visible to the eastward. It was agreed therefore that they would set about building it at once, and should no sail appear in sight, push off as soon as it was completed. On the east side of the rock was a bay sheltered from the view of the other part. Here a number of spars and planks were driven in, as well as rope and canvas. Hemming thus had soon a raft constructed capable of carrying twice as many men as wished to trust themselves on it. He also had a supply of provisions and water carried down to it without being observed by the drunken seamen. When all was ready, he invited the Spanish officers to accompany them, but they declined, saying that they could not leave their men, though from the glances they cast on the raft, it was evident that they did not wish to entrust themselves on it. They, however, did not object to the Englishmen taking the water and provisions, the latter promising that if they got safe to any European settlement they would send them assistance.

"Now, my lads, we'll launch our raft," exclaimed Hemming, when all their arrangements were made.

The Spaniards had not been aware of the nature of their proceedings, but unfortunately two or three of the more sober, who had begun to scramble about the rock, caught sight of them. Believing naturally that they were about to make off with the provisions and water, summoning their comrades, they rushed fiercely towards them.

"Now, my boys, a hearty shove altogether, and we'll have the raft into the water before the scoundrels can come up to us," shouted Hemming, setting an example by putting all his strength to the work. The Spanish seamen, brandishing their knives, were close to them.

"One shove more and the raft will be afloat," cried Jack.

"Hurrah, hurrah, she's afloat," sang out Terence. Their two sick shipmates were speedily placed in the centre of the raft, and the rest leaped on to it. The Spaniards were close to them; one seized a rope which still held the raft to the shore. Quick as thought Hemming took one of the paddles they had prepared, and springing on shore, used it with such good effect that he drove the wretches back before him, then leaping again on to the raft, he shoved it a dozen yards off from the shore. As the Englishmen vigorously plied their paddles they saw the Spaniards making all sorts of frantic gestures at them, shaking their fists and hurling abuse at their heads. When they got from under the lee of the rock, they hoisted sail and found that the raft steered very well, and with the aid of the paddles made good way towards the land. Gradually the rock sank lower and lower in the horizon, till it was almost hid from sight; but when they looked towards the shore, that appeared almost as far off as ever. They had hoped to reach it before sunset, but that hope gradually faded away, as the breeze which had hitherto favoured them grew less and less, and finally sank into a calm. However, that was better than a gale, and they could still paddle on their raft in the direction in which they wished to go. They were also far better off than they had been on their former raft. It was more strongly made, they had better provisions, and the prospect of reaching land in a short time. The sun, however, went down, and they were still far from it. Jack and Terence sat side by side, and endeavoured to keep up each other's spirits during that long, long night. It came at last to an end. The sun rose; they looked round the horizon; no sail was in sight. Some of the seamen began to grumble, as even the best will at times, and to complain at having been enticed off the rock. Hemming overheard them.

"What think you, my lads, would have been our lot had we remained with those madmen?" he said. "I'll tell you; by this time not one of us would have been alive." As the sun rose, the breeze came strongly off the land and drove them once more away from it. "Never fear, my lads; we shall have the sea-breeze soon to send us back again," he cried out cheerfully to keep up their spirits. It did not come as soon as he expected. At last a rock appeared rising out of the water. It rose higher and higher. The raft drifted slowly by at a distance; still the atmosphere was so clear that they could discern figures on the top. They all looked earnestly. There could be no doubt of it; the people were struggling like madmen. Now and then one of them, it appeared, was cast off the cliff into the water, but the distance was so great that it appeared rather like some dreadful dream than a reality. While they were gazing at this spectacle the wind fell; then in a short time the breeze came from the west, and hoisting their sail they once more rapidly approached the shore. For the remainder of the day they made good progress; still they knew that they could not hope to reach it that night, and once more the sun went down and left them in darkness. The night passed as the former had done. No one now expressed a wish that he had remained on the rock. Jack and Terence had kept up their spirits wonderfully. At length, leaning on each other's shoulder, they fell asleep. They were startled with a cry of "A sail ahead!" In an instant every one roused up. As they looked out they saw a large brig on the port tack, standing to the southward across their course. In a few minutes more she would have shot ahead out of hearing. "Now, my lads, shout, shout, till you crack your voices," cried out Hemming; "she is a man-of-war brig; one of the cruisers on the station. I know her by the cut of her canvas." Weak as all on board the raft at this time were, they raised a shout such as Englishmen only know how to give. They listened eagerly. Directly afterwards a cheer came in answer towards them. The rattling of blocks was heard, and the brig's helm being put down, and her maintopsail backed, she came up into the wind. In another instant they were alongside. Cramped and half starved as they all had been, they had great difficulty in getting on board. Hemming was the only man who went up by himself, and his knees trembled so much when he gained the deck that he had to lean against the bulwarks for support. The officer of the watch came forward to receive them. Hemming gave his name as a lieutenant of the *Ranger*.

"Delighted to see you," exclaimed the lieutenant of the brig; "we heard at Sierra Leone that you were lost, for several vessels have been sent to look for you, and not one could gain tidings of you. But come below; you want sleep and food, and dry clothes."

The captain of the brig, hearing what had occurred, turned out, and had berths made up for the two midshipmen in his own cabin, while one of the lieutenants gave up his berth to Hemming in the gun-room. The doctor was soon in attendance on all the party, and sleep, which they all so much required, soon sealed their eyelids. Jack and Terence slept for a long time. When they awoke the sun was shining right down the cabin skylight. At the cabin table was sitting a midshipman reading. They could not see his face, but there was something in his figure and attitude which made them both sit up and exclaim, "Hallo! who are you?" The midshipman sprang from his seat, and in another instant Alick Murray was shaking them warmly by the hand. "This is jolly, this is delightful," exclaimed Jack; "tell us all about it, though." Alick accordingly told them that the brig was the *Archer*, of sixteen guns, that she was commanded by a relation of his, Captain Grant, who had got him appointed to her, and that she had only just come out direct from England. Murray then got his friends to give him an outline of their adventures, which they had to repeat to Captain Grant himself, who shortly after came into the cabin. Meantime the steward had brought them some breakfast; for midshipmen are not heroes of romance, and require feeding before they are fit for much. After breakfast they felt wonderfully recovered, and were able to get up and go on deck. Hemming had before this explained to Captain Grant his promise to bring relief to the Spaniards, and the brig was accordingly beating up towards the rock. As they drew near they looked out for signals, but none were made. They got still nearer. "Where can the people have got to?" exclaimed the captain, looking through his glass. As the brig approached the rock the lead was kept going, but the water was found to be quite deep. She sailed round and round it, but not a human being was seen there alive. Whether some dreadful catastrophe had occurred after the English left the spot, or whether some vessel had visited it and carried off the survivors, was never ascertained. Jack and Terence did their best to banish the dreadful scenes which had occurred from their thoughts, and it was with infinite satisfaction that the three midshipmen found themselves once more together. "This is the station for adventure," exclaimed Jack; "depend on it before long we shall have lots to do."

Chapter Eleven
Life on an African Cruiser

That naval officers do not idle away their time when at sea, on beds of roses, the adventures of my three old schoolfellows will, I think, convince all my readers. Who would have thought when we were together at dear old Eagle House, that they would, ere many years had gone over their heads, have actually crossed swords with real red-capped or turbaned Mahomedans, fought with true Greek romantic pirates, hunted down slavers, and explored African rivers with voracious sharks watching their mouths, hungry crocodiles basking in their slimy shallows, and veritable negroes inhabiting their banks; yet here were all the three, Alick Murray, Jack Rogers, and Terence Adair, collected on board Her Majesty's brig of war *Archer*, commanded by Captain Grant. Alick had come out in the brig from England, the other two, after being shipwrecked, nearly drowned, murdered, and starved, eaten up by sharks, and having undergone I do not know how many other terrible dangers, had at last been picked up by the *Archer*, their own ship, the *Ranger* frigate, being they did not exactly know where. This last circumstance did not probably weigh very much with them. Midshipmen are not generally given to suffer from over anxiety from affairs terrestrial; but Rogers certainly did wish that he could let his family know that he was well, and picked up again, after having, as was supposed, gone down in a slaver the frigate had captured off the African coast. They were capital fellows, those three old friends of mine. Rogers was a good specimen of the Englishman—genus middy—so was Paddy Adair of Green Erin's isle, full of fun and frolic; and a more gentlemanly, right-minded lad than Alick Murray Scotland never sent forth from her rich valleys or rugged mountains. He too was proud of Scotland, and ever jealous to uphold the name and fame of the land of his birth.

The *Archer* was a fine brig, and Captain Grant was a first-rate officer. When naval officers or seamen go on board ships of war they have to take their share of the duty with the rest of the crew; so Rogers and Adair found that they should have plenty of employment, even though they might not for some time be able to join their own ship. Captain Grant considered that idleness is the mother of all vice, so he took care that no one in his ship should be idle, and certainly he had the knack of making good seamen of all who sailed with him.

The midshipmen's berth in the *Archer* was a very happy place, because the occupants were, with few exceptions, gentlemanly, well-disposed, and, more than all, well and religiously educated young men. I do not mean to say by that, that they always acted with the wisdom and discretion of a bench of judges. Far from that. They were merry, light-hearted fellows, full of fun and frolic, but they could be grave, and treat serious things as they ought to be treated, with reverence and respect. Jack and Paddy quickly found themselves perfectly at home among them. The *Archer* had been standing off the coast of Africa under easy sail, when, just as the cold grey light of day stole over the waters, a vessel was seen inside of her, evidently making for a harbour in the neighbourhood. As the light increased, she was discovered to be a schooner.

"All hands make sail," cried the officer of the watch, who had just made his report to the commander.

"All hands make sail," echoed the boatswain, giving with his shrill pipe the well-known signal. "Tumble up there, tumble up there," roared out the boatswain's mates, with their gruff voices, to the sluggards who seemed inclined to stick in their hammocks.

In a few moments the watch below were rushing up on deck and flying to their stations, and then, as if by magic, the masts and yards of the brig were covered with the broad sheets of canvas which had been furled during the night. Topgallant-sails, royals, and studding-sails being set in rapid succession, away glided the brig with her head towards the land, through the calm, leaden-coloured water. Jack and Terence had with the rest sprung on deck, not taking many moments to slip into their clothes. Few landsmen can understand how quickly that operation can, by constant practice, be performed. They had there joined Alick, who had the morning watch. Together they all went aloft to take a look at the chase.

"She's a slaver, from her evident wish to avoid us, and from the way she is standing," observed Alick, after having taken a long look at her through his glass. "We may prevent her from embarking her slaves, and save the poor wretches the horrors to which they are always exposed, when once they get on board these iniquitous prison-ships. To look down on a slave-deck crowded with human beings, is quite sufficient to make a man abhor slavery for ever after, and to desire to put an end, with all his might, to the system which can produce such horrors."

Jack and Adair agreed that they should have great satisfaction in capturing or destroying every slaver on the coast. The stranger soon discovered that the brig of war was in chase of her, and having crowded all sail, kept away directly for the land. From the wide spread of her white canvas, and from the way she had behaved, there was no doubt she was a slaver. Everybody felt certain that they should capture the stranger; the *Archer* was undoubtedly overhauling her, and she could not escape either to the north or south without their perceiving her, and cutting her off. An hour's chase brought them in sight of the land. It was a low, uninviting shore, lined with a dense belt of mangrove bushes, a few tall palms appearing here and there above them; then the ground rose slightly, with some ranges of blue hills in the distance. As the sun rose, a mist was drawn up which floated just above the water and shut out the lower branches of the mangrove-trees, though their tops, forming a wavy dark line, could just be seen above it. None of the officers of the *Archer* had been on the coast before, and as she had no pilot, it was necessary to approach it with caution. The lead was therefore kept going. The schooner stood boldly on.

"The fellows will, I am afraid, run her on shore, if they can find no other means of escaping," observed the captain, after scrutinising the chase and the coast she was approaching through his glass.

"We shall have her, she can't escape us, that's one comfort," cried Jack Rogers.

On flew the schooner. The wind freshened somewhat. Suddenly she entered the belt of mist. Everybody on board the brig rubbed their eyes. Where was she? Not a vestige of her was to be seen. As they approached the land, the roar of the surf on the shore reached their ears. There could be little doubt that the schooner had been run on shore, and would probably soon be knocked to pieces, while her crew had made their escape to the land. Captain Grant was anxious to stand in as close as he could.

"By the deep nine," sang out one of the men in the chains.

"By the mark seven," soon repeated another.

To approach nearer would not have been prudent. The canvas was therefore flattened in, and the brig's head was once more turned to seaward. Scarcely had she hauled her wind, than the sun having risen high above the land, the mist lifted, and the whole line of coast fringed with mangrove bushes, and here and there with a white belt of sand, appeared in sight. But the chase, where was she? Not a sign of her appeared on the shore, while neither to the north nor to the south was she to be seen. Jack looked at Adair, and Adair looked at Jack, and together they discussed the matter with Alick, but neither of the three could offer any satisfactory explanation of the matter. Captain Grant and the rest of the officers appeared equally puzzled. As the brig stood closer in-shore there was a chance of the mystery being solved. The hands in the chains were kept heaving the lead, which showed that the brig was slowly shoaling her water. At length she was hove-to, and two boats were lowered. Their own lieutenant, Hemming, who had escaped with them from a sinking slaver, volunteered to take charge of one of them, and Evans, the second lieutenant of the brig, went in the other. The former, as the senior officer, had charge of the expedition.

"As she cannot have escaped along shore, and certainly has not evaporated into the air, the chase must have got into some creek or inlet, the mouth of which we cannot distinguish," observed the captain. "You will therefore search for such an entrance, and pursue, and bring her out if you can."

"Ay, ay, sir!" answered Hemming, delighted with the work in prospect.

The three midshipmen got leave to go in the boat. Jack accompanied Evans, the other two went with Hemming, as did Jack's old follower Dick Needham. Away they pulled in high spirits. As they approached the shore they observed that a long line of white surf was breaking heavily on it. Hemming stood up and scanned the coast narrowly, thinking that after all the schooner might have been run on shore, and as slavers are but slightly put together, might have speedily been knocked to pieces. As he stood up, and the boat rose to the top of the swell, he saw not what he expected, but a piece of clear water inside a narrow spit of sand, and a little to the south he observed a spot where the surf broke less heavily, and which he concluded was the entrance to the creek or river.

"I have little doubt that this must be the place where the schooner has taken refuge; and as she has gone up, so may we," shouted Hemming, pointing it out to his brother officer.

Evans agreed with him, and the two boats pulled away in the direction indicated. That there was an entrance was evident, but it required great caution in approaching it. A capsize would probably prove fatal to all hands—for had any escaped drowning, they would have fallen a prey to the sharks, which in southern latitudes generally maintain a strict blockade at the mouths of rivers, to pick up any offal which the stream may bring down. The boats rose and fell on the smooth swells as they came rolling in. At last Hemming observed a space on the bar clear of broken water. He gave the signal to go ahead.

"Now, my lads, now pull away," he shouted.

The boats dashed on, the surf roared and foamed on either side of them, and not only did the three midshipmen, but most of the older men in the boats, hold their breath till they were well through it, and once more floating in smooth water inside the bar. Instead of being in a mere creek, they found that they had entered a broad deep river which seemed to come down from a considerable distance in the interior. They pulled on more certain than before of finding the chase. However, after they had gone some distance, they arrived at a spot where the river formed two distinct branches, or, rather, it might be, where another broad stream joined the main current. Up which the schooner had proceeded it was impossible to say.

"I'll take one stream, you take the other," shouted Hemming to Evans; and the boats dashed on.

It was important to overtake the schooner before she got higher up, and perhaps hidden away in some narrow creek where it might be no easy matter to find her. The scenery was far from attractive. Little else on either side was to be seen but long lines of mangrove bushes, and as the tide fell black banks of mud began to appear, which it was evident would soon narrow the width of the stream. Evans and Jack took the branch of the stream which came from the southward. It wound about a good deal, so that they were aware they might any moment come on the schooner. They kept their muskets by their sides ready loaded.

"I say, Mr Evans, I wish that we could see the chase some time before we get up to her," observed Jack. "What are we to do should we find her, sir?"

"Jump on board, and knock every fellow down who resists," was the lieutenant's answer. "Depend on it she is a slaver or pirate, probably both, and her crew will not give in without a tussle."

"With the greatest pleasure in the world," replied Jack, who was very practical in his notions about fighting, and had no idea of half measures.

The current was now making down very strong, and the boat consequently progressed but slowly. Still Mr Evans persevered. The men bent lustily to their oars, and reach after reach of the river was passed, but there was no sign of the chase. Now and then there were openings in the mangrove bushes, and more than once Jack felt certain that he saw some dark figures running along parallel with the river, and evidently watching their movements. Jack pointed them out to Mr Evans.

"That looks as if we had enemies in the neighbourhood," observed the lieutenant. "Be ready, my men—marines, look to your arms."

The boat pulled eight oars, and there were two marines in the bows, and two in the stern-sheets, sitting with their muskets between their knees. In the bows of the boat was a small swivel-gun, and all the bluejackets with cutlasses and pistols. Besides the lieutenant and Jack, there was the coxswain, and there were some half-dozen long pikes which, as the latter observed, would come in handy, if they had a fight with another boat or had to attack a fort, but for boarding he would not give a rush for them. The ebb-tide rushed past the boat dark and smooth, but with swirling eddies, which showed the strength of the current against which they had to contend.

"I wonder whether the other boat has fallen in with the slaver."

"I envy them if they have," observed Jack, who didn't much like being silent just then.

There was something very oppressive in the atmosphere, and in the dark solemn scenery which surrounded them. The sea-breeze had by this time set in and blew up the river, but it had not yet been strong enough to make it worth while to hoist the sail.

"I scarcely think the schooner could have got up so far as this," observed Mr Evans. "But we will pull on a little farther, and then if we do not see her, we will go back, and join the other boat."

They had just then arrived at the end of a reach. The extent of the next one was hidden from their sight by a point of land thickly covered with trees. They pulled on, and soon doubled the point. Directly they did so there appeared before them, pressing up the stream, under all sail, the object of their search. The men required no urging, but, bending to their oars, away they pulled in hot chase after her. The schooner stood on steadily, as if no one on board was aware of the presence of the boat of a British man-of-war. The boat rapidly came up with her. As they drew near, Jack remarked that her decks were crowded with a very ill-looking set of ruffians, but he cared little for that, and he knew that every man in the boat would be ready to attack even twice as many as there were there. They had got up to within a hundred yards of the schooner without any notice being taken of them.

"Give way, my lads; we'll be alongside in a moment," shouted the lieutenant.

Scarcely had he uttered the words, when a couple of guns were ran out at the schooner's stern ports, and a shower of langrage, nails, bits of iron, lead, and missiles of all sorts, came rattling among them, accompanied by a volley of musketry. One or two of the seamen and one of the marines were hit, but the boat pulled on as fast as before.

"Marines, give it the scoundrels," cried Mr Evans. The red-jackets, turning round, deliberately picked off several of the people who had fired at them. They had scarcely time to load again before the boat was alongside the schooner, and the seamen, cutlass in hand, began to scramble up on her decks. Pikes were poked out at them, pistols were flashed in their faces, and cold shot hove into their boat, but fiercely as the pirates fought, they could not prevent the British seamen from gaining the deck of their vessel. Desperate was the struggle which took place there. Both parties fought for their lives. The English knew that they should receive no quarter. The pirates did not expect it either. Jack was soon knocked down, but he got up again with a somewhat ugly gash on his arm, and went at it as hard as ever. At length Mr Evans and his men gained the afterpart of the vessel, and were thus able to command her movements, but the pirates still clustered thickly in the bows, and were evidently preparing to make a rush aft. The English had left their boat, which was alongside, with her painter made fast to the fore-chains. This was an oversight. The pirates perceived it, hauled her ahead, and instead of attempting to regain their vessel, the greater number, jumping into her, made off, leaving four or five of their companions in the hands of the British. These few threw down their arms and sang out for quarter. This was granted them, little as they deserved it. Meantime the rest of the pirates pulled away for the shore, and were soon concealed from view behind a wooded point.

"See the cable ranged, to bring up, Mr Rogers," was the first order given by the lieutenant.

"Ay, ay, sir," answered Jack, but he found that he could not obey the order, as there were neither cables nor anchors on board. It was therefore necessary to keep the vessel under weigh, and to endeavour to beat down the river. Had the English known the channel, this might have been a more easy task than it was likely to prove. They were obliged to make very short tacks for fear of getting on shore, and in whatever reach they were the wind always seemed to head them, so that their progress, notwithstanding the strong current in their favour, was but slow. Their victory had not been gained without considerable loss: a marine had been killed, and three other men, besides Jack, had been wounded, two of them so badly that they were unable to help in working the vessel. This made Mr Evans not a little anxious, and he kept looking out ahead, in the hopes of seeing the other boat coming to his assistance. Jack also, who never failed to make good use of his eyes, was not altogether comfortable, for he had observed in the openings where he had before seen people, a much greater number, evidently keeping a watch on the movements of the schooner. As long as she could be kept moving, there was no great cause for fear; but should she get on the mud, it was difficult to say what might happen. Jack was stationed forward. At length the schooner entered a reach which ran nearly north and south, and the wind enabled her to lay nearly down it.

"No sign of the boat yet, Mr Rogers?" sang out Mr Evans, from aft.

"No, sir," answered Jack; "but there are a number of dark objects in the water which look remarkably like canoes. They seem to be waiting for us at the end of the reach, where we must go about."

"We must run some of them down, and give the rest a taste of the pirate's guns," replied Mr Evans. The guns were got forward, but neither shot nor powder was to be found. Still undaunted, the seamen and marines stood ready to receive the expected attack. Things looked serious. Jack soon made out not less than twenty canoes full of men, with a couple of large boats so posted that it would be almost impossible to avoid them. The schooner was but a very little way from the junction of the two rivers, and the other boat might come to her assistance, but her best chance of escaping was by getting a strong breeze, so that she might dash past the fleet of canoes before they could manage to catch hold of her. There was a prospect of this. The wind had for some time been blowing in fitful gusts, and now it came down on them stronger than ever. To shorten sail was out of the question, but in another minute Jack and his companions found that they had more than the little vessel could well stagger under. That was all right though. On she flew towards their enemies.

"Why, there is our boat among them," exclaimed Jack; "she must have got down by some other channel. We shall have a hard tussle for it." The critical moment was approaching. They could already see the faces of their enemies, and most villainous-looking ruffians they were. Many of them were blacks, but there were several white men among them.

"Steady, my lads, now. Don't throw a shot away till they attack us," sang out Mr Evans. "Stand by to go about." Down went the helm. The jib was shivering in the breeze. A loud shout arose from the canoes and boats, and, making a dash at the schooner, many of the villains began clambering up on each quarter. At that moment a violent gust coming down between an opening in the trees struck the vessel. It was not a moment to start sheet or tack. Every one, indeed, was engaged in the desperate conflict with their assailants. Jack was rushing forward to drive back some fellows who had just hooked on their canoe at the lee fore-chains. The marines were thrusting away with their bayonets. A huge mulatto had grasped Mr Evans by the throat, and several of the seamen were grappling with their opponents. Over heeled the vessel. Just as she was in midstream another gust, more furious than the first, struck her. In an instant Jack felt that she had gone over not to rise again. He scrambled up over the bulwarks into the weather-chains, where he hung on while the rest of the combatants, English, pirates and negroes, were precipitated into the rapidly running stream. Two or three of the canoes were swamped. Some of the blacks swam to the other canoes, and were picked up, but numbers of the combatants, grappling with each other, went down in the dark whirling stream, their shouts, cries, and struggles quieted only by the water which closed over their heads. Jack climbed up to the bottom of the vessel and looked around. His heart sank within him. Where were his late gallant comrades, Mr Evans and the rest? Not one remained. The capsized schooner was drifting rapidly down the stream.

Jack, however, found that he was not alone; but he would gladly have dispensed with his companions. Two blacks had hung on by the rudder-chains, and now, as they climbed up, they caught sight of him. Their eyes flashed vindictively. They had their knives in their belts, but no other weapons. He had retained his grasp on his cutlass, and he had a pistol in his belt, but he feared that the priming must have got wet. The blacks began to creep slowly towards him. They grinned horribly, and were evidently intent on his destruction. Jack saw that he had not the slightest prospect of escape, and must depend entirely on his own exertions. He had no notion, however, of giving in.

The schooner rapidly drifted away from the place where she upset, and none of the canoes were following her. Jack grasped firm hold of the keel of the vessel while he held his weapons in his hands ready for action. Fortunately the blacks could only move on by following each other. They shouted to him in fierce, rough tones, but what they said he could not understand. He was not alarmed, but he held his pistol very tight. The ruffian got close to him; Jack cocked and presented his pistol: if it missed he had his cutlass ready. The negro smiled or rather grinned. He thought the pistol would not go off. Jack pulled the trigger; the negro fell over and over down the side of the vessel into the water. He tried to swim and to regain his lost hold, but his strength failed him, and, with a cry of disappointed rage, he sank under the tide, a small circle of ruddy hue marking the spot where he had gone down.

Jack had not, however, a moment to think about this; he had just time to grasp his cutlass in his right-hand, before his enemy made a spring on him. Jack was still only a boy, though a good stout one, but his nerves were well strung and his muscles were strong. He swung his cutlass round with all his might till the blade met the neck and shoulders of the black, and over he went into the water, where he at once sank, without even attempting to strike out for his life, indeed Jack's blow had almost severed his head from his body. A very short time had been occupied in this encounter; still the schooner had drifted down some way, and neither the pirates nor their allies seemed inclined to follow her. Notwithstanding this, Jack's position was far from a pleasant one. If the vessel drifted on to either bank of the river, he would probably be murdered, and if she continued in the stream, she would soon be among the heavy breakers on the bar, where he would, in all probability, be washed off and devoured by the sharks. With straining eyes he looked out for Hemming's boat, but she was nowhere to be seen. He soon drifted past the channel up which she had gone: not a sign of her could he perceive.

On drifted the schooner. The channel must be very deep, he knew, or the masts must have stuck in the bottom. Should this latter happen, he was afraid that the current gathering round her would speedily wash him off his hold. He felt very grave and sad, and though he was certainly not afraid, he could not help being aware that the life he had found so pleasant and so cheerful, and to which he had so many ties, was slipping away from him. The courage of an older man might well have given way. Jack sighed deeply, but his courage did not give way, for he said to himself, "God's will be done." In that feeling was his strength and support. "I am in God's hand, He will preserve me if He thinks fit."

On drifted the schooner. The current, strengthened by the additional stream, grew more rapid. The vessel kept in mid-channel. He might have gained nothing had she verged on either side, unless he could have got near enough to catch hold of a stout branch of some mangrove bush, where he might have hung on to it till the boat came by, when, should anybody see him, he might be rescued, otherwise a lingering and painful death would be his lot, instead of the speedy one he had every reason to expect. The roar of the breakers on the bar sounded mournfully on his ears. He could see the white surf dancing less high above the sandbank, and he knew that in a few minutes he must be among those roaring, hissing, raging breakers. He thought that he could see the white sails of the brig in the offing, but she was much too far off to render him the slightest assistance. There was, he thought, one chance more. The current might set against the sandspit which crossed its course, and if so, he might be washed on shore. He watched eagerly to ascertain if any logs or branches floating down took that direction. There was nothing to give him assurance of this. For a minute he thought that she was going towards the spit, but the current again seized her, and whirling her round, sent her driving rapidly onwards towards the boiling breakers. Jack felt the wreck rise and fall. He clutched firmly hold of the keel, useless as he believed it to be. The foaming waters sounded in his ears, the foam washed over him, and he knew that he was on that terrible bar, in the midst of the raging breakers.

Chapter Twelve
Adventures on Shore

While Jack Rogers, with Lieutenant Evans and his unfortunate boat's crew, took the southern branch of the river, Mr Hemming, with Murray and Adair, pulled away in the boat up the northern channel, each party believing that they were following the track of the schooner of which they were in search. On dashed Lieutenant Hemming's boat, the crew, as British seamen always will when work is to be done, bending bravely to their oars. They also, as had the other boat, met a strong current.

"Hurrah, my lads, hurrah!" shouted the lieutenant, bending forward almost mechanically to give time to their strokes. "If the chase has gone up the channel, we must take care that she does not creep away from us, that is all."

"Ay, ay, sir," answered Dick Needham. "No fear but we'll hunt her up if she is above water."

In a chase on shore some signs discernible either by the eyes or the olfactory nerves are perceptible by which the pursuers may be guided, but the gallant seamen had only hope on this occasion to lead them on. That, however, was enough. The scenery of this branch was as monotonous as that of the other. Mangrove bushes, with a few tall palms appearing over them, lined the banks, and here and there an opening left blank by nature, or perhaps made by the dark-skinned natives.

"I wonder if, after all, the schooner did come up this way," observed Paddy Adair sagaciously. "If she went up the other, I don't think she could."

His remark of course produced a laugh. No great amount of wit was required to do that. They looked about in every direction, to discover some one from whom they might obtain information, but no one was seen.

"It is not very likely the black fellows would trouble themselves with telling us the truth, so it doesn't much matter," said Paddy. "They are all in league with the slavers, from the king who dresses up on great occasions in a cocked-hat, top-boots, and an old blanket, to poor Quasho, who has never had his nakedness covered since he was born."

Notwithstanding their want of success, still they perseveringly pulled on.

Suddenly Murray put his hand on Adair's shoulder, pointing at the same time with the other ahead. "I say, Terence, what do you see away there at the end of the reach?" he asked. "Does it not look to you like the stern of a vessel?"

"So like it that it must be one," said Hemming. "Hurrah! the slaver must be ours after all."

Just at that moment the sound of firearms coming from a distance was heard, borne faintly on the wind through an opening in the mangrove bushes. Shot after shot followed. "The other boat must have fallen in with some of the rascals; the two channels cannot be far apart," exclaimed Mr Hemming. "Give way, my lads, give way."

He could not help in his eagerness saying this, although the men were already pulling as hard as they could. He was eagerly looking about all the time for some passage through which they might get to the assistance of their comrades. The boat dashed on up the river, and very soon they came in sight of a schooner moored close to the bank of a small creek. They were quickly up to her and mounting her sides. No one opposed them, and not a human being was to be seen. There were, however, evident signs that people had only just left her. A stage of planks led from her deck to the shore. Her sails were bent, her anchor stowed, she was in perfect readiness for sea. A hurried glance below showed that she was undoubtedly a slaver, and about probably that very day to receive her human cargo on board. In her hold were leaguers or huge water-casks filled with water; a large supply of wood and provisions, especially of farina, on which slaves are chiefly fed. Then there was the slave-deck, scarcely thirty-six inches in height, and large coppers for boiling the slaves' food, and some hundred pairs of slave irons or manacles for confining their legs or arms; indeed, nothing was wanting to condemn her. Although Hemming guessed that the crew would soon be back, he was so eager to go to the assistance of Mr Evans, that leaving Murray and a couple of men on board the schooner, he leaped again into his boat and pulled up the creek, thinking that he might get through it into the other channel. It narrowed, however, very rapidly. The trees grew closer and closer together till the branches touched, and finally arched so much overhead as to shut out the view of the sky. It was almost evident that there could not be a navigable passage into the other stream, and Hemming felt that he was not doing a prudent thing in thus pushing on into what might prove not only a hornets' nest, but a hornets' trap, where he and those whose lives were entrusted to him might be stung to death without the power of defending themselves. Still he did not like to abandon his purpose. To push over land would be still more dangerous. The question about proceeding was settled for him. The boat, although in mid-channel, ran her stem into the mud. With a falling tide it would have been madness to proceed farther.

"Back all!" cried the lieutenant.

There was barely room for the oars between the two banks. It seemed doubtful, at first, whether the boat could be shoved off. Delay in this case, as it is in many others, was dangerous. Paddy Adair and several of the men on this instantly leaped out, but sank very nearly up to their middles in slime and water. With their weight, however, out of her the boat floated, and the rest standing up and shoving at the same time, they got her a little way down the stream. Paddy, who was always ready to do anything, however unpleasant, for the sake of setting an example, continued in the water shoving the boat along; the black banks on either side showing the importance of getting out of the trap into which they had gone as quickly as possible.

"Jump in Adair—jump in—she'll freely swim now," said Hemming.

"We'll just get her past this log of wood and give her a shove off from it," said Paddy, making a spring on a dark brown object close to them. He jumped off again, however, very much faster, and sprang towards the boat, for the seeming log opened a huge pair of jaws, exhibiting a terrific row of teeth, with which it made a furious snap at the midshipman's legs. Happily Mr Hemming, leaning over, caught him by the arm and dragged him in, while one of the men gave the monster a rap with the end of his oar, which somewhat distracted his attention, and allowed the rest of the men to scramble on board, which they did in a very great hurry, and no little consternation exhibited in their looks. The alligator first vented his rage by gnawing the blade of the oar, and then made a terrific rush at the boat.

"Shove away, my lads—shove away," cried Hemming, not wishing to waste time in a contest with the beast.

The men, standing up, urged on the boat with their oars as fast as they could; but the savage brute still followed, biting at the blades and trying to get in between them. Terence, however, who very speedily recovered from his alarm, seized a musket, and, watching for the moment when the alligator next opened his huge mouth, fired right down it.

"A hard pill that to digest, if it does not kill him," cried Paddy, when he had done the deed.

At first the brute seemed scarcely aware that anything unusual had gone down his throat; but, as he was making another dart at the boat, he suddenly began to move about in an eccentric way—as Paddy said, "as if something troubled him in his inside," and then, turning away, buried his huge body in the mud, while his tail lashed the water into foam. Round the spot above where his head was probably hidden, a red circle was formed, which, whirling round in the eddies of the current, came sweeping past the boat, proving that Adair's shot had not failed to take effect. Well content to get thus easily rid of their unpleasant antagonist, the men shaved the boat on rapidly down the creek. They had not quite come in sight of the slave schooner when a shout reached their ears. It was repeated. It sounded like a cry for help.

"It is Murray's voice, sir," exclaimed Adair; "he is shouting to us; he is attacked, depend on it."

So Mr Hemming thought. The boat was got round, the men sprang into their seats, and, getting out their oars, dashed away down the stream. The sound of several pistol-shots reached their ears and increased their eagerness to get on. They soon came in sight of the schooner. Murray and his two companions were on her deck, and keeping at bay a dozen Spaniards and blacks, who were attempting to force their way across the platform. Several other people were coming up, and in another instant Murray and the two seamen would have been overpowered. Even when united the Englishmen were far outnumbered by the Spaniards and blacks. Murray heard the shout of his friends as they drew near, and it encouraged him to persevere in his hitherto almost hopeless defence of the prize. In another instant the boat dashed alongside. The crew quickly scrambled on board, and, whirling their cutlasses round their heads, with loud shouts they charged the enemy, and drove them off the platform.

They next set to work to cut it away. They were not long about it. Not a moment was to be lost. More people were coming up, blacks and whites, armed with muskets. The warps which moored the vessel to the shore were speedily cut. Three hands jumped into the boat, and the end of a hawser being heaved to them, they towed round the schooner's head—the current caught it and helped them. Meantime the topsails were loosed and the jib run up; a puff of wind also came down the creek. Away glided the schooner—the boat dropped alongside. The slave-dealers, now mustering strong, began firing at them. They fired in return, so as to drive the villains to seek shelter behind the trees. It might well have enraged the Spaniards to see their vessel carried away from before their very eyes. They did their best to revenge themselves by trying to pick off the Englishmen; but though two of the latter were slightly wounded, no one was disabled, and the schooner held her course unimpeded down the stream. Our friends found, however, before long, in one of the reaches, the wind heading them; and, looking astern, they saw that several large canoes and other boats had put out from the shore, and were in pursuit of them. The slavers probably calculated on their getting on shore, to enable them to come up with them. The current, however, was strong, the wind was tolerably steady, the schooner went about like a top, and a few tacks carried them through each of the reaches, when the wind headed them. Thus they made good way; but still there were many dangers to be encountered. They might, for the present, easily keep ahead of their pursuers; but, unless they could get a free wind, to cross the bar, they must bring up, as it would otherwise be madness to make the attempt. They had gone a long way up the river, and it was difficult to say how the wind might be at the mouth. At last, in a long reach, they ran the pirates out of sight. They, however, suspected that the latter were stopping to collect more of their forces before coming on to the attack. At length the schooner reached the main channel of the river. Hemming and Murray and Adair looked anxiously up the other stream in the hopes of seeing Mr Evans' boat.

"Perhaps she has come down, and will be waiting for us at the bar," observed Hemming. "If she has got hold of the schooner we were looking for, we shall very likely find her ahead of us; at all events we must keep on till we find her."

The little vessel was accordingly kept on down the river. Great was their disappointment, on coming in sight of the bar, to find a heavy surf breaking over it, while the breeze which came in set very nearly up the stream. It was absolutely necessary to bring up. The anchor was dropped, and as the vessel swung to the tide the dark waters came whirling and eddying by with a force which made Hemming thankful that he had not attempted to cross the bar. As soon as he had brought up, he made every preparation for defending the vessel from the attack to be expected. Having got all their arms ready, he had ropes passed round and round the vessel above the bulwarks, so as to serve in the place of boarding-nettings, and then, not without great difficulty, they hoisted their own boat on board, and stowed her amidships. These important preparations being made, they lighted the fire in the caboose and cooked a dinner, for which an abundance of provisions was found on board. A couple of hours passed away. They were anxious ones to Hemming—so they were to Murray, and perhaps to

Adair, though the men did not probably trouble themselves much about the matter. A constant lookout, however, was kept—up the river, lest the pirates should come on them unawares, and down the river, in the hopes of seeing the surf diminishing on the bar and the wind set more out of it. What could have become of Mr Evans, Rogers, and their party, was also the constant subject of conversation.

"Hurrah!" at last cried Murray, who had been looking out astern, "the bar is getting quite smooth. See, there is scarcely any current passing us, and the wind is setting almost out of the river."

"And here come the canoes in battle-array," cried Adair from forward. "They will be down upon us before many minutes are over."

"Heave up the anchor, my lads," shouted Hemming; "let fall the topsails. Run up the jib and fore-staysail. Set the foresail and mainsail." These orders followed in rapid succession. The men did not require to be told to be smart about the work. Round came the schooner's head. Her sails filled, and, under complete command, she stood towards the bar. A clear piece of water showed the only passage she could take with safety. The slave-trader's fleet of canoes came on, but they were just in time to be too late. The schooner stood on, and, well piloted, dashed through the dangerous passage; the surf boiling up still on either side, but not breaking on board her. In another minute she was over it, and floating free in the open ocean.

The brig was at a considerable distance, in chase of a vessel in the offing; but there was no sign of the other boat, or of the schooner, which it was hoped she might have captured. Not knowing the sad fate of Mr Evans and his party, Murray and Adair were eagerly on the lookout for them. Occasionally they turned a glance astern to see what had become of their pursuers; but the pirates seemed to have considered it useless or too hazardous to attempt to cross the bar, and had given up the chase.

"I say, Alick, what do you make out that dark object to be there?" exclaimed Adair, pointing to the southward. One after the other examined it through the glass.

"It's a whale or a ship's bottom," answered Murray, after a long scrutiny. They reported what they had seen to Hemming.

"No whale is likely to have floated into these latitudes," he remarked; "some vessel must have been capsized. Keep her away towards it." The schooner, with a fair breeze, rapidly approached the object they had seen.

It was soon ascertained that Hemming was right in his conjectures. They got close up to the wreck. There was no one on her! "By the set of the current here, I judge that she may have come over the very bar we have just crossed—not very long ago either," observed Hemming, thoughtfully. Twice he sailed round the wreck, examining her narrowly. "I am afraid something has happened," he observed at last; "I am not happy on the subject. It cannot be helped though. It may be the lot of any of us. Keep her up once more for the brig."

Alick and Terence became very sad when they heard these remarks. They scarcely liked to ask Hemming what he meant. As they talked over the matter, they felt very much alarmed on Jack's account. Still they could not believe that he, their old friend and companion, could possibly be lost.

"No, no, he'll turn up somewhere, I'm sure," cried Paddy.

"I trust he will," answered Alick, gravely; but he felt very sad and depressed in spirits.

Hemming seemed doubtful what to do; whether he would across the bar, make a dash at the pirates, and run up the river and look for his friends, or stand on at once and get greater force from the brig. The latter was the wisest course, and he determined to follow it. The *Archer* had stood away in chase of another vessel of a suspicious appearance, and when night fell she was nowhere to be seen. Hemming, therefore, hove the schooner to, to wait till her return. Had he gone after her they might very probably, in the darkness of night, have missed each other.

Never, perhaps, had my two old schoolfellows passed a more anxious night, even when they were wrecked on the coast of Greece; then the three friends were together; now their minds were racked with doubts of the most painful description as to what had become of Jack and his companions. Had they known of the destruction of the boat and her crew, they would, if possible, have been still more anxious.

Hemming also kept pacing the deck all night long, looking out on every side, like a good officer, as he was, who felt that the lives of the people with him were entrusted to his care. He did not dread any attack from boats, but he knew that armed slavers might be attempting to run in or out of the river while the brig was away, and that if they attempted to molest him, he should find them very difficult customers to dispose of. Still he was not the man to allow a slaver to pass him without attempting to capture her, inferior as he might be to her in force. The night was very dark, now and then a few flashes of phosphorescent light played over the ocean, or were stirred up by the bows of the schooner, as she slowly worked her way through the water; but even the sharpest eyes on board could scarcely distinguish anything two or three hundred yards off. Terence and Alick could not bring themselves to lie down nor take any rest, even though Hemming urged them to do so. They were leaning together over the bulwarks. They neither of them could have said whether they were asleep or awake. The wind had dropped considerably, and at intervals the sails shook themselves and gave a loud flap against the masts. Terence felt a hand suddenly resting on his shoulder.

"What is that? Do you hear a sound? Did you see anything?" said a voice in his ear.

The voice appeared so deep and hollow and strange, that he did not at first discover that it was Murray speaking to him. Alick repeated the question twice before he replied. He had, in truth, been fast asleep, but he did not know it.

"No—what? see, hear what? I don't see anything," was his somewhat incoherent answer.

"There it is again; music—some one singing," continued Alick. "Can you see nothing?"

The two midshipmen peered eagerly out into the darkness, but nothing could they discern. They, however, drew Hemming's attention to the circumstance. He had been walking the deck, so the noise of his own footsteps prevented him from hearing the sound. He now listened with them, but after some time, hearing nothing, was inclined to think that they had been deceived by their fancy. Murray thought not, and, keeping his eyes on the point from which he believed the sounds had come, was almost certain that he could distinguish the sails of a square-rigged vessel passing at no great distance off, standing in towards the coast. He called Hemming's attention to it, but whether or not the night mists had at the moment he was looking lifted up, and again sunk down, and allowed him to see a vessel really there, or that his fancy still misled him, it was impossible to say. Certainly no sail was to be seen, nor was a sound again heard. Slowly the hours of that night seemed to pass away. Day came at last, a gloomy coast of Africa morning, with a thick damp ague-and-fever giving fog. In vain they looked out for the *Archer*. They began to fear that she might have followed the vessel after which she had gone in chase to a considerable distance, thus delaying the expedition they were so anxious to undertake in search of the other boat. As the sun rose, however, his rays began a struggle with the mist, and, aided by a light breeze which sprung up from the northward, finally triumphed, and rolling off their adversary, they beamed forth on the dancing blue waters, and on the white canvas of the brig, which came gliding on majestically towards them, followed by another vessel, which she had overtaken and captured. The prize had half a cargo of slaves on board, and was on her way up to another place where her owners had agents to complete it. The first question which Alick and Terence asked on getting on board the *Archer*, was for Rogers and the other boat's crew. Their hearts sank within them, when they found that nothing had been seen of the boat. Captain Grant listened to all the information they could give, and promptly formed a plan, the execution of which he entrusted to Hemming and the two midshipmen, complimenting them at the same time for the gallant way in which they had captured the slaver and brought her out of the river.

Chapter Thirteen
To fight his Friends

Poor Jack Rogers! His lot was indeed a hard one. We left him clinging to the keel of the schooner, while she was carried on by the rapid current over the bar, amidst the raging waters and blinding foam. Every moment he expected to be torn from his hold; but life was dear to him, and he exerted every particle of strength he possessed to hold on. Now a sea would come and wash over the vessel, almost drowning him, and completely preventing him from seeing; then he felt that he was whirled round and round, till he looked up—but it was only to see another huge breaker rolling up ready to overwhelm him. He felt the terrific dash of the wave, its roar sounded in his ears—he was almost stunned. He prayed that he might be preserved from the terrible danger to which he was exposed. The roller passed on, leaving him still firmly clutching the wreck. Again he looked up. The blue sea danced cheerfully before his eyes; the sun shone brightly; the wreck had drifted clear of the influence of the breakers. Most grateful he felt at having been thus far preserved. Still he knew that he was not out of danger. The schooner might any moment go down, and he might be left, without a plank to rest on, to the mercy of the ravenous sharks which swarmed around. His first impulse was to look out for the brig. She was in the offing, standing away to the westward. He had no hope from any help she could render him. Then he looked back over the bar, in the expectation of seeing the other boat coming out; but nowhere was she to be discovered. He saw, meantime, that the wreck was drifting to the southward down the coast, and at no great distance from it. He calculated the distance, and thought to himself that he could swim on shore. If he delayed, the vessel might drift farther out to sea, and the feat might be impossible.

"The sooner it is done, the better," he thought to himself. "I have swum as far in a worse sea before now." Before slipping off into the water, he commended himself with a hearty prayer to the care of a Merciful Providence. He was on the very point of letting go his hold, when, as he looked into the water, his eye fell on a dark triangular object, just rising out of it, slowly moving past. He looked again with a shudder, for he recognised the fin of a shark. Another and another passed by. Truly thankful did he feel that he had not trusted himself voluntarily within the power of their voracious jaws. If the vessel sank though, where would he be? He could not help thinking of that. He got up and gazed around. He was beginning to feel very hungry, and to his other dangers the risk of starvation was now added. Still, he did not allow himself to despair. He hoped that his old schoolfellows and Hemming would soon recross the bar, and, seeing the wreck, come and find him. After a little time, as he was casting his eye to the southward, he thought he saw a dark object moving along close in-shore, just outside the surf. He soon made out that it was a canoe, and then that she was manned by blacks. As they drew near, it was evident that they saw him on the wreck, for they at once pulled towards him. He scarcely knew whether to hail them as friends or foes. They were very ill-looking fellows he thought. There were also two white men in the stern-sheets of the canoe. He did not like their looks at all either. They were soon alongside, and when they saw his uniform, they looked up at him with no very friendly eye. Having held a short parley among themselves, they hailed him, but what they said he could not make out. Dangerous as his present position was, he felt no inclination to entrust himself to their care. However, they made signs to him to come down into the canoe, and after a little reflection, and thinking it better not to show any fear or mistrust of them, he complied with their demands, and as he slid down over the side of the vessel, they caught him, and hauled him in. He saw them minutely examining the vessel, and then they asked him a number of questions in Spanish, or a sort of mongrel Spanish, which he could not clearly comprehend, and he thought it more prudent not to show that he understood them at all. He made out, however, that the strangers were inquiring how the vessel was capsized, and how he came to be on board her. He guessed also that they knew that she was a slaver, and had been captured by the party to which he had belonged. When they found that he did not reply to their questions, they let him sit down at the bottom of the canoe, while the two whites and one of the black men talked together among themselves. They every now and then cast glances ominous of evil intentions towards him. Poor Jack did not at all like their looks, still less the tenor of the few words whose meaning he caught. "Knock him on the head at once," said one. "Throw him overboard, and let the sharks have him," proposed another. "Shoot him with pistol," quoth the big negro,—grinning horribly. These words were uttered with the most cold-blooded indifference, as if the act proposed by the speakers was one of everyday occurrence with them. Jack, as he listened, longed to make an effort to save his life; anything was better than to sit there quietly and be murdered. Far rather would he die struggling bravely for existence. Still, as the pirates did not make any further demonstration, he thought it would be wiser to appear unconscious of their threats, and remained where he was without moving. Jack, however, every now and then, looked over the gunwale of the canoe, to ascertain where they were going. They quickly arrived off the bar, but the slave-dealers or pirates, or whatever they were, seemed to think that there was too much surf to allow them to cross it. They therefore pulled back a little way to the south. Jack observed a patch of sandy beach, with a clear channel up to it, between two rocks. They waited for a short time, and then the canoe, mounting on the top of a roller, was carried rapidly forward, the foam hissing and bubbling round her, till she grounded on the beach. In a moment the crew, jumping out of her, ran her up out of the reach of the succeeding roller, which roared angrily, as if disappointed of its prey. Jack was going to walk on, but he felt a hand laid heavily on his shoulder, and his arms, being seized by two of the black fellows, were bound behind him, and he found himself a prisoner on the coast of Africa, without the slightest prospect, as far as he could see, of making his escape from his ruffian captors.

Poor Jack was dragged along by his savage companions, the muzzle of a pistol or the point of a long knife every now and then being shown him, as a hint that he must keep up his spirits and move on. This was no easy matter without stumbling, for the ground was strewed with decayed timber, while creepers and parasitical plants of numerous species formed traps to catch his feet. He saw, too, the grass frequently moving, as a hideous snake or some other reptile crept away among it. Overhead were birds of every variety, and of the richest plumage; parrots, trumpet birds, pigeons, whydahs, green paroquets, and numberless others, which he was in no humour just then to admire, while monkeys of all sorts skipped about among the boughs of the lofty palms, and chattered away, as if to inquire where the stranger had come from. In one or two openings between the giant palms, bananas, and other lofty trees, Jack caught sight of some blue ranges of mountains in the far distance, and towards them, as they pushed their way through the dense underwood, his captors seemed to be proceeding. The dreadful thought occurred to him, that he was being carried off into the interior to be turned into a slave, and perhaps that he should never be able to make his escape. The jungle grew thicker and thicker, and the forest more gloomy as they proceeded, till he could scarcely work his way along, and even the Spaniards and blacks, with their arms at liberty, had no little difficulty in making progress through it. At last they came to a standstill, and a talk among themselves. Poor Jack caught the very ominous words, "*mata el chico*," which he knew too well meant "kill the little chap."

"He is not worth the trouble he costs us," added the ferocious Spaniard who had spoken. "This knife of mine will settle him with a blow."

"It is a pity we did not do it in the canoe, and save ourselves trouble," growled out his companion, drawing his long knife from his belt.

Jack felt that his last moments had come. He, however, eyed his captors boldly, and tried to nerve himself for the expected stroke. A short time before, some villains of the same character as those into whose power he had fallen had murdered a young midshipman, whom they had found on board a prize they had retaken, and he knew that they would have no scruple about killing him. The blacks stood by, enjoying, apparently, his agony; for, brave as he was, it was a bitter thing thus, without cause, to be cruelly murdered in cold blood. No one spoke. Jack tried to offer up a prayer to Heaven, but, at such a moment, even to pray was difficult. His heart, though, was praying, and One who knows what is in the heart heard him. Suddenly there was a rustling of leaves, a crashing of boughs. A loud shriek was uttered, and a huge animal leaped through the brushwood, and, seizing one of the negroes, again bounded off into the thicket. The unfortunate wretch cried out piteously for help. The Spaniards and the negroes turned to pursue the wild beast. From the glimpse Jack had of it, he believed it to be a tiger. The negro who had been seized was the smallest of the party, and of light weight; and the savage brute was more accustomed to make his way through the tangled underwood than were his pursuers. On he went, bounding through the thicket, his miserable victim in vain crying for assistance. The rest pursued as fast as they could, apparently forgetting Jack altogether. They were soon hid from his sight by the trees. He had no wish to follow them, even had he possessed the power of so doing. His arms were bound, and before he could do anything he must contrive to get them loose. He tugged and tugged away frantically. He was afraid his captors would be back before he could get free, and execute their murderous threats. By what means he was to escape, he could not just then tell. The first thing was to obtain the use of his limbs. He worked away for life and death.

At last he twisted the rope round so that he could reach one of the knots with his teeth. He pulled away lustily. He found that he was slackening it. He listened for the shouts and cries of the pirates. He thought that their voices sounded louder and nearer again. He was every moment getting the ropes looser. One more tug, and his hands were at liberty. He struck out on either side to assure himself that he had the free use of them. He looked round; no one was in sight. His first impulse was to set off and run back to the coast, but then he recollected that he might be easily pursued, that it must be seven or eight miles off at least, as three or four hours had passed since he and his captors had left it. After a moment's reflection he determined to find his way as soon as possible to the banks of the river. He was certain that the boats would be sent in to look for his party, and, by watching for them, he hoped to be able to make some signal to call their attention to himself. He still heard the voices of the pirates. A tall palm-tree was near. He thought that the safest plan would be to get to the top of it. He could easily hide himself among the wide-spreading leaves, and the Spaniards, believing that his arms were bound, would never think of looking there for him. He would also have the advantage of watching all that was going on below. He had seen blacks climb a tree with a band partly round their stem and partly round their waists. The rope he had just got clear of his arms would help him up in the same way. He rapidly fitted it, and, with knees and hands working away, up he went the smooth stem. He had got nearly to the top, when he heard a chattering, and looking up, he saw a very ugly face grinning down upon him. An ape had previous possession of his proposed stronghold. He was not to be daunted, however, but, swinging himself up on the bough, prepared to do battle for its possession. He had still a pistol in his belt, though it was not loaded. The pirates had forgotten to deprive him of it. He held it by the muzzle, and Master Quacko, who seemed to be a very sensible monkey, thought that it would be foolish to pick a quarrel with so well-armed a stranger. As Jack advanced, he retreated, till Jack reached the centre of the tree, where he could coil himself away without the possibility of any one below discovering him. He looked round before sitting down. Below him was a dense mass of foliage, with only here and there an opening. To the west, in the far distance, was the sea, looking bright and blue; to the east were ranges of mountains, the most remote evidently of considerable elevation; while to the north he caught a glimpse of the river, to his great satisfaction, not very far off. He could still hear the voices of the pirates, but he could not discover whether they had succeeded in rescuing the wretched negro from the fangs of the tiger. Meantime the monkey sat on the farther end of a branch watching him.

"I hope you have formed a favourable opinion of me, Master Quacko," he said, looking at the ape, for even in the dangerous predicament in which he was placed he could not resist a joke.

"Quacko, quacko, quacko," went the monkey, in a tone which Jack thought was friendly.

He felt about in his pockets, and found a piece of biscuit. He nibbled a bit, and then held it out to his companion. The ape drew near, at first, hesitatingly; Jack nibbled a little more of the biscuit. Quacko thought that it would all be gone if he did not make haste, so he made one or two more hops up towards Jack. Jack nibbled away, then once more held out the biscuit. The monkey made one spring, and nearly caught it, but Jack drew it back, that the animal might feel that it was given him. Then he held it out, and the ape took it quite gently, but ran off to the end of a bough, that he might examine this new sort of food, and eat it at his leisure.

The pirates had now found their way back to where they had left Jack. He could plainly hear them asking one another what could have become of him. They were under the tree in which he lay so snugly ensconced.

"He must have hid himself in the brushwood; he cannot be far off," said one.

"If he had had his hands at liberty, I should say he would have got up one of these trees," observed another. "Those English sailors can climb anything. I have seen them go up the side of a slippery rock without a hole in which to stick their nails."

"He cannot be up this tree," remarked the first. "See! there is a monkey quietly eating a nut on one of the branches. There is no other tree near in which he could hide."

After this the men hunted about on every side, and Jack hoped that they would then go away.

"He must still be near," exclaimed one of them. "Sancho, do you climb that tree and look about you. You will soon find out where he is by the shaking of the bushes as he moves along. Up! man, up!"

Jack knew, by the voice which replied, that one of the negroes was climbing up. The monkey had finished his biscuit, and, liking it very much, came back for some more, not observing what was occurring below. Jack had now won his confidence; and by giving him a very little bit at a time kept the animal close to him. Up climbed the black. Jack knew that he could knock him down again with the butt end of his pistol, but if he did he would only hasten his own destruction, as the others would quickly find means to get hold of him. He felt that the black was close under him. He caught sight of his woolly pate working its way through, the leaves. "Now or never," thought Jack. He seized the unsuspecting ape, and threw him down directly on the negro's head. The monkey, as much astonished as anybody, laid hold of the woolly crop with his claws, and scratched and bit, chattering away with all his might.

"Fetish! fetish! fetish!" screamed out the negro, sliding down the tree a great deal faster than he had come up, coming down the latter part by the run, and reaching the ground more dead than alive; while the monkey clambered up again, and, not daring to approach Jack, took his seat at the end of a bough, chattering away in the greatest state of agitation.

Jack lay snug. He had hopes that none of the other blacks would attempt to climb the tree after the reception their companion had met with; and from what he heard them say he had great hopes that they really believed they had seen a fetish. The Spaniards too, though pretending to laugh at the superstition of the negroes, having no real religion of their own to supply its place, were very strongly impressed with the black man's superstition, and would on no account have attempted to climb up the tree. Jack therefore began to hope that he should escape from his intending murderers, and he did not despair of ultimately getting back to his ship.

In a short time the Spaniards and negroes, uttering loud oaths at their ill luck in having lost one of their companions as well as their captive, set off once more; and Jack watched them as they worked their way through the brushwood to the eastward. He felt truly glad when they were no longer to be seen. He was now also in a hurry to be off. "Good-bye, Mr Quacko," said he, turning to the monkey, and making him a profound bow, for Jack was the pink of politeness. "I am much obliged to you for the accommodation your tree has afforded me, and for the assistance you have rendered me, and if you will ever venture afloat I shall be very happy to see you on board our ship. Good-bye, old fellow, give us a paw." He felt in a curiously excited state, and ready to talk any nonsense. Quacko, who thought he was to have some more biscuit, came near, but when he saw that there was none he hopped off again and chattered away louder than ever.

Jack now descended in the same way that he had got up. His first care was to cut a thick stick to serve as a weapon of defence, for he thought to himself, "If the tigers about here are so bold as to carry off a black man, they are just as likely to attack me." He accordingly kept his eyes about him, and, steering as well as he could by the sun, he pushed away towards the north. He could not help expecting to see a tiger spring out towards him, and every now and then he was startled by a snake crawling across his path; while the cawing of parrots and parrakeets, and the chattering of monkeys, made him feel like one of those knights in fairy stories, who have to traverse a forest haunted by evil spirits, who do their utmost to turn him from his gallant purpose of rescuing a lovely princess from the enchanted castle in which she has been shut up. Jack, however, was not to be turned from his intention of getting down to the banks of the river. He forgot that he would have to cross through a mangrove swamp, unless he could hit upon one of the few paths used by the negroes for the purpose of crossing it. Night was now rapidly approaching. He saw that unless he would run a very great risk of serving as the supper of some hungry wild beast, he must get up into a tree and pass it there. He was getting very hungry also, and he had but a few scraps of the biscuit he had shared with the monkey. Still, as long as there was daylight, he was anxious to push on, for he was sure that the boats would be sent in to look for him the first thing in the morning, and he wanted to be near the river to signalise to them. So he pushed on, beating down the bushes with his thick stick. Many a snake, lizard, and other creeping or crawling thing hissed or croaked at him as he passed. At last he saw before him an open space. "Ah! now, at all events, I shall be able to push on rapidly," he thought to himself. So he did, and he went on some way, when on a sudden he found himself in front of a pailing with some grotesque-looking figures carved in wood grinning above it, and within it a bamboo-leaf-covered hut, before which stood a remarkably big ugly-looking blackamoor. Jack looked at him, and he looked at Jack, and uttered some words which clearly were meant to express, "Hillo, youngster, where are you hurrying to?" Jack followed a very natural impulse, which was to run as fast as he could. Under other circumstances this might have been a wise proceeding, for he certainly could run faster than the black man, who was not only big but fat. He had scarcely begun to run when a piece of painted wood came whizzing through the air after him, which would certainly have knocked him down had it hit him. He dodged it, however; but the next moment he heard the gruff voice of the black hounding on a dog, and when he turned his head he saw a huge Spanish bloodhound leaping over the pailing, followed by the negro. To attempt to escape was now hopeless, so he ran forward, flourishing his stick in the hope of keeping the dog at bay. When the negro saw he was coming back he called the hound off him.

"For why you run so?" exclaimed the negro, who saw that he was an Englishman.

"For the same reason that a pig does, because I was in a hurry," answered Jack, who saw that his best course was to put a good face on the matter.

"Ah, you funny young ossifer, you laugh moch," observed the negro.

"Yes, it runs in the family, we are addicted to laughing," replied Jack with perfect coolness. "And now, old gentleman, I'm very sharp set, and as I doubt not that you have, plenty of provender in your house, I shall be much obliged to you for some supper."

The negro evidently could not make out what Jack was about, and seemed to have an idea that he had run away from his ship. Jack was not sorry to encourage this. The black was evidently balancing in his mind whether he should make most by giving him up and claiming a reward, or helping him to hide, and then getting possession of any wealth he might have about him. He, in the most friendly way, led Jack into his house. It was very neatly built of bamboo, of considerable size, oblong in shape, and divided into four or five rooms. In one was a table, with some chairs; and the negro, having given some orders in a loud voice to several ebon-hued damsels, who appeared at the door, in a short time several dishes of meat and grain were placed on it. "Come you eat," said the host. Jack stuck his fork into the meat. It was not a hare, or a rabbit, or a pig, or a kid. He could not help thinking of his friend Quacko, as he turned it over and over. However, he was very hungry, and he thought he would taste a bit. It was very tender and nice, so he resolved that he would not ask questions, but go on eating till his appetite was satisfied. There was a sort of porringer of farina, and some cakes of the same substance. He ate away, and felt much more satisfied than at first with the state of affairs. His host informed him that he was a grand pilot of the river, and showed him a variety of certificates which he had received to prove the fact, from the masters of English, American, Spanish, Portuguese, and French traders. Some praised him, but others remarked that he was one of the greatest rascals unhung, and that he would cheat and rob whenever he had the opportunity, and tell any falsehood to suit his purpose. "A nice sort of gentleman," thought Jack, but he did not express his opinions, and tried to make himself as comfortable as he could. The negro placed wine and spirits before him, but he partook sparingly of them.

"You say I good man," observed his host. "Go off to fight ship. Tell moch. Ah, ah!" And he winked and nodded and turned his eyes about in a curious way.

Jack concluded that he proposed going off to the ship, and would give some information about the slavers, and that he wanted him to vouch for his character.

"All right," answered Jack; "you come on board; we shall be very happy to see you, and bring your book of certificates—remember that." Considering the small vocabulary possessed by the negro, he managed to carry on a good deal of conversation with his guest. At last he made a sign that it was time to go to bed, and, pointing to a bundle of mats, he told him to lie down, and that no harm would come to him. Jack did as he was bid, and, having a good conscience and a good digestion, was very soon asleep.

The household was astir by an early hour. When Jack opened his eyes, he saw that two or three strangers were in the room. They looked at him askance, with no friendly glance. His host soon after entered, and it was very evident that a change had come over the man's feelings towards him. Jack, however, got up, and, shaking himself, tried to look as unconcerned as possible. The bloodhound also, which had been very good friends with him the previous evening, walked in and stalked, snuffing, and growling round and round him. Jack did not like the look of affairs. Some food at last was brought in for breakfast—baked yams, fried fish, farina, and other delicacies, of which his host invited him to partake, but was evidently inclined to treat him with very little ceremony. When the meal was over. Jack intimated that he should like to begin his journey to get on board his ship. The negro laughed and said something to the other men. "You no go dere now, you go wid dees." Jack's countenance fell. The other blackamoors grinned, and without ceremony took him by the shoulder to lead him off. The midshipman's impulse was to resist, and he began to lay about him with his stick, which he snatched up from a corner, but the blacks threw themselves upon him, while the horrid bloodhound sprang at his legs, and in an instant he was overpowered, and his hands once more bound behind him. Jack thought that before he was carried off, he would try and induce the big negro to help him, so he exclaimed, "I say, friend pilot, perhaps you can't help this; so just let them know on board ship where I am, and you will be well rewarded." He saw the negro grin, but before he could get an answer, he was hurried off by his new masters. They conducted him along over ground very similar to that which he had passed the previous day. Now and then he saw fields of Indian corn, and small patches cultivated with other grains, but otherwise the country was covered mostly with a dense jungle, very narrow paths only being cut through it. After travelling five or six miles, they reached the river, and having dragged a canoe from among the bushes on the banks, all the party got into it, and paddled away up the stream. The cords were by this time really hurting Jack's arms, and he made all the signs he could think of to induce the negroes to remove them. To his great satisfaction, after talking together, one of them got up and slackened the knots, so that he could throw the rope off. He expressed his thanks to the negro, and placed it gently by his side. Scarcely had he done so, when his eye fell on a piece of board floating by. He stretched out his hand and got hold of it. That instant the idea flashed into his mind, that this board might enable him to communicate with his shipmates. It very soon dried, and then, as if to amuse himself, he took out his knife and began cutting away at it. If he could carve but a few words, they might be sufficient to signify where he had gone. He carved, in no very regular characters, "A prisoner, up south branch.—Jack R." As soon as he had done this, pretending to be tired of the amusement, he threw the board into the stream and watched it floating down towards the sea. "It is a hundred to one whether it is picked up," he said to himself with a sigh, "I'll double the chances though." So he looked out for another board or piece of stick; and having before long got one, carved that in the same way. The blacks did not seem to suspect his object, and allowed him to continue the operation. After paddling about an hour, they ran up a small creek with black mudbanks; and when they had drawn the canoe on shore, Jack found himself standing before a strong stockade or fort with a deep ditch round it. There was no gate on the side turned towards the river, but going round some way, they arrived at an entrance over a rough drawbridge. The negroes talked a few minutes together, and then led Jack in. The object for which the fort was used was very clear. In the centre stood a large barracoon full of slaves. This barracoon was a shed built of heavy piles driven down into the earth, lashed together with bamboos, and thatched with palm-leaves. Jack, as he passed, looked in. Sad was the spectacle which met his sight. The negroes who had charge of Jack did not appear to have found the person of whom they were in search; for after waiting some time they led him again out of the fort and took the road up a hill away from the river. After walking some way they reached a village or town. It was surrounded by a bamboo fence. They entered by a narrow gateway at the end of a street. The houses, or rather huts, were all joined together, forming one long shed of uniform height on each side of the road. Each habitation had a small low door, which alone showed the number of separate dwellings in a row. The sides were composed of broad strips of bark, and bamboo leaves served for the thatch. Here and there were larger houses built of bamboo, with raised floors, marking the residences of chief men. At last they reached a house nearly a hundred feet in length, and, having ascended some steps, Jack found himself ushered into the presence of a burly negro, who was sitting in oriental style on a pile of mats smoking a pipe. He had on a cocked-hat and a green uniform coat covered with gold-lace, wide seamen's trousers and yellow slippers, a striped shirt, and a red sash round his waist. From his air he evidently considered himself a very important personage, and Jack did not doubt that he was in the presence of some Indian potentate. Round the room were several mirrors in gilt frames, and on a table stood a large silver bowl, while there were a couple of chairs and a sofa covered with damask or silk. The king, for so he called himself, looked at Jack sternly and said, "For what you come to my country, eh?"

Jack answered that he had been brought there against his will, and that he had no intention of coming. But his Majesty seemed to doubt him, and asked him a number of questions to elicit the truth. At length, however, he seemed satisfied. Jack was in hopes that he had made a favourable impression, and as he was getting hungry, he intimated that he should like some dinner. The king seemed pleased at the request, and ordered it to be brought into the room. It was a very good repast, and Jack was getting very happy, and hoping that there would be no great difficulty in making his escape, when the aspect of affairs was once more changed by the appearance of the two Spaniards who had picked him off the wreck of the slaver. They looked very fierce, and made threatening gestures at him, and abused him to the king for running away from them, and he discovered that they knew all about the expedition of the *Archer's* boats up the river, and the capture of the schooner. He, however, went on eating his dinner, and tried to look unconcerned about the matter. This enraged them still more. What they might have done he could not tell; but suddenly a man rushed into the room, and gave some piece of information which seemed to put them all into a state of great agitation. They seized upon Jack and dragged him off, and they and a number of other people, headed by the king, rushed down the bill towards the fort. From the few words dropped which Jack could comprehend, he understood that they expected an attack to be made on it for the purpose of rescuing the slaves, and that they were resolved to defend it to the last. He found himself dragged along till he was carried into the fort with the crowd; he was then shown a gun, and it was intimated to him that if he did not do his best to fight, he should forthwith have his brains blown out—a dreadful alternative, but from which he could discover not the slightest prospect of escaping.

Chapter Fourteen
In the Negro Prison

Jack Rogers stood near the gun at which he had been placed in the slavers' fort. He had plenty of time to consider how he should act; but, turn the matter over in his mind as much as he would, he could not arrive at a satisfactory decision. The alternatives left for his choice were to fire at his friends or to be shot himself. The slave-traders and their assistants, and the slavers' crews who stood around him, were fellows whose very ill-looking countenances showed that they would not scruple to execute with very scant warning any threat they had made. An older man than Jack might have felt very uncomfortable under such circumstances. A more evil-disposed band of ruffians could not often have been collected together. They were of all colours, from those who called themselves white to negroes of the most ebon hue. Not that the whites had much claim to the distinction, for they were so bronzed by sun and wind that they were almost as dark as the Africans, and certainly they were not the least villainous-looking of the gang. Two of them especially, who had belonged to the crew of the schooner Jack had assisted to capture, seemed to have recognised him, and paid him very particular and disagreeable attention. One of them politely handed him a rammer, and showed him how he was to load his gun, while the other put a pistol under his nose, and exhibiting the perfect condition of the lock, explained with a mild smile that it was not at all likely to miss fire. Jack smelt at the pistol, and flourished the rammer.

"Very good powder I have no doubt," he remarked, looking as unconcerned as possible, "but I cannot say that I admire its odour. If any of you have a pinch of snuff to offer me now, I should be obliged to you. I want something to overcome the smell of the mud, which is anything but pleasant, let me assure you."

The Spaniard, though he did not understand what Jack said, comprehended his signs; and, thus appealed to, could not resist pulling out his snuff-box and offering it to him, though he fully intended, in case of any sign of insubordination, to blow out his brains at a moment's notice. Jack dipped his fingers into the snuff-box with all the coolness and as great an air as he could command. He knew that his best chance of escape was to throw his captors off their guard. *"Bueno, bueno,"* he remarked, scattering the snuff under his nose as he had seen Spaniards do, for in reality he had no wish to take any up his nostrils. The slave-traders could not help shrugging their shoulders, and thinking that they had got hold of a very independent sort of young gentleman. They talked together a good deal, and from what they said Jack made out that they were proposing to invite him to join them. "A very good joke," he thought to himself; "the rascals! I'll humour them in it, however; it will certainly afford me a better chance of escape."

During this time a number of blacks were pouring into the fort, carrying all sorts of arms, most of them matchlocks of very antique construction, though some were muskets which had probably not long before left the workshops of Birmingham. Jack, hoping that he had thrown his captors a little off their guard, shouldered his rammer, and walked about to try and obtain a more perfect notion of the state of affairs. Looking through the stockades, he saw that the fort commanded entirely the reach of the river, at the extreme upper end of which it was situated. The stream there made a sudden bend, nearly doubling back on itself; and as the fort was placed almost on this point, the guns in it could fire point-blank right down the stream. No boats had yet appeared, but from the look of intense eagerness exhibited on the countenances of all the blacks, he had no doubt that they were near at hand. The whole fort was in a great state of bustle, if not of confusion. The black warriors were running about here and there, chattering away to each other, and examining not only their own arms, but those of everybody else. Some of them Jack saw squinting down the barrels of their companions' muskets, to try and ascertain the cause, apparently, of their not going off, while the man at the other end would snap the lock without giving the slightest warning. One of them after this came up to Jack, and, by signs and a few words of English, requested him politely to look into the muzzle of his musket and ascertain why it would not "fire! bang!" as he expressed it, intimating that he had already put in several charges.

Jack declined that mode of proceeding, but begged to look at the other end. Jack burst into a fit of laughter. "The reason, *amigo*, is this *intendez ustedes*," he answered, as soon as he could find breath to speak. "There's no flint to your lock, and if there had been, the touch-hole is well stopped up with rust, so you had two very secure preventives against its going off. I only hope that the rest of you have arms of a like character. Not much fear for my friends then." He picked out the touch-hole, however, for the negro, telling him that he must put a match into the pan when he wanted to fire it. He resolved, however, to stand clear of the negro when he fired it; for he had little doubt that when he did so the barrel would burst, and do much more damage to the defenders of the fort than to the assailants. Jack was in hopes that the guns mounted in the fort would prove to be in a similar condition; but on examining them he soon saw that they were ship's guns, and were in very good order. He had managed by his independent manner, by this time, to throw the slave-dealers off their guard. He waited for an opportunity when they were not watching him, and then hurried back to the gun of which they had given him charge. As he could not manage to withdraw the shot, he knocked in a wedge, which gave it an elevation calculated to carry it far over the heads of any of the attacking party. He looked round when he had done this, to ascertain whether he had been observed, but the white men had turned round for some purpose, and the blacks did not seem to comprehend what he had been about. "At all events, I shall not have to fire at my friends," he thought to himself, "and now the sooner they come on the better for me." Scarcely had these words passed through his mind than he observed a great commotion among the motley garrison of the fort, and, looking through the embrasure at which his gun was placed, he caught sight of several boats just rounding the point at the other end of the reach. He could not make out who was commander-in-chief of the present gang of villains with whom he was associated. The two Spaniards, who had at first paid him so much polite attention, were evidently not even officers. A huge black man, with a very ugly visage, seemed to have considerable authority. He was engaged in marshalling the negroes, and posting them at the stockades ready to make use of their firearms. The burly sovereign of the territory was nowhere to be seen. He probably thought discretion the best part of valour, and had retired again to his capital, to await the results of the contest. At last Jack's eyes fell on a little wizened old Spaniard in a straw hat, nankeen trousers, and a light blue coat, who, as soon as he made his appearance, began to order about everybody in an authoritative and energetic manner, and very quickly brought the confused rabble of defenders into order. Two or three other Spaniards, who from their appearance seemed to be officers, came with him. He had evidently just arrived from a distance, summoned in a hurry, probably, to defend the fort. He went round, looking at the guns, and Jack was very much afraid that he would examine his. Just, however, as he was about to do so up went a rocket high into the sky, let off probably as a signal for some purpose or other. It had the effect of calling off the old man's attention from him. The people in the advancing boats seemed not to have any notion that they were so near the fort, for they pulled on, without in any way quickening their speed, right up towards the guns.

Jack had remarked the mode in which the place was fortified, so likely to lead strangers into a trap. In front of the stockades was a deep broad ditch, and then beyond it rose a low bank of soft slimy mud, held together by reeds and aquatic plants, and which sloped away again down to the river. This bank was covered at high water, but even then Jack doubted whether a boat could be got across it. The slave-traders and blacks grinned as they thought of the trap into which the British seamen were about to fall. Jack watched the approach of the boats. Oh! how he longed to warn his friends of the danger threatening them. He would have shouted out to them, but they could not have heard him; and then he thought that he would climb up to the top of the stockade and warn them off; but he knew that the moment he was seen by the blacks to make any signal, a pistol-bullet would be sent through his head. Jack was perfectly ready to run any risk for an adequate object; but after a moment's reflection he felt perfectly sure that the boats would come on notwithstanding anything he might do, and that the moment for sacrificing his life had not yet arrived.

As the boats drew near so did the flurry and excitement among the blacks increase: the white men looked along their guns and prepared for action; the little wizened old Spaniard posted himself in a position whence he could observe all that was going forward. Jack saw that he was watching him, and he also heard him tell one of the Spaniards, who had before paid him so much polite attention, to keep an eye on his movements. The old man, probably, had no great confidence in Jack's honesty of intentions. Luckily no one found what Jack had been about with the gun, or it would have fared ill with him. Jack cast many an anxious glance through the embrasure, to catch the movements of the boats. There were a good many of them—that was one comfort. His friends were not so likely to be overpowered as he at first feared. Evidently another ship, or perhaps more, had joined the *Archer* and accompanied her boats up the river. He could not help also turning round to see what the old Spaniard was doing. There he stood on his perch surveying his motley crew—the impersonation of an evil spirit—so Jack thought. Yet he looked quite calm and quiet, with a smile—it was not a pleasant one, however—playing on his countenance. In a moment afterwards his whole manner changed; he sprang off the ground and clapped his hands, crying out loudly, "*Tira! tira, amijos.*" "Fire! fire, my friends! and send all those English to perdition." He was under the belief that the boats had just come in a direct line with his guns, and that every shot would tell on them. The Spaniards and blacks were not slow to obey the order. Off went the guns, and the small-arm men began peppering away till the whole fort was in a cloud of smoke. Jack delayed firing as long as he could, that he might be more certain that his shot would fly over the heads of his friends. He would have waited still longer, had he not seen a Spaniard near him cocking his pistol and giving a very significant glance towards him. He had already begun to stoop down to fire, when a bullet whistled by his head, and he heard the sharp voice of the old Spaniard, "Take that, young traitor, if you don't choose to obey orders."

Jack felt that he had had a narrow escape of his life. Looking along his gun, and seeing that the arc he believed the shot would make would extend far beyond the boats, he fired. He could not see where his shot went, for at the same moment the British, though at first not a little surprised at the warm reception they had encountered, had brought the guns in the bows of the boats to bear on the fort, and had opened a hot fire in return.

With loud cheers they advanced; but Jack guessed that they had something in store which would astonish the blacks much more than the round shot; nor was he mistaken. Up flew, whizzing into the air, a shower of rockets, which came down quickly into the middle of the fort, and made both Spaniards and negroes scamper here and there at a great rate, knocking each other over, shrieking out oaths and prayers in a variety of dialects, and trying to hide themselves from their terrific pursuers. It was as if a number of wriggling serpents had been turned loose among a crowd of people. The old Spaniard stamped and swore with rage, calling the people back to their guns, abusing them, and firing his pistols right and left at them to bring them to order. Jack ran a great risk of being shot in the *mêlée*, either by friends or foes. Oh, how he wished that the former knew the state of affairs inside the fort, and would make a dash at that moment and get into it! It was high tide, and the water covered the mudbanks. The favourable moment was however lost, and by the fierce energy of the little old Spaniard the defenders of the fort were driven back to their guns. Jack pretended to be very busy loading his. He had managed to get in a shot during the confusion, and one of the blacks next rammed in the powder and put another shot in after it. "All right! now blaze away, my hearty!" he sang out. He had piled up a good quantity of powder over the touch-hole, so there was an abundance of smoke, and the negro whom he addressed fully believed that the gun had gone off.

"Now more powder and shot, old boy," cried Jack; "ram away!"

Jack's gun was not likely to hurt his friends, but had the old Spaniard seen his tricks, he would very likely have had another bullet fired at him. Fortunately the old fellow was too much engaged. The whole fort was full of smoke, and the defenders, having got over their first alarm at the rockets, were blazing away with all their might. Jack caught sight of the boats for an instant, separating on either hand so as to avoid the direct fire from the fort, and then he heard in another minute that true hearty British cheer, which has so often struck terror into the hearts of England's enemies. On either flank there came pouring into the fort a fresh flight of rockets, and almost the next instant Jack saw the boats' bows run stem on to the mudbank, which almost surrounded the fort. In vain the seamen endeavoured to shove the boats over it—they stuck fast. Jack shouted as loud as he could, in hopes that his voice might be heard, for he caught a glimpse of Alick Murray in one of the boats and Paddy Adair in another, using every effort to get up to the stockade. Perhaps they heard him, for he saw them leap overboard, followed by their men, with the intention clearly of wading up to the stockade, ignorant of course of the deep ditch between them and it. Jack felt sure that they would be shot down by the blacks if they made the attempt. He could restrain himself no longer, but ran towards them, shouting out, "Back, back! you can't get in that way!" Whether they heard him or not he could not tell, for a heavy blow on the head was dealt him by the butt end of a pistol, the owner of which, one of his Spanish friends, would certainly have shot him had it been loaded, and he fell to the ground, stunned and helpless.

How long he thus lay he could not tell. It could not have been for any length of time, for the battle was still raging when he came to his senses. He instantly crawled to one of the embrasures, and looked out. The English had suffered severely. One boat lay on the mud, disabled, and the dead bodies of several men strewed the mudbank, which the falling tide had left dry. Then he turned his head, for he heard loud cheers and shouts, and cries and howls, on one side of the fort. A fresh attack, he suspected, had just been made. It was resisted with all the desperation of despair by most of the Spaniards and many of the blacks. The British were forcing their way in. He caught sight of the heads of the seamen surmounting the stockade, and then he saw that it was Alick Murray leading them on. The spectacle gave him fresh life. He jumped on his legs and gave a loud huzzah.

He had better have been silent. The old Spaniard, who had been flying about in every direction with the most wonderful activity, encouraging the people, pointing the guns, and showing himself the leading spirit of the gang, caught sight of him. It had now become evident that the fort would be taken; there was but one outlet by which the gang could escape; the ruffians began to give way. Numbers were wounded; many lay dead on the ground. Several of the fugitives passed him. He was hoping that the moment of his deliverance was at hand, when he felt his shoulder grasped by the little old Spaniard, and found himself dragged along by a power he could not resist. He struggled, but struggled in vain. Small as the old man was, he was all sinew and muscle; his clutch was like that of a vice. There was a fierce rush, blacks, Spaniards, and mulattoes were all mingled together; and good reason they had to run, for at their heels came fast a body of English seamen, slashing away with their cutlasses, and firing their pistols. Hemming, Murray, and Adair were leading them, and Jack recognised some of the officers of his own ship, the *Ranger*. He now knew how it was the expedition had been strengthened. He sought to escape from his captor. "If you shout, I'll shoot you!" said the old man, in English, grinning horribly. He was in hopes his old schoolfellows would have recognised him. Back he was hurried. Still he felt sure that his friends would overtake him. The retreating villains had got close to the barracoon, and not far from the last entrance to the fort. The seamen pressed on. There was still some space between the parties, when the old man fired his pistol into a cask sunk into the ground; a thick smoke came out of it. Back, back the pirates pushed. In an instant more a dense mass rose before them of earth, and stone, and timbers, horribly mingled with the arms and legs and bodies of human beings;—a mine had been sprung. Jack was in an agony of fear for the fate of his friends. He could see nothing of them. He observed only that the mine had taken effect under one end of the barracoon. The terrible shrieks and cries of its wretched inmates rang in his ears. A large number of them had been liberated, and with loud yells were following in the rear of the slave-dealers, for whom they served as an effective shield against the shot of the seamen. The slaves had been told that the English would kill them, so they ran away as soon as they were let out of the barracoon, as fast as the rest. The piratical crew, for such they really were, took their way up the hill, towards the king's residence, followed closely by the slaves and all the rabble who had escaped out of the fort. Jack expected that his friends would have pursued, and should he escape the pistol of the old gentleman who had him by the arm, he hoped before long to be rescued. They had not, however, got far up the hill when he saw flames burst forth from the barracoon, in which he knew, judging from those following, that a number of poor wretches had been left in chains, and he truly guessed that his countrymen were stopping to try and rescue them. The flames burst fiercely, and blazed up high, as they caught the dry inflammable timber of which the building was composed. Nothing could arrest their progress. The gallant seamen, he knew, would be dashing in among them in spite of the hot smoke, and doing their best to rescue the unfortunate wretches, but he feared that few would be saved. Even where he was he could hear their piteous shrieks, as the flames caught hold of them, chained as they were and unable to escape. As was too likely the pirates had set fire to the barracoon on purpose to delay the English; this plan succeeded perfectly. Often the same sort of thing has been done at sea, and when a slaver has been hard-pressed, blacks have been thrown overboard by the crew, to induce the English cruiser to stop and pick them up, and thus enable them to escape. Jack was dragged away up the hill, through the gateway of the town, and into the king's palace. That worthy was seated where Jack had first seen him, and employed much in the same way—smoking a pipe.

"Why have you brought him?" inquired his sable majesty of the little old Spaniard, whom Jack heard addressed as Don Diogo.

"He will serve as a hostage—they have got some of our people," was the answer.

"But will they give us back any of the slaves?" asked the king.

"Not one—whatever we may threaten," replied the Don, grinding his teeth. "They will not have got many, that is one comfort. A considerable number came with us, and most of those we were unable to set loose have been burnt. Our enemies have not gained much by their victory in any way, for we killed a good many of them, and destroyed some of their boats. We have had a desperate fight of it, though."

"It may be as well, then, not to kill the youngster, though it might be a satisfaction to you," said the king, looking at the Don.

"Not for the present," said Don Diogo. "We will keep him for a short time, and see how high his friends value him. If they refuse to give enough in exchange for him, as he can be of no use here, we can then shoot him!"

Jack, of course, could not understand all this conversation; but he made out enough to comprehend its tenor, which was certainly not of a character to enliven him. After a little time he found himself hauled out of the king's presence and thrust into a small hut by himself. A black, with a brace of pistols in his belt, and a musket which looked as if it would go off, was placed sentry over him. He either would not, or probably could not, reply to any of the questions Jack put to him, whenever he thrust his head in at the door, apparently to ascertain that his prisoner was all safe.

Thus passed the day. Towards the evening Jack began to be very hungry and very sick, and to wonder whether he was to be starved to death. He pointed to his mouth, and made every sign he could think of to show that he was hungry, but the sentry appeared to take no notice of him. At last, however, another man opened the door and placed a bowl of farina before him. It was not very dainty fare, but he was too sharp set to be particular, and so set to on it at once and gobbled away till he had finished it. He was wondering whether he should have to sleep on the bare ground, when the same man appeared with a bundle of Indian corn and other leaves, and threw them down in the corner, making a sign that they were to serve him as his bed. "Thank you, old fellow, I might go farther and fare worse." His spirits rose somewhat, for he judged rightly that his captors would not take so much trouble about him had they intended to murder him. He did not forget how mercifully his life had been preserved during the day, and he offered up his thanks on high before he threw himself on his bed of leaves to go to sleep.

He slept as soundly as a top all night, and when he awoke he could scarcely remember what had occurred during the previous day. Before long his former attendant appeared and placed another bowl of farina before him. "If they were cannibals, I might have some suspicions of their intentions," he said to himself; "they don't propose to eat me; but I know that I shall grow enormously fat if I go on long ramming down such stuff as this." However, as he was very hungry, he did swallow the whole of it. Hours passed away; no one else came near him. He fully expected to find the town attacked by the English, and waited impatiently to hear the sounds of the commencement of the strife; but, except that occasionally he heard tom-toms beating at a distance, and a few shots fired, everything in the town was quiet. It was sometime in the afternoon when two armed blacks appeared, and marched Jack out of his prison up to the king's palace. The king scarcely took any notice of him as he entered the reception-room. Soon after Don Diogo appeared.

"Will they give up the slaves?" asked the king.

"Not a bit of it," answered Don Diogo. "They say that if we kill that lad, then they will kill six times as many people of ours."

"That can't be helped," observed the king. "The people were born to be killed."

"Certainly," answered Don Diogo; "but there are some Spaniards among them, and I require their services."

"But is it not possible that they may come and burn my town? I have no wish for that to happen, even for your sake, my friend," said the king.

"Shoot the midshipman if they do," answered Don Diogo, turning a not very pleasant glance at Jack. "At present, however, they do not seem disposed to attack us. We have given them enough to attend to for the present. We killed a good number, and the boats have gone back with the wounded and prisoners."

"Then the young jackanapes of an officer may be shut up in prison again," said the king.

Scarcely had the order been given when a Spaniard rushed with fierce gestures into the room. "Those English have killed some of our friends, and we are resolved to have our revenge," he exclaimed, looking savagely at Jack, and handling his long knife.

"Don't kill him yet, though," said Don Diogo, with his usual coolness; "it will be time enough when he is of no further use. Take him away now."

These were not exactly the words Jack heard used, but he made out that such was their tenor.

Poor Jack! He was thrust rudely back into his dark, dirty hut, and the only food he received was a bowl of the ill-dressed farina, of which he was getting heartily tired. His spirits began to fall lower than they had ever before done. He saw no hope of escape; for he was certain that should the English threaten to attack the town, that instant he would put be to death, even should he escape the long knives of some of the Spaniards who had evidently a hankering for his blood. At last he fell asleep. Midshipmen have a knack of sleeping under the most adverse circumstances. His powers in that way were very considerable. It was daylight when he awoke; but there were no sounds to indicate that the negro population was astir. He could not help fancying that some attempt would be made by Captain Lascelles and Captain Grant to rescue him; but the day passed on, and no one except the man who brought him his insipid farina came near him. If he had had any mode in which to employ himself, he could, he thought, have the better borne his imprisonment and the dreadful state of suspense in which he was placed. All he could do was to walk about or sit on his bed of leaves with his head resting on his knees. Now and then, as the evening approached and his weariness increased, he jumped up and thought that he would force his way out and make a run for it: but then the feeling that he would most certainly be killed if he made the attempt, besides recollecting not knowing where he should run to, induced him to sit down again and chew the cud of impatience. Night came again. He was more melancholy than ever. He thought that he was deserted, or that probably his friends fancied he was killed, and would not trouble themselves further about him. He had no inclination to sleep even after it grew dark. He listened to the various noises in the village, or rather city it should be called. They amused him somewhat—the odd tones of the negroes' voices, the shouts, the laughter, the cries of babies, the barking of curs, the beating of tom-toms. At last, however, even they ceased, and he dozed away till he forgot where he was and everything that had happened. How long he had slept he could not tell; or rather, had he been asked he would have asserted that he had not been asleep at all, when he opened his eyes and saw by the light of the moon, which shone through a hole in the roof, the round face of a black boy looking down upon him with a friendly and compassionate expression.

Chapter Fifteen
In Search of Jack

Three of the *Archer's* boats were manned, and under the command of Lieutenant Hemming, Murray having charge of one and Adair of the other, were about to shove off and proceed up the river to search for their missing shipmates, when a sail was seen from the mast-head standing down toward them. She was quickly made out to be a large ship, and in a short time little doubt remained that she was an English frigate. Captain Grant, therefore, ordered the boats to delay their departure that a more powerful expedition might be forthwith despatched to compete with any enemies with whom they might fall in. "Hurrah! she's our own ship the *Ranger*," exclaimed Adair, who had gone aloft to have a look at the stranger, and now came below to make his report to Hemming; "Captain Lascelles is just the man to back up Captain Grant; if he knows of any barracoons or slavers' strongholds of any description, he will be for going in and blowing them all up without a moment's delay."

To prove that Adair was right, the *Ranger* soon after made her number, and at the same time another sail appeared to the northward. She turned out to be a brig-of-war, the *Wasp*. Captain Grant immediately went on board the frigate. Captain Lascelles entered fully into his plan, and instead of three, as soon as the *Wasp* came up, fortunately ten boats started on the expedition. Hemming was much gratified when Captain Lascelles declined to supersede him, assuring him that no one was better qualified to be entrusted with the command. There is always something very exciting in an expedition, no matter what the object, but when there is some uncertainty and danger, and a prospect of fighting, everybody gets into the highest possible spirits. Murray and Adair would have been in high spirits also had they not been anxious about Jack. Not that they were very unhappy. They had all so often missed each other, and been in difficulties and dangers, that they thought he would turn up somewhere before long. The boats dashed over the bar, and pulled up the south branch. As it was flood-tide they made rapid progress. They had gone some way up when they saw some one on the bank of the river beckoning to them. "A mere naked nigger," said Adair, looking through his glass, "not worth waiting for him I should think." Hemming seemed to be of the same opinion, for the boats continued their progress. Seeing this the negro set off running as fast as he could go, and was soon lost to sight in the jungle. Not long after they came to the end of a reach, and then it appeared that the river doubled back as it were on itself.

"Hillo, there is something in the water ahead of us," sang out Adair to Murray.

"It is a negro swimming off to us. Do you see him, sir?" said Murray to Hemming, whose boat was near his.

The negro lifted up his hand, as if trying to make a signal to them, and wishing to be taken into one of the boats. Hemming told Murray to pull towards the negro, and ascertain what he wanted. In a few minutes Murray had hauled a young negro lad into his boat. "What is it you want, my lad?" asked Alick, in his usual kind way. The poor negro evidently wanted to speak, but could not find English words enough to express himself, though he was very voluble when employing his own language. No sooner, however, had Murray returned to the line of boats and retaken his place near Hemming, than the black lad's countenance brightened up. "Ah, Massa Hemming, Massa Hemming," he exclaimed, trying to spring into the lieutenant's boat. He would in his eagerness have jumped overboard, had not some of the seamen held him back.

"He seems to know you, sir," said Murray.

"Is, is—me know Massa Hemming; is, is, kind massa," exclaimed the young negro, eagerly catching at the words.

"Let him come into my boat, and I'll hear what he has got to say," said Hemming, greatly to the delight of the negro, who clearly understood him. No sooner was the black lad on board Hemming's boat, than he seized his hand and kissed it, and showed every mark of affection. Then with evident eagerness and haste he made all sorts of signs, aiding them by such few words as he knew. "Man come—bad, no, no," he said, pointing up the river. Hemming understood that some one would come and try and mislead them, and that they were not to trust to him. Then Hemming tried to ascertain the fate of the missing boat's crew. His heart sank when the negro explained by signs that he could not mistake that they had all been murdered.

"No one escaped?" he asked.

The negro shook his head, no, not one survived, it appeared. Murray and Adair were soon made acquainted with the information, and then indeed they began to fear that Jack Rogers, their gallant jovial companion, was lost to them for ever. Grief and indignation, and a desire to punish the perpetrators of the deed, took possession of their hearts. That was but natural. It is difficult to distinguish between revenge, which is wrong, and a desire to punish evil-doers, when we ourselves are affected by their misdeeds.

The young negro, after talking away and making signs to Hemming for some time longer, desired to be put on shore. Murray was ordered to convey him there.

"Good man—good man, Massa Hemming," he kept saying all the time. "Take care, bad man come off shore."

As soon as he landed, off he darted again through the mangrove bushes, and was lost to sight.

"He seems to be an old friend of yours, sir," observed Murray when he got back.

"Yes, I find that he is a lad I once, when he was a young boy, jumped overboard to save in the West Indies after he had been taken out of a slaver," answered Hemming carelessly. "He made me out when we were in the river before taking the Spanish schooner, and has ever since been watching for an opportunity to speak to me. I cannot make out exactly what he wishes to guard us against—some treachery, I conclude. I could not fancy that he would have recollected me so long. It shows that blacks have grateful hearts."

Hemming sympathised much with Murray and Adair, for he knew of their attachment to Jack, and he fully believed that he had been lost with the rest. Bitter and sad were their feelings. "Oh, Jack, Jack!" muttered Adair in a tone of grief, "are you really gone?" The flotilla of boats proceeded some way farther, when a large canoe was seen paddling out towards them from the shore. A burly negro sat in the stern and made a profound salaam with his palm-leaf hat as he approached.

"Me first pilot in dis river," he shouted with a stentorian voice, "take me board—me come show way."

Hemming ordered his crew to cease rowing, and took him into his boat to hear what he had got to say for himself. He had, however, exhausted nearly all his vocabulary in his first address, and there was some difficulty in understanding him. In vain Hemming tried to gain some information about the missing boat and her crew. The negro either knew nothing or was resolved not to tell. At last he produced a book of certificates, and when Hemming had glanced over them he burst into a fit of laughter, and handed them back. The big negro looked exceedingly indignant, and, striking his breast, repeated vehemently—

"Me good man—me show way."

Many of the certificates had been far from complimentary to the negro, but still Hemming thought that he might be useful as a pilot, till he recollected the warning he had just before received.

"This is undoubtedly the very fellow I was to expect," he said to himself. "No, no, you go on shore; we can do without you," he exclaimed, addressing the negro.

The burly savage blustered and protested, but he was made to step into his canoe, which had been paddling alongside, and Hemming signified to him clearly that he must take himself off. They observed him watching them for some way; then he hauled up his canoe, and taking a path inland, they saw no more of him. They had pulled on for half an hour or more when Murray caught sight of a board floating in the water. He could scarcely account for the impulse which made him steer towards it and pick it up. His eye brightened as he looked at it.

"Hurrah!" he shouted joyfully; "hurrah! Jack Rogers is alive; here is a note from him. There is no doubt about it. It is short though—he says, 'A prisoner. Up south branch. Jack R.'" The shout was taken up by his own crew and the crews of all the other boats, and the banks of the stream rang with their loud hurrahs. This brief notice instigated all hands to make still greater exertions to try and recover Jack, wherever he might be. On they went; reach after reach of the winding river was passed, and they had got a long way up, higher than any of them had been before, when a shot, seeming as if it came out of the bank, flew over their heads. Another and another followed.

"We are just in front of the pirates' battery," exclaimed Hemming; "on, lads, on! we'll storm it without delay." The seamen required no further encouragement. A shower of rockets was first fired into the enemy's fort, and then on they dashed, in spite of the heavy fire of musketry, as well as of grape-shot and langrage, which was opened on them in return. To their rage and disappointment, the boats stuck on the mudbank just outside the stockades, which they only then discovered. Many of the seamen leaped out of the boats and attempted to wade onwards, but they either at once sank into the mud or fell forward into the deep ditch, where several were shot down before they could be rescued by their comrades, while others were drowned or smothered in the mud. It was horrible work. An enemy whom they despised was close to them, and yet could not be got at. Hemming, his heart burning with anger and grief at the loss of so many poor fellows and the almost hopelessness of success, ordered the boats to shove off, with the intention of making an attack on some other part of the fort. The blacks continued firing away under cover without much fear of being hit in return. It was melancholy to have to retire, and to see the bank, from off which the water had begun to recede, strewed with the bodies of those who a few minutes before were as full of life and energy as themselves. Before getting to any great distance, Murray thought he saw a channel to the right, which must run near the fort. He pointed it out to Hemming, who told him to lead the way. He was right; the negroes had neglected to fortify it, and in a few seconds the boats were close up to the stockades. Not a moment was lost in storming them and hauling them down. In rushed the gallant bluejackets, led on by Hemming, Murray, Adair, and other officers, and at length they got their black enemy face to face.

"There's Rogers, there's Rogers!" shouted Murray and Adair, for they both saw him at the same time. They were certain of it, though his features were considerably begrimed with powder, smoke, and dirt. This was incentive enough to make them push on with still greater haste, had they not been eager to punish the abominable slave-dealers and their crew of ruffians. The brave fellows little knew the terrible trap prepared for them. Murray and Adair had sprung on ahead, and believed that in another minute they would have rescued Jack from the grasp of his captors, when they felt themselves suddenly pulled back by Hemming and Will Needham.

" The hot flames were raging around them, and almost prevented them from performing their work of mercy."

The Three Midshipmen | 173

"Back, back, lads, back!" sang out the lieutenant. At that moment up ascended right before them a mass of earth and stones and wood, with a dense cloud of smoke and dust, accompanied by a terrific roar, and they felt themselves lifted off their feet and sent heels over head, while down upon them came showering all the more solid portions of the above-mentioned materials about their ears, as they lay half stunned and stifled and vainly endeavouring to rise. Another foot in advance, and they would have been blown to destruction. Hemming had seen the old Spaniard fire his pistol into the tub, and guessed what was coming. Murray and Adair felt themselves very much hurt, so indeed were Hemming and Needham; while several poor fellows were maimed or killed outright. The two schoolfellows, after lying stupefied for a few seconds, lifted up their heads and began to crawl out from the mass of ruins which surrounded them.

"Where's Jack?" exclaimed Murray.

"Where's Jack?" cried Adair, getting upon his legs and helping Murray, who was hurt more than he was.

These were the first words they uttered. He had not been out of their thoughts, in spite of the dreadful commotion. As the smoke cleared away they caught sight of the group of fugitives, among whom they supposed he was, ascending the hill which rose beyond the fort. They were eager to pursue, but when they looked round and saw so many of their companions disabled, and Lieutenant Hemming himself on the ground, they could not help fearing that pursuit would be hopeless. Still they were moving on, when Hemming, recovering himself, called them back.

"It is of no use, lads," he cried. "The scoundrels have escaped us this time. See, see, too, we have work here," As he spoke, flames burst forth out of the barracoon, part of which had been blown up by the mine. The seamen who could stand, wounded or not, rushed forward, led by their officers, to help the miserable slaves. They hacked away desperately to get them free of their manacles, trying to cut through the solid iron or the beams to which the chains were secured. Meantime the hot flames were raging around them, and almost prevented them from performing their work of mercy. Still, in spite of the fire, the heat, and the smoke, and the possibility of being again blown up, the undaunted fellows laboured on. Numbers of the poor slaves had been liberated, and several children had been carried off who would otherwise have been left with their mothers to perish; but at last the terrific element gained the upper hand. The seamen's clothes were literally scorched off their backs before they would quit the work of humanity on which they were engaged, but even they were at last obliged to retreat, leaving the miserable captives to their fate. Again and again, however, now one, now another, would make a dash in among the flames, and try to haul out some poor burning creature whose imploring cries their tender heart could not withstand. One gallant fellow was killed by the falling of a burning beam before they would desist altogether from their brave efforts.

By this time the retreating slave-dealers had got completely out of sight, and when Lieutenant Hemming looked round and saw the number of men he had lost, and the disabled state of some of his boats, and of so many of his followers, he felt that he could in no way be justified in attempting to continue the pursuit. An officer often shows his bravery and fitness for command as much by his discretion and by holding back as by pushing forward.

Hemming was just one of these men. If he thought a thing ought to be done, he did not stop to consider what others would say about it, he did it. He now ordered his party to collect, and having conveyed some of the lighter guns to the boats, and spiked and turned the others over into the mud, and set fire to what would burn in the fort, he ordered all hands to make preparations for embarking with the rescued slaves, as well as with four Spaniards, three of whom were wounded, and several negroes who had been captured. He had formed a plan which he hoped to carry out. Some time, however, was occupied in repairing two of the boats; one was so completely destroyed that he could not carry her off. Before all these arrangements were concluded and the party were prepared to embark, it was late in the day. Hemming wanted, by a show of retreating, to throw the slave-dealers and negroes off their guard; and then to make a sudden dash up the stream and to come upon them unawares, having previously sent down the river to the ships some of the boats with the captured slaves. The rest of the officers agreed to the plan as soon as he propounded it to them, and Murray and Adair were consoled at the thought of soon being able to return and attempt Jack's rescue. The state, however, of his wounded men, and the difficulty of navigating the river in the dark, compelled Hemming to bring up sooner than he had intended. A spot of high ground near the river which he thought might be easily defended induced him to land. Some bamboos and young trees were cut down to form a stockade, fires were lighted, sails were spread to form tents, and every preparation was made for passing the night.

"I only wish that Jack was here; he would enjoy this," observed Paddy to Alick. "I say, by hook or by crook, we must get him out of the hands of those ruffians. I've been turning the matter over in my mind, and I am resolved, if Mr Hemming does not think fit to go back and try and rescue Jack, that I will make the attempt myself. I could very soon black myself all over, and a nigger's costume will not take long to extemporise. I would soon frizzle up my hair, and with an old palm-leaf hat on the top of it, and my shirt with the tails hanging down, and tied round the waist by a piece of rope-yarn, I should look every inch of me a blackamoor."

"Capital," observed Murray; "I'll accompany you if we find better measures fail; but still I fear that we should run a great risk of being discovered by the blacks."

"Not a bit of it," answered Adair; "the very daring of the thing would throw them off their guard. They would never expect that two white people could so speedily turn themselves into niggers. Of course we must pretend to be dumb: though we can talk first-rate nigger gibberish in the berth, it won't pass current, I fear, among the natives of these parts."

"Not very likely. However, your idea of pretending to be dumb is good. I think I had better pretend to be an idiot," answered Murray. "But the question is, who will they take us for? where do you fancy they will think we have come from? My idea is that we should rather try and find where Jack is, without falling foul of any of the natives. I want to set off directly it is dark, clamber up the hill where we saw him last, and cut him out. It is to be done, I am certain, and Jack is well worth all the risk we should have to run."

"That he is," exclaimed Adair warmly. "There's nothing I wouldn't do for him, and I'm sure he would do anything for us."

The subject was fully discussed, and then the midshipmen went to Hemming, and asked leave to put their plan into execution. Hemming might on another occasion have been inclined to laugh at the proposal, but he was too anxious to get Jack out of the slavers' power, for he felt his hands tied somewhat with the fear of what the blacks might do to the midshipman should he attack their town. He was, therefore, ready to try any plan, however desperate, to recover Rogers. Having obtained the leave they wanted to put their plan into execution, Murray and Adair set to work to devise the details. As they could only hope to carry out their scheme at night, they agreed that they need not be very particular as to the correctness of their masquerade. There was no time to get any dye, but burnt cork well rubbed in with oil they agreed would answer the purpose. It was too late, however, to take any active steps that night. It was settled that the next morning the flotilla, with some parade, should proceed down the river, while they, with Dick Needham and a picked crew, should lie hid in the smallest boat till dusk the next evening; then they were to land and try and find out where Jack was.

Once discovering the locality of his prison, they fully believed that they could, as they called it, "cut him out as easily as many a rich Spanish galleon has in days of yore been cut out from an enemy's fort, even though protected by the guns of the fort."

The night passed away quietly. The party had expected an attack from the slave-dealers, but these gentry had received a sufficient notice of the warm reception they were likely to encounter, not to make the attempt. In the naming, however, Murray, who had the lookout while the rest were preparing to strike their tents, observed a party approaching with a white flag. He reported what he had seen to Lieutenant Hemming.

"The impudent scoundrels," he exclaimed; "no flag of truce ought to shelter them. However, while poor Rogers is in their power we must treat with them as we best can."

The party soon arrived at the temporary encampment. The most prominent person was the burly negro who had introduced himself down the river as a pilot, and there was a Spaniard and several blacks. The big negro was spokesman, as he professed to know more English than any of the rest. Hemming received them in a very haughty way.

"What is it you want? Have you come to excuse yourselves for firing on my boats and killing my people?" he asked in a stern voice.

It was difficult to understand exactly what the negro said in return, but Hemming made out that he knew nothing about firing on the boats, as he had not been at the fort, but that he had been sent by the king of the country to demand back some prisoners who had been taken while defending the territories of the said king against an unlawful attack made on them by the English boats. Also, there were some Spanish cavaliers, his honoured allies, who must be likewise restored to liberty: there were some slaves too, who must be given up, or the king would visit the English with his intense displeasure.

The long rigmarole speech, of which this was the substance, would have made Hemming laugh on any other occasion. However, now he merely replied, "Listen. Tell the king, or whatever he calls himself, that the English are here to punish evil-doers, to set slaves at liberty, to put a stop to the slave-trade, to encourage commerce, and to prevent wars. If the people we have caught are found to be pirates, as such they will be hung. We keep no terms with people who, like him, support piracy and the slave-trade."

Hemming said something more to the same effect. The negro had, however, a last card to play, which he fancied would win the game.

"Ah, then, if you kill our people, the king says he will kill a little officer we have of yours. His life may not be worth much, but he shall die." The negro grinned horribly as he said this.

"If he does," exclaimed Hemming furiously, "tell the king that we will never rest till we have pulled him off his throne and his town about his ears, and burnt up all his country. Now you have got my answer. Go." Hemming wisely would not condescend to say another word after this. He knew pretty well how to treat such barbarians. The sable ambassador and his motley suite, finding that nothing more was to be got out of the English officer, took his departure. Scarcely had he gone, when a figure was seen to creep out from among some bushes in the neighbourhood. It proved to be the negro lad who had warned them of the black pilot's intended treachery. He ran forward and threw himself at Hemming's feet, showing every sign of delight at finding him again. Hemming at once thought of asking him about Jack. The very thing it proved he had come about. He had heard of him, had gone and discovered where he was shut up, and understood that his captors talked of killing him should any harm befall their people who had been taken prisoners.—Hemming felt sure that he might be fully trusted, so did Murray and Adair. They therefore explained their plan to him, and asked him to assist them. This he at once joyfully undertook to do. Very little change in their plan was necessary. He agreed to act as their guide. They were to assume the character of slave boys belonging to a distant tribe whom he was conducting to his uncle, a chief of some influence in the country, and who was secretly favourable to the English. Wasser, the negro lad, assured them that he was very glad they had not ventured to make the attempt by themselves, as their detection would have been almost certain. Hemming delayed as long as he could before embarking, and he promised to wait for Murray and Adair some way down the river while they went on their expedition. Their boat, with Dick Needham, their new friend Wasser, and three other picked men, all well-armed, shoved off with the other boats, and soon darting in towards a sheltered nook, which they had before observed, lay as they believed perfectly concealed from all passers-by. Wasser, however, advised them to cut down boughs, and to fasten them in front of the boat. This they did, and, as Paddy observed, they could not desire to pass the day in a pleasanter way than in a shady bower with nothing to do and plenty to eat.

Chapter Sixteen
A Flight for Life

The time passed slowly by while the *Archer's* boat, with Murray, Adair, and Dick Needham aboard, and the young African lad Wasser, lay hid under the bank of the river, waiting for the time when they might sally forth to the rescue of Jack Rogers. Everybody was eager for the moment, for all longed to have him safe among them.

Wasser's deep gratitude to Hemming was very remarkable, after a separation of so many years, as was also his recollecting him. Murray felt sure that if any one could rescue Jack Rogers, Wasser was the person to do it. The day at length passed away, and after the party had taken a supper, as soon as Wasser thought it was safe, they issued forth from their leafy bower, and with rapid strokes pulled up the stream towards the fort which had been the scene of contest. Wasser remarked that none of the blacks would be venturing there at night, and that it would be the best place for the boat to remain at. Murray and Adair only landed. Needham had directions to wait for them till within an hour of daylight, and then, if they did not appear, to conclude that they were taken, and to pull down as hard as he could to inform Mr Hemming, and to bring him up to their assistance.

Wasser led the way, Alick and Paddy following close after him. Little would any of their friends have recognised in the two half-naked blackamoor lads the neat midshipmen who were wont to walk the deck of Her Majesty's ship *Ranger*, in all the pride of blue cloth, gold-laced caps, and gilt buttons. Now, except a pair of scanty drawers, a shirt fastened round the waist with a piece of rope-yarn, and a tattered straw hat, clothes they had none. Their feet were tolerably hard, from the custom in which they indulged, in common with most midshipmen, of paddling about without shoes or stockings when washing decks. They were not however unarmed, for both of them had a brace of pistols and their dirks stuck in belts concealed by their shirts. It was curious also to see one of the despised negro race taking the lead as Wasser did on the present occasion.

They landed close to the fort, when without hesitation he led the way inland, and then after a little time they found that they were going up hill.

Up, up they went for a long distance, it seemed a mile or more, over a well-beaten path.

It was not so dark as it had been. The light was increasing, it was that of the rising moon. They found that they had arrived in front of some palisades. They formed the wall to the negro city. Wasser signified that they must get over it to see their friend, and conducted them to the left, along the outside of the palisade. At last they got to a spot where he showed them that they might climb over, and whispered that there were no houses near whose inhabitants might discover them. The moon, as I was saying, was rising, so there was no time to be lost in reaching Jack's prison before the light might render the approach more difficult. Cautiously they crept on under the shadow of the houses. The inhabitants appeared to be asleep. Now and then a dog barked, but they saw no one. At last, at the end of a street, they came to an open space, in which stood a solitary hut. Wasser pulled up, and said, "Dere your friend." How Alick's and Paddy's hearts longed to get at him! Their impulse was to run across the square and to let him out, but at that moment a sentry appeared from the other side of the hut with a musket on his shoulder. Though they did not fear the musket, they knew he might possibly let it off and alarm the town, so they stood under the dark shade of a wall, deliberating what was to be done. They watched him for some time, and ascertained that, like a clockwork figure, he always made the same round at the same pace.

"We shall have time to get across the square and to seize him before he makes his round," observed Murray. Adair signified that he thought the same, as did Wasser.

"Then," added Murray, "you and I, Paddy, will seize him, while Wasser lets Jack out of the prison, and he can come and help us bind and gag the sentry."

"Now is our time," whispered Murray. "One, two, three, and away!" Down the square they dashed at full speed. Paddy leaped like a wild man of the woods on a sudden on the astonished sentry's back, and pressed his hand tightly over his mouth, while Murray grasped his musket, putting his hand on the pan, to prevent it going off (he need not have taken so much trouble, as it had no flint in it), while Wasser climbed up to the top of the hut, where he had ascertained there was a hole. It was his honest countenance Jack saw looking down upon him. Jack little thought all the time how near his friends were, and what essential service they were rendering him. Wasser put down his hand, and Jack catching it, Wasser, with a strong tug, enabled him to grasp some of the rafters. Jack very quickly was on the roof, and seeing two negro lads struggling with the sentry, guessing that they were in some way trying to serve him, leapt down to help them. The sentry had very little chance against four stout lads, and so they soon had him down and gagged, and dragged inside the hut.

"Now run, run," whispered Wasser, "no moment lose."

Away they all ran as hard as they could pelt. They reached the palisade and began to scramble over it. Jack had not recognised any of his deliverers, but he was much obliged to the little black fellows for the help they had afforded him. Just then a dog barked, then a man's voice was heard shouting, then another and another joined in the outcry. There could be no doubt that the town was aroused.

The wild hubbub in the negro town increased. The midshipmen and their sable ally had too much reason to fear that they should be captured. Wasser led the way over the palisade, Jack followed, Alick and Paddy brought up the rear. Jack had not yet discovered his friends, as in consequence of their dread of being discovered no one had spoken. Jack only thought that some negro lads, for some reason or other, had come to his assistance.

"Run, run!" cried Paddy, as they jumped down on the outside of the palisades. There was little necessity for his saying this though.

"Who are you?" exclaimed Jack, the truth breaking oh him.

"Alick—Terence," they answered.

"Oh, capital! just what I should have thought you'd have done, if I had fancied it possible," said Jack. "Then let's stop and fight them."

"No, no," said Wasser, "too many men come to fight. Run on, run on!" His advice was evidently the wisest, so run they did, and at a very great rate too. It was clear that by some means or other the sentry had made himself heard. He probably did not describe, in the most complimentary of terms, the people by whom he had been knocked down, gagged, and bound. Some horrible fetish had done it, that of course he believed and asserted. The blacks must have thought that their town was attacked, and very quickly tumbled up from their beds (they had not many clothes to don) and flew to their arms. Shots were heard in different quarters, and the previous stillness of the night was rudely broken by shouting and hallooing of men, barking of dogs, and crying of children, and screaming of women to each other to inquire what it was all about. The noise, however, was not a thing to be much-dreaded. It showed that the negroes were awake, but it was also pretty evident that they had not yet begun the pursuit, so Jack and his companions thought. Wasser led them back into the chief pathway up the hill. There was no other by which they could reach the boat. They had, therefore, to pass very close again to the principal gate of the city. There was a great chance of their being seen as they did so. There was no help for it, so on they dashed. Never had any of them ran faster in their lives, for they were running for their lives. Down the hill they went. They heard a shout; some men were rushing out of the gate of the city in pursuit.

"On, on—mans come—neber fear," cried Wasser.

"I should think not," observed Jack, but he did not slacken his speed. Their pursuers came on at a great rate. They knew the ground and their feet were accustomed to it. Alick and Paddy found theirs hurt horribly, while Jack, having on shoes, could not run as fast as the negroes. It was a long way to the boat. Happily, however, the path wound about a good deal, or probably their pursuers, who had arms, would have fired, that is to say, if the arms had locks and were loaded—slight points in which negro soldiers are not always very particular. Luckily they had to go down the hill instead of up it. At length they reached the bottom; still they had some way to go. The voices of their pursuers grew louder and louder. They fancied that they heard some Spaniards among them, uttering their usual horrid oaths. They knew that those wretches were far more barbarous than their black brethren. With the negroes they might have had some chance of escape, with the Spanish pirates none. On they went. They dared not look round. There was a sharp report of a pistol—a bullet flew by them. Another and another followed. Happily, as their pursuers were running, they could not take steady aim; still they were getting dreadfully near. Another enemy was added to the pursuers. The midshipmen heard the baying of a bloodhound. There could be no doubt about the sound. The brute was still at a distance though; probably let loose by some of the Spaniards not roused till late to join in the chase. Murray and Adair remembered their pistols, and it was a satisfaction to feel that they might possibly shoot him before they were torn to pieces. Not that the task would prove an easy one though. Just then appeared before them through the dark foliage a sheet of silvery hue; it was the river. The sight nerved their limbs afresh; they had need of something to encourage them. Scarcely thirty yards behind them came the savage rabble. The fugitives had difficulty to keep ahead of them. Fierce were the shouts of blacks and Spaniards, and more savage was the baying of the bloodhound. Paddy, who brought up the rear, could scarcely help shrieking out, for he felt the brute close at his heels. He cared much more for it than he did for the bullets. He was certain that in another moment the animal would have hold of his legs, when up there started, just in front of the fugitives, honest Dick Needham and two seamen, well-armed with muskets and cutlasses. Dick, springing forward, made a cut at the savage brute, which almost severed its head from its body, and then shouted, "Back, back, you villains, or we'll blow you into the sky!" and then, in another tone, he cried out, "Run for the boat, young gentlemen, we'll cover your retreat." No one required to be told this a second time, and Needham and the seamen, facing the crowd of blacks, and firing as they retreated, kept the enemy completely at bay till the midshipmen and Wasser had reached the boat. They were not long in jumping in after them, and, shoving off, away they pulled, shouting with delight at their success, and leaving their enraged pursuers swearing and grinning with rage on the shore.

"A miss is as good as a mile," cried Paddy, as he seized one of the oars; but they were not altogether out of the fire. Many of the people collected on the shore had muskets, and began blazing away at them, several of the shots striking the boat, and others coming uncomfortably near; this only made them pull the faster however. While some of the slave-dealers' people were firing, others ran along the bank, and, launching several canoes, paddled off in pursuit. This was much worse than their shooting. The British boat, a light gig, pulled well, but the canoes would probably paddle faster. Nothing daunted, however, Jack and Murray set to work to reload all the muskets and pistols, to make as good a fight of it as they could, should they be overtaken. They could count the canoes as they appeared darting out from among the bushes on the banks—one, two, three, four, five, six, came out one after the other. It was a long way down to the spot where Hemming had said he would await their return. Before they could reach it the blacks must have overtaken them, unless Jack and Murray could manage to pick off some of their chief men, and so perhaps frighten them back; both said that they would do their best to effect that object, however. Wasser sat quiet; he could do no more for the present—not all men even *can* sit quiet. The canoes drew nearer and nearer. However, a sailor feels very differently on the water and on shore, for even when compelled to run away on his own element, he can face his enemy and show fight: this Murray and Rogers now did to some effect. The canoes had got well within range of their muskets: the sooner, therefore, they began to fire, the better chance they would have of stopping their pursuers. Old Brown Bess, however, was never celebrated for carrying very straight, and neither Jack nor Alick did much execution. At the same time, now and then, they saw the negroes bob their heads as the bullets whistled unpleasantly near them. Some of the people in the canoes fired in return, but, as Dick Needham observed, they might as well have been firing at the moon for all the harm they did.

The English boat pulled on, the canoes following. A long reach was before them. Surely and steadily the canoes were gaining on the boat. The greater portion of the distance to the end of the reach was got over, and now in another five minutes, perhaps less, the canoes would be up with her. "While there is life there is hope;" so thought Jack and his companions, and so they continued making every effort to escape. The voices of the negroes chattering away in the headmost canoe, sounded very loud. Jack and Murray had ceased firing—for the best of reasons—they had come to the end of their ammunition. Perhaps it was fortunate; they could have done no good, and would only the more have enraged the negroes. The latter also had not fired for some time, probably on the same account.

"I feel somewhat inclined to squeak, as a hare does when a greyhound catches hold of her, but I won't," said Jack, as the headmost canoe got almost up to them. "You two in the bows, Johnson and Jones, keep pulling, while all the rest lay about them to drive off the blacks. We are not going to be beat by a parcel of pirates and niggers."

The men cheered at Jack's address, and, grasping their cutlasses, stood ready to obey his directions. Now came the tug of war. The other canoes got up and crowded round them, but again the undaunted seamen cheered, and firing their pistols right and left among the pirates, laid about them most lustily with their well-sharpened cutlasses. As they cheered, what was their surprise to hear their cheers answered, and at the same moment five dark objects on the water were seen coming round the next point. Murray exclaimed that they were men-of-war boats. They must have made out that their presence was much needed. On they dashed towards the canoes. The pirates saw them coming, and dared not stand their onslaught. Before they turned to fly, they made a desperate attempt to capsize the boat, and to carry off some of the English as prisoners. They very nearly got hold of Paddy, whom, in spite of his costume and colour, they had discovered not to be a negro; but Jack and Alick hauled him back, with the loss only of part of his shirt. Poor Wasser was in the same manner saved by Needham; had they got him they would, to a certainty, have killed him. The other boats, now dashing on, put them to flight, and off they went at a great rate up the stream. Hemming himself had come to their rescue. He had felt some misgivings about them, and had returned, intending, if he did not meet them, to land and threaten to ravage the black king's whole territory with fire and sword if they were not given up. Jack was received with warm congratulation by his friends; but there was not much time for compliments, as Hemming instantly went off in pursuit of the canoes. The canoes paddled fast, but the men-of-war boats pulled just then faster, and the negroes and their Spanish allies, finding escape problematical, ran the canoes in on the bank, and, leaping on shore, left them to their fate. As they were undoubtedly employed to assist, directly or indirectly, the nefarious slave-trade, Hemming set fire to them all with the exception of one, which he carried off as a trophy. As it was important to get on board as soon as possible, Hemming pulled at once back to the place where the rest of the boats, with the prisoners and liberated slaves, had been left. They were all safe, and by noon the next day the expedition returned once more to the ship. Sad indeed was the loss they had to report—so many fine fellows cut down in a nameless fight with a band of rascally pirates. The captives not only exonerated Hemming of all blame, but assured him that they believed he had done all that a man could do under the circumstances of the case. Everybody on board both ships welcomed Jack, and poor Wasser was highly delighted with the way he was received and praised for the assistance he had afforded in rescuing him from the slave-dealers; nor did Murray and Adair fail to get their meed of applause.

"I am much obliged to you for all what you have to say," answered Paddy, laughing, "but I wish some of you would tell me how to wash a blackamoor white. I have heard that it was a difficult operation. The burnt cork would have come off by itself, but Dick Needham rubbed in the oil and grease so hard that soap and water won't do it."

Doctor McCan, when applied to, looked rather grave, and, after he had heard the circumstances of the case, delivered a long lecture to prove that black powder rubbed in in that way, in such a climate, when the pores were open, would take root and become ineradicable.

Terence saw a twinkle in the doctor's eye, which made him suspect a quiz, and the laughter of Jack, Alick, and some of his other messmates who stood round, confirmed this suspicion. At first he felt that he ought to be very indignant, but his good-humour seldom kept away many seconds together, and he quickly joined in the laugh against himself. He then accompanied Alick into the hospital, where, in a tub with some hot water and soap, and some alkali the doctor gave them, they very soon got washed white, and returned on deck as spruce-looking midshipmen as they usually appeared. Theirs and Jack's great regret was, that as Alick had to go back to the brig, and they must join the frigate, they would again be separated. Rogers and Adair were once more or board the *Ranger*, with Lieutenant Hemming and Needham, and the rest of the people who had escaped the various dangers to which they had been exposed since they quitted her. Captain Lascelles was of opinion that it would be necessary to inflict a severe punishment on the slave-dealing king and his white allies, and accordingly resolved to send another expedition up the river without delay, to burn his town and any other barracoons which might be in the neighbourhood; or to induce him to break off all intercourse with the Spanish slave-dealers. The Commodore was able to carry out his object even sooner than he expected, by the arrival of two other brigs, the *Rambler* and the *Tattler*. Jack and Terence were very much disappointed when they found that they were not to go. To their earnest request to be allowed to volunteer, Captain Lascelles replied, "I admire your spirit, my lads, but as you are not made of iron, and I cannot afford to expend my midshipmen, others must take their share of the work. You are both of you already as thin as thread-papers."

Certainly by this time they had become very brown and wiry, and bore but a slight resemblance to the rosy, jolly-looking midshipmen they were when they left England. Hemming, however, again went in command, and Wasser begged that he might accompany him as interpreter. With somewhat of an envious feeling the midshipmen saw a considerable flotilla of boats cross the bar and pull up the river.

The day passed away, and so did the greater part of the next, and still the boats did not reappear. Captain Lascelles became somewhat anxious. Hour after hour went by. "There they come, there they come!" was shouted by several who were on the lookout on deck. Not only were all the boats seen, but several large canoes were in their company. In one of the latter, as they drew near, Jack recognised his friend, the negro king, seated in the stern and dressed in the same magnificent uniform in which he had appeared in his own palace. He seemed perfectly happy, and was smoking a pipe with true regal dignity. The side was manned to receive him, and with a grand air he stepped on deck, making a profound bow and a wide flourish with his cocked-hat. Captain Lascelles, on this, went forward to meet him, and, ordering up some cushions from the cabin, begged him to be seated and to continue smoking his pipe, while he ascertained from Hemming the particulars of the expedition. The expedition had proceeded up the greater part of the way towards the fort without meeting any one. When near it a canoe appeared approaching them. In it were the stout pilot, Jack's friend, and three other blacks rigged out in what they considered full fig. They came, they said, as ambassadors from the king. He wished to inform the English that Don Diogo and the rest of the Spanish slave-dealers had gone away overland, to the south—he could not tell where—and that, as he wished to be friends with everybody, he hoped that no further harm might be done to his country. Hemming replied that he was very glad to hear this, but that profession was not practice, and that he must have stronger proofs of his sincerity. The pilot said the king hoped all the English would visit his capital. Hemming answered, that half would go and half would stay to look after the boats. Whether treachery was intended or not, the idea was, it appeared, abandoned, and Hemming, with thirty of his men well-armed, proceeded up the hill to the king's capital. They found it to be a tolerably strong place, and though they might have taken it by storm, not, perhaps, without difficulty and loss. The king received them very courteously, and seemed to be really a sensible fellow, perfectly alive to his own interests. During a long palaver, Hemming explained to him that if he persisted in carrying on the slave-trade, the English would destroy his barracoons, and injure and annoy him in every possible way; but that if he abandoned it, and refused to have anything to do with slave-dealers, but would engage in commerce, encourage agriculture, well treat his people, and act like an honest man, they would assist and encourage him in every possible way; that the Queen of England would be friends with him, call him her well-beloved brother, and send him presents of far greater value than any he got from the Spaniards. So eloquently, indeed, did Hemming put the case before him, that his negro majesty expressed his eagerness to come off to the good queen's big ship and ratify the treaty, which he desired might forthwith be drawn up. Captain Lascelles lost no time in clenching the matter. All sorts of presents were bestowed on the black sovereign; a gun, some crockery, a pair of boots, a tooth-comb, a pair of epaulets, and half a dozen gaily coloured pocket-handkerchiefs, the pilot and the other chiefs coming in for a share of the good things, the captain hinting that this was only a forestalment of what they might expect if they behaved well. Highly pleased with all that had occurred, under a salute of eleven guns from the frigate, and more than half-seas over, the negro potentate and his great ministers of the realm, and other followers, betook themselves to the shore.

"They are slippery as their own skins," observed the Commodore; "we must have a sharp look on them, to keep them to their engagements."

The *Ranger* had captured several slavers, and sent them away to Sierra Leone for adjudication, and had driven many more off from the rivers into which they were bound to take in their cargoes, when, being under easy sail, about six miles off the coast, a large schooner was seen in-shore of them. Though all sail was made in chase, as the schooner increased her distance, Captain Lascelles ordered two boats to be manned in order to pursue her. To their great delight Jack got command of one, the cutter with eight men, and Adair of the other, a gig with six, many of the other officers being away in prizes. Their chief object was to come up with her before the setting in of the sea-breeze. Both boats, however, pulled badly, being soddened from having been so constantly in the water, besides which they leaked not a little. However, Jack and Paddy had learned that perseverance conquers all difficulties. Hot, as usual, was the sun. "Another warm day, Jack," cried Terence, as they pulled away; "I wonder how much marrow we shall have left in our bones and how much fat outside them when we get home."

Two hours and a half passed before they got up with the chase. The gig, from pulling best, was ahead. Jack did not grudge his messmate the honour, though he liked to be first when he could. The schooner, with all her sweeps out, as the boats neared her, put her helm up, and tried to run them down, opening at the same time a sharp fire of musketry. They, however, were too quick for her, and, pulling on either side, each man seized his musket and let fly in return. Loading again with the greatest coolness, as they passed her, they poured in another volley. The sweeps being rigged out, prevented them from climbing up by the chains.

"Never mind," cried Jack, "let us try the quarters." He pulled up to one quarter, Adair to the other, and before the slavers knew where they were going, the boats had hooked on, the seamen, led by their two gallant young officers, were springing over the low quarters of the schooner. Adair, however, got a severe lick on the shoulder, which would have sent him back into the boat had not one of his men given him a shove up; while Jack got an ugly gash on his arm from a cutlass, and would have had his head laid bare, had not Dick Needham's trusty weapon interposed to save him. All this time the slaver's crew were firing away down into the boats. One of the cutter's men was shot, and fell over. A messmate, Brown, attempted to lift him up, but he sank down like a piece of lead.

"It's all over with him," cried Brown, springing over the bulwarks, and resolved to avenge him. It was too true. He had been shot through the heart. A like fate befell one of the gig's crew. Still, with diminished numbers, the British fought on, but the odds were fearfully against them. They had, however, gained a footing on the slaver's deck, and as they had cutlasses and pistols in their hands, which they well knew how to use, they felt themselves to be on equal terms with six times their number of the sort of mongrel wretches who made up the slaver's crew. The latter at the same time seemed in no way daunted, and fought on with the greatest desperation. Hitherto neither Jack nor Adair had made out who were the officers of the wretches opposed to them, for the smoke hung so thickly over the deck, crowded as it was with people of every hue and every variety of costume, that it was difficult to distinguish one from the other. At last Jack caught sight of a little man, urging on his companions. The voice too he had heard before. A puff of wind cleared away the smoke: Jack recognised his old enemy, Don Diogo. The Don knew him also. "Ah, ah, have you come to be killed?" sang out the little man, with a horrid grin. "Cut him down, cut down the little spy, my men. He was one of those who destroyed our barracoons and deprived us of our property. The sea-breeze will soon be up to us, and we may laugh at the frigate. Revenge, revenge!" Instigated by these shouts from their fierce chief, the slaver's crew, uttering loud imprecations, made a desperate rush against the English, and Jack, in spite of the gallant defence made by those around him, found himself brought on his knee to the deck.

Chapter Seventeen
Aboard the Prize

Don Diogo and his companions did not know what Englishmen were made of if they thought that they were going to win the day without a hard fight for it. Adair, wounded as he was, threw himself before Jack, and, aided by Needham and some of his best men, pistoled some of the Spaniards and cut down others, hurrahing so loudly, and charging so fiercely, that the rest, in spite of the little Don's exhortations, gave way before them. They pushed on till they reached the mainmast, where a resolute stand was made by the slaver's crew. During this time Jack recovered sufficiently again to join in the conflict. The little Don, seeing how things were going, rallied a number of his people around him, evidently prepared to make a stand to the last, and Jack, from what he had observed of his character, was fully convinced that he would make some desperate attempt to destroy them, even perhaps by blowing up the schooner and all on board.

Fortunately the hatches of the schooner's decks were open to give air to the unfortunate slaves confined below. They all the time were uttering the most fearful shrieks and cries, not knowing what was going to happen. Pressed backwards, several of the pirate's crew were tumbled down the hatchways among the negroes, adding to the confusion and dismay below. Others, pressed by Jack, who was fighting his way forward on the starboard side, leaped overboard, and, to avoid the cold steel of the avenging British, found that death from the ravenous sharks to which they had consigned so many of their black fellow-creatures. Although some gave way, others kept rallying round the mainmast, and so Adair had to keep them engaged to prevent them turning and attacking Jack in the rear. So hotly was he engaged, however, that he had no time to look about him. A loud shout made him turn his eyes for a moment forward, and then he saw Jack, who had gained the forecastle, waving his cutlass in triumph. The Spaniards, who had hitherto shown a bold front, on hearing the shout, and seeing that their chance of victory was gone, threw themselves pell-mell down the hatchways among their companions, who had by this time regained their legs. What was bad, they had also kept possession of their arms, and began to fire upon the English. The seamen could easily have shot them, but the cowardly scoundrels retreated among the chained slaves, believing that their enemies would not dare to fire, for fear of wounding the poor blacks also. They counted, however, without their host. Never was there a cooler fellow than Dick Needham, and, getting his musket ready, he ran forward, and judging where the Spaniards had stowed themselves, picked out a couple of them from the very middle of the blacks; then leaping down, cutlass in hand, followed by three of his shipmates, they very soon made the rest of the wretches cry out for quarter. When Jack and Terence looked around the deck they found it cleared—not a little to their surprise. What had become of Don Diogo?

"The villain must have gone below, and will be blowing us all up!" exclaimed Terence, rushing aft.

Forward he certainly was not, or Jack would have seen him. They both, pistol in hand, rushed into the cabin, expecting to have a desperate encounter with the fierce little Spaniard. The door gave way before them.

"Hillo! the fellow is not here," cried Jack.

"Then he's concealed somewhere," answered Paddy. "It's very unpleasant to feel that any moment he may be sending us up like rockets into the sky. I wish that we could rout him out before he commits any mischief."

Just then they were recalled on deck by the shout of one of their men. They hurried out of the cabin, and, looking over the quarter, they saw what they would have perceived before had they looked in the right direction. The Don, with six or seven of his followers, had jumped into their own gig, and was pulling away with might and main towards the shore. Jack and Terence at first thought of following him in the cutter, but then there was the danger of the Spaniards left on board rising, and overpowering the rest of the English. He also would certainly not yield without a most desperate resistance.

"The Don will say that exchange is no robbery," exclaimed Paddy, "we had better let him go. He has got our gig, and we have got his schooner, and a very magnificent craft she is, with 400 or 500 slaves on board. We can well spare him the gig."

Jack agreed to this, but suggested that if the sea-breeze reached them soon, they might still catch the Don by the ear. Meantime they set to work to secure the slaver's crew. Many of the villains had stowed themselves away among the slaves, and were endeavouring to let them loose, telling them that the English had come to murder them, and that their only chance of saving their own lives was to rush upon deck and to murder the English instead. Happily the attempt was discovered before many of the negroes were set at liberty, and the slaver's crew were all knocked down and, having both hands and feet lashed together, were brought on deck and placed in a row under the bulwarks.

Jack saw the breeze coming, and gave an order to trim sails to take advantage of it so as to go in pursuit of the gig with Don Diogo in her. The frigate lay about eight miles off and of course had not perceived the escape of the Don. She being more in the offing, would get the sea-breeze first. Jack and Terence watched her trimming sails, and then her white canvas began to bulge out, and on she came gliding proudly towards them. Not long afterwards they got the breeze. To tow the cutter would have impeded them, so they dropped her to be picked up by the frigate and stood after the gig. Don Diogo had got a long start, but still, from the gig pulling heavily, as they knew to their cost, they did not despair of overtaking her. Everything was done to increase the schooner's speed, as it was important to get hold of one of the most daring slave-dealers and slave-captains on the coast — a man whose head had grown grey in the vile traffic in which he was engaged, and who had already spent half a dozen fortunes made by it.

"Paddy, I believe we shall catch the Don after all," exclaimed Jack, who had been watching the gig through a glass, and at the same time inspecting the coast beyond. "I can make out no creek for him to run into, and if he attempts to beach that boat he will be swamped to a certainty."

"And serve him right too," answered Terence. "But, hillo, what is that for?" As he spoke a shot fired from the frigate came whizzing over their heads. Another and another followed in rapid succession. One of them flew directly between their masts.

"I don't like to heave-to, or we shall lose our chance of catching the Don," observed Jack; "but this is getting rather too serious to be looked upon as a joke." It was, indeed, for in another second, three or four more shot came crashing through the sails and against the spars of the schooner, one of which, the foretop-gallant yard, was shot away.

"We must signalise them, and beg them to be aisy," cried Terence. "But, hillo, I say, Jack, who could have left that abominable flag flying at the peak?" There, sure enough, at the peak of the schooner flew out the often disgraced flag of Spain.

"We'll haul it down, and settle that point afterwards," said Jack, suiting the action to the word and hauling down the flag. He was but just in time to save the schooner from a tremendous peppering, which the frigate, now ranging close up astern, had prepared for her. Jack ran up the rigging nearest the frigate, and pointed ahead to show that he was chasing something;

indeed, by that time the gig when looked-for must have been seen clearly from the deck of the frigate.

"I am glad we did not fire into you, my lads," shouted Captain Lascelles through his speaking-trumpet. "You've done well—very well, but why did not you haul down the slaver's flag?"

"We'd so much to do, we never saw it, sir," shouted Jack in return. "There's the slaver's captain—we're after him."

"Stand in as close as you can, but don't get on shore, though," cried the captain.

"Ay, ay, sir," answered Jack, well pleased to follow the orders given.

The frigate stood on for some distance after the gig, but she had to be hove-to that the depth of water might be ascertained, and this gave the Don an advantage of which he did not fail to profit. Though guns were continually fired at him, the gig was too small an object at that distance to enable even the best of marksmen to hit her with any certainty. When the frigate hove-to, the schooner once more passed her. Nearer and nearer she drew to the shore.

"We must take care not to wreck our well-won prize," observed Jack to Terence, and a lead and line having been found, he wisely sent a hand into the chains, to heave it as soon as he had rounded the schooner to. Well was it that he did so, for in a very few minutes more the schooner would have been on shore. It was provoking, however, to see the wicked old Spaniard pulling on triumphantly. They watched the gig as long as they could with their glasses. She disappeared amid a cloud of foaming surf, which seems ever, even in the calmest weather, to be breaking on that shore.

"The old fellow has escaped us now, but we will still have him some time or other—depend on that," said Jack, shutting up his glass. "However, we have destroyed his barracoons, and now we've captured his schooner— that's one consolation. He can't love us, though."

Truly, indeed, did Don Diogo nourish a bitter desire for revenge against the British generally, and the officers and the crew of the *Ranger* especially, which he was one day destined to have an opportunity of gratifying to the full. The frigate's studding-sails being rigged in, she, with her prize in company, shaped a course for Sierra Leone. Both Jack and Terence had been so severely handled when boarding, though they did not feel much of their wounds during the excitement of chasing the Don, that it was necessary for them to return on board the frigate to be under the doctor's hands, while another officer was put in charge of the prize. This was a great disappointment, but Captain Lascelles promised them that they should have command of the next prize the frigate might take. Having seen the prize some way on her course, the *Ranger* stood back to her cruising ground to the southward. In consequence of head-winds and calms she made but slow progress, and thus some weeks slowly passed away after the events I have described, before her people had much work to do. This was a great advantage, as it enabled Jack and Terence and the sick and wounded men to recover, away from the noxious air of the coast.

At length it became advisable to communicate with King Bom-Bom, whose prisoner Jack had been, and as both he and Terence knew the river, they were ordered to proceed up it, to deliver the message, and to return as soon as possible. I ought to have said that Wasser had attached himself to his old friend Hemming, and had entered regularly as a seaman on board the frigate. A very steady and careful lad he was too. He now went with the expedition to act as interpreter. The boat crossed the bar safely. Several traders were in the river, exchanging Manchester goods and cutlery for palm-oil, ivory, gold-dust, and other articles of value. King Bom-Bom received the midshipmen most politely, and gave them a handsome feast, though, as Paddy remarked, the cookery was rather dubious. He then frankly assured them that he was growing far richer as an honest trader, keeping a monopoly of the chief articles himself, by-the-by, than he had by all his connexions with the slave-dealers, taking into account the occasional burning of his barracoons, and the hot water in which he was continually kept. Of course King Bom-Bom was a sensible fellow, and saw things in their true light.

"What we have heard from our regal friend fully reconciles me to all the hard work we have to go through on this coast," observed Jack, as he and Terence were talking the matter over on their return down the river. "One thing is clear, this abominable slave-trade must be put down, and I believe that we are setting the right way to work to do it. First make it unprofitable and very dangerous, and then show the natives the advantages of civilisation and commerce." When the boat reached the mouth of the river, the frigate was nowhere to be seen. "Then, Paddy," exclaimed Jack, clutching his rifle, "let us have a cruise on our own hook. You remember the prize you took among the Ionian Islands, old fellow?" How merrily they laughed at the recollection of that early freak of theirs. Paddy, of course, was delighted to join in any scheme of Jack's. They could not tell in which direction the frigate had gone. They, at a hazard, steered to the southward. They had a good supply of provisions in the boat, and King Bom-Bom had given them still more. All that day they looked out anxiously for a sail, but sighted none. The greater part of the next passed much in the same manner.

They were growing impatient. It is not pleasant to have to sit cramped up in a small boat under a burning sun off the coast of Africa with nothing to do.

At last the sea-breeze set in, and soon afterwards Paddy jumped up and, in his delight, almost toppled overboard, exclaiming, "A sail! a sail!" As the stranger approached, Jack made her out to be a long, low, black brig; he ordered the boat's sail to be lowered, and the people to lie down in the bottom of the boat, and to cover themselves up with the sail.

They both thought that the approaching brig was a slaver, but to make more sure they called Wasser to them. He crept along under the sail, and put his eyes up over the gunwale: "Yes, big slaver, no doubt," he observed; "but no get slavie in yet."

"Then we'll follow and board her," cried Jack. "If she won't heave-to, we'll make her."

This seemed rather a vaunting boast for two midshipmen and six men in a small boat to make, but Jack was perfectly in earnest about the matter. The men had their oars all ready to ship at a moment's notice. The brig stood on till she was within about 400 yards of the boat, and Jack, who was watching her from under the sail, thought that he should have to get out of her way to prevent being run down. Suddenly she changed her course, and hauled more off the land. Perhaps her people suspected a *ruse*. In an instant, as Jack gave the order, up sprang his men, out went their oars, and away after the brig they pulled. The character of the brig was soon shown, for no sooner did her crew see that they were pursued than they began peppering away at the gig, while a gun was run out at a port on her quarter, which opened a fire of round and grape-shot. Her low bulwarks afforded no protection to the crew working the gun, so Jack stood up, and taking deliberate aim, shot one of them just as he was about to fire.

"Terence, give me your rifle, and reload mine," he exclaimed. Terence did as he was bid. Another of the gunner's crew fell; a third and a fourth shared the same fate. The slaver's people could not understand how this had happened, but terror seized them, and they refused to go to the gun. This, however, did not save them, for the unerring rifle picked out several on different parts of the deck. The breeze was freshening, and the slaver made all sail away from the boat. But as a thresher pertinaciously pursues a whale till it has destroyed it, so did the little gig follow the large brig, which looked large enough to destroy a hundred such pigmy cockle-shells. Jack felt that everything depended on his coolness and the steadiness of his aim. Aided by Terence, well did he do his work. The astonished crew of the slaver must have fancied that they were pursued by evil spirits rather than by men. Once more they kept away dead before the wind, and, crossing the bows of the boat, stood towards the coast, it became evident that their intention was to run the vessel on shore and abandon her. Jack and Terence had no fancy that they should do that, as they did not wish to lose their prize. The breeze, however, increased so much that they could hardly keep way with her. Still they followed, firing as rapidly as before. At last Jack found that his shots were no longer telling, and as he was afraid of expending all his ammunition, he ceased firing, but still followed hard after the slaver. A sandy little bay was ahead, sheltered somewhat by a reef of rocks from the roll of the Atlantic. Towards it the slaver was steered. She grounded in smooth water. A boat was lowered, and into it some of her crew tumbled, while others appeared to be swimming on shore.

By the time they got up to the brig's quarter and climbed on board, all the crew had escaped with the exception of two men, one of whom was dying, the other was dead.

"Oh, Terence," exclaimed Jack, as he looked at them, "this is very dreadful!"

"What?" asked Adair, surprised.

"That my hand should have done that," answered Jack, gravely; "to know that one has been killing people is bad enough, but to see them afterwards—oh, I wish that I hadn't done it!"

"Then, you see, Jack, the slaver would have got off, and taken 300 or 400, or more, poor black people away from their homes and families, a third of whom would have probably died miserably on board, and the rest would have been destined to spend their lives in abject slavery, and to become the parents of a race of slaves. Those Spaniards, or Portuguese, or whatever they are, have brought about their own deaths. Every shot you fired contributed to prevent a vast amount of wretchedness and suffering."

Leaving the wounded man to Wasser's care, they went below to examine their prize. They found that she was fully equipped for carrying 700 or 800 slaves, instead of only 300 or 400, as Terence had supposed. She had two brass guns, an ample supply of arms and ammunition of every sort, so that she was as well able to act the pirate as the slaver. They could not decide what to do with her. They feared if they left her that her crew would return and burn her, while at the same time they were anxious to get back to the frigate. After waiting some time their course was decided by seeing the *Ranger* in the offing.

"Terence," said Jack, "you must go off to her. Leave me and the rifles, with Dick Needham to load them; and if the pirates appear I will keep them at bay till you return."

In vain Terence expostulated. Jack would have it so, and he was compelled to obey.

Thus were Jack and sturdy Dick Needham left alone on board the stranded vessel. They watched the gig as she pulled away, till she was lost in the distance.

"Now, Needham," said Jack, "if the pirates come back, which is more than likely, we must be prepared to give them a warm reception. See you load the rifles and I'll fire them." Jack very quickly got over his scruples about killing his enemies.

"Ay, ay, sir," answered Dick, not at first quite comprehending what a warm reception meant. "But, sir, as they've left plenty of ammunition on board and these two brass guns, besides no end of muskets, we might give 'em a warmer still. If you think fit, sir, we'll load the guns with langrage, and range the muskets along the deck; and then any spare moment when you are using the rifles I might be popping them off."

Jack highly approved of Dick's notion, and only wished that the slaver's crew would come back, that he might carry it into execution. They both had been so busy that they had not thought of the poor wretched Spaniard. Suddenly Jack recollected him. He had been placed in the shade, under the poop-deck. He was still breathing.

"*Eu moro de sede* (I die of thirst, I die of thirst)," groaned the miserable man, showing his glazed eyes. His parched lips showed how much he was suffering.

"Dick, bring some water for this poor fellow," cried Rogers.

"Oh! senhor, you are very kind. I am a wretch, I know; but, as I hope to be forgiven, I forgive the man who shot me."

These were very nearly the last words the Spaniard uttered. A cry from Needham called Jack out on deck. There appeared on the beach the whole crew of the slaver, and in addition some twenty or thirty others, white men and negroes. They evidently did not perceive that anybody was on board, and began deliberately to launch the boat by which they had reached the shore, and which Terence had neglected to tow off before he left the brig. Jack waited till they had shoved off.

"Now, Dick," said he, creeping to one of the ports, "stand by to load, and hand me the rifles while I—do my duty." He was going to say, "pick them off."

Shot succeeded shot, and three men were hit before the pirates knew where their enemies were concealed. The boat was seen to put back, the people in her leaping in a desperate hurry on shore.

"It won't do to let them fancy that they are safe yet," cried Jack. "Hand me another rifle." He continued firing away, seldom failing to hit the man he aimed at.

"Hurrah! hurrah!" shouted Needham. "They are running off, they are running off." So they were, but they had not gone far before a man was seen galloping up on horseback. Jack thought he looked remarkably like Don Diogo. He began striking right and left with a sword at the fugitives, and was evidently urging them to make an attempt to regain the brig. At last he succeeded in inducing another party to embark, but he himself remained on shore. Several times Jack had aimed at him, but he seemed to bear a charmed life. None of the bullets took effect. Jack was afraid of firing at him again, for his rifle ammunition was almost expended. Finding the firing cease, the pirates gained courage and pulled boldly towards the brig.

"Now's the time for our dose of langrage, sir," cried Needham. Jack nodded his consent. Dick ran out one of the guns. Jack pointed it and fired. Then they sprang to the other, and fired that. Shrieks and cries followed, and the boat in a sinking condition put back to the shore. Don Diogo got off his horse, and stamped with rage. He could not make it out, but the men would not make another attempt. In a minute more they had all disappeared. As soon as they were clear off Jack and Needham set to work to examine the vessel more minutely, in the hopes of discovering some small quantity of water, or other liquid which they could drink. Vain again was their search, but on opening a locker Jack observed a box thickly bound with brass. He tried to pull it out, but could not move it alone, so he summoned Needham to his assistance. It was very heavy.

"We'll see what is in it," said Jack. Perhaps had he reflected, he might have waited to deliver it over unopened to Captain Lascelles. However, this did not occur to him at the moment. A cold chisel and hammer were soon found, and on the chest being forced open rolls of glittering gold coin lay exposed to view.

"Here is a mint of gold," cried Needham. "I wonder them pirate chaps didn't try to walk off with it."

"It shows what a fright they must have been in to leave it behind if they knew it was here," answered Jack. "However, we must shut the box up again. It is lawful prize-money, and will be divided in due proportions among all hands, that's one comfort."

"By-the-by, Needham," said Jack, after the box had been closed, "it strikes me that old Don Diogo must have known that the gold is on board, and that makes him so anxious to get hold of the vessel to recover it. Oh, how thirsty I am. For my part, just now, I would rather have a quart of water than that box of gold."

"So would I, sir," answered Needham; "may be, though, we shall find it cooler on deck, where there is a breath of air."

Fortunately Jack took Needham's hint. On looking towards the land the whole beach was covered with men carrying among them six or eight large canoes, while the little Don appeared as before on horseback, directing their movements. Jack, knowing the incentive which was influencing his enemies, and seeing the preparations made to attack the brig, might well have despaired of successfully resisting them. He and Needham were not people to sell their lives cheaply. As before, they loaded the brass guns, and all the muskets and rifles. He waited, however, to fire till the canoes were launched. Then he immediately opened on them. The canoes came on. Don Diogo was in one of them. He was eager probably to secure his gold. Jack took a steady aim at him, down he sank to the bottom of the canoe. Still that same canoe came on, and Jack fancied that he could see the old man's arm lifted up and still pointing at the brig. He could not bring himself to fire at him again, as he thus lay wounded and almost helpless. Needham, however, had marked the canoe; and, pointing his gun at her, let fly a whole shower of langrage about the heads of the negroes paddling in her. Many were knocked over; and the remainder, turning her round, made the best of their way to the beach. The other canoes stopped and wavered. Jack plied them well with bullets. The people on shore seemed to be beckoning them back. Jack bethought him of taking a glance seaward to ascertain if assistance was at hand, and there he saw the *Ranger* under full sail, standing towards him. His danger was not yet over. The pirates made another desperate attempt to regain the brig, but were as gallantly repulsed as before, the negroes not being able to withstand the hot fire kept up on them. Jack and Needham set up as loud a cheer as their parched throats would let them give, when, in a short time, they saw Hemming in a boat and Adair in another, approaching the brig. Fortunately she had taken the ground so softly that she was hove off that very evening. Adair, however, in consequence of the exertions he had gone through, was too ill to accompany Rogers in charge of her to Sierra Leone; and so Jack, much to his regret, had to go by himself, not forgetting his faithful rifle.

Meantime the *Ranger* stood to the southward. Adair had got almost well: he was on the lookout aloft, when his eye fell on a dark object floating on the water. At first he thought it might be a rock, then a dead whale. At length he felt convinced that it was a vessel, either capsized or with all her canvas lowered. He descended below, and reported the circumstance to Captain Lascelles. The ship was steered towards the object, and his last conjecture was found to be the right one. As they got close to the vessel, a small schooner, one person only was seen walking the deck.

"That's a midshipman, sir," said Adair to Mr Hemming. "And I can't make him out quite, but he looks very like Alick Murray."

The frigate was hove-to, a boat was lowered, in which Adair went; and sure enough, Alick Murray was the person seen. He looked ill and thin.

"My dear fellow, how do you come to be this in plight?" asked Terence, as he jumped on board the little craft.

"It's a long story," said Murray. "We took her to the southward off Benguela, and Captain Grant put me in charge of her to carry her to Sierra Leone. She had the fever on board, I have no doubt, at first. It broke out the other day after we parted company with the *Archer*, and one after the other my poor fellows died. A black man and boy, whom we took in the prize, are the only survivors, and they are still below sick with the disease. I have been waiting in hopes of their getting well and strong enough to make sail to proceed on my voyage. I'll give you a fuller history another time."

"The best thing you can do is to let the little craft go her own way, and come on board us," observed Adair.

"What, Paddy, would you counsel such a course?" exclaimed Murray. "Captain Grant put me in charge of the vessel to carry her to Sierra Leone, and while I've life in me that is what I am bound to do."

"Then, old fellow, I'll go with you, if Captain Lascelles will let me," answered Terence, warmly. "That's settled; I'll go on board and get leave, and bring Dr McCan to have a look at your people, and to leave some physic for them to take."

Away went Terence. He had a hard battle to fight with his captain, who, however, expressed his admiration of the spirit evinced by Murray. Needham and Wasser, and another man and a boy, were directed to go on board to act as crew. Dr McCan came on board the schooner: and having prescribed for Murray and his two negroes, and pronounced them in a fair way of recovery, took his departure. Murray then made sail and shaped a course for Sierra Leone, much happier than he had been for a long time.

Chapter Eighteen
An adventurous Voyage

Who would not rather command a gunboat, or even a despatch vessel or fire-ship, than be a junior lieutenant, mate, or midshipman on board a line-of-battle ship or the smartest frigate afloat? Such were Murray's feelings as he and Adair paced the deck of the somewhat unseaworthy little schooner of which he had been placed in charge by Captain Grant. While he stood away towards Sierra Leone, the *Ranger* continued her course to the southward.

"I can't say much for your accommodation," observed Terence, after they had stood watching the fast-receding frigate, and Murray had shown him over his craft.

"I won't boast of it, and if I had to fit out a yacht, I should choose something better," answered Murray, laughing. The whole cabin was only eight feet long, and though it was five high in the centre, under a raised skylight, it was scarcely more than three at the sides, which being right aft, it decreased rapidly as the stern narrowed. There was a fore-peak, in which the two poor negroes lay, but there was no room in it for more people, so that the rest of the crew were obliged to live in the after-cabin. Adair certainly did not know the discomforts to which he was subjecting himself when he undertook to accompany Murray. Not a particle of furniture was there in the cabin, the beams and sides were begrimed with dirt and cockroaches, and a considerable variety of other entomological specimens crawled in and out of every crevice in the planks, and found their way among all the provisions, as well as into every mess of food cooked on board.

The schooner was laden with tobacco and monkey-skins, which latter she had taken on board at one of the ports, in exchange for some of her tobacco, the remainder of which she was about to barter for slaves.

"Negro-head for negroes," as Paddy remarked, when Murray gave him the account.

Several days of the voyage had passed with light winds and smooth sea, and not unpleasantly, though but little progress had been made, when as Adair, who had the first watch at night, was walking the deck, thinking that all was right, he heard a roaring noise on the port quarter. He looked astern. A long white line of curling foam came rolling up at a rapid rate towards them.

"Lower the peak, slack away the main halyards, in with the mainsail, brail up the foresail! Murray, Murray! on deck here; all hands on deck! In with the jib and down with the fore-staysail!"

The sudden quick jerking of the little vessel would soon have awakened all the watch below had his voice not done so. The sails were not lowered a moment too soon. On flew the schooner under bare poles, the seas roaring up on either side, and often breaking over her. Every man had to hold on for his life; away, away she flew; every instant plunging more and more, while the foaming seas seemed still more eager to make her their prey. Murray, attended by Wasser, disappeared below. He soon returned.

"Paddy," he said, touching Adair on the shoulder, "I've bad news. We've sprung a leak, and I fear that the vessel is sinking."

Both Murray and Adair had gone through so many dangers, that neither of them were inclined to despair, even when they found themselves on board a little rotten vessel, plunging along through terrific seas with a leak in her bottom, which was letting in the water at a rate which must speedily send her far down to the depths of old ocean. Away flew the little craft under bare poles, the dark seas, with thick crests of white, rolling up on either side of them, with loud roars, and threatening to come right down upon the deck and swamp them. Tumbling about as the vessel was, it was no easy matter even to get the pump rigged in the dark. That task, however, was at length accomplished, and all hands set to with a will in the hopes of clearing the vessel of water. At first it seemed to be rushing in as fast as it gushed out.

"I believe after all it was only the water which got down the hatches when the first sea broke aboard of us," said Murray, and with this idea both he and Terence were much comforted. Drearily and wearily drew on the dark hours of that tempestuous night. Daylight came at last, and only exhibited the scene of wild commotion around; the leaden sky, the dark grey waves broken into strange shapes, leaping and rolling over each other, and covered with masses of white foam. Off that strange African coast, storms and calms succeed each other with but scant warning. By seven o'clock the wind suddenly dropped, and in another hour the sea went down, and the lately wave-tossed bark lay perfectly becalmed.

"Terence," said Murray, "look over the side of the vessel; doesn't she strike you as being much lower in the water than she was?" Terence feared so. The well was sounded, and three feet of water was found in the hold.

"Man the pump!" cried Murray. This was done, but before many minutes had passed the pump broke. The damage was considerable; but Needham was a handy fellow, and could manage nearly any work. The two young officers lent him a hand. All sorts of devices were thought of, all sorts of things were substituted for those which were wanting; but with the quantity of water in the hold, and in the way the craft was tumbled about by the swell, the operation took much longer time than might be supposed. It is very exciting to read of a ship sinking with the pumps out of order, and half a dozen leaks in her bottom; but the reality, though it may also be exciting, is very far from pleasant. People under such circumstances are inclined to labour away rather in a hurry, and not to stand on much ceremony as to what they do. Night was coming on rapidly. They laboured and laboured away. It was difficult enough to do it with daylight: it was a question whether they could make any progress at all in the dark.

"There, sir!" exclaimed Needham, giving a hearty blow with his hammer, and relieving his pent-up feelings by a loud outletting of his breath between a groan and a sigh; "I hope that will do." Without stopping a moment, he and Wasser, with White, the other seaman, seized the break, and began labouring away with all their might. To the great joy of all hands a clear full stream came gushing upon deck, and ran out through the scuppers. The blacks, and all not immediately engaged in mending the pump, had been baling away all the time with buckets. They pumped and pumped away, and after half an hour's toil they found on sounding that they had much lessened the water in the hold.

"Huzza!" shouted Needham; "we'll do now, never fear, lads!" Nearly three hours, however, passed before the vessel was completely cleared of water. It was Adair's watch.

"I shall sleep more soundly than I have done for many a day," said Murray, as he prepared to turn into his horrible little berth. "We have been so mercifully preserved that I trust the same Almighty hand will protect us to the end of our voyage. Paddy, my dear fellow, do you ever pray? I never see you on your knees."

"Pray!" answered Adair, with some hesitation, "of course I do; that is to say, sometimes—when I recollect it. I dare say I ought more than I do."

Murray took his shipmate's arm as they stood together near the taffrail of their little craft, looking out over that heaving ocean whose smooth, glass-like undulations reflected ever and anon the bright stars which glittered in the dark sky above their heads. "Tell me who but One whose hand is powerful to save could have preserved us from the numberless dangers into which our duty, but how often our thoughtlessness, has led us. Were it not by His mercy, we should even now be sinking beneath those glassy but treacherous swells on which our vessel floats securely; then should we not, my dear Adair, pray to Him, not only now and then, when we may think of it, but at morning and evening, when we rise and when we sleep, and oftentimes during the course of the day? Remember what the Bible says, it tells us to pray always."

"You are right, Murray, you are always right," answered Adair, with a sigh. "I know, too, that you practise what you preach, or I would not listen to you. I'll try to follow your advice. I'll pray when I turn in by and by. I'll thank God that we have not gone to the bottom, and I'll pray that we may be saved as we have been all along in the dangers we may have to encounter."

"Why not pray at once?" exclaimed Murray. "All on board here have been equally preserved. The same God made us all, the same God will hear our prayers."

"Yes, yes, all right—I'll do what you like," said Adair.

The young midshipmen called the crew around them, after Needham took the helm. They and Wasser and the other seamen knelt on the deck, and though in no set phrases, offered up their hearty thanks for their preservation from the dangers which had threatened them; and earnestly did they pray that they might be carried in safety through those they might yet have to encounter. Murray was one of those people who could think well, and when he wrote had no difficulty in expressing himself, yet when he came to speak aloud, and more particularly to pray aloud, found that the exact words he might have wished to use were not forthcoming. The two poor blacks who, perhaps, had never in their lives seen white men praying before, stood by astonished at what was taking place. They asked Wasser what it was all about. He was rather more enlightened than they were. He told them to the best of his knowledge. They listened attentively. They said that they should like to know more about the matter, and he promised them that he would ask Mr Murray to speak to them on the subject. Thus was a way opened into the hearts of these two benighted sons of Africa to receive the good seed of the truth by this unpremeditated act of the young midshipmen. How many other midshipmen might do the same, with the most blessed results, if they themselves did but feel the importance of performing boldly and fearlessly their duty as Christians.

With the return of daylight the weather promised to be fair, and, making sail, they again shaped their course for Sierra Leone. As may be supposed, even in calm weather they had no very great amount of enjoyment. When the sun shone they were almost roasted by its burning rays, and when it was obscured they were pretty well parboiled. Do all they could, also, they could not keep the cabin clear of cockroaches and numberless other creeping things. A meal was anything but an easy or pleasant operation. The only chance of not having half a dozen live creatures sticking to each mouthful was to keep not only the dishes but the plates covered up. Disagreeable as it was, Murray and Adair could not help laughing at each other as at every mouthful they had to pop in their forks under the covers, which were instantly clapped down again, and what was brought out thoroughly examined before it was committed to the mouth, while, as Adair remarked, the soup was more properly "beetle broth" than anything else. The schooner rejoiced in the name of the *Venus*, though, as the midshipmen agreed, she was the very ugliest Venus they had ever seen. She had, besides tobacco, a quantity of monkey-skins on board.

They were sitting at dinner one day, for the sun was too hot to keep on deck, and they had no awning.

"I say, Murray, is there not a somewhat disagreeable odour coming out from forward?" observed Adair, sniffing about. "Tobaccoish, I find it."

"Rather," answered Murray, laughing. "I have perceived it for some days. It is enough to cure the most determined smoker of his love for the precious weed. It is from the tobacco we have on board. After being thoroughly wetted it has now taken to heating. However, we may hope for the best, at present it is bearable."

A bright idea struck them soon after this. They might turn the monkey-skins to advantage. They had needles and a good supply of twine, so they set to work and neatly sewed them together till they had manufactured an awning sufficiently large to cover a good part of the deck. They could now take their meals and sleep occasionally, when the weather was fair, in fresh air, which was a great luxury. At length Wasser, who had the lookout one morning, shouted, "Land! land!—land on the starboard bow!" Everybody in a moment jumped up. After examination, Wasser declared his conviction that it was somewhere off the Gold Coast, not far from Cape Coast Castle. Still Murray and Adair agreed that it would be far better to stand on, because if they could manage to weather Cape Palmas they might have a quick run to Sierra Leone. The schooner was soon afterwards put about. No one complained, though they might have cast a wistful eye at the harbour they were leaving astern.

"We are doing what is right, depend upon it," observed Murray. "If so, all will turn up right in the end."

The provisions had, they knew, been running short. They now carefully examined into their stock, when, to their dismay, they found that they had only a supply remaining for three or four days.

"Never mind," was Murray's remark. "We will go on half allowance. In three or four days at most we shall weather the cape, and then we shall have sufficient provision to keep us alive till we get in."

No one even thought of complaining of this arrangement, but took with thankfulness their half allowance of food. Murray was much pleased with the way the men bore their privations. He never thought about himself, and took less than any one.

"I remember hearing an account given by some friends of ours of the behaviour of their servants during a famine in England many years ago," observed Murray. "Corn was very scarce, and bread being consequently at an enormous price, they determined to put their household on an allowance, and to allow so many slices to each servant in the day, giving them rice and other things instead, not stinting them, therefore, in their food. This excessively enraged the pampered menials, and their old butler, who was the most indignant, ate so much meat and puddings of various sorts, and drank so much beer, that he actually brought on a surfeit, and died from it. How angry most of the fellows at school would have been if told that they could not have butter, or sugar in their tea. Never mind if the butter was not to be procured, and the sugar had by chance not come from the grocer's. How differently do these poor seamen and the ignorant blacks behave. Not a grumble is heard, not a look even of annoyance is seen."

Day after day they stood on, thinking that they must sight Cape Palmas before many hours had passed, and then, after making the land, they found that they could not be many miles farther to the west than they were before.

"Still we might do it, if we could but get a stiffish breeze," observed Murray. "I think the wind is drawing out more from the north-west and east. What say you, Paddy?"

"Let's keep at it to the last moment. I'm ready for what you are?" answered Adair.

The schooner was once more put about with her head to the westward.

Everybody whistled as they walked the deck—even the blacks did so—though they did not know the reason why.

The breeze did not come a bit the faster on that account. However, at night it blew pretty strong off the land, and their hopes again revived. But as the sun rose, it backed once more into its old quarter, and once more they had to tack. On making the land, there were the identical hillocks and clumps of trees they had before seen. Murray and Adair agreed that there must be all the time a strong current setting them to the eastward, and this, on running in closer, heaving-to, and trying the bottom with the lead, they found to be the case. Provisions for two days, and less than half allowance, was all they had now got. Murray and Adair consulted together.

"We shall have to make for the nearest port, I fear, after all, or run the chance of starving," said Adair.

"There is no alternative," answered Murray, with a sigh. "We have done our best."

"That we have," replied Adair quickly. "There is no doubt about that. You have, that is to say—I should have given up long ago. The sooner we shape a course for Cape Coast Castle the better."

The schooner was kept away to retrace her steps to the eastward. But now the wind fell altogether, and they began to fear that after all they should get nowhere. The little food they had left was very bad. Gradually it disappeared, and at length they literally had nothing eatable on board.

"We must take a reef in our waistbands, and suck our thumbs," said Paddy. "I see no other remedy for it."

He said this in the hearing of the men, to encourage them as much as he could.

"We cannot be far off Cape Coast Castle, that is one comfort," added Murray. "We will keep a sharp look out for it at all events."

The day passed, and so did the next, and still the calm continued. They searched about in every part of the vessel, in the hopes of discovering a store of farina or rice, but nothing could they find but the rotting tobacco and the monkey-skins, and, starving as they were, they could not manage to eat them. Even when reduced to this extremity the young officers themselves did not despond, nor did their men, who looked to them for example, do so either. Murray calculated that if they could but get a breeze, they might reach the port for which they were steering in less than twenty-four hours. It was very tantalising to be so near it, and yet not to be able to get there. Had they had any fish-hooks, they would, they thought, be able to catch some fish, but none were to be found, nor had they a file with which to manufacture any out of old nails, as they had often heard of being done.

"Necessity is the mother of invention," exclaimed Adair suddenly. "Here's a piece of tin. I have some scissors in my dressing-case, and I think I could manage to cut out a hook or two before they are quite blunted. Let's try, at all events."

The scissors were produced, when, to their great delight, a file for finger-nails was discovered at the back of the blades. Not only were two tin hooks cut out, but three more were manufactured out of some nails before the files were rendered completely useless. Bait was the next thing to be procured. As there was nothing eatable on board, how was it to be got? That was the question. Adair solved it by trying one of his hooks without any. "Hurrah!" he exclaimed in less than five minutes, "I have a bite. Hurrah!" Up came a curious-looking monster in the shape of a fish. It was a question whether or not it was poisonous. A fire was made and a pot put on to boil, into which the creature, part of it being cut off for bait, was immediately popped. They would rather have caught a young shark, with whose character they were acquainted; but starving men are not particular. Before the pot had begun to boil, a fresh breeze came in from the offing, and away flew the little schooner with more liveliness than she had displayed for many a day. The lines were hauled in. Murray and Adair agreed not to touch the strange fish. They also advised the men not to eat of it. The sun went down, and all night they ran on at a fair rate. The next morning land was in sight. They hoped that it might be near their destination. Adair had just relieved Murray, who had turned in to go to sleep. He observed the black man looking very miserable, and presently the black boy complained of being very ill.

"What have you been about, Sambo?" asked Adair, looking into the caboose.

"Oh! massa, massa, me eat fish," groaned the poor lad.

"It ought to have been thrown overboard, to have removed temptation out of your way," observed Adair, taking the pot with the intention of suiting the action to the word, but on lifting the lid he found it empty. The negroes had eaten up every particle of the fish. They groaned and rolled about for some time evidently in some pain and in considerable alarm. It was no wonder they were ill, but it was evident also that the fish could not have been of a very poisonous character, or they would have been much worse. Indeed they speedily forgot all their sickness on hearing Wasser exclaim, "Dere, dere! dose hills above Cape Coast Castle!"

The words indeed had a great effect on all on board. Murray, who had been there before, the instant he came on deck pronounced Wasser to be right, and in a short time the schooner was running in towards a collection of conical and wooded heights, with the strong and formidable-looking fortress of Cape Coast, built on a mass of rock, in front of them, with the sea washing round a considerable part of it. It looked a very large fortification; indeed it covers several acres of ground, mounts upwards of a hundred guns, and is kept in the most efficient condition. The old castle stands in about the centre of the fortress, and is four storeys in height. The Governor and his suite, as do most of the public officers, find ample accommodation within its walls. It is garrisoned by black soldiers, chiefly from the West

Indies, but their officers are all Englishmen. As soon as the schooner's anchor was let go, Murray and Adair hurried on shore to report themselves to the Governor, and to obtain his assistance. The moment he heard of the state of the schooner's crew he sent off provisions, insisting on the midshipmen remaining to dine with him, that they might relate their adventures.

"But you young gentlemen are probably hungry, and would rather not wait for dinner," observed the Governor.

"Slightly so," answered Adair, "seeing that nothing has passed our lips for the last two days. We were in a hurry to get food for our people, so had no time to eat before calling on your Excellency."

The remark in a very few minutes procured the midshipmen an ample luncheon, to which they did full justice, and would very likely have done more than justice, had not the good-natured Governor stopped them, and hinted that they would spoil their appetites for dinner.

"No fear of that, sir," answered Adair, laughing, "midshipmen make it a rule always to be ready to eat two dinners if called upon to do so in the way of duty. However, I dare say we can hold on now till dinner-time."

Murray and Adair had no intention of spending the interval in idleness. Though they would have gladly gone to sleep, or taken a bath, they again hurried on board their craft, to ascertain that the provisions had arrived, and that their men were made comfortable. Needham had done all that they could wish, and was very proud of being left in charge of the schooner while they were on shore. The first thing to be done was to refit their vessel before she would be in a fit state again to put to sea, and to effect this they without delay took the necessary steps to procure rope and other stores. On returning to the port the Governor received them with the greatest kindness and hospitality, and as they sat in the cool dining-room in the castle, they agreed that it was a perfect paradise compared with their stuffy little cabin when the noonday sun was striking down on the deck.

"All things are by comparison," observed Adair sententiously. "Some people now at home would not think this old fort on the African coast much of a paradise." Several guests, merchants, and others were present, and they had to recount their adventures to all the party. On returning on board, having moored the vessel in a safe position, they turned in and slept as midshipmen thoroughly worn out with anxiety and fatigue, with good consciences and a comfortable dinner inside them, can sleep. The next morning all hands set to work with a will to refit the schooner. By heaving her down they got at what they believed to be the chief leak, and caulked it, and in four days they considered their craft once more ready for sea. The Governor supplied them with provisions for forty days, and very kindly sent them some extra luxuries for themselves. By the Governor's advice, they took one entire day's rest for themselves and their crew. Then, in high spirits, anticipating no further difficulties, they once more put to sea. They had arms and powder, and a six-pounder gun which had belonged to the schooner, and, as compared to their previous condition, they felt themselves in a condition to encounter any gale of wind or any enemies they were likely to meet with. When they went to pay their farewell respects to the Governor, he said that the state of their little vessel had been reported to him, and that he would really advise them to give up the attempt to take her to Sierra Leone, and to wait till a man-of-war should call off the castle to receive them on board. Murray's answer may be supposed, though he thanked the Governor for his advice. The day was remarkably sultry and close. There was a haze, but not sufficient to obscure altogether the sun's beams, while the only wind which blew came off the hot sands in the interior. They agreed that they would be better off at sea than roasting on shore, and so, getting on board, they hove up the anchor and made all sail to the westward.

"Paddy," said Murray, as they were walking the deck after dinner, almost gasping for breath, "I don't quite like the look of the weather; what do you think of it?"

"That we should stand by to shorten sail at a moment's notice," answered Adair. "See that white line of foam curling away over the glassy surface of the water out there. Here it comes."

"I see it. All hands shorten sail!" shouted Murray, as he and Adair ran to help execute the order. They were but just in time when the tornado came thundering down upon them. The main and peak-halyards were let go, and the mainsail was handed while the topsail and jib-sheets were let fly, and round spun the vessel, almost capsizing as she did so, for the foresail was not yet brailed up. It was hard work to brail it up, fluttering as it was in the gale, but at length away she flew before the gale. Some people have an idea that the climate on the coast of Africa is all sunshine and heat. Hot enough it is, but at the same time the sky is often dark, lowering and gloomy in the extreme. Nothing can have a more depressing effect than the atmosphere at such times on all not thoroughly acclimated to it. Everything was made snug on board, but for three entire days they could scarcely show a stitch of sail, while the little vessel tumbled about so much that it was with difficulty they could light a fire for a short time in the caboose. They got some salt beef boiled, and then a sea came in and put the fire out, and though they tried hard, they could not light it again. However, the beef was pretty well done, and lasted them some days. Murray and Adair passed the time as they best could. They had but a small supply of books. The cabin was so close and hot, and on the deck the wind blew so hard, that it was a somewhat difficult undertaking to attempt to read. They did not manage therefore to add much to their stock of knowledge during the period of the gale. The vessel, however, happily held together, and at the end of three days the weather gave signs of moderating.

"That's a comfort," exclaimed Adair, as once more they were able to make sail, and the schooner, with everything she could carry, was put on her proper course; "it will be hard if we do not reach Sierra Leone before long now." They, however, on taking an observation, found that they were much farther from their destination than they were when at Cape Coast Castle. At it again they went, however, but the wind fell, and for several days they made but very little progress. Still they were going in the way they wanted, and that was something. For about a week they stood on thus, with the wind not only light but very scant. One afternoon Wasser's sharp eye discovered a sail to windward. Murray went aloft with his glass to have a look at her.

"What do you make her out?" asked Adair.

"A brig or brigantine; a two-masted vessel of some sort," answered Murray. "She is standing this way. I do not altogether like her looks. She has a widespread of white canvas, and so, if she is not a man-of-war, she is a slaver, of that I have little doubt." The crew heard what was said. Murray remained some time longer aloft. When he came down he looked grave and determined. "My lads," he exclaimed, after exchanging a few words with Adair, "I have very little doubt that the craft in sight is a slaver or pirate, and that at all events she will treat us with scant ceremony. We must beat her off. I know that you all will do your best to do so."

"That we will, sir, never fear," answered Needham, in the name of the rest.

"I know that, my men; there's no time to be lost in getting ready though," said Murray. "Hand up the arms, and we'll try to give the fellows, whoever they may be, a warm reception if they attempt to molest us." All hands were instantly employed in getting ready for the enemy. The gun was loaded, and several shot placed in a rack near it; the muskets and pistols were also loaded, and cutlasses were buckled on. They had no boarding-nettings, and their only hope of victory was by showing so bold a front at first, that the enemy might be driven off without coming to close quarters. As the stranger drew near she was seen to be a most wicked, rakish-looking brigantine, and neither Murray nor Adair had any longer the slightest doubt in their minds that she was a slaver. They hoisted the English ensign, but she showed no colours in return.

"We shall have to fight for it," observed Murray to Adair; "but though the odds are fearfully against us, I have a strange feeling of satisfaction in contemplating such a contest. I cannot help trusting that we shall come off victorious, in spite of the apparent strength of our enemy."

"I am sure I hope so," said Adair, who did not quite understand the thoughts which were pressing through his messmate's head. "We will fight away as long as we have hands to fight with and an ounce of gunpowder for our muskets. It was a craft like that brigantine out there captured poor Hanbury, and murdered him and his boat's crew. I only wish that we had a few more guns and men, and if that is the very pirate, we might avenge his death."

"No, no, do not talk of vengeance, Adair," said Murray gravely; "vengeance does not belong to man. It would be our duty, if we had the power, to take the miscreants and to bring them to justice; as it is, I trust that, though with infinitely inferior force, we may beat them off. But we must not, as Christians, allow ourselves for a moment to indulge in the idea that we are avenging the death or the wrongs of even the dearest of our relations or friends."

"I had not seen the matter in that light," answered Adair.

"Then, my dear fellow, try and do so. It is the true light depend on that."

Who would have supposed, when looking at the two vessels, that those on board the little half-crippled schooner could for a moment have contemplated with confidence a conflict with the well-found, powerful brigantine? But there was just this difference. The midshipmen felt that they were, to the very best of their means, performing their duty, and they felt a perfect confidence in Heaven's protecting power, while they knew that the slaver was engaged in the most nefarious of callings, and that the most abandoned miscreants composed her crew. On she came, as though triumphing in her strength. Hitherto the little wind blowing had been to the northward and east. As Adair was looking out to the northward, he observed a dark blue line coming rapidly along over the water. He pointed it out to Murray. "Trim sails," was the order promptly given. In another minute the little schooner, close hauled with her sails like boards, was standing away to the westward, while the brigantine lay dead to leeward at the distance of at least two miles and a half. Some minutes passed even before she felt the breeze, and when she did it was pretty evident that it would take her many a weary hour to catch up the schooner. The midshipmen agreed that with the opportunity thus afforded them of getting away from the slaver, it would be the height of rashness to wait and encounter her. They felt grateful for having been thus preserved, and when the brigantine was seen to fill and keep away on her course, they could not help joining their men in giving vent to their feelings in a shout of joy. They stood on all night. Eagerly the next morning they looked out—not a sign of the brigantine was to be seen. For several days after this they were knocking about, making often very little way, and sometimes drifting back again during a calm double the distance they had made good during the last breeze.

"I do hope, sir, as how this voyage won't last much longer," observed Needham to Adair, pointing to numberless rents and torn places in the sails. "I don't think this here canvas would stand another stiffish gale without flying into ribbons. I've been hunting about, and I've found a spare boat's sail and some other stuff to mend them. To my mind, it's the best thing we could do before another squall catches us."

Needham's advice was immediately taken, and the wind being very light, the sails were lowered, and all hands set to work to mend them in the best fashion they could. Needham having once belonged to the sailmaker's crew, was a very fair hand at the work, but the rest were anything but expert. However, all used their needles to the best of their abilities. Adair pricked his fingers very often, and, as he observed, he left indisputable traces of his industry. So important was it to get their sails set again before night, that they scarcely allowed themselves time for their meals. Having done little else than drift about all day, it was with no little relief to their minds, that, just as the sun went down, they once more got the sails bent and hoisted. Murray's sextant had been broken, and as he was leaving the *Archer*, a shipmate offered him his quadrant. It was a very indifferent one at best, and in one of the gales to which the *Venus* had been subject, it had received yet further damage, so that it was often ten or even twenty miles out of adjustment. Murray and Adair never lost an opportunity of taking an observation, while they kept their reckoning with the greatest care; but, after all, they often could only guess at their position. The weather, too, was very uncertain. Day after day down came torrents of rain—not merely English spring showers—but, as Adair observed, regular bucketsful, which compelled them to open the ports to let the water run off the decks, for fear of swamping the vessel. No people could behave better than did their little crew. Murray allowed no one to be idle. They were employed either in cleaning their arms, mending their clothes, repairing the rigging, and, when the sea was sufficiently calm, in fishing. Needham kept up his own spirits, and did his best to keep up that of his messmates. However, they were to be again severely tried. One evening, early in October, scud was seen flying rapidly across the sky, while thick masses of cloud banked up densely in the horizon. It was Adair's first watch; Murray had been about to turn in. He cast his eyes around.

"Depend on it, Adair, we are going to have a heavy blow, a regular tornado will be down on us before long, and the sooner we make everything snug the better."

Adair doubted whether there would be anything more than a squall. Just then the sails flapped ominously, and there was a perfect calm. The flame of a candle brought on deck would have ascended straight upwards.

"Adair, I tell you it will be down on us in a few minutes, and with terrific force too," exclaimed Murray. "All hands shorten sail!" Not a moment was to be lost; Needham and the rest saw that. With the exception of the fore-staysail every sail was lowered and carefully stowed; the topmasts were struck, and everything on deck was lashed and secured. All the time a dead calm continued, the atmosphere was dreadfully close, so that even on deck at times it seemed difficult to breathe, while all around became darker and darker. Suddenly a sound, like heavy thunder, was heard in the distance.

"It is the beginning of the strife—the first gun fired in action. Look there, what do you say to that?" He pointed to a bank of foam which was seen rolling up through the dense gloom towards the devoted little vessel.

"Why, I suspect that we shall find ourselves in the midst of a sea which will pretty nearly swamp us," answered Adair.

On it came, rolling and leaping, as if eager to destroy the little craft. No sooner did her head feel the force of the gale than off, like a sea-bird on the wing, she flew before it. The fore-staysail was now stowed, for, from the fury of the tornado, it would either have been torn out of the bolt-rope or run the vessel under water. On flew the little craft, the sea every instant getting up and the wind freshening.

"Hold on, all of you; hold on for your lives!" sang out Murray with startling energy.

The caution was not ill-timed. On came a monster sea, roaring astern. High above her quarters it rose, and down it rushed on her decks, wellnigh swamping her. All the hatches had before been secured; but, had not the ports been open, so as to allow the water immediately to run out, it would have swamped her. The half-drowned crew shook themselves as they once more emerged from the weight of water above them. Happily, none were washed away.

Chapter Nineteen
In perilous Condition

The little half-sinking schooner dashed on amid the raging seas, now lifted up to the summit of one surrounded by hissing foam, now sinking down into the gloomy hollow between others which seemed as if they were about instantly to engulf her. Again another sea struck her; and had not every one held on tight to the rigging or bulwarks, her deck would have been cleared, as it made a clean wash fore and aft.

"We must not run this risk again!" exclaimed Murray. "All hands go below; one on deck is enough. I'll take the helm. No expostulation, Adair; remember, I am commanding officer. I am determined to do it."

Adair, with a bad grace, was obliged to obey with the rest. They all went below, and Murray battened down the hatches. Lashing himself to the helm, he alone remained on deck through that fearful gale. The sea roared around the little vessel, the wind whistled through the shrouds, fierce lightnings darted from the dark heavy clouds, the thunder rattled in deafening peals, while deluges of rain and spray flew about his head and almost blinded him. Yet, undaunted as at the first, he stood like some spirit of the storm at his dangerous post.

Those below tried to sleep, to pass away the time, but so fearful was the tumult that sleep refused to visit even the seamen's eyes. Hour after hour passed by. Still, by the noise and the movement of the vessel, it was too evident that the gale continued. Adair calculated that it must already be almost day. Just then the vessel became more steady, and the noise of the storm considerably diminished. Adair was surprised that Murray did not take off the hatches. He was anxious to go on deck to relieve him. He knocked and knocked again on the skylight. He called and called out again and again. There was no answer. With frantic energy he attempted to burst open the skylight. The dreadful idea seized him that Murray, his brave and noble friend, had been washed overboard and lost.

He and his companions again knocked several times. Still there was no answer. They themselves were almost stifled with the heat of the atmosphere and the odour of the rotting tobacco and monkey-skins. "This will never do," exclaimed Adair, becoming more and more alarmed for Murray's safety. "We must force the hatches off, or break our way through the skylight." They groped about and found a handspike which had been chucked down below. "Now, lads. Heave he!" cried Adair, and getting the end under the skylight, with a loud crash they prized it off, and one after the other sprang on deck. There stood Murray lashed to the helm, and looking more like a man in a trance than one awake.

"Hillo, where am I?" he exclaimed, gazing wildly around.

"On the deck of the *Venus*, old fellow," answered Terence, taking him by the hand. "Right gallantly you steered us through the gale, and as soon as it fell calm you dropped asleep, and small blame to you. We did the same below, and I cannot tell you how glad I am to see you safe: we all thought you had fallen overboard." Murray was very much surprised to find that he had slept so long and so soundly, but he soon gave evidence that he had not had enough rest, for Adair had a mattress brought up and stretched under an awning on deck, and the moment he placed his head on it he was off again as soundly as before.

"We must turn to at the pumps, sir," observed Needham, coming from below. "If we don't bear a hand, I fear the craft will sink under us." Such it appeared would probably be the case, but no one was daunted. All set to work and laboured away as manfully as before. When Murray awoke he found that the schooner was again almost cleared of water. The last man to leave the pumps was Wasser. He was still labouring away, when down he sank on the deck. Murray and Adair ran to lift him up. He could scarcely open his eyes, and looked thoroughly worn out. They lifted the poor fellow to the mattress from which Murray had just risen, and as soon as the fire, which had gone out, could be lighted, they made some beef broth, which they poured down his throat. They also gave him a little rum. Alick and Terence differed as to which was the best restorative, but, unlike doctors in general, they agreed to administer them alternately. Paddy wanted to give them in equal proportions—that is to say, for every cup of broth Alick gave, he wanted to give a glass of grog; but fortunately to this arrangement Murray would not consent. He argued that one tumbler of grog, half and half, was stronger than a dozen basins of broth, and he would therefore allow only half a tumbler in the day. When Wasser was at length able to speak, to Adair's astonishment he declared in favour of the remedy of the rival practitioner, and Murray and his broth carried the day. In spite of the heat, Wasser had to be carried below, and all who could were glad to take shelter there, for down came the rain with terrific force, and continued without intermission, almost swamping the little vessel. Her crew had work enough to do all their time in keeping her clear of the water, which poured in through the leaks in bucketsful. For days and nights together no one had on a dry jacket. By such observations as they could manage to make, Murray and Adair began to suspect that all their seamanship was set at nought; for though they at times made some way through the water, they as quickly lost all the ground they had gained, and thus it became evident that there was a strong current against them.

"This is dreadfully trying," exclaimed Terence, after they had become convinced of this disagreeable fact. "Let us try and make the land again, and see whereabouts we are. Perhaps by hugging the shore we may be able to get round Cape Palmas after all." Murray agreed to this proposal, although he was not very sanguine of success. He knew that the currents were probably as strong in-shore as where they then were, but he hoped that they might possibly get a slant of wind off the land, which would enable them to stem the current, and help them along round the Cape. Murray had been making his calculations on paper.

"I could scarcely have believed that we could have been so unfortunate," he observed, looking calmly up. "For the last six days we have not made good more than four or five miles—perhaps scarcely so much. I have no wish to pay another visit to Cape Coast Castle, though I dare say the old governor would be as kind to us as before."

"I agree with you," answered Adair. "Let us stick at it. We must get the wind in our favour some day or other It does not always blow from the nor'ard, I suppose."

Like true British sailors they did stick at it. Such is the spirit which has animated the numerous brave voyagers who have explored the arctic regions, the southern seas, and the wide-spreading Pacific. At length the land was made. It was a long way, however, to the southward, or rather to the eastward of Cape Palmas. The wind fell soon afterwards, and slowly they drifted in toward the shore. Their glasses as they approached were directed at it, and they could see a number of blacks collected on the beach and evidently watching them. The part of the coast they were now off is called the Ivory Coast. As far as the eye could reach it was flat and monotonous, but along its whole extent appeared rich groves of cocoa-nut trees, extending a considerable distance inland. Here and there, embosomed by the cocoa-nut groves, they could see small villages and separate buildings, the cottages with high conical roofs, thatched with palmetto leaves. To the east appeared a long thin spit of sand, separated from the main beach by a lagoon, into which several rivers and streams appeared to fall. As they approached the shore a terrific surf was seen rolling in towards it, and breaking with a loud roar on the sand.

"What will become of our little craft if we get in among those breakers?" said Adair. "She will have hard work to swim, I suspect."

"I doubt if she will ever float through them," answered Murray. "If she does, and we are stranded, which is the best fate we can then hope to happen to us, I fear that those black gentry on the shore will not give us a very friendly reception. They are flourishing their spears as if they would like to dig them into us."

"We shall be completely in their power, and, what is the worst, we have not the means of showing fight," said Adair, watching the people on the shore through his glass. "They have some big canoes hauled up on the beach, and they seem disposed to launch them, and come in chase of us, should the rollers not send us to them."

"I wish that there was a chance of that," exclaimed Murray; "I should have very little fear of them if they came to attack us. Ah! there's a puff of wind off the shore. Our blacks have discovered it. They are wetting their fingers and holding up their hands. We may yet be able to stand off the land."

The minutes passed slowly by. They were full of the most anxious suspense. Now the promised breeze died away, and the little vessel floated helplessly in towards the dreaded surf. Now it came on again, and she was able to get a little farther off, again to be left to drift back towards the land. Then, just as her case seemed hopeless, another puff would come, and once more her sails would fill, and all on board hoped that she would make a good offing. Had they possessed sweeps, with the help of the transient breeze, they might have got to a safe distance from the land. As to anchoring, that was out of the question. Even had there been bottom to be found with such an inset, their cable would not have held them for an instant. When the schooner got near enough to the shore, they saw that the natives were still watching them eagerly, and no sooner did the breeze return, than preparations were made to launch several of their canoes. From the gestures of the blacks, Murray and Adair agreed that their intentions did not appear to be friendly, and therefore it would be wise to avoid them altogether if they could, and at all events to be prepared to receive them warmly, should they overtake the schooner. Her progress was very slow, and there appeared too great a prospect of their doing this. Every preparation was therefore made for such a contingency. The wind was light, but it appeared to be increasing, and by degrees it was evident that the little craft was forging ahead more and more rapidly through the smooth shining ocean. The negroes on shore must have seen that their chance of overtaking her was every moment lessening, and they were observed to make several strenuous efforts to launch their canoes through the surf. The first two were capsized and sent back on the beach, which the people in her (or rather out of her) very easily regained, as if perfectly accustomed to that mode of proceeding. Again, however, the canoes were righted and launched, and this time four gained the open sea. The fifth was driven back, and probably received some damage, for she was not again launched. Four large canoes full of strong active negroes, completely armed according to their own fashion, were antagonists not to be despised; still it was evident that they had not firearms, or that if they had, they must have been rendered completely useless from the thorough drenching they must have got. Night was drawing on. The wind in a few minutes drew more round to the eastward, and gave signs of once more dropping. Of course every inch of canvas the little *Venus* could carry was set on her, so that unless the breeze, increased it was impossible to make her go faster than she was doing through the water. As yet she was keeping well ahead of the canoes. The two midshipmen anxiously watched the proceedings of the latter. The blacks in the stern-sheets were standing up and gesticulating, and flourishing their clubs and lances, and encouraging their companions. The sun at length went down, and with the last gleam of light shed by his rays they could see the canoes still in pursuit. Darkness, however, now rapidly rose over the deep, and hid them from their view. Murray wisely bethought him of altering the schooner's course more to the southward for a short time. Nearly an hour passed, and there were no signs of the canoes. They had therefore little apprehension that they would overtake them. The schooner was hauled up again on a wind. The night passed away, and when morning broke neither the canoes nor the land were in sight.

"If the breeze lasts we may hope to regain the ground we lost last night," observed Murray. But it did not; and when once more they reached in towards the land, they found that they had made as little progress as before. Again, too, their provisions were running short. Though they might catch some fish, the supply was uncertain.

"We shall have to bear up again for Cape Coast Castle after all, I am afraid," observed Adair to Murray. "And really, Alick, if I were you, I would leave the old craft there, and let us find our way as we best can to Sierra Leone. Yet, of course, if you resolve to continue the voyage, I'll stick by you. You'll not think I hesitated about that point."

"I know full well that you'd not desert me, Paddy, even if things were ten times as bad as they are," answered Murray. "But you also know me well enough not to suppose that I would disobey my orders and abandon the schooner while she holds together. If she gets a slight repair, with a fresh supply of provisions, she will be as well able to perform the voyage as she was at first. There is no use starving, though; and as we have scarcely anything left to eat on board, we'll keep away at once for Cape Coast Castle."

The order to put up the helm was received with no little satisfaction by Needham and the rest, and in less than three days the schooner was riding safely at anchor before the old fort. The Governor received the two midshipmen with the greatest kindness.

"Well, my lads," said he, "I suppose you have had enough of this knocking about in your rotten old tub, and will not object to leave her this time. We shall soon have a man-of-war here, which will carry you up to Sierra Leone, and I will bear you free from all blame with your captain or any one else. You should no longer risk your own lives or those of your people in such a vessel."

"I am much obliged to you, sir," said Murray. "I've made up my mind long ago on the matter, but I am willing to let any of the people leave me who wish it, and will try to get others in their stead."

The Governor, who really was anxious about the safety of the young officer, whose perseverance he very much admired, the next day went on board the schooner, hoping to persuade the crew to abandon her; and expecting to gain his point under the belief that no other people would be obtained to go in her. They assembled on deck. The Governor addressed them. Murray said nothing.

"I sticks by my officers," said Needham, touching his hat and going behind Murray. Not another word did he utter.

"So do I, sir," said White, doing the same. Wasser and the other blacks, grinning from ear to ear, and scratching their woolly pates, followed Needham and White. Murray felt much gratified.

"There, sir," said he to the Governor, "you see that my men will not desert me or the ship. We are bound to continue the voyage."

"I give up all hope of preventing you," said the kind-hearted Governor, with a sigh. "However, as go you will, we will try to make you as comfortable as we can."

The Governor was as good as his word, and provisions and stores of all sorts were sent on board. There was little chance of their starving this time, though that of their going to the bottom was not much diminished, as few means were procurable of giving anything like a substantial repair to the little craft. Among other gifts Alick and Terence received a couple of parrots and a monkey. The first two were presented to Murray, the latter to Adair. The little craft was once more pronounced ready for sea. They had been employed all day in setting up the rigging, and in bending sails, when one of the men proposed a swim overboard, to cool themselves after the heat to which they had been subject. In an instant all hands were in the water swimming about round and round the vessel. The boat was in the water on the starboard side. Murray, intending to bathe afterwards, was alone on deck. Suddenly he saw the ill-omened fin of a shark rising above the water at no great distance off, and then his snout appeared, and his wicked eyes were visible surveying the scene of action. Murray shouted to Adair and the rest of the people to come on board. No one lost an instant in attempting to obey the order. Wasser alone was on the port side at the moment, and nearest to where the shark had appeared. He was a good swimmer as he had before shown, and instead of singing out for a rope with which to climb up on that side, he struck out to pass round the schooner's stern. It was a fatal resolve. Murray was watching the ominous fin. It disappeared. "Swim towards the stern! swim towards the stern! splash about with your legs, Wasser!" he cried out, running aft, and heaving the poor negro a rope. "Catch hold of this, my lad, catch hold of this!" Wasser made a spring at the rope, for instinctively he was aware what was behind him. He had half lifted himself out of the water, when he uttered a fearful shriek. The monster shark had seized him by the legs. In vain he struggled; in vain Murray hauled away to drag him out of the water; the ferocious fish would not let go his hold; the poor negro shrieked again and again. By that time Terence and Needham had climbed on board, and, coming to Murray's assistance, they leaned over the counter, and seizing Wasser by the arms, pulled him up still farther out of the water, and then White, joining them with a boat-hook, drove the point into one of the monster's eyes, when he at length opened his jaws, and retreated to a short distance, still, however, watching his writhing prey, as if ready to make another attack. It would be too horrible were I to describe the dreadful condition in which the shark had left poor Wasser's legs. One foot was entirely gone, while the other leg was bare to the bone. A mattress was got up on deck, and Murray and Adair, with all the skill they could command, set to work to doctor the negro lad, while they sent off to the port for assistance.

"No use, thank ye, massas," said Wasser, shaking his head. "Doctor no do good. My time come. Me die happy. Once me thought fetish take me, now me know where me go—who wait for me."

He pointed solemnly upwards as he spoke. The deathbed of that poor black lad might well be envied by many a proud white man. Wasser's predictions proved not unfounded. When the doctor came on board he pronounced his case utterly hopeless, and as Wasser himself entreated that he might not be sent on shore, he was allowed to remain where he was. All night the two midshipmen and Needham sat up watching him, and doing their best to relieve his pain. At daybreak they were to get under weigh, and with the dying lad on board they once more left Cape Coast Castle and shaped a course for Sierra Leone. The wind still continued light, and in order to keep them from gloomy thoughts or apprehensions, Murray set all hands to work to fish. They had plenty of lines and bait this time, and as they sailed along the sea seemed literally alive with fish of every description. There were bonettas, and dolphins, and skipjacks without number, all affording sport and very pleasant provender; while the seaman's arch-enemies, the sharks, cruised round them as if they had made up their minds that they were to become their prey. Poor Wasser had lingered on from day to day, it appearing that each hour would prove his last, when, just at daybreak on the fourth morning, after leaving harbour, he called Murray, with a faint voice, to his side. "Me go, massa! me go up dere, good-bye," he whispered, and with his hand pointing upwards, he fell back. His arms dropped by his side, and Murray saw that the faithful lad was dead. A funeral at sea is often an impressive ceremony. That of poor Wasser was short, for though there were few in attendance it was not the less sad; for by his gentle and obliging manners, and his coolness and courage in danger, he had won the affection and respect of all with whom he had sailed. The body was sewn securely up in his blankets and hammock, with such heavy weights as could be spared fastened to the feet; and when launched overboard, after Murray had read the funeral service, it shot quickly out of sight.

"Well, Tom, I don't think as how Jack Shark will be able to grab the poor fellow before he gets safely down to the bottom."

I do not know exactly what sort of a notion sailors have of the bottom of the ocean, but I rather think they have an idea that it is a comfortable sort of a place, where people can spend their time pleasantly enough, if they can but once contrive to reach it without being caught by a shark or other marine monster.

When they had got over the feelings produced by Wasser's death, the little crew managed to amuse themselves tolerably well. Murray taught his parrots to sing and whistle, and to talk, till they became wonderfully tame and fond of him; while Paddy contrived to instruct his monkey Queerface, as he called him, so well, that he fully rivalled his old friend Quirk on board the *Racer*. Paddy used to observe that as Queerface could act like a human being, while the parrots could talk like one, their united talents would enable them to make a very fair representation of a young savage; or indeed of some of his acquaintance who considered themselves polished young gentlemen, but often acted no better than monkeys, and scarcely knew the meaning of what they were saying more than did the parrots. There was no fear of the parrots flying away, so they were allowed full liberty, and in calm weather they used to sit on the rigging, nodding their heads and cleaning their feathers, and talking away with the greatest glee till Queerface, who had been watching them from the deck, would take it into his head to spring up the rigging after them and chase them from shroud to shroud, or they would keep out of his reach by circling round and round the vessel, completely laughing at his beard. One day a huge shark was seen following the vessel.

"I wonder what he wants with us?" exclaimed Paddy, gravely. "If we do not catch him, perhaps he will catch one of us."

"Such a notion is a mere superstition," observed Murray. "However, we will try and catch him."

A bonetta had just been caught, and that, it was agreed, would serve as a good bait for the shark. There was no hook on board large enough to secure him, so another plan was adopted by Needham's suggestion. The bonetta was secured to a small line, while with the end of the peak-halyards a running bowline-knot was formed and placed over it, or rather round it. The fish was thus in the very centre of the hoop, or slip-knot it might be called, but a short distance before it, "We shall have the gentleman, no fear of it," observed Paddy, as he watched the shark dart forward towards the bait. Murray managed the line with the bait, Paddy kept the bowline to draw it tight when the shark should get his head well into it. Silently and cautiously the monster glided on, his cruel green eye on the bonetta, which Murray gradually withdrew till it was close up to the counter. Then suddenly the shark, afraid of losing his prey, made a dart at the fish till the bowline was just behind his two hind fins, when Paddy, giving a sudden jerk to it, brought it tight round him. The men, when they saw this, endeavoured to catch a turn with the rope to secure the monster, but, quick as lightning, he gave a terrific jerk to the rope and tore it through their hands. Out flew the rope. Unhappily, Paddy was standing in the middle of the coil, and before he could jump out of it a half-hitch was caught round his leg.

"Hold on! hold on, lads!" he shrieked out; "oh, Murray, help!" It was too late. He was drawn up right over the gunwale, but just as he was going overboard he seized hold of the peak-halyards, where they were belayed to the side, and held on like grim death. The shark tugged and tugged away terribly. He could hold on no longer. He felt his fingers relaxing their grasp, and in another moment he would have been dragged under the water with small chance of escape, when Needham seized him firmly by the jacket. Ned, however, forgot that it would be necessary for him to get a grasp at something; but before he had done so, he found himself dragged over with

Paddy. At that moment White sprang up, and grasped hold of his legs just as they were disappearing over the gunwale; and at the same time Sambo, the other black, caught hold of White, who would inevitably otherwise have followed Needham, and thus poor Murray saw himself in a moment about to be deprived of his brother officer and crew. He himself now sprang to their assistance. All I have been describing took place within a few seconds of time. With a boat-hook, fortunately at hand, he got a hold of Paddy's jacket, which considerably relieved Needham; and at the same moment, the shark coming up again towards the schooner, he and Needham were hauled on board again, his leg being happily released from the coil which had caught it without the necessity of cutting the rope. Poor Paddy's leg was, however, dreadfully mangled; and, unable to stand, he sank down with pain on the deck. Queerface was all the time chattering and jumping about in a state of the greatest excitement, evidently understanding somewhat of his master's danger; and no sooner did Adair regain the deck than he ran up, and, squatting down by his side, made so ludicrous a face that in spite of his pain Terence could not help bursting out into a fit of laughter, which, as he afterwards remarked, must wonderfully have relieved poor Queerface's mind. The shark meantime was hauled on board, though when they had got him thus far he flapped about and struggled so violently that he almost took the deck from the crew. Little mercy had he to expect from their hands. His enemies now attacked him with anything which first came in their way, but they made little impression on him while his head was the chief point of assault. Queerface chattered away and skipped about, taking very good care, however, to keep clear of him; and the parrots, Polly and Nelly, sang and talked as vehemently as if very much interested in the scene, till Sambo, the black cook, watching his opportunity, rushed in with his cleaver and gave the monster a blow on the upper part of his tail, which in an instant quieted him. Not another flap did he give with tail or fin, his huge jaws closed, and he was dead. After all their trouble, he was of no great use to them. They cut a few slices out of him for frying; for seamen will often eat shark's flesh with much the same feeling that a Fejee islander or a New Zealander a few years ago used to eat their enemies taken in war. His skin, however, was of some value, and that accordingly they took off and preserved.

Poor Paddy suffered very great pain from his hurt. The only remedy any one on board could think of applying was oil, and with that they continued to bathe it liberally, as it did just as well afterwards to burn in the lamps. The wet season was not yet over. Day after day they had torrents of rain, so that no one on board had a dry rag on their backs. The schooner too grew more and more leaky and the cargo of tobacco more and more rotten, till the odour arising from it was scarcely bearable, and at length they were completely driven out of their cabin. Often they wished to heave it overboard, but they dared not; for had they done so the vessel, already somewhat crank, would certainly have capsized. Still, whenever the two midshipmen could get a glimpse of the sun they took their observations; and they found that they were making progress, though slowly, to the northward.

"Can you believe it, Paddy?" exclaimed Murray, "you have been on board here upwards of three months, and four have passed away since I was placed in command of her. Still my motto is 'persevere,' and I intend to stick to it." Right gallantly did the little crew follow his example.

A few days after this, on taking their observations, they found that they had in this last twenty-four hours made good no less than forty miles, and two days after that they went over fifty miles of ground. This put all hands in good spirits; and Adair's leg getting better, he was once more able to move about as before. They even began to fancy that all their trials were over, and that they should make an easy passage to Sierra Leone, but they were mistaken. That very evening the sky gave signs of a change of weather. The wind began to moan in the rigging, white crests rose on the summits of the seas, which increased rapidly in size as they rolled tumultuously around them. All the canvas was closely reefed, when the gale came down upon the schooner. She stood bravely up to it on her course till it increased in strength, the lightning darting from the clouds with a vividness, and the thunder rattling and crashing with a fury which no one on board had ever before experienced. Sometimes so intense was the heat of the electric fluid as it passed round and about them, that they expected to be actually scorched by it if they happily escaped being struck dead. The rain all the time came down in torrents, leaking through the deck and half filling the vessel, which was also letting in the water at every seam. They had thus not a moment for rest, for they soon found it necessary to keep the pumps going all the time. At length the gale ceased; but it left them in a deplorable condition, with the leaks much increased and their sails in tatters. All the canvas had been expended, and it seemed impossible to repair them, till they bethought them of the monkey-skins in the hold; and as soon as the wind fell they were lowered down, and all hands turned to for the purpose of mending them with this novel contrivance.

"We shall do very well now," exclaimed Adair, when once more they were set. "But my friend Queerface does not seem quite to understand the joke of seeing his brothers and sisters stretched out there before him, and I should say feels remarkably uncomfortable in his own skin lest we should some day think it necessary to make use of his hide in the same way."

For three or four days they ran on to the northward, when down came another gale upon them, which gave every sign of being heavier even than the first.

"I will have no man's life exposed unnecessarily to this fearful lightning," exclaimed Murray, as flash after flash darted vividly around them.

Night had just come on. Between the intervals of the flashes the darkness was such as could be felt. Adair attempted to expostulate, and the rest would gladly have disobeyed orders; but Murray was firm, and insisted on being left alone as before.

"Well, my dear fellow, mind you don't go to sleep," observed Adair, as with the crew, Queerface, and the two parrots, he dived down into the noisome little cabin.

Hour after hour Murray gallantly stood to the helm, the little schooner dashing through the foaming seas, for he judged it better to keep her on her course than to heave her to. Terrifically the thunder rolled. Crash succeeded crash almost without cessation, while the lightning darted from the sky and played with even more fearful vividness round the little vessel than on the former night. Still Murray undaunted stood at his post with perfect calmness. Though he scarcely expected to escape, it was not the calmness of despair or stoicism, but that which the most perfect trust in God's mercy and all-just government of human affairs can alone give. "If He thinks fit to call me hence, His will be done," he repeated to himself over and over again during that dreadful night. Several times Adair, anxious for his safety, lifted a little scuttle which had been contrived in the skylight, and inquired how he got on, and at times wondered at the fearless tone in which he replied. Still the danger of foundering was to be feared, for, what with the torrents of rain from the skies, and the opening leaks, the little vessel was rapidly filling with water. Dawn was at length breaking and the wind was decreasing, when, as Murray looked around, he thought he saw a vessel to windward bearing down upon them. Just at that instant a cry arose from below that the schooner was sinking, and Adair and the crew leaped on deck. The pump was instantly rigged, and they worked away at it with a will. Still the water appeared to be gaining on them. On came the stranger. She was a large and fine schooner. As the wind had decreased she was making sail; rapidly she neared them. There could be little doubt from her appearance that she was a slaver. To offer any resistance, should she wish to capture them, would be out of the question. Their hearts sank within them. Just then the glitter of some gold-lace on the cap of an officer standing on the schooner's poop caught Adair's eye. He seized his telescope, and directly afterwards a cheer came down to them, as the schooner, shooting up into the wind, prepared to heave-to. "Huzza! huzza!" exclaimed Adair. "It's all right!—there can be no doubt of it!—There's Jack Rogers himself."

Chapter Twenty
Slave-Hunting

The big schooner and the *Venus* were soon hove-to, and while the two vessels were bowing and bobbing away at each other, a boat was lowered from the quarter of the former, which came dashing over the seas urged by four stout hands towards them. Jack Rogers sat in the stern-sheets. He sprang on board and grasped Alick's and Terence's hands. For nearly a minute he could not speak. He looked at one and then at the other.

"My dear fellows, you do look terribly pulled down," he exclaimed at length. "Still I am glad to see you even as you are. The truth is that it has been thought you were lost, when week after week passed and you did not appear. Many of them gave you up altogether, and thought that you and the schooner had gone to the bottom, but I never entirely lost heart. I couldn't have borne it if I had, and I was certain that you would turn up somewhere or other. What have you been about?" Their story was soon told. "That's just like you," cried Jack, again, wringing Murray's and then Paddy's hand. "You are right. A fellow should do anything rather than desert his colours. I am glad, indeed, that you've got safe through it. But, I say, the craft seems to be moving in a very uneasy way. What is the matter?"

"If we don't keep the pumps going, she'll be going down in a few minutes," put in Needham, touching his hat.

Jack called his crew out of the boat, and all hands set to work at the pumps. It was high time, for the crazy little craft was settling fast down in the water. Four fresh hands pumping away while the rest baled once more got the leaks under, and in a couple of hours, Jack returning on board his schooner, sail was made for Sierra Leone. The schooner was a prize lately captured by the *Ranger*, and Captain Lascelles had put Jack in charge of her to carry her up to Sierra Leone, while the frigate continued her cruise to the southward. He was to find his way back to his ship by the first man-of-war calling at the port. Jack wished very much that he could remain on board the *Venus*, to keep up, as he said, his friends' spirits, but as he had two or three hundred slaves on board his prize, he had to return to her to preserve order.

He promised, however, to stay by the *Venus*, come what might, and Alick and Paddy had no fear that he would desert them. He lent them a couple of hands to work at the pumps, but even with this assistance they had the greatest difficulty in keeping the schooner afloat.

"If another gale should spring up, I really do not think the craft would keep afloat an hour," exclaimed Adair, with a ruthful countenance, after he had been pumping away for an hour, till he was, as he said, like Niobe, all tears, or a water-nymph.

"Then we must let her sink," answered Alick, calmly. "We have done our best to keep her above water, though it would be hard to bear if, after all, we should be unable to carry her into Sierra Leone."

"Never fear, Alick," exclaimed Paddy, warmly. "As long as any of us have life in our bodies, we'll pump away, depend on that. If pumping can do it, we'll keep the old craft afloat."

Not the least anxious of the many anxious hours they had passed on board the *Venus* were those they had now to endure. Jack Rogers, however, kept close to them, so that they had no fear about their lives. It was with no slight satisfaction, therefore, that at length they heard the cry from the foretopmast head of the *Felicidade*, Jack's prize, of "land ahead," and soon afterwards the high cape of Sierra Leone hove in sight. They ran up the river above five miles, when they came to an anchor off Freetown, the picturesque capital of the colony. It is backed by a line of lofty heights of different shapes and sizes, which are covered to their summits with trees, and add much to the beauty of the scenery, the Sugarloaf rising in the distance behind them. The river immediately in front of the town forms a bay, which affords good anchorage to vessels of all classes. The town rises with a gentle ascent from the banks of the river, and presents a very good appearance for nearly a mile long, and the streets are broad and intersect each other at right angles. The town is open to the river on the north, but on the east, south, and west it is hemmed in by the wood-crowned hills, which are about a mile or so from it, the intervening space being filled up with undulating ground, forming altogether a scene of great beauty. Here and there in the distance could be seen the palm-thatched roofs of the cottages, which form several villages scattered about on the sides of the hills, and all united by good roads.

"What a pleasant place this would be to live in if it wasn't for the yellow fever, and the coast fever, and a few other little disagreeables," observed Adair to Murray, as they stood on the deck of the *Venus* waiting for Jack Rogers, who was coming to take them on shore. Meantime Needham and the rest of the crew were still hard at work at the pumps, to keep the craft afloat. The schooner's sails being stowed, Rogers was soon alongside. With no little satisfaction they stepped into his boat. Just as they were shoving off, Queerface, who had hitherto been looking over the side, chattering in the most voluble manner, made a spring and leaped in after them, and took his seat aft as if he thought himself one of them, as Paddy remarked. He looked about him in so comical a way that they all burst into fits of laughter, and when they tried to catch him to put him on board again, he leaped about so nimbly, that they were obliged to give up the chase and allow him to accompany them on shore.

"If Master Queerface was asked, I have not the slightest doubt but that he would say there were four of us in the boat now," said Paddy, laughing. "Just see what a conceited look the little chap puts on; eh, Master Queerface, you think yourself a very fine fellow now."

"Kack, kack, kack," went Queerface, looking about him in the most self-satisfied manner.

"Hillo, who comes here?" cried Jack, as the boat was nearing the shore. He pointed at the *Venus*, whence two large parrots were seen flying towards them.

"Those are my pets," exclaimed Murray, laughing. "We should in England be looked upon as the advertising members of some travelling menagerie."

When they got on shore Queerface walked alongside Paddy with the greatest gravity, except that he every now and then turned round to grin at the little negro boys who followed, making fun at him in a way he did not approve of. One of them, more daring than the rest, tried to tweak him by the tail, when he made chase in so heroic a manner that he put them all to flight. Meantime Polly and Nelly, the parrots, kept flying above their heads, and occasionally alighting to rest on Murray's shoulder. Sometimes for a change one of them would pitch on the head or back of Master Queerface, with whom they were on the most friendly terms. The dangers they had gone through together seemed to have united them closely in the bonds of unity. Thus the party proceeded till they reached the governor's house. They in vain tried to keep out Queerface and the parrots, but the governor, hearing the disturbance, desired that all hands should be admitted. He was highly amused at the pertinacity with which the parrots and monkey stuck to their masters, and still more interested with the account Murray and Adair gave of their voyage. Indeed, they gained, as they deserved, great credit for the way in which they had stuck to their vessel. All three midshipmen were treated with the greatest kindness by the residents at Freetown, so that they had a very pleasant time of it, and were in no hurry for the arrival of a vessel to carry them back to their ships. They made friends in all directions, both among the higher as well as among the less exalted grades of society; indeed, they were general favourites. Even Queerface and Polly and Nelly came in for some share of the favour they enjoyed, for although neither monkeys nor parrots can be said to be scarce in Africa, their talents were so great and of so versatile a character, that their society was welcomed almost, Adair declared, as much as that of their masters. Queerface more than once, however, got into disgrace. The three midshipmen were spending the day at the house of a kind old gentleman a short distance from the town. It was as cool and airy a place and as pleasant an abode as could be found under the burning sun of Africa, surrounded with broad verandahs, French windows, and Venetian blinds. The hour of dinner arrived, and all the family assembled in the dining-room, but Mr Wilkie, the host, did not make his appearance. They began to get anxious about him, and some of the ladies hurried off to call him, when at length he came up the room laughing heartily with a white night-cap on his head. "I must apologise, ladies and gentlemen," he said, "but the truth is, I wear a wig, a fact you are probably aware of; but while I was taking my siesta somebody came and took my wig away. Sambo and Julius Caesar and Ariadne have been hunting high and low and on every side without success, and what is extraordinary my dressing-gown disappeared at the same time. However, I hope that you will excuse me, for I thought it better to appear as I am than not at all; for, I confess it, I have but two wigs, and my other one has been left at the barber's to be refrizzled."

Some dreadful suspicions came over Paddy's mind when he heard this, and his fears were not allayed when he heard a loud chattering, and presently Queerface, with Polly and Nelly, appeared at the open window, the former with the missing wig on his head and the dressing-gown over his shoulders. In he popped, nothing daunted, and seeing an empty chair—the intended occupant had died of the coast fever that morning—he squatted himself down in it, and began bowing and grinning away round to all the company.

Paddy began to scold him, but Queerface merely lifted a glass which stood near him and nodded his head at him in the most cool and impudent way, as much as to say, "We understand each other perfectly—we are both men of the world." Then he turned to the master of the house, and steadfastly looking at his white night-cap, adjusted the wig he had stolen in the most comical manner. Everybody present all the time was roaring with laughter, in which no one joined more heartily than did the master of the house.

"Come, come, Master Queerface, I want back my wig," he exclaimed, at last; "my wig, old fellow—my wig—ha—ha—ha!"

But not a bit of it. Queerface was evidently too much delighted with the ornament on his pate to think of abandoning it, and the more vehement were the signs Mr Wilkie made the tighter did he haul it down over his ears. As he sat up in a big chair, with the coloured dressing-gown over his shoulders, and the wig hanging down on each side of his head, Paddy declared that he looked exactly like a judge on the bench.

"Will you or will you not give me up my wig?" at length exclaimed the owner of it—but Queerface held it tighter than ever. "Take that, then!" cried Mr Wilkie, recollecting a well-known story of his youth, and seizing his white night-cap he flung it at Queerface. The monkey was not slow to imitate the example, but whipping off the wig, he threw it at the owner with one hand while he caught the white cap with the other, and soon his ugly mug was grinning with delight from under it. Mr Wilkie, having delivered over his wig to one of his negro servants to be brushed and cleansed, begged his guests and family to begin dinner. Adair and his brother midshipmen apologised for the behaviour of their companion, but he assured them that he would not have missed the fun on any account, and that his wig was not a bit the worse for having been worn by the monkey.

After dinner they strolled out to see a monkey bread-tree, the baobab, a huge monster which Mr Wilkie asserted was three or four thousand years old. It was not more than seventy feet high, but the stem was close upon thirty feet in diameter, with immensely long roots, while the boughs hung down to the ground, forming altogether a wonderful mass of verdure.

"A jolly abode for the monkeys," observed Adair. "I wonder whether my friend Queerface would like to take up his lodgings there, if I were to leave him on shore?"

Queerface seemed to understand the remark, and jumping up on Adair, showed no inclination to leave him. Murray had held up wonderfully during all the hardships he had undergone, and even after he came on shore he was able for some time to go about, but a few days after this the fever, which had been hovering about him, seized him. He would have had to go to the hospital, but Mr Wilkie sent a litter for him, and had him carried to his own house, and nursed him as if he had been his son. Jack and Terence went there every day, and assisted in nursing him, but for long he appeared to be hovering between life and death. Often his two messmates left him with sad and sorrowing hearts, believing that they might never see him again. At last he rallied, and seemed to be getting better. Now they longed for a ship, because they hoped that breathing again the pure sea air, unmixed with any exhalation from the land, might restore him. He was at last able to accompany them about the town.

Everybody will remember old Hobnail, the coloured boot and shoe-maker at Freetown. What a jolly, good-natured, genial-hearted man he was! Every naval officer was welcome at his shop, not because he wanted to make customers of them, for it seemed all the same to him whether they bought his boots and shoes, but really from his genuine kindliness of heart. He had a little room, cool and at the same time airy, with the last newspaper from England, and lemonade, or some other refreshing beverages, and not unfrequently a cigar of a quality rarely to be surpassed. Hobnail's shop, as may be supposed, was often visited by the three midshipmen. They were good customers too, for Murray and Adair had worn out their shoes before landing, and Jack very soon finished off his with walking about.

The first ship which looked into the river was the *Ranger* herself, and as it was very important for Murray's health that he should get afloat, Captain Lascelles carried him off, as well as his own two midshipmen, with, of course, Queerface and the two parrots. The *Ranger* went away to the southward, where she cruised without much success. Those only who have been long on the coast know what dreary work it often is, how homesick many poor fellows become, how easily, when the coast fever gets hold of them, the destroyer gains the victory. They had been some two or three weeks at sea, when a man-of-war schooner fell in with them, and handed a letter-bag from England, with some letters from Sierra Leone. Murray got several. One from the latter place. It was from no less a person than Mr Hobnail, who had taken a great fancy to him. It ran as follows:—

"Honoured and respected Sir,—You are a member of that profession which I deem the noblest and most praiseworthy of any in which man is employed, and more especially that branch of it which is engaged, like that of the squadron on this coast, in relieving suffering humanity, and thus I feel a great satisfaction in the privilege I enjoy of inditing a few lines to make inquiries respecting you. I trust, dear sir, that you may now be enjoying that *seabreezetical* health which a residence on the bounding billows of the free ocean is calculated to bestow. May you soon again return to this truly charming and delectable, though much and unjustly abused town, when I may again have the pleasure of holding those agreeable conversations on subjects of interest which have formed the solace of many hours which might otherwise have been spent in the society of ungenial spirits, whose base-born spirits cannot soar to those exalted heights of poetical sentiment in which I, it must be confessed, with due humbleness, delight to roam. Hoping soon to receive a response congenial to my heart, no more at present from your attached friend, if I may take the liberty of so calling myself,

"Peter Hobnail."

The worthy shoe-maker's epistle caused great amusement in the midshipmen's berth, and Murray lost no time in replying to it in a strain which he hoped would be congenial to Mr Hobnail's heart. The ship was some way to the southward, and had stood in for the land at a place called Elephant Bay. The boats were sent on shore to bring off water, the weather being fine, and the state of the surf allowing of a landing. Paddy and one of the assistant-surgeons were in one boat. While the casks were being filled, they came to a shallow pool, where the medico discovered a quantity of leeches.

"These will be most welcome on board," he exclaimed. "We have been out of them for some time, and Dr McCan will be most thankful for a supply."

Paddy had been carrying a jar for Frazer, the assistant-surgeon, for the purpose of holding any aquatic specimens of natural history they might fall in with. They were all now turned out, and the jar filled with leeches. They had got further than they intended, and when they returned to the beach they found all the boats gone, and only one canoe manned with Kroomen left to bring them off. The surf had in the meantime got up; however, the canoe was as well able to pass through it as any of the other boats.

"We must not run the risk of losing the leeches," observed Paddy. "I will fasten the jar with a lanyard round my neck, and then, if the canoe is capsized, that will be saved at all events, as we can easily scramble into her again."

This was done, and into the surf the canoe was launched. She breasted the rising seas bravely, for she was very light, and her black crew handled her beautifully. Both Adair and Frazer thought the last rollers passed, and were congratulating themselves on being certain to get on board without a ducking, when unexpectedly a white-topped sea rose directly upon them, and in a moment they found themselves rolled over into the water. They clung to the canoe, and the black crew swam round her, and striking out before they attempted to right her, towed her away entirely from the influence of the breakers. Paddy and Frazer had some unpleasant misgivings about sharks, but the blacks shouted and shrieked so loudly, that if there were any they were kept at a distance. They were soon, however, again seated in the canoe; and as the frigate had stood in to meet them, it was not long before they were close to her.

"I say, doctor, I feel some rather unpleasant sensations about my neck," observed Paddy. "I can't help thinking that some nettle-fish must have got hold of me in the water. I feel the stinging all over me, right down my breast. What can it be?"

"Bear a hand there and get that canoe up alongside," sang out the officer of the watch from the deck of the frigate.

The order was speedily obeyed, and the dripping officers and black crew were soon standing on the deck.

"Hillo, Paddy, why what's the matter with you?" exclaimed Jack, who had been watching the canoe, "you are all streaming with blood."

"It's a jelly-fish got hold of me, I conclude," answered Paddy; but looking down he saw the jar into which he had put the leeches dangling at his neck, but the cork was out, so were the leeches, and they, of course, had fixed themselves to the first body with which they had come in contact. This was Paddy's neck. They had just now begun to drop off, and streamlets of blood were running down from him in every direction. Poor Paddy was indeed a most pitiable object, with his hair all lank and wet hanging down his face, for he had lost his hat, and he had on only a linen jacket over his flannel shirt, inside of which some of the greedy leeches had crawled, while the rest hung round his neck and throat, their black bodies quickly swelling out and looking like so many pendants of polished ebony.

No sooner did Queerface, who happened to be up the rigging sunning himself, recognise his master, than down on deck he scuttled and hurried up to him. He seemed very much astonished at the look of the leeches, and evidently could not make out what they were. Adair held out his hand, when up he jumped, and thrusting his paw down his shirt pulled out a leech which had not yet fixed itself. The monkey's first impulse was to put it to his nose, towards which the creature made a twist and fixed itself firmly. Poor Queerface opened his paw, and not knowing what had happened, off he scuttled again up the rigging with the leech hanging to his nose, and apparently not liking the feel of it, he had not the courage to pull it off till it dropped off itself on the deck. Everybody laughed, so did Adair, in spite of the pain and annoyance he was suffering.

"A pretty sort of a necklace for a nice young Irish gentleman of polite manners and respectable connexions," he exclaimed, still laughing away. "But I say, doctor, do bear a hand and get these brutes off me, for they are becoming remarkably troublesome."

"That I will, my boy," answered Dr McCan, to whom he had spoken. "You are suffering in my service, and I am bound to do my best for you."

The doctor at once got Adair below, and by applying salt to the tails of the leeches made them let go. And then a little cooling ointment set him all to rights, while the bleeding did him no particular harm. It was many a day, however, before he got rid of the marks of the bites.

As the appearance of the frigate off the coast put all the slave-dealers on the alert, Captain Lascelles adopted a plan which has frequently been successful. Standing in-shore, he would suddenly make all sail away, either to the northward or southward, as if in chase of some vessel, and then when the ship could no longer be seen from the land he would heave-to and send the boats in-shore, when very frequently they would pounce upon slave-vessels totally unsuspicious of their presence. While the boats were on shore watering, Hemming had with a few hands walked along the coast and ascertained that a number of blacks, prisoners-of-war they were called, were collected in the neighbourhood, and there could be no doubt that a vessel would soon be coming to take them off. Accordingly the usual ruse was put in practice, and the pinnace, under the command of Hemming, with Jack Rogers and Adair, left the ship to watch for her. Murray was still too unwell to engage in any such duty. They left the ship in the evening, so that it was dark by the time they neared the land. Hemming had fixed upon a spot among some high rocks where the boat might remain completely concealed either from people on the shore or from any one afloat. The only difficulty was finding the way into it among the rocks at night, still he hoped to effect that. There was a slight crescent moon, which shone on the calm waters and showed the white sandy breach and the tall wide-topped palm-trees rising up against the clear sky. There hung also over the land a slight gauze-like mist, which somewhat distorted objects. They rowed steadily on with muffled oars, making as little splash as possible.

"Starboard a little," said Hemming to Jack, who was steering. "I think that I can make out the opening I want to find; yes, that's it, I'm sure." In a few minutes the boat glided in between high ocean-worn rocks, round from the waves of the Atlantic dashing against them for thousands of years past. A grapnel was hove on to the rocks, and there she lay as snug as any on board could desire. The boat was furnished with a little stove for cooking, and they had a good supply of eatables and drinkables on board, the latter being, however, more in the shape of tea, coffee, and cocoa, than spirits. Having supped, all hands turned in to sleep except two, an officer and man, who sat up to keep watch. Jack, Adair, and Hemming succeeded each other, but though they kept their ears open not a sound could they hear to indicate the approach of any vessel. At length the sun rose, but Hemming determined to remain where he was all day, hoping that, should a breeze spring up, the looked-for slaver might make her appearance. Hour after hour passed pleasantly enough, however, for they had no lack of provisions, and books, and chess, and games for the men. Captain Lascelles thought that his seamen, wearing out their days under the broiling sun of Africa, required being amused just as much as the gallant fellows who have been shut up for many dreary months amid the snow and ice of the Arctic regions. The consequence of his care in that and in a variety of other ways, was that he lost fewer men than any other ship on the station.

At last Jack suggested that it might be possible to make a lookout place from the top of one of the rocks. He first ordered the men to cut a quantity of seaweed and to tie it up in bundles, and then getting on to one of the rocks he crawled along on hands and knees till he reached the outer edge, when he found a cleft which exactly answered his wishes. Hauling up the bundles of seaweed, he placed them before him, so that he could look out without being seen himself. Without much difficulty he could crawl backwards and forwards to it from the boat. He had gone several times, when at length, early in the afternoon, he made out a sail in the offing. He watched her eagerly through his glass. She was a felucca, and as she drew near he made her out to be a large vessel for her rig, and a most rakish, wicked-looking craft. Her very appearance made him certain that she was engaged in no lawful calling. At last, when he saw her stand into the bay and drop her anchor, he hurried back to give the information to Hemming. Jack was for dashing out at once and capturing her, but his more cautious superior shook his head; "No, no, my boy, wait till she has got all her slaves on board and then we'll have her and them too." The boat, therefore, remained snugly hid. During daylight Jack kept crawling up to his lookout place to see what was going forward. At last he came back reporting that a raft had come off from the shore loaded with slaves, and that they were being shipped on board the felucca.

"All right," observed Hemming, "it will take some time before they get their whole cargo on board, then we'll be up and at them."

"Does it not strike you that they are a long time getting the slaves on board?" said Jack at last to his superior.

"Why, yes, they are somewhat; but it is extraordinary how many poor wretches they will stow away between decks in those small crafts; but they take some time packing," answered Hemming, in a whisper. "Probably too the raft is small and does not carry many at a time." They waited some time longer till the former sounds continued, which showed that the raft was still going backwards and forwards.

"I cannot make it out," muttered Hemming; "the villains are a long time about their work. They little dream that we are close to them, or they would be rather smarter about it."

Some time longer passed, and then Jack proposed returning to his lookout place, to try and make out what was occurring. It was no easy undertaking, scrambling along over the slippery rocks in the dark, with a chance, if he lost his hold, of a tumble into some dark deep pool, or of getting jammed in some crevice, or perhaps being caught by some prowling ground shark or other monster of the ocean. However, he reached the point as which he aimed, but he had not been there a minute before he heard that peculiar sound of heavy blocks working, *cheep, cheep, cheep.* He made out clearly the tall pointed lateen sails of the felucca rising from her decks, and then the sound of the windlass working reached his ears; while a breeze, not felt below and every moment increasing, fanned his cheeks. He hurried back as fast as he could to the boat. As he sprang on board, he exclaimed, "The felucca is under weigh, and there's a breeze off the land."

In a moment the crew threw up their oars, the boat was shoved off from the rocks, and emerging from their hiding-place, away she started in chase of the slaver.

Chapter Twenty One
Desperate Fighting

On flew the felucca, urged by sails and oars. The *Ranger's* boat dashed after her.

"Give way, my lads, give way," cried Hemming; not that his crew required the slightest inducement to pull as hard as they could lay their backs to the oars.

The felucca had got considerably the start, and was going through the water somewhat faster than the man-of-war's boat; the more also she drew off the land the stronger she got the breeze.

"There's no use longer attempting concealment," cried Hemming, "the chances are she has made us out already. Get a blue-light ready, Adair. The frigate will see it by this time, and be on the look out for her. Rogers, see to the gun forward. You may be able to send a shot into the felucca and knock away a spar, perhaps."

These orders were promptly obeyed. While Jack sprang forward to fire the gun, Adair's blue-light, blazing up, cast a lurid glare over the figures of the crew as they tugged at their oars, and which also extended far away across the surface of the ocean, while at the same moment the sharp report of the gun broke the hitherto almost perfect silence of the night. Jack could not see whether his shot had taken effect, but he had some hopes that it had. Again, at Hemming's order, he fired, while, as soon as the first blue-light had gone out, Adair lighted another. Their eyes all the time were ranging the offing to try and discover the whereabouts of the frigate.

"There is her light, sir," shouted Jack from forward, and when their own blue-light grew dim, hers was seen shining like a star floating on the water in the far distance.

Thus they went on, burning blue-lights, at longer intervals though than at first, and firing shot after shot at the felucca. The slaver bore it at first without attempting to return the compliment; but at length, when Rogers hoped that he had hit her, her captain seemed to lose patience, and she opened fire on the boat in return. The latter, however, especially in the night, offered too small an object to be easily hit. Still one shot came whistling over their heads, and another struck the water close to them, showing them, as Paddy said, that they were comfortably within range.

"I think that I have winged her," shouted Jack; "if so, even should the breeze increase, and she escape from us, the frigate will get hold of her."

Thus time sped on, the frigate and her boat showing at intervals their blue-lights, while the slaver, caught between them, continued pretty rapidly firing away at the latter. Still Hemming, at all events, did not feel at all certain that the felucca would be caught. Though the light on her deck could be seen, she was growing more and more indistinct as she increased her distance from them. At last she ceased firing. The breeze too was increasing.

"Do you still see her, Rogers?" asked Hemming.

"No, sir," answered Jack. "She's vanished altogether into thin air."

"Then there's no use firing at her, I suppose," said Paddy to himself.

Some little time longer had passed, when Jack shouted that he again saw her light. Away the boat pulled towards it. The frigate, by sending up a blue-light, showed that she saw it likewise.

"We'll have her this time, at all events," cried Adair, rubbing his hands.

"Don't be too sure of that, Paddy," said Hemming; "still, towards the light we must pull."

It was rather heavy work, for the people had been now some time at their oars without a moment's rest. On they pulled, however, with renewed vigour, fully believing that they were about to pounce down upon the slaver. Nearer and nearer they drew to the light.

"The felucca must have hove-to," cried Adair. "It's strange, after getting so well ahead she should have given in."

What Hemming thought he did not say. Some grave suspicions crossed Jack's mind.

"There she is though. Starboard a little," he sang out, "or we shall run into a tub with a light in it."

"Oh, the scoundrels!" broke from many lips. Jack was about to douse the light, but Hemming told him to let it burn on. "It will serve as a beacon to us, and the felucca's people will not know whether or not we have been deceived by it," he observed.

It now became a question in which direction the slaver had gone. On they pulled, therefore, once more towards the frigate. Hemming wished to let Captain Lascelles know what had occurred, that he might thus steer a course on which he was most likely to come up with the slaver. With the increasing wind the boat would have little chance of overtaking the felucca, but by staying where they were the lieutenant hoped that they might possibly cut her off. The blue-lights and the flashes of the guns had dazzled their eyes, and the night seemed darker than ever. In vain Jack peered for some time into the darkness to make out the frigate. A thick bank of mist, blown off the land, lay upon the water. Suddenly, like a dark phantom stalking over the deep, the frigate's hull, with her tall masts towering up into the sky, appeared, and he had barely time to shout out, "Port the helm, pull round the port oars," before the boat was close under her bows, very narrowly escaping being run down. In another minute they were on the quarter-deck, and Hemming was reporting to Captain Lascelles all that had occurred. He suggested, that while the frigate stood after the felucca in one direction, he should be allowed to cruise in an opposite direction, to double the chances of falling in with her. All he wanted was a further supply of water, fuel, and provisions. To this the captain consented, and the boat being furnished with what was required, Hemming and the two midshipmen again shoved off from the frigate's side. Jack had of course his faithful rifle with him, and he felt pretty certain that, should he once get a sight of the enemy, he should be able to use it with good effect. "I have not the slightest compunction about picking off those slaving scoundrels," he observed, as he was busily employed in loading his piece. "They seem to be completely lost to all sense of what is right and just, such perfectly abandoned sinners, that there can be no hope of their reforming, so I only feel as if I was destroying a wild beast to prevent it doing further mischief."

"All very right," observed Hemming; "most people act from more than one motive, and it's well that both should be good. It's enough for me that it's my duty to kill the fellows if they don't give in."

It wanted still nearly an hour to daylight. The boat had lost sight of the frigate for some time. She had made good way to the northward under sail. At length, when the first faint streaks of sunlight were observed breaking forth over the land, Hemming ordered the sail to be lowered. By this they had a better chance of seeing the felucca without being seen. The lieutenant stood up and slowly moved round, scanning every part of the horizon. The land breeze had now completely died away, and there was not a ripple on the water, though the slow moving glassy undulations which came rolling in and constantly rocking the boat, showed that they were not floating on an inland lake. Jack and Adair began to fear that the felucca was not in sight, when Hemming slowly sank down into his seat again, saying quietly, as he cast eyes on the boat's compass, "There she is, though; out oars. Starboard the helm a little, Rogers, west-north-west. That will do. Give way, my lads."

Away glided the boat, urged on by sturdy arms, in the direction mentioned. After pulling some time the light increased, and the tops of the felucca's sails appeared above the limited horizon of the rowers. Once more Hemming stood up. The slaver lay perfectly becalmed. He ordered all hands to breakfast. The cocoa was quickly heated, and the meal was soon despatched with good appetite. Then he allowed those who wished it to smoke for a few minutes, and once more, the oars being got out, away went the boat in the direction of the slaver.

Before long they themselves must have been seen from her deck; but, to his surprise, as Hemming looked at her through his glass, he saw that her sweeps were not got out, nor was any attempt made to escape. There she lay rocking slowly on the slow undulating water, as if no human being was on board to rule her course. As they drew closer still, only one person indeed was to be seen on her deck. He was walking up and down it with a glass tucked under his arm, apparently scarcely noticing their approach. Hemming naturally suspected treachery. He well knew that the slavers were capable of the greatest atrocity. He was, therefore, prepared for any emergency.

"Why, sir," exclaimed Jack, as they got almost alongside, "I do believe that is my old acquaintance Don Diogo. He'll do us a mischief if he can."

"Be ready, lads, to spring on board the moment the boat touches her side," cried Hemming. Just before this three or four other men came up from below rubbing their eyes as if lately awoke out of sleep. The bowman the next instant hooked on, and the British sailors, led by their officers, sprang on board. The slaver's people ran forward and aft to get out of their way, except the man at first seen, whom Jack had no doubt was no other than the old pirate, Don Diogo, as he called himself.

"Good morning, gentlemen," said he, quite coolly, making the politest of bows to the lieutenant. "May I request to know what brings you on board here at this early hour in the morning?"

"You are known to be a slaver, and we have come to capture you," answered Hemming, bluntly.

"Ho, ho, ho," cried the Don; "there may be two opinions about that. You British officers don't go upon surmises. You want proofs, and you are welcome to all you can discover."

The Don's coolness rather staggered Hemming and the two midshipmen. Jack was certain that he had seen the slaves carried on board in Elephant Bay, and he had no doubt as to the felucca being the same vessel he had seen in Elephant Bay. To settle this point, they lifted off the hatches.

"Don't disturb my poor men. Some of them are asleep below," said the Don, in an ordinary tone of voice.

Hemming, however, paid very little attention to his remarks, but ordered Jack and Adair to keep a sharp lookout on his movements on deck while he descended below. Hemming looked round the dark hold of the supposed slaver, but there was no sign of a slave-deck, nor, after a careful search, could he find anything to warrant him in detaining her. In the fore-peak a rather numerous crew for the size of the vessel were asleep, or pretending to be asleep, for some lifted up their heads even to have a look at the intruders. At length Hemming returned on deck.

"I told you so, gentlemen," said the Don, making another excessively polite bow. "Suspicions, as I remarked, are not proofs. I might now ask by what authority you ventured on board this craft and nearly frightened some of my poor men out of their wits; but we are honest, peaceably disposed people, and have no desire to quarrel with strangers."

"Do you mean to say that you hadn't your vessel full of blacks last night, whatever since you have done with them?" exclaimed Jack, stamping on the deck with indignation, as he felt somewhat compromised in the matter.

"Be calm, young gentleman," said the Don. "As I remarked, suspicions are not proofs. I am not accustomed to answer questions as to my movements, and therefore would advise you to be silent."

There was no more to be done on board the felucca. Although Don Diogo was known to be a slave-dealer and guilty of numberless atrocities, he could not be touched, nor could his craft be detained. As the English returned to their boat he bowed and scraped, his mouth grinning, and his countenance wearing at the same time an expression of the most intense hatred. "We may meet again, gentlemen, before long, but perhaps you may not find me in so placable a mood as at present."

Hemming made no answer, but the Don was seen bowing away and nourishing his sombrero as long as they could see him. Not a little vexed at the fruitless result of their expedition, Hemming and his companions pulled to the northward in search of the frigate.

"I cannot make it out," observed Jack, after having been lost in thought for some time.

"I can, though," said Hemming. "I have not the shadow of a doubt that, somehow or other, the Don got notice that we were in the neighbourhood, and that, as the slaves were taken in on one side of the vessel, he sent them back again by the rafts over the other. Had we made a dash at the felucca at once, we should have found some of them on board, and she would have been condemned. We will be wiser in future."

It was not till late in the evening that they fell in with the frigate. She kept cruising off the bay, and two other boats were sent in to watch for the felucca; but the old Don was too wary a bird to be thus easily caught, and nothing was seen of the felucca. Soon after this a steamer hove in sight, and her commander, coming on board the *Ranger*, informed Captain Lascelles of an unsuccessful attack having been made on Lagos; at the same time delivering to him despatches from Mr Beecroft, the British Consul for the Bight of Benin, residing at Fernando Po, asking for further assistance. Sail was instantly, therefore, made for the northward, and, the wind holding favourable, they were not long before they got off the slave-coast in the neighbourhood of the place proposed to be attacked. Great was the satisfaction expressed by all hands, both in the gun-room and midshipmen's berth, and throughout the ship, at the prospect of some real work being done. In the midshipmen's berth, perhaps, the satisfaction was more vehemently expressed.

"There's nothing like getting a real enemy right before you, and having an honest slap at him," exclaimed Jack Rogers. "It is all very right hunting down those slave-dealers and chasing slavers, but the scoundrels are such slippery fellows, it is difficult work to get hold of them."

"Or to keep them if you have got a grip of them," observed Adair. "But I say, does anybody know who it is we are going to fight, and what we are going to fight about?"

"Something about the slave-trade," said Hobson, one of the mates.

"The blacks hereabouts want a thrashing, so we are going to lick them," remarked Lister, another midshipman, who was never very exact in his notions.

Just then Murray, who had had the forenoon watch on deck, came below. He was, on the point I have mentioned, a great contrast to Lister. He was forthwith applied to. "As soon as I have taken the sharp edge off my appetite I will tell you all I know about the matter," he answered. The edge of people's appetites on the coast is not very sharp, in the dog-days especially, so Murray was soon in a condition to begin.

"Now just look here," he commenced, collecting some crumbs and bits of biscuit, which he began to place about on the table. "To the north and east of us is the slave-coast. Inland, due north, or thereabouts, is Dahomey, the king of which is something like a king, for he can cut off his subjects' heads at pleasure; he has got several regiments of Amazons, who fight most furiously, besides other troops armed with matchlocks. To the east is the

Yoruba country, and to the south, further round the bay, is the kingdom of Benin. The Yoruba country is between the other two I have mentioned. Its chief river is the Ogun. At the mouth is Lagos, a large town, held by an independent chief or king of considerable wealth and power. About seventy miles up is Abeokuta. Abeokuta is a very remarkable place. About twenty-five years ago the remnants of the inhabitants of a number of villages which had been broken up by the attacks made on them for the purpose of carrying away these people as slaves, betook themselves to a large cavern on the banks of the Ogun about seventy miles from the coast. In this place of concealment they remained for some time undiscovered, living on roots, and berries, and other natural productions of the ground, till they were joined by other fugitives from the hated slave-dealers. At length, their numbers increasing, they ventured forth from their cavern, and began to cultivate the ground and to build themselves houses. They chose as their chief a liberal-minded, talented man, called Shodeke; and it is said that at present there are upwards of 80,000 people in their community. They have built a large town, which they have called Understone, or, in their own language, Abeokuta, in memory of the cave under which they first took shelter. Now, if the blockading squadron had never done more than what I am going to tell you about, they would have performed a very great and blessed work. Among the thousands of negroes they have captured and liberated were many hundreds who had been taken from the Yoruba country, and who were settled at Sierra Leone. Here many of them had grown rich, and a considerable proportion had been converted to Christianity. Among them was a man named in their language Adgai, but called in English Crowther. He had been embarked as a slave on board of a slaver at Badagry in 1822. That slaver was captured by one of our cruisers, and taken to Sierra Leone. At that place he was well educated, was converted, and ordained as a minister of the Gospel. Now, several of the Yoruba natives I have spoken of, who had become possessed of property, purchased a vessel, and visited Lagos and Badagry to trade. At those places they heard of Abeokuta and the stand it had made against the slave-trade. On their return to Sierra Leone, from the accounts they gave of the new settlement, a considerable number of their countrymen resolved to go there. Among the first was Mr Crowther. He is, I am assured, a man of high intellectual powers, and of eminent piety. He persuaded other Christian Africans to accompany him. Nearly the first people he met on arriving at the new city were his mother and sisters, and they were his first converts. The greater part of the inhabitants are now Christians, and Mr Crowther is engaged in translating the Bible into the Yoruba language.

"The King of Dahomey looked with an evil eye on the growing power of Abeokuta, and led his army to destroy it; but he and his forces were, however, most signally defeated. On this he instigated the King of Lagos to attack Abeokuta. That chief has got a hundred war canoes, fully five thousand men all armed with muskets, and sixty guns.

"Happily the old King of Lagos lately died. He left his crown to a fellow called Akitoye, the younger of two sons, the elder, Kosoko, being a ragamuffin and banished. Akitoye, on coming to the throne, recalled Kosoko; but, true to his character, the elder brother managed to bribe the army, and to turn poor Akitoye out of the country. Akitoye took shelter in Badagry, which place Kosoko was preparing to attack, being promised a thousand men by the King of Dahomey. If he succeeds he will undoubtedly attack Abeokuta. To prevent this, Mr Beecroft applied for a naval force to bring Kosoko to reason.

"Accordingly, the *Bloodhound* and a squadron of boats was sent off to Lagos to reason with the usurper. He, however, did not understand what they wanted, and, as they approached, opened a heavy fire on them from a number of concealed batteries, both with great guns and small-arms. Several poor fellows were killed and wounded, and at length the expedition had to retire, there not being enough men to hold the town had it been captured. The commodore has now resolved to send one of ample strength to drive the slave-dealing sovereign, Kosoko, from his throne and his stronghold altogether. This is the business we are called on to perform. If we succeed, and there is no doubt about that I should hope, we shall preserve Abeokuta, and enable the Christian missionaries to labour on without interruption; we shall punish the usurper, and restore the right man to his government; we shall rout out a nest of slave-dealers, and put a stop to slave-dealing in Lagos; and we shall teach the King of Dahomey to be cautious, lest the same punishment we inflict on his friend there may overtake him. All these things are well worth fighting for, you'll acknowledge."

All hands agreed that it would be difficult to have a better object than that Murray had described for the proposed attack.

"Yes, indeed, it is a truly satisfactory feeling, to be sure, that the cause you fight for is a righteous one," repeated Murray. "Still I do not hold for one moment that it is not our duty to fight, as long as we remain in the service, whenever we are ordered by our superiors. The difference is this, in one case we fight heartily, in the other we do only just what we are ordered; at all events we don't do it in the same hearty way we would like."

"We'll fight heartily now, at all events," exclaimed Adair, with even more than his usual enthusiasm. "If there is one cause more than another in which I would rather expend my life, it would be that of getting rid of this abominable slave-trade. No scoundrels are greater, in my opinion, than the fellows who engage in it. No country can prosper or be happy which allows it."

The conversation was cut short by the announcement that several sail of men-of-war were in sight. The ships began working away with their bunting, and, when they had collected, the commanders assembled on board the Commodore to arrange the plan of attack.

The next day, by the evening, everything was ready. The squadron, composed of steamers as well as sailing ships, brought up off the mouth of the Ogun river. It has a bar across it. Inside it, on an island about two miles in circumference, near the right bank, stands the slave-dealing city of Lagos, whose houses could just be distinguished peeping out among the cocoa-nut trees. It was known that the place was strongly defended with stockades, some sixty guns, and from 1,500 to 2,000 men with firearms, and gunners trained by the Spaniards and other slave-dealers to serve the artillery. All hands watched eagerly for the signal to commence operations. The three midshipmen were delighted to find that they were to be in the first squadron of boats. Preceded by a steamer, they dashed across the bar, and then anchored inside, out of reach of shot from the town, to commence operations the next morning. Soon after sunrise men were seen assembling on the banks of the river, and, on pulling over to them, they found that Mr Beecroft, with the ex-king, Akitoye, had arrived, bringing with him 500 men from Abeokuta and Badagry. That they might be known, they had white neckcloths distributed among them, with which the black volunteers were highly delighted. A number of canoes were then discovered at a slave station on the left bank, and these having been brought off, the black auxiliary force, now considerably augmented, was passed over to the right bank. The steamer next dropped up the river with the tide to reconnoitre the fortifications, and it was found that, at all points where boats could land, stakes in double rows were driven in, while an embankment had been thrown up with a ditch in front of it, and that twenty-five guns were trained to guard all the narrower parts of the channel. On the north side of the island were the houses of Kosoko and the slave-dealers, and it was here accordingly, as it was right that they should be chiefly punished, that the commander of the expedition resolved to commence the attack. The following day being Christmas-day, he determined, in order that that holy day should be spent as quietly as possible, and be a day of rest, to wait till the 26th. This it was, except that the slave-dealers wasted a large amount of ammunition by firing at the squadron, which was far beyond their range. With infinite satisfaction, soon after daybreak on the 26th, the order was received to proceed to the attack. The scene may be easily pictured. Before them lay the island surrounded by stockades, with palm-trees, and the huts and houses of Lagos rising beyond them; the broad river in front full of shallows, narrow channels only between them.

Towards the island the steamers and the squadron of boats now advanced. At first all was calm and smiling. Jack and Paddy were in the same boat.

"I wonder whether the scoundrels will give in without fighting," observed the latter; "I shouldn't be surprised."

"Not a bit of it," answered Jack. "They want first to be taught a lesson or two which they cannot forget."

"But what can these miserable black fellows do against us? I should think that we should blow them and their town up into the sky in a dozen minutes or less," exclaimed Paddy, with a laugh.

Scarcely had he spoken when, from the whole line of stockades, showers of round shot and bullets came rattling about the steamers and boats. On dashed the whole squadron, the steamers keeping up a hot fire from their great guns in return, though so well sheltered were the blacks that not one of them could be seen. This sort of work continued for some time, several officers and men being hit, when one of the steamers grounded. She then became, of course, a target for the enemy, and several people were wounded on board her. The boats meantime had opened their fire to protect her, but so well were the batteries of the negroes concealed that it was difficult to find out a point at which to aim. A division of the boats was now sent round to the north-east point of the island to ascertain the position and strength of the guns on that side. These boats, after a hot fight, during which they upset some of the enemy's guns, returned, and then made a gallant attempt to force the stockades in order to land and spike the guns bearing heaviest on the steamer. Away they dashed; they could see the barrels of the negroes' muskets gleaming through the stockades, and a terrific fire was opened on them. Still on they went, right up to the stockades. Axe in hand the works were attacked, but in vain they hacked and hewed at the tough posts. No sooner was one party of blacks driven from the defences than others took their places. Many of the seamen were hit; some poor fellows sank never to rise again. The British seamen cheered and loaded and fired as rapidly as they could; the blacks shrieked and shouted, and kept banging away in return. Jack heard a cry close to him. It came from the boat next to his. He saw an officer fall. His heart sank; he thought it was Murray. He sprang into the boat to lift him up—but no—it was another gallant young midshipman, whom he had seen an instant before bravely cheering on his men. Assistance was useless, he had ceased to breathe. He placed him in the stern-sheets of his boat and regained his own. Once more a desperate assault was made on the stockades, but without effect, and, with numbers wounded, the boats were compelled to haul off.

What to do with the steamer on shore was now the question. It was resolved, to avoid the necessity of blowing her up, to land with a strong force to destroy the guns annoying her. Till the tide rose there seemed no prospect of getting her off. Some little time was expended in arranging the expedition. Again the signal was given, and in line they pulled gallantly up towards the stockade. As they approached a fire from fully 1,500 muskets opened on them, to which they replied with spherical, grape, and canister shot. Hotter and hotter grew the fire of the blacks, but on the boats steadily advanced till their stems touched the beach, when the men, springing on shore, formed in an instant, and, led by their officers, rushed up to the stockades. Axes were plied vigorously—some seized the timbers and hauled them down, and a breach being made, in they rushed and drove the enemy before them. The fort was gained, the blacks fled out of it into the thick bush in the rear, and all the guns were spiked. While this work was being accomplished, a party of the blacks had come down and, attacking one of the boats, had carried her off along the beach, hoping probably to make their escape in her. A party pursued them on discovering this for a considerable distance, when the blacks who had fled into the woods, seeing what was taking place, rushed from their concealment in the woods by swarms, and poured a crushing fire into the boats at pistol range. One poor fellow, who had been left on board the boat, when he saw the enemy coming, made a desperate attempt to spike her guns, and was cut down while so engaged. After all the boat could not be recovered. The Krooman on board Mr Beecroft's boat by mistake let go her anchor directly in front of the enemy's lines, and had not an officer, in the most gallant way, cut her chain cable with a chisel, under a fearfully hot fire, during which he was several times hit, she also would have been destroyed. Everybody during the action behaved admirably, and no one deserved more praise than did the surgeons sent on the expedition, who, throughout the day, attended on the wounded, exposed to the hottest fire. Disastrous in one respect had indeed been the result of the expedition, for upwards of sixty men and officers had been wounded, and thirteen men and three midshipmen killed. When it was found that the boat could not be recovered, a mate of one of the ships and the gunner, in the most gallant way, pulled back to the cutter, and by throwing a rocket into her, so well-directed that it entered her magazine, blew her up, destroying at the same time not a few of her captors. Towards the evening the steamer was got off, and the order was then given for the boats to return out of gun-shot for the night. British seamen are not apt to indulge in low spirits or to give way to melancholy, but those engaged in the expedition might well have been excused had they done so. Had they been successful the case would have been different, but as yet nothing had been accomplished; still probably there was not a man who did not feel that before the end of another day something would be done, nor did any one dream of abandoning the enterprise. Jack and Adair looked out anxiously for Murray.

"Can he have been hit?" said Terence. "It surely was not his boat that was taken."

"I trust not indeed," answered Jack, anxiously. "I'll hail the boats as they come up, to learn if anybody knows where he is."

Boat after boat was hailed, but no information could be obtained of Murray. They became seriously anxious about him. Jack had several men wounded in his boat, and one poor fellow lay stark and cold in the bow. The other boats had also several wounded on board them, while the steamer had a still greater proportion. The groans and cries of the poor fellows, as they lay racked with pain in the confined space which could alone be afforded on board the small vessels and boats, sounded sadly in the calm midnight air. The surgeons all the time were stepping from boat to boat, or visiting the vessels in succession, and doing their utmost to alleviate the sufferings of the wounded. Happy were those who could sleep, but many, among whom were Jack and Terence, could not close an eye. How anxiously, as they leant back and looked up to the dark sky studded with its myriads of stars reflected in the calm glassy waters, did they wish for the morrow, though that morrow might bring death and wounds to themselves or their companions. Happy, indeed, is it for all of us that we do not know what the morrow may bring forth.

Chapter Twenty Two
Prisoners

Battles and wounds, death and destruction, and all the other concomitants of warfare, may be interesting matters to read about, but the reality is very far from pleasant or desirable. Even Jack Rogers and Paddy Adair could not help coming to this conclusion during the night they spent off Lagos, surrounded by their wounded, and dead, and dying companions. They were also not a little anxious about Murray, of whom they could obtain no information. The stars kept shining forth from the dark sky, the surface of the river was smooth as glass, on either side around them was the squadron of steamers and boats, while in the distance could be observed the lights of the black city, from which every now and then a flash might be seen as a negro took it into his head to fire off his musket, or perhaps, while handling it, let it explode unintentionally. At length daylight returned. Directly everybody was on the alert, but as yet no signal was made to recommence the attack. Whatever heroes of romance might have done, modern warriors require rest and refreshment, so the men set to work to cook and eat their breakfasts. While this was going on, a boat was seen approaching the squadron. She was the gig Murray commanded. He himself was on board. His shipmates warmly welcomed him.

"Where have you been? What have you been about? We feared you were lost," exclaimed several voices.

"It is a somewhat long story," he answered. "After the retreat was ordered yesterday I saw some negroes pulling off in a canoe to the northward of the island, and not thinking of consequences, I pursued them. Away we went at good speed, but they paddled faster. It did not occur to me at the time that they were making their escape from the town. When I looked astern I found that our own boats had gone to the southward, and that between me and them was a large body of native canoes. To attempt to pass them would have been madness, so I pulled on up the river. The blacks were so engaged in the fight, that I was not perceived. I therefore pulled up the stream till it was dark, and then lay hid for some time to rest and refresh my men. I bethought me that having got thus far, I would employ myself profitably. I therefore dropped an anchor, and let the men take a couple of hours' sleep; then once more getting under weigh, I dropped down, sounding as I came, and passed right round to the west of the island. When abreast of it I saw dark objects moving across the channel, and found that they were canoes crossing and recrossing, and I have no doubt carrying off household goods and other property, and perhaps some of the inhabitants were making their escape. At all events, it looks as if the natives were not very sanguine of success. I had to wait till I had an opportunity of threading my way between them, and it was only just at daybreak that I was able to get clear. I must now go and make my report to the captain."

Not long after this the signal was given to attack, and the whole squadron was quickly in movement. There was not a man engaged who was not resolved to redeem, if possible, the loss of the previous day. The boats, as before, pulled round to the northward, where the houses of the king and his prime ministers, as well as of the European slave-dealers, were situated, while the steamers took up positions on either side of the town. There was no mistake this time as to what was to be done. The sad loss of life which occurred on the previous day arose, it must be remembered, entirely in consequence of the grounding of the steamer. This made it necessary to land in the face of a hot fire and to storm the stockades, while it also brought about the subsequent disasters. The signal was given and the steamers and boats opened a steady and well-directed fire, which soon began to tell. House after house was seen to be in flames. The blacks returned it, but with very different spirits to the previous day. They had fancied after the apparent defeat the English had suffered on the previous day, they would not again venture to attack them. Steadily the boats fired away. "Hurrah! hurrah! hurrah!" A loud cheer ran through the line. A shot had entered the house of Tappis, Kosoko's prime minister, and set it on fire. He was one of the most determined supporters of the slave-trade, and the chief instigator of the first attack on the boats of the squadron. Soon after the gun in a battery below his house was capsized, while the men working it were driven out by a well-directed rocket sent among them. House after house now caught fire. Most of the non-combatants had before this fled, the rest were next seen hurriedly making their escape with cries of terror and dismay. Still the garrison, with a bravery worthy of a better cause, held out. The firing on both sides became more rapid, but the English redoubled their exertions. Showers of shot, and shell, and rockets were flying into the devoted town. Suddenly a fearful roar was heard. Earth and stones, and fragments of timber mixed with human forms, were seen to rise up into the air. One of the enemy's chief magazines had exploded. From that moment the conflagration extended more rapidly and fiercely than before, till the whole city appeared to be in a blaze, the flames rising up in ruddy pyramids and supporting a dark canopy overhead—a fit funeral pall for those who had fallen in the strife. There could be no longer any doubt that the fate of Lagos was decided. A broad creek ran through part of the town. This stopped the flames. Kosoko's house was still standing. A boat was directed especially to destroy it; but the commander of the expedition, influenced by truly Christian motives, resolved, before doing more injury to the town, to give Kosoko an opportunity of capitulating. The next day was Sunday. He resolved, should the blacks commit no act of hostility, to make it also a day of rest. Recalling all the boats, he sent in therefore a flag of truce, by a friendly chief, to Kosoko, allowing him till Monday morning to consider his proposals. Once more, therefore, on Saturday evening, the squadron retired from before the town; but very different were the feelings of those engaged from what they had been on Friday. Now success appeared certain, then a heavy loss and defeat had been the termination of their day's labour. Still, as the three midshipmen met on board Jack's boat, their conversation was far sadder than it was wont to be. So probably was that of the commanders of the expedition.

"To think that we should have spent all this time before a town fortified only by slaving rascals, and manned by blacks, and after all not yet to be masters of it!" exclaimed Jack, with some bitterness in his tone.

"It comes very much of the common English fault of despising our enemies," observed Murray. "We are apt to forget that though fellows have black or tawny skins, they have got brains in their heads."

"Still we don't often find enemies who have the pluck of Britons," said Adair.

"No, and that is the reason why we are ultimately so generally successful," answered Murray. "But that does not prevent us from frequently, in the first place, meeting with defeat and disgrace, and losing numberless valuable lives. I do not mean to say that what happened on Friday could have been avoided, but it is very sad to think of the poor fellows who have lost their lives, as well as of the many now suffering from their wounds; so we won't talk more about the matter."

That night passed like the former ones, and Sunday was gliding tranquilly away, spent in most instances by the crews on board the vessels and boats, after the example of their commander, as a Sunday should be passed, when it was ascertained that the usurper and his prime minister, and the greater number of his troops, had abandoned the city. The English commander, therefore, sent to direct the negro auxiliaries who had accompanied King Akitoye from Abeokuta to escort him into the city, and to install him in his office. This was done, and they took possession of the houses which had escaped the conflagration, while a small portion only of the British forces entered that evening and spiked the guns in the chief batteries turned towards the river. The next morning fifty-two guns were destroyed or embarked. Murray was among those who went on shore. In his letter home he made the following remarks:—

"The greater part of the stronghold of slavery is now little more than a heap of ashes; but enough of the works remain to show the cunning methods devised by the blacks for entrapping us into ambushes had we assaulted it. In truth, the place is a great deal stronger than we had any notion of. One thing I must say, that, in spite of the reverses we at first experienced, every officer and man engaged in the affair did his utmost, and behaved as British seamen always should behave; and it must be the consolation of the relations and friends of the gallant fellows who lost their lives, that a very important work has been performed, and that the capture of this stronghold of the slave-trade will prove one of the severest blows that hateful traffic has ever experienced. It has done much also, I trust, to advance the cause of religion and civilisation in Africa, and will help, I hope, to wipe away the dark stain which is attached to many of the so-called Christian nations of the world. Akitoye is now installed King of Lagos. He professes great friendship for the English, as well as for the people of Abeokuta. If he proves the stern enemy of the slave-trade and the true friend of Christianity, we shall not have fought in vain."

On searching for the Spanish and Portuguese slave-dealers, by whom the Lagos people had been trained to arms, none were to be found. They had fled, and as their property was completely destroyed, they have never since returned. The midshipmen heard that their old acquaintance Don Diogo was one of those who had establishments there, but they could not hear anything of him, nor what had become of the felucca, on board of which he was last seen. One thing was very certain, that his love for the English generally, or for them in particular, could not have been increased when he found that all his property in Lagos had been destroyed. The squadron at length once more put to sea, and Lagos has ever since virtually been under the jurisdiction of the British Government, who retain it for the purpose of keeping in check the traffic in slaves.

The frigate had been some weeks at sea before she at length fell in with the *Archer*, which Murray had then to rejoin. All three of the midshipmen were beginning to look forward to the time when they might hope once more to return to England. Still they were perfectly content, till the time arrived, steadily to go on in the performance of their duty.

When Murray left the frigate he took with him his two parrots, Polly and Nelly, but Queerface remained, and Adair declared that under his judicious system of education he had become one of the most learned and sagacious of monkeys. He said that it reminded him very much of Don Diogo, and so he and Jack amused themselves by rigging him out in a dress similar to that in which they had seen the old Don appear. The imitation was so good that the moment Queerface sprang up on deck the likeness was recognised by all who saw him. When Adair went away in boats he usually took Queerface with him to afford amusement to his men. The frigate had been for some time cruising on to the southward, without meeting with any success, when, there being every appearance of calm weather, Captain Lascelles ordered away two of the boats to cruise in search of slavers, one to the northward and the other to the southward. Jack, to his great satisfaction, got command of the pinnace, and Adair, who would otherwise have remained on board, volunteered to accompany him with Queerface, to make sport for the crew. Dick Needham was also of the party. Away they pulled to the northward, and before sunset they were out of sight of the ship.

"We must have a prize somehow or other," cried Adair; "it will never do to return without one."

"Just such a one as you and I took in the Mediterranean when we first went to sea," said Jack, laughing. "However, we'll do our best: what do you say to it, Master Queerface?" There sat the monkey in the stern-sheets, dressed in a broad-brimmed straw hat, nankeen trousers, a light blue jacket, and a red neckcloth, just as Don Diogo had appeared when Jack had last seen him. Queerface seemed in no way to disapprove of the hat and jacket, but his lower garments at times somewhat puzzled him; however, he altogether behaved himself very well. There was so little wind that Jack did not even step his masts. He thus hoped to get close to any slaver, should he see one, without being discovered. He had his trusty rifle ready, and from frequently practising he was even a better shot than before. Adair had picked up a very fair rifle at Sierra Leone, but he could not pretend to equal Jack as a shot. They both well knew that they could not hope to take a prize without exerting themselves, and they were, therefore, constantly standing up and looking about on all sides in search of a sail. They were off a part of the coast whence numerous cargoes of slaves were still embarked. A short time before sunset they made the land. Soon after this, as Jack was standing up on the stern-sheets, his eye fell on a white spark glistening brightly in the oblique rays of the departing luminary. He brought his glass to bear on the subject. Adair took a look at it, and so did Needham. They all agreed that the sail in sight was a square topsail schooner standing off the land.

"Then she must pass close to us," cried Jack. "We'll be on the watch for her."

Another look they all took before the sun sank below the horizon confirmed them in this opinion. The last few hours of daylight were spent by the crew in examining their pistols, in seeing that their cutlasses were ready at hand, and everything prepared for boarding at a moment's notice. All hands then turned to and had a good supper, after which, as they said, they were up to anything.

The boat floated quietly on the almost calm waters, for though the men lay on their oars, they did not pull a stroke. Not a word was spoken above the lowest whisper. There were sounds, for the ocean itself is never, even in a calm, altogether silent. Ever and anon there was a splash, sometimes caused by the boat as the smooth undulations rose up as it seemed from the depths below, and made her roll lazily for an instant from side to side, or some fish rose to the surface with wide-open mouths, or leaped up into the air, or one of the monsters of the unfathomed waters came to have a gaze at the strange thing which floated over their liquid home. A slight mist came over the land with the night air, damp and unwholesome enough, but Jack and Terence little regarded that point, as it contributed much to conceal the boat from the approaching stranger, though they had little doubt that her more lofty sails would easily be seen above it. Time passed on. They calculated that the schooner must be drawing near them.

Once more Jack stood up. "There she is," he whispered, as he sank into his seat. "Away to the northward. Out oars, lads, as gently as possible. In ten minutes we shall be alongside of her." The oars had been muffled, and with the long, steady strokes made by the men, scarcely a splash was heard. They might well hope to be up to the stranger without being discovered. On glided the boat. It was an exciting moment. The sails of a large topsail schooner rose up out of the mist before them.

Jack and Adair thought they saw a little beyond her the pointed tops of another craft slowly moving over the bank of fog. If they should both prove enemies there would be fearful odds against them. They numbered only eleven people in all—eight pulling, Needham, and themselves. Still they did not hesitate.

"We'll take one, and then be ready for the other," whispered Jack.

Adair nodded his assent. Still discretion might have been the best part of valour in this case.

"That further craft is a felucca," again whispered Jack. "I can see the tops of her lateen sails above the mist. Perhaps she's the old Don's craft. Never mind, we'll be ready for him."

In two minutes more they were close up to the schooner. No notice had hitherto been taken of them by those on board. They flattered themselves that they were not perceived. They dashed alongside.

"Who are you? who are you?" said a fierce voice in Spanish. "Speak, speak, who are you?"

"A boat of her Britannic Majesty's ship *Ranger*," answered Jack, who understood what was said. "Heave-to, I want to come on board you." He said this as the boat was hooking on, and he and Terence, followed by their men, were about to spring on deck, when again the same person who had before hailed, sang out, "Heave, heave, sink the boat and the scoundrel heretics. Have no mercy on them."

At that instant down came half a dozen round shots into the bottom of the boat, rattling through the planks, while pistols were fired in their faces, and pikes were thrust at them, and swords flourished above their heads. They were prepared for opposition, so, in spite of this, cutlass in hand, they sprang up the side of the vessel without much difficulty, as her bulwarks were low, and attacked their assailants. Jack had time to seize his rifle, for he saw the water rushing into his boat, and he felt that she was sinking under their feet. Followed by Queerface, who, through fright, chattered away louder than ever, the English seamen gained the deck of the slaver. Such undoubtedly she was, if not worse. Jack saw that they had nearly taken her by surprise, for but few men were at that moment on deck; but others, some only half dressed, were rushing out of both the fore and after cabins. The first who had received them made so bold a stand that time was allowed for the whole of the Spanish crew to assemble. They far outnumbered the English. Still the gallant young midshipmen and their followers fought on undaunted. Suddenly Queerface, who had hitherto kept behind the rest, jumped up into the rigging and looked over them.

"Don Diogo! Don Diogo!" cried several of the slaver's crew; "how comes he to be with these men? There must be some mistake."

"Quacko—Quacko—Quacko," cried Queerface, and scud up the rigging out of harm's way.

The Spaniards could not make it out. The delay, however, was an advantage to the English, as it enabled them to cast their eyes around and see the state of affairs. The greater number of their enemies were forward, so Jack and most of his party sprang on in that direction, hoping to dispose of them first. The fellows stood their ground, firing their pistols and flourishing their swords, and two of the English were shot, and Jack got an ugly cut across his shoulder. Still he pressed on, and compelled at length the Spaniards to take refuge in their cabin under the topgallant forecastle.

Meantime Terence was keeping the slaver's captain and officers in check, but he had lost a man, who was struck to the deck, and Needham too was wounded. Matters were going very hard with Jack and his followers. Still ten British seamen might well have hoped to conquer the whole of a slaver's crew. The fight had now become desperate. The Spanish captain had probably all his fortune embarked in the venture, Jack and his party had to struggle for life and liberty. Again and again they made desperate rushes at the afterpart of the vessel, and at length they pushed the Spaniards so hard that they almost drove them overboard, when two sails were seen emerging from out of the fog and gliding up alongside. In another instant, not Queerface, but the veritable Don Diogo himself was seen to spring on board, followed by a dozen or more villainous-looking ruffians.

"What's all this? what's all this?" his harsh croaking voice was heard shouting in Spanish. "Down with the English pirates, down with them!"

Hearing the cry, the Spaniards, who had taken refuge forward, rushed out again, and though Jack called to Terence to fight to the last, and that they would sell their lives dearly, they found themselves literally borne down by numbers, and their cutlasses whirled out of their hands.

"We have done our best, Paddy, we can do no more," exclaimed Jack, as he and Terence found themselves standing side by side, with their hands secured and lashed to the mainmast. Needham and the rest of the people who were able to move were treated in the same way.

"Why, my friend, you were very nearly captured by these picaroons," they heard Don Diogo remark to the other Spanish captain. "But where is a lantern?—let me see whom we have caught."

The lantern was brought, and the Don came round and held it up to their faces.

"Ha! ha!" he exclaimed, with a most sardonic grin. "Your obedient humble servant, gentlemen. I told you we should meet again, and we have met. What do you expect after all the tricks you have played me?"

Neither Jack nor Terence deigned a reply.

"Ah, speak, pirates," he exclaimed, stamping furiously on the deck; "the yard-arm, a sharp knife, or a walk on the plank? Whichever you like. I grant you your choice."

Still neither of the midshipmen would reply. What was the use of so doing?

"We must kill every one of them," exclaimed the Don, speaking in Spanish, turning to the other captain. "I have a long account to settle with these English generally, and these lads especially. They have been the cause of nearly all my losses. They cannot repay me, but I can take my revenge, and that is something."

"Certainly, certainly, my friend," answered the other: "you can hang, or drown, or shoot them, as you think fit. It is a matter of perfect indifference to me."

These were the last words poor Jack heard as the two worthies entered the cabin.

"We are in a bad case, Jack, I am afraid," said Adair, "though I could not exactly make out what the fellows said."

"It was not pleasant," answered Jack, briefly. "Terence, have you ever thought of dying?"

"Yes, I have; that is to say, I have known that I was running many a chance of being knocked on the head or finished in some way or other," answered Adair, with some little hesitation.

"Then, Terence, my dear fellow, let us look at it as an awful reality, which is about speedily to overtake us," said Jack solemnly. "These fellows threaten to at once take our lives; depend on it, they will put their threats into execution."

"It is hard to bear, Jack dear," replied Adair; "I am so sorry for you and for all your brothers and sisters at home. I don't think mine care much for me; that's one comfort. But I say, I wish that the blackguards would let us have our arms free, that we might still have a fight for our lives."

"Don't speak thus, Terence," said Jack, who was almost overcome by Adair's allusion to his family. "Don't let us think of the past, but keep our thoughts fixed on the future world we are about to enter, and think how very unfit we are of ourselves for the glorious place we would wish to go to."

Terence listened, and responded in the same tone to his messmate. Much more they said to the same effect, nor did they forget to offer up their prayers for preservation from the terrible danger which threatened them. Then, with the calmness of Christians and brave men, they awaited the doom they believed prepared for them. Such consolation as they could give also they offered to the survivors of their crew. Two poor fellows had been killed outright; another was bleeding to death on the deck, nor would the brutal Spaniards offer him the slightest assistance, while they prevented his shipmates from giving it him. Jack himself was suffering also much pain from his wound, while he felt so faint from loss of blood that he could scarcely support himself. He had told Needham that the Spaniards threatened to kill them all.

"Well, sir, they may do it if they dare, but they will be sure to be caught some day or other," answered Needham. "I wouldn't change places with them. We shall die having done our duty; they will be hung up like dogs. If I knew their lingo I would tell them so."

The English were not long left in quiet. So many of the Spaniards had been wounded that some time was spent by them in bandaging up their hurts, and as soon as this was done they came on deck eager to wreak their vengeance on their captive foes. They now came about them with their long knives, flourishing them before their eyes, and pretending to stab at them. Some indeed, more brutal than the rest, actually stuck their knives into their flesh, but though blood was drawn, the seamen generally disdained even to utter a word, though one or two said, "I'll tell you what, you villains, if I can get my fists at liberty, I'll give it you." At length Don Diogo and the captain of the schooner came out from the cabin. They had apparently made up their minds what to do. The latter gave orders to reeve ropes to each yard-arm, while planks were got up and placed over the sides, secured on board by lanyards. On these being cut, of course the end of the plank overboard would instantly sink down and let the person standing on it into the water. Don Diogo had, it seemed, taken upon himself the direction of the executions. Jack and Adair had supposed that the Spaniards would wait till the morning to kill them, but the little Don evidently had no wish to delay his vengeance.

"Cast the prisoners loose, and bring them aft," he cried out. "Now, you scoundrel heretics, what have you got to say for yourselves? Nothing? I thought so. Well, I will be merciful. You shall choose the mode of your death. What shall it be—will you be hung or walk the plank? There are plenty of sharks alongside who will be happy to entomb you either way."

No one replied to this address.

"Speak, you heretics," he cried, stamping with rage.

The two midshipmen cast their eyes about them to assure themselves that what was taking place was a reality; the whole scene appeared so like some horrid dream that they could scarcely believe it true. As they looked up they discovered that a strong breeze had sprung up, and that the vessel was moving rapidly through the water. The deck was crowded with seamen, many of whom held lanterns, so that the whole ship was lighted.

"It is time to begin," cried the Don. "Come, as you will not choose for yourselves, I must choose for you. Here, seize that lad and run him up to the mainyard-arm."

He pointed at Adair. Several of the ruffian crew rushed forward and seized poor Terence, and dragged him up to the rope which hung from the yard-arm. They were about to take hold of it to adjust it round Adair's neck, when down by it came gliding an apparition which, in the uncertain light cast by the lanterns aloft, looked so like old Don Diogo himself, that the superstitious Spaniards, believing that it was his wraith or ghost, let go the rope and sprang back to the other side of the vessel. The old Don was not less astonished than the rest, but not exactly recognising himself, it occurred to him that some spirit of evil had come on board to watch his proceedings. Queerface, meantime, for the apparition was no other than him, seeing the confusion he had created, shinned up the rope again, and on reaching the yard-arm, finding it slack, hauled it up after him, and there he sat chattering away and wondering what the strangers were going to do to his master. The wicked old Don, though astonished at first, was not altogether overcome, and soon recovering himself, began to get an idea of the true state of the case. Once more he ordered the crew to go on with their cruel work, but no one would venture aloft to overhaul the whip, and Queerface showed no disposition to help them. The Don began to swear and stamp with rage, calling them all by certain uncomplimentary epithets, in which the Spanish language is so rich. The crew swore and abused him in return. In the midst of the confusion a voice hailed them through a speaking-trumpet.

"What schooner is that? Heave-to, or I will fire into you."

"We are in the hands of a set of bloody pirates. I'm Jack Rogers," sang out Jack, at the top of his voice. Never had he sung out louder.

"Take that for speaking," exclaimed the little Don, levelling a pistol at his head. He pulled the trigger. It missed fire, and before he could again cock the lock, Needham, who had been working his hands free, sprang aft, and with a blow of his fist levelled him with the deck. It was the signal for the Spaniards to set upon them, and they would all have been cut down, but the next instant a loud crash was heard, and the dark hull of a man-of-war brig, with her taunt masts and wide spread of canvas, was seen ranging up alongside. The next instant twenty or more stout English seamen, led by Alick Murray, came pouring down on the slaver's deck. The brig which had thus providentially fallen in with them was the *Archer*. She was on her passage to the northward with despatches for Captain Lascelles, recalling him and his frigate homewards. The news was received by all hands with unmitigated joy. The tables on board the schooner were quickly turned. The Spaniards were all handcuffed, and a strict guard set over them. The midshipmen and their followers went on board the brig, where they were cordially welcomed, and their wounds looked to. The felucca escaped, but as she was never again heard of, it was supposed that she was lost in a fierce gale which occurred two days afterwards. The schooner was found to be full of slaves, and proved a rich prize. Don Diogo escaped hanging, but was reduced to abject beggary, for he had not even the means of leaving Sierra Leone, and very soon afterwards was found dead on the beach. This was the last adventure either of the three midshipmen met with on the coast of Africa. They were all three pretty well tired of it, and delighted indeed were they when they once more found themselves in sight of Old England. The frigate and brig were paid off about the same time, and Alick and Terence accompanied Jack to that often-talked-of and well-loved home of his in Northamptonshire. It must not be forgotten that they had in their train the most sensible of travelled apes. Master Queerface, who, by his amusing antics and performances, and extraordinary monkeyish sagacity, gained the admiration of the whole surrounding neighbourhood. There they remained for some weeks, when, after Alick and Terence had paid a short visit to their own friends, they were all once more summoned afloat.

Chapter Twenty Three
Bound for China

Her Majesty's frigate *Dugong* was fitting with all despatch for sea at Portsmouth; so was her Majesty's brig-of-war *Blenny*, just commissioned by Commander Hemming, well-known, as the papers stated, for his gallantry on the coast of Africa, and on every occasion when he had an opportunity of displaying it. The papers spoke truly, and well had our old friend won his present rank. Both the frigate and the brig were destined, it was supposed, for the China seas; but this was not known to a certainty. The *Dugong* had been commissioned by Captain Grant, Alick Murray's old commander in the *Archer*, who had some short time before received his post rank. Captain Lascelles, with whom the three midshipmen first went to sea, commanded at this time a line-of-battle ship on the Indian station.

Who has not heard of the *Blue Posts* at Portsmouth, to be found not far from the landing-place known as the Point, now sadly encroached on by new batteries and a broad wooden pier?

One afternoon, at the time of which I am speaking, a cab stopped at the door of that well-known inn, with a portmanteau outside, and a cocked-hat case, a sword, a gun-case, and several other articles, including a young naval officer inside. He nodded smilingly to the waiter and boots, who came to get out his things, as to old acquaintances, and then, having paid the cabman, entered the inn. No sooner had he put his head into the coffee-room, than another young officer, in the uniform of a mate or passed midshipman, jumped up, and, seizing him by the hand, exclaimed—

"I am delighted to see you, my dear Jack. You've come to join the *Dugong*, I hope."

"If you belong to her, Adair, I wish I was," answered Jack Rogers, for he was the new-comer. "But I am not. The fact is, Hemming has got command of the *Blenny*, and I applied and got appointed to her. It can't be helped now. Any news of Murray? He wrote me word, some little time ago, that he expected to get appointed to a ship. I wish that I could have had him with me; but we three have been on the same station, and mostly together all our lives, and we can scarcely expect the same good fortune to continue."

"We tried to keep together, and we succeeded," answered Adair. "There's nothing like trying, in my opinion."

"You are right there, old fellow; there isn't a doubt of it," exclaimed Jack Rogers, who had been a little out of spirits, and inclined to take a somewhat gloomy view of affairs in general.

No wonder, for he had just left as happy a home as any to be found in Old England. It was a cold March day too, and he was chilled with his journey. He took off his great coat, which, with his other things, Boots carried to his room, and then the two old messmates sat down before the fire. They had been talking on for some time while their dinner was getting ready, when Adair observed a young man sitting at a table a little way off, narrowly observing them. Terence looked at him in return.

"Do you know, Jack, I do verily believe that there sits no other than Bully Pigeon," he whispered. "What can he be doing down here?"

The stranger, seeing them looking at him, got up, and approaching them with his hand extended, said—

"What, do I see some old friends? Rogers! Adair! Very glad to see you. How de do? How de do? You remember me, surely. I'm Pigeon."

Thus addressed, it would not have been in the nature of either of the two midshipmen to have refused to shake hands with their old schoolfellow, bully though he had been. They invited him to join them; and when they had dined they all three sat over their wine together, talking merrily of former days.

"I'm going out to China in the diplomatic line," observed Pigeon, in his old tone. "I have a notion that I shall be able to manage the Celestials. There are few people who can deceive me."

These, and a few other similar remarks, showed that Pigeon in one respect was little changed from what he had been in his early days. When or how he was going out to China he did not say.

They had been chatting away for some time when another cab rattled up to the inn, and presently at the door of the coffee-room who should appear, to the delight of Rogers and Adair, but Murray himself. They dragged him into the room, each eager to know what ship he was come to join. Paddy gave a shout of delight when he heard that he was appointed to the *Dugong*. He told them besides that she was certainly under orders for China, to sail as soon as ready for sea, and that the *Blenny* was also to be sent there.

The old schoolfellows, as may be supposed, passed a very pleasant evening, their pleasure being heightened with the anticipation of being together in whatever work they might be engaged. Even Bully Pigeon was sufferable (as Paddy observed), if he was not altogether agreeable. He had a number of strange adventures to narrate, of which he was the hero. Although his accounts were not implicitly believed, it was agreed that, at all events, they were possible, which was somewhat in his favour.

Two weeks after this, her Majesty's ships *Dugong* and *Blenny* were gliding under all sail across the Bay of Biscay.

"The frigate looks something like a dowager with her small daughter following in her wake, sir," observed Jack, glancing his eye from the brig to her big consort, as he walked the deck with his captain.

"We must try and make the little daughter win a name for herself out among the Celestials," said Captain Hemming in return.

"That we will, sir, if we get the chance," answered Jack.

"Ay, Rogers, but we must make the chance," remarked his captain with emphasis.

"So we will, sir," said Jack warmly. "There is not a man on board who'll not be glad of it."

Captain Hemming had a sincere regard and respect for Jack, as Jack had for him. They had both seen each other well tried and never found wanting, and they could thus converse frankly and without reserve. Neither Hemming nor Jack were people to talk without fully intending to perform. Indeed, those who knew them felt sure that when dash or cool courage, or perseverance and intelligence, were especially required, they would show that they possessed them all. Jack liked his ship and most of his brother officers, as well as his captain, and was a general favourite with them. He had brought two companions, Adair's old African follower, Queerface, which he had given to Jack; and a fine Newfoundland dog, Sancho by name. Jack had intended leaving Queerface at home, as Paddy remarked, to remind his brothers and sisters of him. The compliment was somewhat doubtful. But the monkey had played so many curious tricks, and had committed so much mischief, that no one would undertake the charge of him; and therefore, like a bad boy, he was sent off to sea again in disgrace. As was natural, Sancho and Queerface became very intimate, though not at the same time perfectly friendly. Each, it appeared, was striving for the mastery. Queerface, monkey though he was, gained the day; and one of his great amusements was to mount Sancho's back, and to make him run round and round the deck with him, whipping him on and chattering away all the time most vociferously, to the great amusement of the seamen, if not always to that of the first lieutenant.

Jack had another charge to look after, a young midshipman, Harry Bevan by name, who had been especially committed to his charge. The little fellow had been a petted somewhat spoilt child, an only son, yet go to sea he would; and his parents never had refused him anything, so they let him have his will, though it almost broke their hearts. Jack promised to take the best care of him he could. Harry was not exactly a pickle, but he had very little notion of taking care of himself; so Jack had quite enough to do to look after him, in addition to Queerface and Sancho. Harry and Sancho were very great friends, but Queerface evidently looked upon him as a rival in his master's affections, and bore him no good-will. This feeling of the monkey was increased by the tricks which the young midshipman played him whenever he had the opportunity. At last he was never able to approach Queerface without a rope in his hand, which he held behind his back, or doubled up in his pocket. The monkey, in the most sagacious way, would skip about till he had ascertained whether the weapon was there or not. If it was there, as soon as he caught sight of it, he would spring up into the rigging and sit on a ratline, as quiet and demure as a judge, without attempting to retaliate.

On board the frigate there was little to interrupt the usual routine. Murray had carried one of his parrots with him, and the sagacious bird afforded almost as much amusement as did Bully Pigeon, who soon showed that he was very little altered from what he had been in his youth. He could not bully, but he could give abundant evidence of being still an arrant donkey. Pigeon now called himself a philosopher, and used to be very fond of broaching his philosophical principles, as he denominated his nonsense. One day, when dining in the gun-room, he began as usual. As he drank his wine he grew bolder and bolder in his assertions. At last he declared that he did not believe that there was a place of punishment after death. He had taken it into his head that the surgeon would side with him.

"I'm sure, doctor, a sensible man like you will not assert that such is a fact?" he continued. "What use would there be in it?"

"I'll tell you what, ma laddie, there's one vary good use it will be put to, and that will be to stow away all such vicious, ignorant donkeys as you are," answered the doctor with great emphasis and deliberation.

Pigeon was no way disconcerted at this somewhat powerful rebuke, but continued as before. Indeed, nothing is so difficult as to make a conceited fool cease from talking folly. At last the first lieutenant struck his fist on the table with a force which made all the glasses ring, as he exclaimed—

"I'll tell you what, Mr Pigeon. This ship belongs to a Christian Queen, and while I'm the senior officer present I'll not allow you to sneer against religion, or a word to be spoken which her gracious Majesty would not approve of. Now, sir, hold your tongue, or I'll report your conduct, and have you put under arrest."

The diplomatist, though looking very silly, began again, but another loud rap on the table silenced him. It did not, however, silence Murray's parrot, who had found its way, as it often did, into the cabin, and the moment the voices ceased Polly set up such a roar of laughter, that Pigeon fancied that she was laughing at him. The silly fellow's rage knew no bounds. There was, however, nothing else on which he dared to vent it, except on the loquacious bird. A bottle of port wine stood near. He seized it by the neck to throw it at Polly, who, unconscious of the coming storm, only chattered the louder. The stopper was out. As he lifted it above his head, a copious shower of the ruddy juice descended over his white shirt and waistcoat, and head and face, so blinding him that he missed his aim, but broke the bottle, while Polly gave way to louder laughter than ever, in which everybody most vociferously joined. The wretched Pigeon had to make his escape to his cabin to change his dress, nor did he venture out again for the rest of the day, some of the time being passed in listening to the not very complimentary remarks made upon him and his so-called philosophy. If anything would have cured him of his folly, that might have done so. He had some glimmering suspicion that he was wrong, but he had no hearty desire to be right, and when that is the case a man is certainly in a bad way.

Day after day the two ships sailed on in sight of each other. The brig was very fast, and, though so much smaller, could outsail the frigate, which was not remarkable for speed. Frequently, when they were together, Polly used to take a flight, to pay her old friend Queerface a visit, and he always seemed delighted to see her. He exhibited his pleasure by all sorts of antics, though he could not express what he felt so fluently with his tongue as she did. At length the Cape of Good Hope was doubled without the *Flying Dutchman* having been seen, though the philosopher Pigeon kept a bright lookout for him. One night he declared that he saw the phantom bark sailing right up in the wind's eye, but it was found to be only the *Blenny* following the frigate under easy sail with a fair wind astern. Pont de Galle, in the island of Ceylon, celebrated for the rich spices it exported, and supposed to be one of the most ancient emporiums of commerce, was visited, and at last the most modern and yet the largest emporium in the Indian seas, Singapore, was reached. This wonderful city, which was founded as late as 1824 by Sir Stamford Raffles, on a spot where, though formerly the site of a Malay capital, at that time but a few huts stood, is now the most wealthy and flourishing on the shores of those eastern seas. Here vessels bring produce and manufactures from all parts of the world, again to be distributed among all the neighbouring countries. There are no duties levied of any sort or description, so that people of all nations are encouraged to come there with their goods. The Chinese especially flock to the port, and great numbers are settled in the city and throughout the island, largely contributing by their persevering industry to its prosperity. Who does not know the look of a Chinese, with his piggish eyes, thatched-like hat, yellow-brown skin, black tail, and wide short trousers? The streets swarmed with them, ever busy, ever toiling to collect dollars, the most industrious people under the sun— yet the least lovable or attractive. Their houses may be known by the red lintels of the door-posts covered with curious characters and designs; while at night the persevering people may be seen still working away by the light of huge paper lanterns covered with the strangest of devices. The whole island is not larger than the Isle of Wight, but already there are a hundred thousand people living on it, collected from all quarters of the globe. There are numerous very handsome houses in the town, mostly roofed with red-brick tiles, while the higher spots in the neighbourhood are chiefly occupied by the villas of the European merchants and other principal residents. Such was the place before which her Majesty's ships *Dugong* and *Blenny* brought up, outside a fleet of strange-looking junks, with flags of all colours, devices, and shapes flying at their mast-heads, while in different part of the extensive roads were ships belonging to nearly all the countries in the world, English, American, and Dutch, however, predominating.

Although just then the British and Chinese empires were linked in the bonds of peace, the ships of war of the former had plenty to do in keeping in order the numerous hordes of pirates which infested those seas, and considerably impeded her commerce, plundering her merchantmen, and cutting the throats of the crews whenever opportunity offered.

The frigate and brig had been at Singapore but a few days when an open boat under sail was seen entering the harbour. She stood for the *Blenny*, which was the outer vessel. Jack Rogers, who was doing duty as officer of the watch, hailed her to know what she wanted. A glance at the condition of her crew told him more than any words could have done. Their faces were wan and bloodless, their dresses torn, and several had their heads and limbs bound up. One man sat at the helm, and another forward to manage the sail; the rest lay along the thwarts or at the bottom of the boat, apparently more dead than alive. The boat came alongside, but no one in her had strength left to climb on board. Even the man at the helm sank back exhausted as she was made fast. Jack ordered some slings to be got ready to hoist them up, and then, taking some brandy and water in a bottle, he leaped down into the boat to administer it to the poor people. His restorative was only just in time, for many of them were already almost dead. The surgeon and most of the officers of the brig were on shore. Jack, therefore, signalled to the frigate to send a doctor forthwith. Doctor McCan, who had been appointed to the frigate, accompanied by Murray, soon came on board, and every possible assistance was given to the famished strangers. After some time the man who had steered the boat recovered. He said that he was mate of a ship bound from China to the Australian colonies, and that when she was about three hundred miles distant from Singapore, she had been attacked by a fleet of piratical Illanoon prahus, and her captain and crew had resisted to the utmost, but she was reduced almost to a wreck, and at night by some accident caught fire. The first mate was the only surviving officer; the captain and the rest, with many of the crew, had been killed by the pirates. During the darkness the survivors made their escape unpursued, though they could see the prahus approaching the burning wreck soon after they had left her.

As soon as this information was conveyed on shore, the frigate and brig were ordered to proceed to sea in search of the pirate fleet. No one was sorry to have work to do, though small amount of glory was to be obtained in pirate hunting.

"It's our duty, at all events, and that is one comfort," observed Jack to Adair, who had been lent to the brig in consequence of the illness of her second lieutenant. Thus two of the old schoolfellows were together.

The squadron, sailing to the northward, cruised in every direction where they were likely to fall in with the piratical fleets; but though many traces of them were discovered in ruined villages and stranded vessels, the crews of which had been murdered or carried off into slavery, the pirates themselves were nowhere to be seen. At last it occurred to Captain Grant that in all probability the pirates were receiving constant information of their movements, and had thus managed to elude them. He therefore determined to fit out three boats, which would, by being able to steal along shore, and pull head to wind, be more likely to come on the pirates unawares.

No sooner was the thought conceived than it was put into execution. Each boat was fitted with a long gun on the bows, besides swivels at the sides for closer quarters, and manned with twelve hands armed to the teeth, besides officers; and in the larger boats two or three extra men. Rogers and Adair got charge of two of the boats. Murray would gladly have gone in the third with Mr Cherry, the second lieutenant of the frigate, who had command of the expedition, but two midshipmen had already been directed to get ready to go in her, and he did not like to deprive either of them of the pleasure they anticipated. The boats did not leave the ships till some two or three hours after dark, that none of the friends of the pirates might discover what had occurred.

No one expected anything but amusement from the expedition. Nat Cherry, their leader, was one of the most good-natured, jolly fellows in the navy, and seldom failed to make everybody under him happy. They could not bring themselves to believe that a whole fleet of pirate prahus would ever wait their attack for a moment, they felt almost sure that directly they appeared the enemy would attempt to escape. Just as Jack was shoving off from the brig, Queerface, who had been watching his opportunity, made a spring into the boat, and there was instantly a loud cry from all on board her, that he might be allowed to remain.

"Oh, he's such a divertin' rogue, he'll keep every mother's son of us as merry as crickets," sang out an Irish topman, whose own humour generally proved a source of amusement to all with him.

The request was granted, and Queerface seemed to enjoy the prospect of the trip as much as his companions. Away pulled the squadron of boats. When daylight dawned they were coasting along the shore of an island fringed with cocoa-nut trees, and hills rising in the centre. There were numerous deep indentations, bays, and gulfs, with bluff cliffs here here there, and high rocks scattered about, capital spots in which whole fleets of prahus might lie hid without much chance of being discovered. The weather was very hot, as it is apt to be within a few miles of the equator; and when there was no wind, and the sea shone like a burnished mirror, the sun came down with very considerable force on the top of the heads of the party in the boats. Still their spirits did not flag. Jack and Adair, indeed, had been pretty well seasoned to the heat of the coast of Africa, where, if not greater, it was often far less supportable.

Mr Cherry led: Jack and Terence followed side by side. A constant fire of jokes was kept up between the two boats. Queerface evidently thought that there was something in the wind, and kept jumping about with unusual activity, keeping apparently as bright a lookout as anybody on board. Not an inlet was passed unexplored, still not a sign of the pirates could they discover. On going up one small but deepish river, they came, close to the banks, on a native village. The inhabitants must have taken to flight on their approach, for not a human being was to be seen.

"That looks suspicious," exclaimed Adair. "We ought to burn this village to teach them better manners."

Mr Cherry fortunately had no such intention. He had an idea that burning people's houses was not the best way of making friends of them.

"Indeed, it would be a pity to have to destroy so picturesque a place," observed Jack Rogers.

The houses were mostly separate, built on piles four or five feet above the ground. They were of one storey, with a deep verandah or gallery running round them, a ladder leading up to it. The roofs, which were high and pointed with deep eaves, were covered with a thick coating of palm-leaves, and so were the walls, while the floors were made of bamboo cut in strips and placed nearly an inch apart, being covered with a thick, beautifully woven mat. They appeared strong, but very springy, so much so, that when Adair began to dance a polka on one of them, he very nearly bounded up to the roof. The village was surrounded and interspersed with cocoa-nut and other palm-trees, and with bananas, whose dark-green foliage gave effect to lighter tints of the forest. The thick jungle pressed hard on every side, leaving space only here and there for some small fields and gardens. Mr Cherry would not allow the slightest injury to be done to the houses; for though it was suspected that they belonged to the pirates, no traces of booty were to be discovered.

After spending some time in examining the locality, they were about to embark, when a dark visage was seen peering out at them from among the trees. Instead of making chase to catch him, Mr Cherry stood still and beckoned to him. This gave the native courage, who, seeing also that no injury had been done to the village, after a little hesitation advanced. One of Jack's crew was a Malay, who could speak not only his own language, but that of many of the surrounding tribes. He had no difficulty in entering into conversation with the native, who asserted that his people had taken the British for pirates, and had run away in consequence. To prove his sincerity, he offered to pilot the boats to the chief haunts of the pirates. As there was no reason to doubt him, his offer was accepted. He merely requested time to equip himself for the expedition. He entered one of the houses, and soon returned with a couple of creeses stuck in his sash, and a sword by his side, and the whole party, embarking once more, proceeded on their voyage. Their volunteer pilot was a merry, talkative fellow. What his real name was it was difficult to make out exactly, so Jack gave him that of Hoddidoddi, which it sounded very like, and he at once readily answered to it.

All that day they sailed on without seeing anything of the pirates. They began to last to fancy that Hoddidoddi was deceiving them; but he entreated them not to despair, and promised, by noon the next day at farthest, to bring them in sight of the marauders. They brought up at night in a sheltered bay, where the water was as smooth as a mill-pond. Jack and Adair grew very sentimental as they leaned back in the stern-sheets of Mr Cherry's boat, where all the officers had collected to smoke their cigars, and looked up into the dark sky, sprinkled with stars innumerable. What they said need not be repeated.

"Come, lads, dismount from your Pegasus, and turn in and get a little sleep," cried their commanding officer; "we've a hard day's work before us to-morrow, I suspect."

This warning brought their thoughts back to the business in which they were engaged, and, returning to their respective boats, those not on watch were very quickly wrapped in what, as Paddy said, "might have been 'soft repose,' if it wasn't that the planks were so mighty hard." They were awoke before dawn by a summons from Hoddidoddi, who declared that there was sufficient light for him to pilot them, if they wished to proceed. The anchors were at once got up, and they pulled away along shore.

By daylight they came to a broad channel some miles wide. Their pilot averred that they should find the pirate fleet across it. Away they dashed. A thin silvery mist hung over the ocean; sufficient, however, to conceal them from any one on the lookout on the opposite shore. Only here and there, as they approached, a few palm-trees, rearing their heads above the mist, showed where the shore itself was.

"If the pirates only happen to be there, we shall catch them to a certainty," shouted Paddy to Jack, as they pulled rapidly on.

Soon all were ordered to keep silence, and Hoddidoddi was seen to be indulging in a variety of curious and somewhat violent gesticulations. Just then appeared the masts and yards of a whole fleet of Illanoon prahus. There could be no doubt that they were the pirates. Mr Cherry had no necessity to order his followers to give way. The seamen laid their backs to the oars, and made the boats fly hissing through the water. They thought that they should take the enemy by surprise; but the sound of tom-toms beating, pistols being fired, and loud shouts showed them that the pirates were not asleep, and that they themselves had been heard, if not seen. Just then a puff of wind blew aside the mist, and exhibited some twenty prahus or more drawn up in order of battle, and ready to receive them. A larger body than they were might have hesitated about attacking; still it did not enter the head of their gallant leader that it would be possible to retreat. He ordered Jack to attack on one wing and Adair on the other, while he pulled for the centre of the fleet, firing his long gun as he did so. The pirates were evidently astonished at this bold proceeding, and at the way the shots pitched into them. Probably they thought that the boats they saw were only the advanced guard, and that a much stronger force was following. First one and then another cut their cables, and, getting out their long sweeps, pulled away on either hand. Some four or five stood to the southward, and Jack in hot haste followed them. Adair pursued nearly the same number round the north end of the island, while the main body, with whom Mr Cherry was engaged, showed a disposition to run up a narrow inlet or channel, which appeared astern of them. Jack cheered on his men, and they, nothing loth, gave way with a will. Still the pirates showed that they possessed very fast heels, besides which they could kick, as the British found to their cost, and several shots from their stern guns struck the boat as she got nearer to them. A groan burst from the lips of one of the seamen. He pulled on; but Jack saw his hands suddenly let go his oar, and down he sank. Directly afterwards another poor fellow was hit. This loss considerably lessened the speed of the boat; some little time also was occupied in placing the wounded men in the stern-sheets, and in looking to their wounds.

Chapter Twenty Four
Hot Fighting

With Jack Rogers had come little Harry Bevan; Jack, not believing that there would be any fighting, had got leave to bring his young charge with him. As the shot were flying thickly about, how gladly would he have shielded the young lad with his own body. He wished that he could have ventured to stow him down at the bottom of the boat, out of harm's way; but he knew well enough that Harry would not have remained there a minute had he done so. Not a thought that he himself might be hit crossed Jack's mind. His whole anxiety was for the young boy. Harry, however, seemed unconscious of danger. He was leaning over one of the wounded men, assisting to bind up his arm, when Jack saw his hand drop powerless by his side, while he fell forward. Jack caught him in time. "What is the matter, Harry?" he exclaimed. "Are you hurt, lad?"

"A strange pain about my shoulder and arm and neck," he answered faintly. "Oh, I am very sick, Rogers, very sick." Jack saw that the boy's jacket was torn. He cut away the cloth with his knife; the blood how gushed out freely; there was a desperate wound on the shoulder. No woman could have dressed it with more care and gentleness than did Jack. He poured some brandy and water down the lad's throat, which much revived him, though his suppressed groans showed that he was still in great pain.

Many people would have given up the chase under these circumstances, but Jack Rogers was not a fellow to do that. He found, however, that he could do the enemy more damage by keeping out of the range of their guns, and yet keep them within range of his. Miles were thus passed over. As the sun rose the heat increased. There was a breeze, and the prahus profited by it by spreading all their sails, but it did not serve to cool the air. At length Jack found that he had got round the island, and greatly to his delight he saw the other portion of the pirate squadron followed closely by Adair. The two boats were soon alongside each other. A council of war was held. It was a question whether they should wait for their commander or pursue the enemy. It was quickly decided that they should continue the chase. There were groups of islands ahead, and the chances were that if they did not follow the enemy they would escape among them. So on they pulled. The pirates fired as before, though without doing any further damage. The only person who seemed to wish to be elsewhere was Queerface. He jumped about and chattered incessantly. Then he would try and hide himself; but could not remain quiet, but every time he heard a shot he popped up his head to see where it was going. Suddenly it grew perfectly calm again. A lurid look came over the sky. Evidently there was going to be a change in the weather. The pirates seemed to know what was about to occur. There was an inlet in an island close at hand: towards it they rapidly pulled. Jack and Adair were about to follow, when down upon them came a terrific squall, which very nearly blew both their boats right over. They happily got them before it, and away they flew towards the island they had left. To weather it was impossible. The best chance of saving the boats was to beach them. They prayed that there might be no rocks in the way, but the fierce breath of the tornado was sweeping up such vast masses of foam into the air, that they could see but a few fathoms before them. Side by side the two boats sprang on. Jack stood up. As his boat rose on the top of a sea, he saw the land: close under her bows it appeared.

"Be ready, lads, to spring out, and to carry our wounded shipmates up the beach," he exclaimed. The next instant the boat struck with a force which shattered her almost to pieces. The seething, foaming waters rushed round her, and would have swept her off again, had not her crew, leaping out, seized her gunwale and dragged her up the beach, while the wounded men were carried to a spot where they were safe.

Jack having placed little Harry, whom he carried in his arms, in a place of safety, looked anxiously round for Terence. The boat of the latter had received even greater damage, but his people had escaped with their lives. Some of the provisions had, however, been washed out of her.

"I fear we are on a very *dissolute* island," exclaimed Adair as he came up to Jack. It was certainly a most unpromising spot. There were a few palm-trees to be seen here and there at a distance, but of a stunted growth, as if there was but little soil to nourish their roots, while all around was sand and rock. On hauling up the boats they were both discovered to be unseaworthy; their stock of provisions was much reduced; and what was worst, most of their powder was spoilt, and the boats' guns rendered useless, a very important loss in the neighbourhood of so numerous and vindictive an enemy. The men had their muskets and cutlasses, however, and there was no doubt but that should the pirates attack them, they would fight to the last. The great hope was that the tornado which had driven them on shore, might have treated their enemies in the same way.

"We ought not to wish our enemies ill," observed Terence; "but I suppose that it would not be wrong to wish that they may be no better off than we are."

Jack had nothing to say against this principle. Another source of anxiety was for Mr Cherry. They had left him attacking a very superior force; and even had he come off the victor, how would his boat have withstood the tornado?

Still no one despaired or even lost their spirits, neither were they for a moment idle. The men joked and laughed as much as ever, especially at Queerface, who, delighted to get on shore, leaped and frolicked about in the highest glee. Jack and Terence, after a short consultation, agreed that as they could not get away, it would be safer to fortify themselves, in case the pirates should discover and attack them.

They were not long in selecting a spot among some rocks, where, by throwing up banks of sand and digging holes in which to shelter themselves, they hoped that they might bid defiance to ten times their own number of enemies. The tornado kept blowing very fiercely for most of the time; at length, when their work was far advanced, it subsided considerably. Their labours were, however, not ended till nearly dark, by which time it was again calm. They made an awning with the boats' sails, and were all glad to lie down and get some rest after the fatigues of the day, the necessary guards having been placed to give notice of the approach of an enemy. They prudently would not light a fire lest the light should be seen by the pirates, who might be on the lookout for them.

Jack's chief concern was for Harry Bevan. The men bore their sufferings well, though they groaned in their sleep as wounded men generally do, even when not in much pain; but their pulses kept up, and their minds were collected. Jack and Adair had gone to the highest point of rock in the neighbourhood, to ascertain, if they could, if any enemy was near; but far as their gaze could extend across the starlit ocean, no vessel of any sort floated on its surface. Hoping that they might be left in peace till daylight, and thus give longer time for Mr Cherry to rejoin them, they returned to their encampment. They found poor little Harry talking away vehemently about people and circumstances of which they knew nothing, relating undoubtedly to his far-distant home. His mind was wandering. He thought Jack was his mother, and blessed him for all the care and kindness he was showing him. He fancied, however, that Adair was Queerface; and told him that he would rope's-end him if he came near him, a compliment Paddy did not altogether approve of. The worst part of the business was, that they could do nothing for the poor boy. They had no medicine, and had no notion of what to administer if they had had any. Jack was afraid of giving more brandy, so he let him have as much water as he wanted to drink; and by soothing words tried to calm his mind, and lull him to sleep. At length Dick Needham, who belonged to Jack's boat, woke up and entreated to be allowed to sit by the side of the poor little fellow. Who could wish for a more tender, gentle nurse than a true-hearted British sailor can make when he is aware that grog, however good in its way, is not, under all circumstances, the very best of medicines that can be administered? Leaving Harry therefore to Needham's care, Jack and Terence sat up talking for some time longer, making arrangements, like wise commanders, what, under the various circumstances which might occur, they would do. At length they threw themselves on the ground, and endeavoured to obtain a little rest in preparation for the work before them.

Jack thought that he had been only a few minutes asleep, when he started to his feet on hearing Needham's voice. "What is it?" he exclaimed, looking around. It was daylight, but a thick white mist hung over the sea.

"The enemy are not far off, I suspect, sir," answered Needham, who at that instant was entering the encampment. "My mind misgave me somehow, and I went to the top of the rock." Before he could finish the sentence Jack sprang on towards the place mentioned, followed by Terence, who roused up the moment he heard Jack's voice. On reaching the top of the rock, they cast their eyes eagerly seaward. At first nothing but a mass of white mist could be seen. Jack thought that Needham had been mistaken. While, however, they were still in doubt, a current of air it seemed blew off the top of the mist just as froth is blown from a mug of ale, and the upper sails of a fleet of prahus appeared not a quarter of a mile from the shore.

"The pirates must be looking for us," exclaimed Terence; "it will be fortunate if the mist continues, and they slip by without pitching on us."

"Pitching into us, you mean," said Jack, with a laugh. "Well, if they find us out, we must drive them off, and hold our own till the frigate sends to look for us. Still as they are ugly customers, we'll do our best to keep out of their sight." In this strain the two midshipmen talked on for some time, watching the movements of the prahus. Now the fog closed round them— now it lifted and exposed their sails to view. They seemed to be gliding by the island. Yet they were unpleasantly near.

"If the fog lifts, they can scarcely fail to see us," remarked Terence.

"Then, Paddy, we must fight it out to the last, and I am sure that you are of my opinion too," said Jack.

"That I am, Jack," cried Adair, wringing his hand. "But I say, what is that? I heard the splash of oars." They listened. There could be no doubt of it, and their practised ears told them that it was not the stroke of British seamen. The pirates, it was too probable, had sent on shore, and would land close to the very spot where the wreck of the boats lay. They would in all probability betray them. It could not be helped, so they hurried back to the camp to prepare for whatever might happen. As they passed along the beach, they could still hear the sound of oars, which was borne for a considerable distance over the calm water. The men stood with their muskets in their hands ready for the attack. Even the wounded men begged to be propped up against the bank that they might get a shot at the enemy.

Poor little Harry had dropped off into a deep slumber, and knew nothing of the preparations taking place. Needham volunteered to go down and watch behind a rock close down to the water, so as to give the earliest notice of the approach of the pirate-boats, should they come on shore at that point.

They had not long to wait. Louder and more distinct grew the splash of the oars.

Presently Needham came running up to the fort. "There are pretty nearly a dozen boats in," he exclaimed; "you'll see them in a moment coming out of the fog. They can't very well miss finding us."

"Very well," said Jack, coolly. "They'll be sorry that they did find us, that's all."

As Needham had said, in another minute the long black hulls of the pirate's boats appeared through the fog, and being run up on the beach, the crew leaped out of them. The swarthy savages, with sharp creeses by their sides and long jingalls in their hands, looked about on every side, and seemed surprised at not finding an enemy. They examined the boats, and then looked about again. So well was the fort constructed among the rocks, that in the fog they did not discover it. They began to scatter about; they were evidently persuaded that the English had made their escape across the island. At length three or four Malays wandered close up to the fort. They stood for a moment as if transfixed, and then, as it beamed on their comprehension what it really was, they beat a retreat, shouting to their companions.

The seamen were for firing at the intruders, but Jack ordered them not to throw a shot away, or to fire till they were attacked. They had not long to wait. The whole band of Malays quickly collected, and, with glittering creeses in their hands, rushed on to the attack.

"Now, boys, give it them," cried Jack, and Terence repeated the order almost in the same breath, for he knew that it was coming. Half the seamen only fired, and then began again to load. The other half waited till the first were ready, and the Malays had got close up to the bank. The latter, fancying probably that only a few had firearms, came on courageously.

"Fire, boys," cried Jack, quietly. The seamen jumped up, and the pirates, not expecting so warm a reception, wavered and fell back, leaving several dead and wounded close to the fort.

Jack and Terence began to hope that they would retreat altogether, but, encouraged by their chiefs, once more they were seen to come on. At the same time several more boats reached the shore. Jack and Terence could not conceal from themselves that they were in a dangerous position.

With loud, horrible shrieks, the Malays rushed up to the fort. The noise of the firing woke up little Harry, and, just as the pirates had a second time reached the embankment, Jack found him standing close to him, his clothes bespattered with blood, and his face looking pale as a sheet of paper. For a moment Jack thought it was the ghost of his young charge; but he had no time to think about it, for the next instant the enemy were close to them. Again and again the English sailors fired and kept the enemy back, but the pirates so far outnumbered them that there seemed but little hope of their ultimate success. Again, by their unflinching bravery, they drove the enemy back. The Malays, however, kept up a hot fire at them when they got to a distance, and several of the English were hit and unable longer to fight. Two poor fellows were killed outright. The fog now cleared, and Jack saw that the prahus themselves were drawing in with the land. With their own scanty numbers diminishing, and those of the enemy increasing, Jack and Terence could not help acknowledging that their case was desperate. Still, when the enemy once more came on, they received them with as firm hearts and as hearty a cheer as before. For a short time there was a cessation of firing. Queerface, who had wisely got into a hole, looked out to see what had happened. At that moment a bird was seen flying towards the fort. To the surprise of all, it pitched close to Queerface, who seemed delighted to see it. Adair turned round. "Why," he exclaimed, "there is Polly. Where can she have come from?" It was a question no one could answer. The boats had gone off to the prahus, and now returned with more men. With terrific shrieks and cries of vengeance, the Malays rushed towards the gallant little band of Englishmen, resolved to destroy them.

Chapter Twenty Five
In desperate Condition

The Malay pirates surrounded the fort, uttering the loudest shrieks and cries, in the hope of terrifying the defenders, but they did not know what British seamen were made of; and in spite of the fierce and terrific looks of the enemy, Jack and his little band stood fast, prepared to receive the onslaught. Poor Harry Bevan had sunk to the ground, not through fear, but weakness; and Jack had placed himself over his body, determined to defend him as long as he himself had life or strength. He felt and looked not a little like a lion prepared to do battle for her young. Jack had now grown into a very strong fine young man. He was not very tall, but he had broad shoulders and an expansive chest; and now, as he stood cutlass in hand, with a profusion of light hair streaming back from his honest sunburnt countenance, he was the picture of a true British sailor, and might well have been likened to the noblest type of the king of beasts. Adair was not a whit behind him in courage, though his physical powers were not so great. What hope was there though for them and their gallant men? At that moment there appeared but very little. Both of them knew that braver savages than the Malays were not to be found. Jack, as he stood there, with his muscular arm bared and his sharp weapon in his hand, did not put his trust in either. He knew and felt that the arm of One alone who is mighty to save could preserve him and his companions; and with deep earnestness and perfect faith he lifted up his heart to heaven, and prayed that assistance might be sent them. The British seamen returned the shrieks of the Malays with shouts of defiance, and kept up a rapid fire as they came on. Now their weapons cross. There is the loud sounding clash of steel, the sharp crack of muskets and pistols, the shouts and shrieks of the combatants. There is the thick smoke from the firearms mixed with the mist, rapid flashes of flame, and all the other sounds and appearances of a desperate struggle. Still, though the pirates hemmed them closely round, the seamen stood as before, boldly at bay, and no impression was made on their front.

"Jack," cried Adair, in the middle of the fight, "I don't think Polly came here for nothing. Hold on for a short time, and we shall be relieved, depend on it. She and the monkey have been talking away together, and Master Queerface looks as if he knew all was right."

I rather suspect that Adair was allowing his imagination to run away with him, or that he spoke thus to keep up the spirits of his men. Still the appearance of Polly was very extraordinary, and could only be accounted for by supposing that the frigate was not far off; or that she had accompanied Mr Cherry, and that his boat was in the neighbourhood. The idea might have encouraged the seamen to still further resistance, but the Malays pressed them hard; and, overwhelmed with numbers, it appeared as if their fate was sealed. Even Jack began to fear that this was the case. He saw that the fire of his men began to slacken, and the dreadful report ran round among them that their ammunition was almost expended.

"What is to be done, Rogers?" said Adair in Jack's ear.

"Trust to Heaven, Terence," answered Jack, warding off a blow which a Malay who had leaped forward made at his head. The next moment the savage rolled over, a lifeless corpse, down the embankment. For another minute the desperate struggle continued with unabated fury. Then a sound was heard which made the hearts of the British seamen leap within their bosoms—it was the loud report of a heavy gun which echoed among the rocks. The seamen answered it with a hearty cheer, for no guns but those of their own ship could give forth that sound. Another and another followed. At the same time the breeze which the frigate had brought up blew away the mist; and just above the rocks her topsails could be seen as she stood after the Malay prahus. The pirates saw her too. If they would save their vessels and their lives, they knew that there was not a moment to be lost. At a sign from their chiefs, as if a blast of wind had suddenly struck them, before the English knew what they were about, they rushed away like a heap of chaff before the gale. Jack and Terence, knowing their cunning nature, and fancying that they might rally again, hesitated to follow, and kept back their men.

"They are off," at length cried Terence. "Hurrah, my lads. Let's after them!"

Jack did not spring forward at once. He had not forgotten for a moment his young charge. He knew that, driven to desperation, the Malays were very likely to run amuck, and, if they found him, to kill him. He felt sure that he would only be safe if he had him with him. Stooping down, therefore, he seized the little fellow in his arms, and, holding him as much as possible behind his back, he sprang on, and overtaking his companions, made chase after the retreating Malays. The other wounded men, in the excitement of the fight, had forgotten their hurts, and were pursuing with the rest. Queerface and Polly had, therefore, no fancy to be left behind, so off they set also, though they took care to keep in the rear of their friends.

The Malays had reached the beach, and some were swimming and others wading off to their boats, when the two midshipmen and their followers got up with them. All were too eager to escape to attempt to offer any resistance. Jack had to recollect that they really were most atrocious robbers, or he could scarcely have brought himself to allow his men to fire on them. Not many shots, however, were fired, for the last cartridge in their pouches was expended. Happily, the Malays were in too great a hurry to be off, to turn and let fly at them. The frigate, under all sail, was coming round the point on the left hand, while the prahus were endeavouring to get away out of the range of her shot to the right or south side of the island. They were catching it, however, pretty severely, and more than one appeared to be in a sinking condition. The midshipmen were now eager to try and get their own boats afloat, but they were in an utterly unfit state for launching, so all they could do was to make signals to the frigate that she might return and take them off, after she had destroyed the pirates. This there was very little doubt she would do. In the eagerness of the chase, however, Jack bethought him that those on board would very likely not observe their signals.

"Never mind," cried Adair, as a bright thought struck him; "we'll send Polly off; she'll carry our message." A note was accordingly written on the leaf of a pocket-book, and being secured under Polly's wing, Adair lifted her up, and showing her the frigate, gave her a shove off towards it. She seemed to know exactly what was expected of her, for, giving one glance only round at her friends, away she darted towards the ship. They watched her anxiously till she was lost to sight. Still, they had little doubt about her reaching her destination, and in the course of a very few minutes their anxiety was relieved by their seeing a flag run up to the mast-head of the frigate, while a gun was fired to leeward. She, however, passed before them, and soon disappeared again on the other side of the island. A rapid and continuous fire told them what she was about. Jack and Adair would gladly have gone round to see what was occurring, but the distance was considerable, over hot burning sand and rocks, and they would not leave their wounded and tired men to gratify their curiosity. They very soon remembered, after the excitement of the work in which they had been engaged was over, that they had not breakfasted; so all hands who could move about set to work to collect sticks to light a fire. It soon blazed up, and speedily coffee and cocoa were boiling, and bits of meat were roasting away at the ends of ramrods and sticks. The poor wounded men, when the excitement was over, began to feel not hunger, but the pain of their hurts, and several sank to the ground unable to move. Their shipmates did their best for them, and rigged an awning with the boats' sails, under which they were placed. Some of the men wandered away, and brought back a supply of cocoa-nuts, the milk of which afforded a deliciously cooling beverage to the poor fellows. Jack, meantime, was tending his young charge with as much care and tenderness as a mother would a child. At length he was rewarded by seeing Harry come to himself. The boy looked up in his face, and the first words he uttered were—

"We've beat them, Rogers, have we? Hurrah! hurrah!"

"Yes, Harry," answered Jack, "it is all right. The enemy have taken to flight, and we shall soon, I hope, be on board the frigate. But here, you will be the better for some cocoa. Take this."

Jack sat down under the shade of the sail, and Needham having brought him a mug of cocoa, he broke some biscuit into it, and stirring it up while the boy's head rested on his knee, he fed him as he would have done a baby. Harry, who had soon again relapsed into apparent unconsciousness, opened his lips and ate a little with a dreamy expression of countenance, as if he himself fancied that he was still a baby being fed by his nurse. The food, however, Jack saw was doing him good, for the colour slowly returned to his cheeks, and his pulse began to beat more regularly.

"He will be all right soon," exclaimed Jack to Adair. "It is wonderful what Nature will do if we don't play tricks, and take liberties with her."

Harry Bevan, though delicately nurtured, was of a sound constitution, which he had not injured by either drinking or smoking, or by any other means, as many poor silly lads do, thinking they are behaving in a manly way by so doing. Had he been inclined to do so, Jack Rogers would have taken very good care to prevent him. Thus it was, however, that he did not succumb to the fearful injury he had received. Still Jack was very anxious to get him safe on board, and under the doctor's care. Time went on, and still the frigate did not appear. Adair proposed starting off to the other side of the island to ascertain what had become of her, when a boat was seen rounding the point. "She is Mr Cherry's boat," was the cry. "Hurrah! hurrah!" With hearty cheers, Mr Cherry was welcomed on shore. He had had a severe struggle, and had lost two of his men killed, and three wounded, but had succeeded in putting the pirates to flight. His boat was not large enough to carry all the party, but he had one of the carpenter's crew with him, and some tools; and, after a little examination, Tom Gimlett declared that he could patch up one of the boats so as to make her in a fit condition to launch. All hands helping, and with the aid of some planks from the other boat, this was done, and at length the two boats were on the water, on their way to look for the frigate. When Mr Cherry heard how long it was since she had passed the island, he began to be somewhat anxious about her. The boats, however, were so heavily laden, that they could not make much speed to satisfy themselves as to what had happened. The men did their best, and it was wonderful how they kept up their spirits under the hot broiling sun, which, as Paddy observed, "was roaring away like a furnace, right over their heads." No sooner had they rounded the island than the sound of a gun, booming over the smooth waters, reached their ears. At slow intervals another and another followed. "The ship is in distress," observed Adair to Jack. "What can have happened?"

"Give way, lads," cried Jack, seizing the stroke oar, and bending his back to it with a will. It was the only answer he made to Adair's remark. Little Harry looked up at him with admiration and affection, and the men exerted themselves more than ever. On they pulled, hour after hour. No one proposed resting, even to take any refreshment, except a piece of biscuit, which the men chewed during the intervals that they were relieved at the oars.

"There she is at last," cried Jack, standing up on the stern-sheets. He took a steady look at her through his glass. So did Mr Cherry through his. Her sails were set, but with heavy hearts, they both agreed that, from her appearance, she must be hard and fast on shore, and if on a coral reef there was too great a probability that she might not be got off again.

Chapter Twenty Six
Another fierce Conflict

A ship on shore is, at all times, a melancholy spectacle; but very sad it makes the hearts of those feel who see their own vessel lying among rocks in strange seas, far away from any friendly ports, and surrounded by enemies. Mr Cherry and his companions pulled away with all their might to ascertain the worst. The frigate, during this time, occasionally fired one of her bow guns. As they drew nearer, they perceived that she was doing so at a fleet of war-junks clustering in the distance, but who prudently were keeping out of range of her shot. Still, from their remaining where they were, it was evident that they were meditating an attack on her should another gale spring up, or any other occurrence give them a chance of success. The boats could not be of any great assistance, but still they would be of some use in the exertions to be made in getting her off. The brig would be of far more service; but where she was, it was difficult to say. When last seen, she was in a chase of another fleet of pirates to the northward. When they got alongside, every man of the frigate's crew was busily engaged in efforts to get the ship off. Mr Cherry and his party were warmly welcomed, however, and in spite of the fatigue they had gone through, they all at once lent a hand to effect the desired object. Anchors were got out astern, the anchors and some of the heavy guns were lowered into the boats, and the capstan was manned. Round went the men with the capstan bars, but the cables were soon stretched to their utmost, and there they stood pressing with might and main, but not an inch did the frigate move.

"We shall have to start the water and heave some of the stores and guns overboard, I fear," observed the first lieutenant to the captain.

"We will do anything rather than lose our guns," said Captain Grant. "I have no fancy to have our teeth drawn. The crew may rest for a spell. See, there is a breeze coming ahead," observed the captain, after some time. "Man the capstan again. Set the mainsail, mizen-topsail, and topgallant-sail. Let the people run from side to side as the capstan goes round."

The orders were put into execution. The men strained every nerve as before. Suddenly the capstan went round an inch; then another and another. Was it the anchors coming home? No: the ship herself was moving. Everybody on board felt her move. "Hurrah! hurrah!" There was a general shout. Again the men sprang round with the capstan bars; the frigate was afloat. She was soon hauled off into deep water. The well was sounded, but she did not appear to have received any damage. Night was now coming on, and the master was unwilling to take the ship through the intricate channels, among which she was entangled, without daylight to guide him. She was therefore brought up with a spring on her cables, ready to make sail, should any emergency arise to make this necessary.

The three old messmates were now together again, for the first time since they left England. Jack and Adair had all their adventures to tell to Murray, who was keeping the first watch, and so, though tired as they were, they preferred walking the deck with him to turning in and going to sleep. The night was very dark, but the wind fell, and it became almost calm, so that the only sound was the splash of the water as the swell broke over the reef ahead. All on board had reason to be thankful that they were not on it. The young men had a good deal to talk about; but it did not prevent them keeping their eyes about them, or their ears open. Jack, also, did not forget his young charge, little Harry Bevan.

"It is high time we should be thinking of turning in," he observed. "But I must see first how Harry gets on."

He went below to the berth where the young midshipman had been placed, and found one of the assistant-surgeons with him. The poor boy was very feverish, and was continually crying out for lemonade, and other cooling beverages. Jack sat with him for some time till he became calmer and better, and then went on deck to have another look out before he turned in for the night, as, not belonging to the ship, he had no watch to keep. He found the officer of the watch, Murray, and others peering through the darkness, over the frigate's quarter.

"Some suspicious sounds were heard coming from that direction," remarked Murray. "There were voices, and creaking of blocks, and the splash of oars. It is just to windward, and sounds travel a long distance in a dark night. Our friends, the pirates, are about some mischief. Perhaps they expect to find us napping, and purpose paying a visit."

Everybody on deck was on the alert, and there was not much chance of the crew of the frigate being taken by surprise at all events. Captain Grant was told of what had occurred; they waited and waited, but still nothing more was seen, or rather heard, of the pirate junks. Yet Murray and Mr Cherry, and all the officers who had been on deck, were so certain that they had not been deceived, that it was concluded that the pirates had been really close to them, but finding the frigate afloat, had thought better of the matter and hauled off.

Jack and Adair at last went below. Jack did not turn in, but lay down on one of the lockers in the midshipmen's berth, with a writing-desk for a pillow, and a boat-cloak for a mattress. The instant he put his head on the desk he was fast asleep. It appeared to him but a moment afterwards that he heard the cry, "All hands on deck." Immediately afterwards several shots were fired from the frigate. He was up in a moment. On looking out he saw the dark shadowy forms of numerous large war-junks gliding round the ship, and the next instant a shower of jingall balls and round shot came rattling on deck. The salute was returned by a broadside from the frigate, which, if it did not send several of the pirate's junks to the bottom, must have severely crippled a number of them. They must have thought that the frigate was still ashore, or that she had hove her guns overboard to get off, or they would not have ventured so near.

Still the unseen enemy showed more courage than might have been expected, and from every direction, on each beam and ahead, and astern, a shower of missiles came crashing in which could not fail to do a considerable amount of damage. The cries of several poor fellows showed that they were badly wounded, while one seaman, standing close to Jack Rogers, fell heavily to the deck. Jack stooped to raise him, but the man did not speak, and from the inert weight of the body, he feared too truly that he was killed. The worst part of the business was that, from the excessive darkness of the night and the thick mist which hung over the water, it was only from the flashes of the enemy's guns that the frigate's crew were able to see how to point theirs. By the cries and shrieks which arose every now and then in the distance they had reason to believe that their shot had told with dire effect. Still the pirate's shot was doing them a great deal of mischief, and, notwithstanding all their courage and power, all they could do in return was blindly to blaze away. Still there could be no doubt that the pirates would ultimately get the worst of it, and haul off long before morning. Of course, in daylight they would not venture to remain near her. After the frigate had fired several broadsides, it was discovered that the enemy on each side did not reply, but that all the shot came from ahead or astern. Again, the guns being loaded, Captain Grant hauled in on the spring so as to bring the broadsides in the direction the head and stern had before been. The word "fire!" was given. Instantly the terrific shrieks which rent the air showed that the enemy had there most thickly assembled. Some random shots were fire in return, and then all was silent.

"Really it is difficult to believe that so short a time ago the ship was surrounded by bloodthirsty enemies," observed Murray to Jack, as they stood together looking out into the darkness. "Besides the poor fellows who have been hit, I dare say that our running rigging and sails will show that we have been engaged; yet now how calm and quiet everything is."

"I, for one, would not trust them, though," said Jack; "if they can play us a trick they will."

The night, however, wore on. The pirates had evidently a sufficient taste of the frigate's quality, and had no wish to try it further.

Once more Jack was going below to finish his nap on the locker, when he heard Adair sing out, "There are two big junks close aboard us."

Captain Grant was on deck in an instant, and ordered the capstan to be manned to work the ship round as might be required.

"They are desperate fellows on board those crafts, or they would not attempt to get so near us," observed Adair.

"They are indeed," said Jack. "See, there's another of them. I don't like their looks. I wonder the captain has not ordered us to fire at them."

Just then Captain Grant's voice was heard ordering the boats to be lowered. Scarcely were the words out of his mouth than a bright light burst out of one of the junks, and instantly she was in flames, casting forth rockets and missiles of every description.

"They are fire-ships," cried numerous voices—a very evident fact. Without a moment's delay, Jack and Murray and Adair, with two of the lieutenants of the frigate, and the men nearest at hand, jumped into the boats, and, being lowered, pulled off to tow the fire-ships away from her; as, in consequence of the darkness, they had been brought thus close up before they were discovered, there was little time to spare. One in another minute would be alongside. Jack boldly sprang up her high bow, and making fast a tow-rope, ordered the men to give way. The spring on the frigate's cable was manned, and her broadside was turned away from the approaching fire-ships. Scarcely had Jack got hold of his prize than the flames burst forth from her, and he and the crew were covered with sparks and burning fragments of wood, which several times nearly set their clothes on fire and singed them not a little. Fortunately the rockets and other fireworks on board took an upward flight, but they soon found themselves pulling under a complete cascade of fire. Jack cheered them on: "Never mind, my lads," he shouted; "it's better than having the old frigate burnt, at all events."

He could scarcely bear the heat of the fire; still he persevered. At last he got his unpleasant captive just clear astern of the frigate, and a little way to leeward. Still a shift of wind might send her back, so he was towing her a little farther, when, with a loud roar, some magazine, which had been hitherto preserved at the bottom of the ship, exploded, sending every particle of her which remained high into the air, and as the wreck came down, the fragments very nearly swamped the boat and killed all in her. No one was hurt, however, and he and his brave crew instantly pulled back to grapple with another foe. All the other fire-ships had been seized hold of and were very nearly towed clear of the frigate.

Jack heard Murray's voice calling to him. Alick was fast to one which seemed heavier than the rest, and he had great difficulty, apparently, in moving her. Had not Jack gone to his assistance, in a few seconds she would have been alongside the frigate. When just under her stern, she broke out into the fiercest flames, and Jack, whose clothes were by this time very nearly done brown, was glad enough to cast loose from her. In another moment she blew up with a violent explosion, and as before, fragments of the burning wreck came flaming down into and around the boats, while the other fire-ships were still burning away brightly to leeward. Once more the boats were hoisted up, and the frigate was made ready to get under weigh the instant daylight would allow her to be carried free of the reefs. Just as one of the quarter boats was being secured, a splash was heard, and instantly the cry was raised of "A man overboard!"

Jack Rogers, who was on the quarter-deck, without stopping to ask who it was, kicked off his shoes, and threw off his jacket, and gliding down a rope, struck out astern. There was a strong current running, he had before discovered, and he knew that the man who had fallen overboard would be carried rapidly away from the ship.

"Who are you?" he sang out in a loud voice. "Tell me, that I may know where to swim to you."

There was no answer.

"It was Mr Murray, sir," cried some one from the ship. "We are afraid that he must have hurt himself as he fell."

This was sad news to Jack. Still he determined to persevere. The only light he had to guide him was from the burning fire-ships now drifting away. Should Murray come to the surface, he hoped he might see him and be near enough to support him, till a boat could arrive and pick them up. He heard the sounds of a boat being lowered from the frigate. He raised himself out of the water for an instant to look around, and he felt sure that he perceived a person's head not far off. He made strenuous efforts to reach it. Just then also he saw, the glare of the burning vessel being cast on it, what he would rather not have seen—a large Chinese boat. He was certain that the head was Murray's. His old friend was drifting rapidly down towards the pirates. He had every reason to fear that they would strike at Alick the moment he got near. He knew also that they would equally strike at him, but this did not make him hesitate a moment. He clove the water with all his might, dashing on till he was close up to the drowning man. He hoped that the pirates might not have seen him.

"A few more strokes, and I shall have him," he exclaimed to himself. Just then he saw some of the savage-looking pirates standing up in the boat peering towards him. A gleam of light fell on the head of the person in the water. It was Murray. He seized his friend by the collar and turned him on his back, then struck out once more towards the frigate. Of course he had but one hand at liberty, and in spite of all his efforts he could not stem the current, but found himself and Murray still drifting down towards their relentless foes. Some accident had, apparently, happened to the boat, and he could not tell whether or not she was even yet in the water. He could do nothing but keep himself and his companion afloat. He dared not shout, as his so doing would draw the attention of the pirates towards them, and he felt sure that, at all events, a boat would be sent to look for him. Jack and Alick had now another danger to encounter. They were drifting down on one of the fire-ships, and ran a great chance of being burnt. To avoid the fire-ship, Jack was obliged to approach nearer the pirate-boat, which had been keeping so as to leave the burning vessel between her and the frigate. The miscreants now saw him, and dashing their paddles in the water, were rapidly up to him. He fully expected that the next moment would be his last; but he still held fast the senseless form of his friend. He looked up for an instant, and saw the hideous countenances of the Chinamen glaring down on him over the side of their boat.

Chapter Twenty Seven
Chasing the Pirate Fleet

Adair had just come on deck when Jack jumped overboard to save Murray, and he was on the point of jumping in after him, when his arm was seized, and he found himself held back by Captain Grant.

"You would uselessly risk your life, Adair!" exclaimed the captain. "Lower that gig; be sharp about it: you may go in her."

Several men with Adair had instantly flown to the boat nearest them, and, under the direction of the captain, were lowering her, when the after-fall gave way, and up she hung by the bows, most of her gear falling into the water, as did one of the two men in her. He was a good swimmer, and struck out boldly to keep up alongside the ship, but the current was too strong for him, and before a rope could be heaved to him, he gradually dropped astern. The fall had been injured by one of the enemy's shot. Another boat was now lowered, but in consequence of the darkness, and the disarrangement incidental to the work in which the men had been engaged, more delay than usual occurred. At last the boat was lowered and manned, and Adair and Mr Cherry jumping into her, away they pulled to pick up, in the first place, the poor fellow who had just fallen into the water. They shouted out his name: a faint cry reached their ears. He had already got a long way from the ship; it took some time before they could find him. He must have sunk once, and they caught him just as he came up again; he was insensible when they hauled him into the boat. Adair wanted to go on, but Mr Cherry said that he feared the man would die if they did, and that it was his duty to carry him on board.

"I fear, too, that there is but little chance of our picking up the other two poor fellows," he observed. "They must have drifted a long way by this time, and can scarcely have kept afloat."

"You don't know, sir, what a superb swimmer Jack Rogers is," exclaimed Adair: "he will keep up for an hour or more; I have no fear on that score. Let us get this man on board, and we will soon find him."

Terence had never in his life felt so deeply anxious as he now did. The boat rapidly returned to the ship, the nearly drowned man was hoisted on deck, and then once more they shoved off, and fast as the men could bend to their oars, they pulled in the direction it was supposed Murray and Jack must have drifted.

The fire-ships were still blazing away as the boat approached them. "I think that they cannot be far from here," said Mr Cherry. "Steady now, lads; paddle gently; keep a look out on either side, all of you."

Terence however thought that they might have drifted farther on.

"Rogers, ahoy!" he stood up and shouted; "Jack Rogers, where are you?"

Just then, one of the fire-ships which had been burning most furiously, and concealed everything on the other side of her, blew up with a loud explosion, scattering her burning fragments far and wide around her. Several pieces of blazing timber fell into the boat among the men. One or two were much hurt, and they had enough to do to heave the bits overboard to prevent the boat herself catching fire.

Terence was in an agony of fear for the sake of his friends. A single fragment of the burning ship falling on them would have sent them to the bottom. Still he would not give up all hope, but continued searching. Mr Cherry now agreed that, if they still were on the surface, they must have drifted farther on; so on they pulled slowly, looking out as before. They had gone a little way, when the man in the bows said he saw a boat in the distance.

Mr Cherry made her out also: "Perhaps they may have reached her," he observed. This was very little consolation to Terence, because he did not think it probable, if, as there was little doubt, she was a pirate's boat, her crew would let them live. Still he was eager to go in chase.

Mr Cherry, who was more calm, thought that it would be wiser to look about on every side, to ascertain if Jack was still floating near. Again and again they called to him, but there was no answer.

"Either they have been picked up or are drowned," said the lieutenant.

Terence's heart sank within him. Mr Cherry now agreed to go in chase of the Chinamen's boat. Away they dashed; their shouts of course had given notice of their approach, and the boat was evidently pulling on rapidly before them. Bright sparkles of light fell from the blades of their oars, and in their wake appeared a long fiery line, as the boat glided over the dark smooth water.

Two of the fire-ships were still burning, and their position, with the distant signal-lights of the frigate, enabled them to keep in the direction they believed the two midshipmen had drifted. The Chinamen's boat pulled fast, and they appeared to be very slightly gaining on her. Adair believed that the only chance of saving his old companions' lives was to overtake her. Mr Cherry already gave them up as lost, still he was determined, if possible, to overhaul the boat. The crew bent manfully to their oars.

It did not occur to any one for some time that they had left the ship unarmed; except that two of the men had pistols in their belts, and one had still his cutlass, while Mr Cherry had jumped into the boat without unbuckling his sword.

"Never mind; the boat's stretchers must serve those who haven't better weapons. Very likely the Chinamen in the boats are no better off," exclaimed Terence, in his eagerness. The lieutenant agreeing with him, on they went.

"We shall have her at last," cried Adair; "we are gaining on her, I am certain of it. But hillo! what are those lights there, ahead of us?" he added after some time. The question was soon answered, for looming through the darkness appeared a long line of large war-junks, behind which the boat of which they were in pursuit rapidly glided. They must have been seen from the junks, for directly afterwards they were saluted by a thick shower of jingall bullets, while several round shot came whizzing past them. Terence, in the impulse of the moment, was for dashing on and attacking the nearest junks, but, as Mr Cherry had discretion as well as valour, he ordered the men to pull round their starboard oars, and to get out of the range of the shot as fast as they could. It was rather too much for even six British seamen and two officers to do, to attack a whole fleet of war-junks. Terence was of the same opinion. With heavy hearts they pulled back against the current to the frigate, fully believing that Rogers and Murray were lost to them for ever. As soon as they made their report, Captain Grant expressed his wish to make an attempt, at all events, to ascertain the fate of the two midshipmen. If the frigate was got under weigh with the strong current which was then making, she would most certainly be drifted on to the reefs. A boat expedition was the only means left for doing anything. Immediately all the boats of the ship were manned, with guns in their bows, and this time the crews went well-armed. Away they pulled, resolving, if they did not find the two young officers, to make the pirates pay dearly for their loss. The rest of the fire-ships had burnt out, so it was now quite dark. The men were in their usual spirits when fighting was to be done, and were highly pleased at the thoughts of getting alongside the villains with whom they had hitherto been playing at long bowls—a game to which Jack had a great dislike. Terence had Needham in his boat. They had pulled for a considerable distance, and Adair thought that they ought to be up with the enemy.

"Can you manage to make out the junks, Dick?" he sang out.

"No, sir, I can see nothing ahead whatever," was the unsatisfactory answer.

So they pulled on yet farther. Still no junks were to be seen. On proceeded the flotilla, till they had considerably passed the spot where Mr Cherry and Adair had fallen in with the enemy. Mr Cherry considered that it was not prudent to separate, so kept the boats together. After again pulling some way to the east, they first took a northerly course, and then swept round again towards the south, but not a trace of a boat or vessel of any sort could they discover. Just before dawn, very considerably disappointed, the expedition returned to the frigate. As the sun rose, a breeze sprang up, and once more the anchor was weighed, the sails were let fall, and the frigate stood out of her perilous position. A steady hand in each of the main chains kept the lead going, while the master, with anxious countenance, stood on the bowsprit issuing his orders as to how the ship was to be steered.

"Starboard!" he cried.

"Starboard!" was the answer, with a long cadence.

"Port!"

"Port it is!" sounded from aft.

"Steady!"

"Steady!" the seeming echo answered.

Now the ship was tacked; now she cut into the wind's eye; now she was kept away; now coral rocks rose up close to her; now the channel was so narrow that it seemed as if there was not room for her to pass through it. Everybody breathed more freely when she was at last in clear water again. What had become of the junks it was impossible to say. Not a sail was to be seen from the mast-head. Altogether the affair in which they had been engaged had been disastrous, and an unusual gloom was cast over the ship's company. The frigate stood round the group of islands; a complete archipelago, with numerous intricate passages between them. Sometimes she brought up, and the boats were sent away, and strict search was made for the piratical fleet; indeed no trouble or exertion was spared, but all was without result. No tidings could be gained either of the brig or the fleet of piratical junks. At length the frigate entered the Chinese waters, and anchored off Canton.

One Chinese city is very much like another. They are surrounded by castellated walls, some thirty feet in height, and coated with blue brick, which gives them a very toyshop appearance. The wall is about twenty feet at the base, diminishing by the inclination of the inner surface to about twelve feet. The thin parapet is deeply embattled with intermediate loopholes, but there are no regular embrasures for artillery. The Chinese till lately have seldom used cannon, but have usually stuck to the bow and arrow. At each gate there is a semicircular enclosure, forming a double wall. Over the two gateways are towers of several stories, in which the soldiers who guard them are lodged. Also, at about sixty yards apart along the whole length of the wall, are flanking towers projecting about thirty feet from the curtain. Some of the cities have ditches before the walls. The interiors of most Chinese cities are also very similar. The houses are very low, and the streets, which are narrow, are paved with flag-stones, suited however only for the passage of people on foot, or for sedan-chairs. The road is often crossed by ornamental gateways, with square openings in the centre, one on each side, not an arch. These have been erected to the memory of distinguished individuals. Another feature in the streets are the slabs of stone covered with inscriptions, about eight feet high, and placed on the back of a tortoise carved out of the same slab. The plan of the houses is very similar in all respects to that of those discovered in Pompeii, with open courts and rooms opening out of them. They have more lattice-work and paint, and the ornaments and designs are of course very different. The shops are generally open to the street, those of one description being placed together, as is very much the custom in Russia, Portugal, and other European countries. Suspended high above, like a banner over each shop, is a huge varnished and gilded signboard, with a description of the style of merchandise to be sold within. As these boards hang at right angles from the walls, they contribute much to the gay appearance of the street.

The Chinese delight in placing quaint inscriptions over their shops. Many of the streets are dirty in the extreme, while the shops are dark and dismal, and the shopkeepers far from urbane and accommodating: people these narrow streets, with their signboards and gateways, with an ever-moving crowd of yellow-faced, turn-up nosed, pig-eyed beings in blue and brown and yellow cotton dresses, wide trousers, loose jackets, and thatch-shaped hats, carrying long bamboos with boxes or baskets hanging at each end, or hung over with paper lanterns or birdcages, and all sorts of other articles, and here and there a sedan-chair with some mandarin or lady of rank inside, borne by two stout porters; and we have a fair idea of a Chinese city. Then, of course, there are public buildings of larger dimensions, and temples and towers of porcelain, pictures of which everybody has seen; and then outside the walls are canals and lakes, and curious high-arched bridges, and summer-houses and pagodas.

In the suburbs of Canton, where the foreign factories are situated, the shops are open, and the streets are not so much ornamented as in the city itself, but the plan of the houses and the general arrangements are similar.

No other ship of war was at Canton when the *Dugong* arrived. Captain Grant had fully expected to find the *Blenny* there, and was much disappointed at her non-appearance. He waited anxiously for several days, but she did not appear. At length he determined to sail in search of her.

"To lose our consort, and those two fine young fellows, Rogers and Murray, is very trying," he observed to Lieutenant Cherry, as they walked the deck together, while the ship was standing away from Canton.

"As to the *Blenny*, sir, she'll turn up before long, depend upon it, unless she is hard and fast somewhere on a rock," answered the lieutenant. "Hemming has been routing out some of those piratical scoundrels, and they probably have given him a longer chase than he expected."

Still Captain Grant was not satisfied. As the frigate cruised along she brought to all the vessels of every sort she fell in with, and made inquiries at every island and place where anything like a truthful answer could possibly be procured. They had an interpreter, a Chinese, who spoke English, though rather of a funny sort, and as it required a good deal of cleverness to comprehend it, it may be supposed what he professed to wish to communicate was not always very clear. The man who might most have assisted them, Hoddidoddi, had been missing ever since Rogers' and Adair's battle on the island, and it was supposed that he must have concealed himself for the purpose of returning home. The *Dugong* had been three days at sea, when a clipper schooner, with dark hull, square yards, and a most rakish look, hove in sight early in the morning, and approached the frigate.

"On the coast of Africa, I should say that the fellow was not honest," observed Mr Cherry, who had the morning watch, to Adair; "I wonder what he wants."

"A very pirate or slaver," replied Adair, "but she is only, I suspect, an honest opium-smuggler."

"Honest, do you call her?" exclaimed the lieutenant. "If because a vile system is carried on openly it is to be considered honest, then slaving is honest, and piracy, and highway robbery, for that matter. See, however, her gallant skipper is not afraid of us. Look, with what a self-satisfied air he walks the deck with his gold-lace cap, and glass under his arm. They are preparing to lower a boat, and he'll come to pay his respects as one captain does to another."

In a short time the master of the schooner made his appearance on the deck of the frigate. Captain Grant got up to receive him. He was an intelligent, dashing-looking young man.

"I am glad that I have fallen in with you, sir," he began. "Last night, just before sunset, I heard some firing, and standing in the direction from which the sound came, I observed a brig-of-war apparently almost surrounded by junks not far from the land, to the southward of this—out there. I made sail, hoping to render her assistance; but so large a force of sailing and row junks sallied out from behind a point of land and made towards me, that, as I have lost half my crew with sickness and a former battle with a squadron of the villains, I was compelled to up stick and run for it. I shall be glad, however, to return with you, and assist in piloting you to the spot."

"Thank you, captain—thank you," answered Captain Grant, extending his hand. He wisely never denied nominal rank to masters of vessels, however employed. "I most gladly accept your offer."

"Hudson is my name—my craft is the *Flying Fish*; and when you see her in a good breeze, you'll acknowledge that she does fly along," answered the master, looking with pride at his trim and beautiful craft.

She and the frigate instantly made sail to the southward. In a few hours the sound of an occasional shot saluted their ears and gave them hopes that the *Blenny* was still afloat and able to defend herself. As they got nearer, they could make her out from the mast-head, amid a wide circle of junks which were keeping up a distant fire at her. It at this critical juncture fell perfectly calm. Captain Hudson, who had come on board the frigate and gone aloft, now returned on deck.

"I know the trick of those fellows, sir. They hope to make her exhaust her ammunition and then to board her. They seem pretty well to have done that already. You must go to her relief in the boats, or the villains may have cut the throats of all on board before you can get up to them."

This seemed too probable. All the frigate's boats were now lowered, armed with guns in the bows, manned, and sent away under the command of Mr Cherry, without a moment's delay.

"Poor Jack!" exclaimed Adair to young Harry Bevan. "It was only the other day that he and I were pulling along just as we are now doing. And now—who can say where he is? Still, do you know, Harry, I have an idea that he'll turn up somehow or other. He always has done so, and I can't help hoping that he and Murray may yet be found."

"I hope and pray so, I'm sure I do," said Harry, almost crying, "but I'm afraid there's very little chance of it. Even if the Chinese picked them up, they would be sure to murder them."

Chapter Twenty Eight
The Midshipmen in Prison

Who would have ventured to believe that the fate of the brave, true-hearted Jack Rogers, and the gallant, high-minded Alick Murray, was to be cruelly murdered by a set of ill-conditioned, barbarous Chinese pirates? Yet such has been unhappily the lot of many of the finest fellows in the British navy and army. When Jack, supporting Murray with one arm, looked up and saw half a dozen hideous Chinese faces, with flat noses, grinning mouths, and queer twisted eyes lighted up by the flames of the burning fire-ships, gazing maliciously down on him, he gave up all for lost. Had Murray not been still insensible, he would have swum away, defying the sharks till he could have got hold of something to support him, or he would have attempted to climb into the boat and had a desperate battle for his life. As it was, without sacrificing Murray, he could do neither. A savage was standing up, lifting a large battle-axe, the bright steel of which glittered in the glare of the burning ships, and was on the point of letting it fall with a crushing blow on his head, and already Jack felt the horrible sensation of having his skull crushed in and cleft asunder, when another man sprang forward and seized the wretch's uplifted arm. He could only turn the blow aside, for the axe came down, and the blade dug deeply into the side of the boat. Jack seized it, for it formed a convenient handle on which to rest, and afforded him a support he much required. He fully expected to have another hack made at him, and was considering how best he might avoid it, when the pirates seized him and Murray, and dragged them into the boat. Still he did not feel much more secure than he had been in the water, as he expected that, as they might treat a useless fish, they would throw him overboard again when they had glutted their revenge by knocking the life out of him.

"If poor Murray does not revive, he will be spared much of the unpleasantness," he thought to himself. It is extraordinary how coolly he took matters. He was rather surprised himself at his own indifference to his approaching fate. The Chinese were all chattering and vociferating together over him and Murray, as their bodies lay along the thwarts, for he was so exhausted that he could scarcely move, when he heard a voice say, "Don't fear, English officer. I take care you no hurt."

"Very much obliged to you, whoever you are," answered Jack. "But I say, friend, I wish that you could get me put into a more comfortable position, and lend a helping hand to my poor companion here, who will be suffocated, I fear, if something is not done to him."

"All right, by and by," answered the voice. "Let dese men hab dere palaver out; dey no talk of kill 'ou now."

"That information is satisfactory, at all events," thought Jack. "Well, I must have patience; that never hurt any one, and has saved many a life. Only I do wish these fellows would bring their palaver to an end, and let me find out who my friend is."

The pirates at last brought their conference to an end. They probably came to the conclusion that, as a live donkey is of more value than a dead one, and as profit more than revenge was their object, it would probably better answer their purpose to keep the young officer? alive, and endeavour to obtain a ransom for them, than to kill them, and in consequence be hunted down with even more pertinacity than before. As to being influenced by any feelings of humanity, such an idea never for a moment crossed their brains.

Jack and Murray were now carried to a platform in the afterpart of the boat, when the former was allowed to sit up with his friend's head in his lap, and to apply such means of restoring him to animation as he could devise. He turned him round on one side, so that the water might run out of his mouth, and was rubbing away as briskly as he could, when he heard the same person who had before addressed him say, "All right, I told you; I come and help you now." On looking up, who should he see, but one of the crew of the frigate, the Malay who spoke English, who went by the name of Jos Grummet, and his friend Hoddidoddi, who, it now appeared, had deserted with him on the island. It was Jos who had saved his life from the man with the battle-axe, and Hoddidoddi who had advised the pirates not to kill them at all, but to keep them for the more satisfactory object of obtaining a ransom.

After a little time, by their united exertions, Murray recovered, and was able to sit up and understand what had occurred. Jack was now much happier as to the future. "Well, thank you heartily, Jos, for what you have done for us," said he. "And I can assure you, that if you go back to the frigate, you will not be flogged, or even have your grog stopped."

"Tankee, sare," answered Jos. "But spose me no go back, no hab fear of floggie at all."

"Please yourself," said Jack. "Remain a wandering Malay, or become a civilised British seaman, with Greenwich in prospect. However, you have done me a great service, and I wish to recompense you to the best of my power."

"Really, Alick, I think that there ought to be a fund for pensioning those who assist in preserving midshipmen's lives; we do run so many risks of losing them," he observed to Murray, who fully agreed with him.

"I say, Jos," he exclaimed, after a little silence, "do just hint to these polite gentlemen, that we shall make the amount of our ransom depend on the condition in which we are returned to our friends, and that if we are starved, they will not give much for us. I am getting very peckish; are you, Alick? I thought it was just as well to make those remarks in time; besides, it is always wise for people in our circumstances to put a good face on matters; it shows the villains that we are not cast down or afraid of them."

Jos told Hoddidoddi, who interpreted their request in his own fashion, and the reply was, that they should have some food when they got on board the junk. At that moment the sound of oars was heard, and an English boat hove in sight. Some of the pirates were for fighting, but Jos represented that the British sailors were such desperate fellows, that they would not hesitate to attack a big junk, and would take her and make mincemeat of every one on board; and that such a boat as theirs would be treated with still more scant ceremony. So, much to the midshipmen's disappointment, they wisely pulled away as hard as they could go, till they go under shelter of the fleet of junks.

The boat belonged, it appeared, to one of the smaller junks, on board which Jack and Alick were at once carried.

The piratical squadron now instantly made sail, and a favourable breeze having sprung up, they steered for the northward. Their notable scheme for destroying the English frigate having failed, the fleet separated, some taking shelter among the neighbouring islands, others standing out to sea in quest of prey; but the greater number returning to their accustomed haunts in the neighbourhood of Canton, localities most frequented by traders in the China seas.

The vessel on board which Jack and Alick found themselves formed one of the latter fleet. Their captors were, Jos explained to them, great diplomatists. They argued that if they gave them up at once, a small sum only would be offered for them; but if they kept them for some time, and made their friends suppose they were lost, they would be ready to pay any amount demanded for their ransom. They were not treated with much ceremony or civility, but Jack's hint about their condition when reckoning for ransom had one good effect; and somewhat for a similar reason that an ogre or a slave-dealer would sufficiently feed his captives, they were amply supplied with rice and other provisions. Sometimes the dishes had a very suspicious look.

"They don't eat babies, do they?" said Jack, dipping his chop-stick into the tureen placed before them, and producing a limb of some creature which certainly had a very odd appearance.

"No, I fancy not," answered Murray, "but we had better not ask questions."

They agreed that it was in all probability only a monkey which had been seen on board, but was no longer visible; and as the captain and his officers partook of the same dish, they had no cause to complain. They soon learned to relish lizards and snakes well stewed with curry powder and rice; and they came to the conclusion that a dish of snails was not in any way to be despised. As they could take no exercise except a walk up and down the curious little narrow cabin in which they were confined, they both declared they were growing so fat that perhaps the pirates would, after all, demand a higher ransom than Captain Grant would be able or willing to pay.

"I am really afraid that we are caught in our own trap," said Jack. "I thought that pig-tailed, pig-eyed skipper of ours, when he looked in on us just now, smiled very complacently at our sleek skins. We must get Jos to tell him that if we grow too fat we shall be worth very little. There is nothing like moderation in all things."

"There is nothing like honesty and telling the truth," said Murray.

"We should have starved if we had strictly stuck to it in this case," answered Jack.

"No matter, we should probably have been much sooner liberated," answered Alick. "Depend on it, whenever a person tells an untruth he sets a trap to catch his own feet."

"You are always right, Alick," said Jack, with honest warmth. "And suppose all this time they have been giving us stewed babies and young alligators to eat, how doubly punished we should be."

The junk on board which the midshipmen were prisoners was a curious piece of marine architecture. She was flat-bottomed, flat-sided, flat-bowed, and flat-sterned. She was of course narrower at the bow than at the stern, where indeed she was very broad. The rudder was wide and fixed in a hollow in the stern, to which it was hung by ropes or hawsers, so that it could with perfect ease be lifted out of its place and slung alongside. There was no stem, but a huge green griffin or dragon, or monster of some sort, projected over the bows, on each side of which were two large eyes— Chinaman's eyes in shape: and as Jos remarked about them, "Ship no eyes, how see way?"

The sides, though flat, extended gradually outward as they rose, so that on deck there was considerable beam. The deck was composed of loose planks easily removed. At the poop and forecastle were a succession of little sloping decks, gradually narrowing as they rose in height, and enclosed to form cabins. The bulwarks were high and surrounded with large round shields of wood, and leather, and brass knobs, and curious devices painted on them. The anchors were curious contrivances, made of some hard wood, very large and cumbrous, the flukes only being tipped with iron. Outside at the bows was a wonderfully awkward-looking winch for getting up the anchor; and as Jack observed, when he came to be made Lord High Admiral of the Chinese fleet, there were a good many things he saw that he should have to alter. The sails were made of matting, with laths placed across them. When it was necessary to reef or lower the sails the seamen climbed up these laths, and standing on the upper yards pressed them down, no down hauls being necessary. Bowlines, however, were used to stretch them out. Had Jack and Murray not been prisoners, with the possibility of the pirates changing their minds and cutting their throats, they would have been excessively amused at watching the proceedings of the crew, and rather enjoyed their cruise on board the pirate. On deck there was an erection like a diminutive caboose, but which was a temple or joss-house. The sailors were constantly making offerings before it, apparently as the caprice seized them, by burning gilt paper, or thin sticks, or incense.

One day the junk was caught in a calm, and as a sail appeared in sight in the distance which the Chinamen thought might be an enemy, they were very anxious for a breeze to make their escape. The midshipmen saw that they were very busy about something, and soon every man appeared with a model junk, which he had constructed of gilt paper. A boat was lowered and these frail barques were carefully placed on the surface of the deep, the men endeavouring to blow them away, so that they might be clear of the ship.

Jack was much amused, and asked Jos the meaning of the ceremony. Jos answered—

"For why you don't know? Dere is one great lady, queen, they call her, lives up in de sky, and she like to see dese paper junks; and so when she see dem, den she send breeze to blow junk along."

Jack was highly amused at this account.

"Well, I never thought much of a Chinaman's wit," he observed; "but I did not think he was such a goose as to fancy that a breeze would be sent merely because he put some twisted-up bits of paper on the water."

Jos, who understood some of these remarks, looked at him, and remarked—

"When I 'board English ship I hear sailors whistle, whistle, whistle when dere is calm. I ask why dey do dat? Dey say, 'Whistle for a wind.' Now, I tink Chinaman just as wise as English sailor. Anybody whistle, cost nothing. Chinaman spend money, buy gold paper, make junk, much trouble. Dat please Chinaman's lady-god more dan empty whistle can Englishman's fetish, or whatever he whistle to."

"Excellent," exclaimed Murray. "The Malay has hit us very hard. That whistling for a breeze is, in most cases, merely a foolish trick, but it is too indicative of unsound principles to be witnessed without pain. If we really considered the matter rightly, we should feel that every time we whistle for a breeze, we are offering a senseless insult to the Great Ruler of the universe. It is a remnant, I suppose, of some superstition of our Scandinavian ancestors, who thought by whistling they were addressing some demon or spirit of the elements."

"That is taking the matter seriously, Alick; but I suppose you are right," said Jack.

"Nothing that leads to error, or that encourages superstition, or that leads a person to rely on any other power or influence than that of God's merciful providence, can be treated too seriously, my dear Jack," answered Murray. "Here have we, worthless fellows, had our lives providentially preserved; and we ought to do our utmost in every way to employ them in His service, and to do His will and to make known His truth. Depend on it that it is a very useless sort of religion, or seriousness, which a man adopts only when he is on the point of death or feels himself too ill to enjoy life."

"Well, well, Alick, I will do my best to log that down in my memory and stick to it," answered Jack, who always felt the force of Murray's remarks, which had already had a very considerable influence on him for good; more, probably, than Murray himself was aware of. However, he went on in faith, speaking faithfully to his friend, assured that he was doing his duty.

Jack and Murray did their best to make out in what direction they were going, and from the very rough calculation they were able to form, they conjectured that they had arrived at a group of islands within some hundred and fifty miles of the latitude of Canton. They were not allowed to go on shore, but were permitted occasionally to quit their little cabin in the stern and to walk about the deck; but the crew had communication with the land and brought off all sorts of provisions, by which they benefited.

Once more the fleet, consisting of about a dozen junks, put to sea. The next morning it was almost a calm; and as daylight came on a brig was seen, apparently a merchantman, with her foremast gone and otherwise much disabled. There could be little doubt that she had got into her present condition from having encountered one of those partial squalls which occasionally occur in those seas. A long consultation was held among the captains of the pirate fleet, in which the crews as well as the officers took considerable part. There was an immense amount of talking and gesticulation, and flourishing of creeses, and daggers, and swords, and various other weapons; and at last the sweeps were got out, and the junks began to move in a body towards the devoted brig. Jack asked Jos, the Malay, what the Chinamen were about to do.

"Cut de troat of ebery moder's son of dem, take de cargo, and burn de brig, den no one get away to tell news," was the answer.

"Kind and pleasant intentions, but what do they think we shall do?" observed Jack. "I don't like the look of affairs. They will be for cutting our throats, to prevent our giving an account of their doings."

"Perhaps the Malay is mistaken," answered Murray. "They may not intend to murder the people; or if they do, they will keep us shut up in the cabin while the operation is going forward, or they will make us swear before they set us at liberty not to give information. I have no fears about our safety."

"Nor have I in reality," said Jack; "but I wish that we could render some assistance to the poor people on board the brig. We might warn them of the fate intended for them; but even if we got Jos and Hoddidoddi to stand by us, I am afraid we could not do much in the way of fighting."

"I am afraid not, indeed," said Murray; "we must be prepared for any emergency. It is impossible to say what will occur."

"I like the feeling," said Jack. "I wish that we were on board the brig though, we would have a fight for it. But we are drawing near. Had the pirates intended much mischief they would have sent us into our cabin, I suspect."

The pirate junks had now completely hemmed in the helpless brig. She was American, for just then the stars and stripes of the United States flew out from her peak. Two men, apparently the captain and his mate, were seen to come on deck with revolvers in their hands. They turned round, and shouted in English and Spanish, and Malay down the hatchway, to the crew to come up on deck, and defend themselves and the ship and passengers like men. No one appeared.

"Cowards, wretches, brutes, will you have your throats cut like sheep without an attempt to defend yourselves? Take that, then!" cried the captain, and in his rage he hove his pistol at their heads and stood prepared for his fate. The mate threw his overboard, which was a wiser proceeding, and then, folding his arms, stood ready to bear whatever might occur.

"Those are brave fellows," cried Jack; "we must try and save their lives at all events."

The pirate crews now burst forth into the most terrific and unearthly shouts, and, urging on their junks, dashed up to the brig, and simultaneously threw their grappling irons on board her. At the same time those nearest to her hove fire-balls, and stink-pots, and stones, and bits of iron, and missiles of all sorts on board, and then reiterating their shrieks, sprang on to her deck. The captain and his mate, who had hitherto undauntedly stood at their post, were borne down; and the pirates, throwing themselves on them, seized their arms and bound them to the mainmast. There seemed to be a hundred or more pirates from the different junks: their persons garnished with pistols and daggers of all sorts stuck in leathern belts, and their heads surmounted with red turbans, which increased the natural hideousness of their countenances. Some of the savage crew joined hands and leaped and danced round and round the deck, with the most violent contortions of the body, shrieking all the time at the top of their voices, while others, flourishing their daggers and shrieking louder than ever, rushed below. At that instant a cry very different from that of the pirates ascended from the cabin. Jack and Alick heard it.

"It is the voice of a lady, or a female at all events," cried Jack. "Alick, we must go and assist her. Jos, my boy, come along. Tell Hoddidoddi he is wanted. The Chinamen won't stop us, they are all too busy."

"I am with you," answered Murray, as they picked up two Chinese swords, several of which lay about, and, followed by the Malay, leaped unopposed on the deck of the brig.

Chapter Twenty Nine
The Night Battle

The Chinese pirates were so busily employed in the agreeable occupation of plundering the American brig, that they did not observe the two midshipmen leaping in among them. Jack and Alick had on, it must be remembered, turbans and Chinese jackets and trousers like the rest, so in the confusion they easily passed unnoticed.

"I really think that we might drive the scoundrels out of the brig and retake her," observed Jack as he sprang on.

"No, no, sare, one ting at a time, if oo please," answered Jos the Malay, who heard his remark.

Jos was right, as Jack afterwards confessed, for though they might have swept off the heads of a good many pirates engaged in collecting booty, the rest would soon have come to their senses and cut off theirs.

Again the female cry was heard. Jack and Murray sprang into the main cabin. It was full of Chinese rifling the lockers and searching in bed-places or wherever anything could be stowed away. No females were there, but there was a hatchway and a ladder leading to the deck below. The cries proceeded from thence, so they jumped down, leaving Jos and Hoddidoddi, who had joined them, to guard the entrance. There, in dim uncertain light, they distinguished two ladies, apparently one old and stout, the other young, struggling in the hands of half a dozen or more pirates, who were endeavouring to draw the rings from their fingers, and their earrings from their ears. One lady was somewhat stout and oldish, the other was young and slight, and Jack thought very pretty. Whether ugly or pretty would not have mattered just then. She and the old lady were in distress, and that was enough to make the midshipmen eager to fight for them, whoever they were. They were very much terrified, but not so much so as to prevent them from endeavouring to repel the indignities offered them.

Not a moment was to be lost. There was no room to use their swords without running a great risk of wounding the ladies, so Jack knocked one fellow down with his fist, and another with the butt end of his pistol. Murray did the same. They then both planted such thorough honest English blows under the ribs of the other two miscreants, that they sent them reeling backwards among the casks and packages which filled the after-hold, and there they lay sprawling, unable to get up again.

"It won't do to stop here, Alick," cried Jack. "Haul along the old lady, I'll carry the young one; and we'll stow them away in our berth till we see what's best to be done. Come along, miss. Beg pardon—hadn't time to ask your leave; it's all right, though." Jack said this after he had lifted the young lady in his arms, and was carrying her up the ladder. As he remarked, there was no time for ceremony. Everything depended on the rapidity with which they could accomplish their enterprise.

"Thank you, thank you, sir; I trust you," said the young lady in a foreign accent.

Murray, who always admired Jack's plans when anything dashing was to be done, followed as fast as he could, helping the old lady along. He would have had great difficulty in making progress, had not Jos the Malay comprehended what was required. So he seized her under one arm, while Alick lifted her under the other, and thus, without molestation, they followed Jack on board the junk.

Jack rushed into their cabin, and placed his fair burden on a chair, when Alick and Jos bundled the old lady in after her, with a very scant ceremony; indeed there was no time for any; and then they closed the door and walked a little way off, and tried to look as unconcerned as if they had done nothing to merit the anger of the pirates.

"I begged the young lady not to be alarmed, and entreated her to try and keep the old one quiet, promising to defend them with our lives," observed Jack.

"Of course we will do so, and Jos will stick by us, won't you, Jos?" said Murray.

"Yes, sare," answered the Malay; "but if Chinese come aboard, dey cut all our throats. Stay do—Jos know what he do."

There was a peculiar, fierce, vindictive look on the countenance of the Malay as he spoke, which boded mischief. Without uttering another word he sprang on board the brig, and disappeared among the crowd who were hurrying to and fro below, removing the cargo.

Just then Murray pointed out to Jack the brave captain and mate of the brig sitting on deck, lashed with their hands behind them to the mainmast.

"When those wretches have glutted themselves with booty, they will indulge their evil tempers by tormenting those poor fellows. Could we not manage to release them while no one is watching us, and let them hide themselves on board their junk? We may, perhaps, by and by be able to form some plan to escape together."

"With all my heart," answered Jack. "No time like the present. Here goes."

Saying this, he and Murray seized their swords, which they had stuck into the bulwarks, and a few springs brought them up to where the captain and mate were sitting. In an instant the knives were at work, and the ropes were cut.

"Leap on board the junk, my men, we'll cover your retreat."

The captain and mate did as they were directed, and had just reached the junk when several of the pirates saw what had happened and sprang after them.

Had not the midshipmen undertaken to defend them, their heads would have been off that moment. Jack and Alick had fortunately gained the side of the vessel, and there stood at bay. They had cut down three of their assailants, but others were coming on, when the Malay rushed past them, crying out, "Leap, leap on board; cast off, or we shall all blow up." A back-handed blow which he gave with his short sword cut down the nearest of their assailants, and enabled them to accomplish his advice. He and they, without questions asked, instantly cast off the grapnels, and shoved the junk away from the brig before the Chinese saw what they were about.

Scarcely were they free, when a rush of flame burst out of the hold of the merchantman, and up went her decks with a terrific explosion, carrying masts, and spars, and sails, and cargo, and the many hundred human beings, who, like ants in a granary, were swarming in every direction, rifling her of the treasures she contained. The numerous junks surrounding her did not escape; some were blown up, others had their sides blown in, and several caught fire or were more or less injured. For a moment there was perfect silence; every one stood aghast, and then down came clattering on their heads, limbs, and trunks, and heads of human beings, and fragments of spars, and burning bales, and canvas, and packages burst open like shells, scattering their contents on every side. Next arose shrieks, and groans, and shouts, a hubbub most terrific, the cries of the wounded, and the imprecations of those who had escaped and been baulked of their prey.

"Dat is just what I tort it would be," said Jos, quite coolly, watching the effects of the catastrophe, as he assisted to shove the junk out from among the crowd of burning vessels. The pirate captain and crew, most of whom had got on board, thought that they were very much indebted to him and the white men for having been the means of saving their vessel. As they also had been the most busily at work, and had collected a good deal of booty, they did not at all take to heart the accident which had happened to their pirate companions. They shrugged their shoulders, and blinked their little pig-eyes, and seemed to think that it was just as well as it was, seeing that they themselves had come off better than anybody else. A few more junks having blown up, and others burnt to the water's edge or sunk, those that had escaped sent their boats, not so much for the chance of saving any fellow-creatures who might be struggling for existence, as to pick up any articles of value which might be still floating. The fleet then made sail away from the spot, lest the explosion might be the means of bringing down an enemy upon them to interfere with their proceedings.

The midshipmen were now placed in a somewhat difficult position with regard to the ladies in their cabin. How to account for their being there was one puzzle, and how to save them from annoyance or insult was another. The pirates seemed inclined to treat the American captain and mate as well as they had done the midshipmen. They had seen them very active in saving the junk, but it was probably not gratitude so much as the hope of obtaining a ransom which made them civil. Jos having intimated that they were hungry, in a short time a mess of food was brought for the whole party to the upper raised deck in the afterpart of the vessel. While discussing this meal, they also discussed the means likely to be most serviceable to the ladies. The American captain told them that his brig was the *Wide Awake*, that his name was William Willock, that of his mate, Joe Hudson; that they were bound to Sydney in Australia, where the two ladies, who were French, and mother and daughter, were proceeding.

"I know what!" cried Jack, as if a bright thought had struck him. "The pirates seem to treat men civilly enough; could we not manage to rig up the ladies in men's clothes? There is a chest of Chinamen's coats and trousers in our cabin, and the old lady would make a very tolerable mandarin."

"I should think it would very speedily be discovered what they are," answered Murray. "It will be better if we get Jos to talk over the old pirate skipper, and having excited his cupidity in suggesting a good ransom, produce our captives, and charge him to treat them well. What do you say. Captain Willock?"

"A very good plan, I guess," was the answer; "there is nothing like making it the interest of a man to do what you want him. Just let the ladies show themselves. I suppose Chinamen have hearts like other people, and will have some compassion on them, when they see their distress."

"But how are we to account for their being on board, and in our cabin?" asked Jack.

"Let your Malay friend, then, settle that; he'll know what will be most likely to go down with the Chinamen," answered Captain Willock.

"I think, rather, that we should boldly say that we brought them, and claim them as our share of the loot as the Indians call it—the booty," said Murray. "Now all the miserable wretches from whom we rescued them have, in all probability, been destroyed, there will be no one, unless any of our own crew saw our proceedings, to witness against us. When the pirates find that they are to get a ransom for the ladies, they will be very much obliged to us for having saved them, and, depend on it, will treat them properly."

Murray's plan, which was certainly the wisest, as it was the most straightforward, was agreed to. They, however, said nothing till late in the evening, when the fleet of junks dropped their ponderous wooden anchors close to the shore in a beautiful little bay, surrounded by green hills covered to the water's edge with trees.

"The pirates are fellows of some taste to choose this beautiful spot for their harbour," observed Jack, looking round.

"Not they," answered Captain Willock with a laugh. "I guess now they choose it because it hides them pretty securely, and they can sweep out and pounce down on any unfortunate craft which they may catch unprepared for them in the neighbourhood. But here's our skipper; Fi Tan you call him, don't you? Well, he's a mild, decent, quiet old gentleman; don't look as if his trade was cutting throats. You'd better tell him about the ladies, or he will be finding it out himself."

Jack and Alick agreed to this, and calling Jos, begged him to open the subject to the pirate captain, which he did with no little circumlocution; and very considerable departure from the real facts of the case, notwithstanding Jack's charge to him to adhere to them. The Malay had two reasons for this. In the first place, he had got so completely into the way of telling falsehoods, that he could scarcely speak the truth had he tried; and in the second place, he knew that, speak the truth or not, he should not be believed. Old Fi Tan having heard Jos to an end, and watched the dumb-show of the midshipmen and Americans, desired to have the cabin-door opened. The old lady, who had thrown herself into a bed, started up, and was going to shriek out, when Captain Willock's voice reassured her. Her daughter, who had been watching while she slept, stood trembling by her side, but tried to look as composed as she could. Captain Willock and the midshipmen soon made them understand what had occurred, and begging them to be no longer alarmed, promised that they would do their best, either to effect their escape, or to obtain their ransom.

"Oh! but our friends are all in Australia; we have no one at Canton to care for us," cried the young lady, wringing her hands.

"Never fear, miss," said Jack. "I beg your pardon, but I don't know your name; but I don't doubt the merchants there will come down with all that is required; and if not, the midshipmen on the station would be delighted to pay your ransom, and take it out of the pirates afterwards, when we catch them."

The young lady, who did not exactly understand who midshipmen were, or what taking it out of the pirates meant, nevertheless thought Jack a very polite young gentleman, and thanking him warmly, told him that her name was Cecile Dubois, and that her mother was Madame Dubois, but that she only spoke French, and as she was now too old to learn English, she hoped he would learn French to talk to her. Jack, with a flourish of his turban, which head-covering he and Murray wore instead of their caps, which they had lost, assured her that he should have unbounded pleasure in so doing, if she would undertake to teach him. "But, Miss Cecile," added Jack, "now I know your name, it is pleasant to call you by it; before we begin, wouldn't you like a little food? You and your mamma must be peckish, I suspect, and she doesn't look as if she was accustomed to starve." This want being made known to Jos, he in a short time procured an inexplicable sort of mess not altogether unattractive, to which, at all events, the old lady seemed perfectly ready to do justice, though the younger one, with a taste which Jack admired, only ate some of the rice, and the less oleaginous morsels.

Altogether the midshipmen were pretty well satisfied with the turn affairs had taken; but poor Captain Willock had to mourn over the loss of his ship and cargo, as also, probably, most of his crew. Some he had seen taken prisoners, and dragged off on board the junks. Whether their throats had been cut, or whether they were to be found among the pirate fleet, he could not tell; others he had too great reason to fear had been blown up. "They were cowards some of them to be sure, or they would have stuck by us, and we should have beaten off the pirates; but still I cannot bear to think of them all being cruelly murdered," observed the captain to his mate.

"I guess you're not far wrong, captain," answered Joe Hudson. "If it hadn't been for these British officers, we should have been where they are, pleasant or unpleasant."

"We only did for you what I am sure you would have done for us," answered Murray. "We liked to see the brave way you met the pirates, and we are very glad to have assisted any Americans, whom we look upon as cousins, the next thing to our own countrymen."

"Thank you, sir, thank you," said Captain Willock warmly, taking Alick's hand. "If the Britishers and Yankees were always together, we might flog all the world, I guess, who might try to oppose us." Thus harmony prevailed among the captives.

For the next two days the fleet lay at anchor, those junks which had suffered by the explosion of the brig being engaged in repairing damages.

Jack got on very rapidly with his French, for, having nothing else to do, he studied very hard, and Mademoiselle Cecile happened to have a copy of *Paul and Virginia* in her pocket when the vessel was attacked. It served as a capital lesson-book.

As Murray already knew French, he did not require Miss Cecile's lessons, and so he was able to look philosophically on, and, like a wise monitor, he told Jack to take care what he was about, neither to take possession of the young lady's heart nor to lose his own. Whether he would have taken this advice, which was sage and sound, it is impossible to say; but other stirring events happened which put a stop to the French lessons.

One evening the midshipmen observed the pirates in a great state of commotion. Those who were on shore came off and armed themselves after their fashion, by sticking pistols and daggers in their belts, and hanging swords over their necks, and then all hands set busily to work to get their ships into fighting order. Jos, who had been on shore, came off among the others, and informed them that another pirate fleet had hove in sight, and that it was expected that it would come into the bay to attack them for the sake of making them disgorge the booty they had collected.

"Pretty scoundrels," said Jack; "there is not even honour among these thieves themselves."

"No, sare," answered Jos quietly. "Big man in dis country always cut little man's throat, if little man got any ting worth having."

"Pleasant," remarked Jack; "I would rather be an English ploughman than a Chinese mandarin."

While the midshipmen were talking to Jos, Captain Fi Tan came up, and intimated to the latter that he should expect his prisoners to take an active part in the battle, and to assist in defending the junk.

"A cool request," remarked Jack; "however, as fight we must probably to defend our own lives and those of the two ladies, we may as well make a virtue of necessity. You agree with me, Murray, and so do you. Captain and

Mr Hudson? Well, then, Jos, tell Captain Fi Tan that we will fight for him, but that he must give us any recompense we may demand."

Jos spoke to the pirate captain, and immediately said that he would agree to their terms.

"That's to say, he'll take the fighting out of us first, and then, if he finds it convenient, change his mind," remarked Captain Willock. "I know the way of the Chinese. You cannot trust them."

"Perhaps when we have taught them to trust us they may learn to be trustworthy themselves," observed Murray; "besides, these fellows are professed pirates. What can you expect of them?"

"They are all alike, all alike; all rogues and vagabonds together," answered the skipper.

After this somewhat sweeping condemnation of a whole people, their conversation was interrupted by the pirates bringing them a heap of pistols, daggers, knives, and swords, with which to cover their persons in Chinese fashion to be ready for battle. Darkness now came on, and in a short time lights were seen in a pretty dense line, reaching across the entrance of the harbour. The dark outlines of a fleet of junks soon after this appeared through the gloom, and forthwith gongs and cymbals began to clash, and shrieks and shouts ascended, and guns, and jingalls, and pistols went off, while fire-balls, and rockets, and stink-pots, and other Chinese devices for warfare, filled the air, and truly made "night hideous."

Chapter Thirty
An Attempt at Escape

Rogers and Murray, and their companions, watched with considerable anxiety the approach of the fresh horde of pirates. From the number of lights they showed, and the noise they made, it was very evident that their fleet was much more powerful than the one which had captured the brig.

"If we were on shore now, I should little care if the result of the fight was like that of the two Kilkenny cats Adair tells a story about, who fought so desperately that at the end of the battle only their tails were to be found," said Jack; "they having, in a way none but Irish cats could have succeeded in doing, eaten each other up. Paddy sticks to his story, and declares it is a truth, but does not exactly explain how it happened."

Rogers' remarks were cut short by one or two shots striking their junk, on which the crew set up the most terrific shouting, and began blazing away from all their guns, jingalls, and other firearms. Jack and Alick, and Captain Willock and his mate, loaded their muskets and began to fire away, and to make as much noise as the Chinese, but they none of them at first took much pains to aim at the other pirates, their object being to make their companions suppose that they were fighting desperately. However, before long a jingall ball grazed Jack's shoulder, and that put up his blood.

"I say, it won't do, we must drive these villains off," he exclaimed; "if we don't, we shall be getting the ladies' throats cut, and our own too."

"I am afraid so," answered Alick; "it isn't pleasant fighting either way." So they now loaded faster than ever, and took the best aim they could. All the firing and shouting did not stop the advance of the enemy, and jingall balls and other missiles came flying thicker and thicker round their heads.

"Those poor ladies! What will become of them? They must be very much frightened," cried Jack. A considerable number of the crew were by this time hit; many were killed outright, and as far as the midshipmen could judge, their side was getting the worst of it. Still the shrieks and cries in no way diminished, but rather grew louder and more unearthly. One large junk appeared to have singled them out, and was steadily approaching to board. Their crew evidently did not like this state of things. The old captain had just come up to them, with Jos the Malay as interpreter, to make some proposal or other to them, when, as the words were coming out of his mouth, a round shot took his head off, and his body was sent flying half across the deck. What he was saying Jos could not tell, and gravely remarked that no one was now likely to discover. The crew, on discovering that their chief was killed, and that they had lost so many of their companions, showed signs of unwillingness to fight. At last one ran to the side, and overboard he jumped, and began to swim towards the shore. One after the other followed like a flock of sheep, all taking the water exactly in the same way, till not a pirate remained on board. The midshipmen entreated Jos to remain, and Hoddidoddi engaged to stick by them.

"The ladies, probably, can't swim," observed Jack; "but if we could manage to launch a boat, we might get away before the big junk can scull alongside." There was a boat, but on examining her, they found that she had several holes in her side, which was the reason the pirates had not taken her.

"That's pleasant," cried Jack. "Now if those fellows board us in a hurry, before Jos has time to explain who we are, we shall get knocked on the head to a certainty."

"We must stow ourselves away, I fear, till the first rush is over," said Alick. "We must keep outside the ladies' cabin, so as to protect them."

"I am afraid so," said Jack, and he ran and told Madame Dubois and her daughter what had occurred, and entreated them not to be alarmed—advice which was more easily given than taken. Jack then ran back to Murray, who was trying to induce Jos and Hoddidoddi to remain with them, they very naturally wishing to swim on shore, under the belief that they should be knocked on the head if they remained. On came the huge junk, and in another instant would have been alongside, when, as the midshipmen began to feel that too probably their last moments had arrived, a loud roar was heard, up went her decks and masts and sails, and fierce flames burst out from every part of her—the same event which had happened to the brig had occurred to her; she had blown up. The bodies of the poor wretches belonging to her, and the burning fragments of the vessel, fell close alongside them, and nearly set their junk on fire. Had they possessed a boat, they would have done their best to render assistance to the drowning wretches; as it was, they ran to the side of the vessel, and got such ropes as they could lay hands on to heave-to the people who were swimming about. The pirates, however, believing that if they came near the vessel they were about to attack they would simply be thrust back again into the water, or be knocked on the head, or have their throats cut, or be disposed of in some similarly unpleasant way, kept at a distance, and the midshipmen saw them one by one disappear beneath the surface. All this time the battle was raging on every side round them, and the attacking fleet drew closer and closer to the junks at anchor, and appeared to be gaining the victory. As soon as they could, the midshipmen ran to the ladies' cabin to tell them what had occurred, and to give them such consolation as they had to offer.

"But could not we manage to make the vessel sail and run away?" exclaimed Cecile, with considerable animation, as if a bright thought had struck her.

"I wish we could, Miss Dubois," said Jack; "but there is no wind, and we have not strength to hoist these heavy mat sails of the junk."

"Ah! but I will help you, and so will mamma, I am sure," answered the young lady.

"Mamma would be of great assistance in hoisting, I doubt not," said Jack, looking with an expression of humour, which he could not repress, towards the weighty dame. "We'll try what can be done." They could not venture to remain long in the cabin, so they hurried back on deck. They were as much puzzled as ever to know what next to do. Their great fear was that the pirates would return from the shore and prevent any attempt they might make to escape. When they told the American captain what Miss Cecile had proposed, he said that she was a brave young lady for thinking of such a thing; that perhaps a breeze might come off the land, and that if it did, they would try and sway up the foresail. Scarcely had they come to this resolution, when, by the flashes of the guns, they saw a boat pulling a short distance ahead of them. The American captain hailed. A voice answered immediately in English. "Why, that's one of my men, as I'm a freeborn American!" exclaimed the captain. "Come here; be smart now." In less than a minute one of the boats of the brig came alongside with three seamen in her. They had been captured by a junk, and, finding the boat floating astern, they had taken the opportunity, during the confusion of the battle, of jumping into her and pulling off. The boat was too large for the three men to manage, and they would probably have been lost had they got outside. Not a moment was wasted in bringing the two ladies from the cabin, and in lowering them into her. Captain Willock and his mate, and Jos and Hoddidoddi followed, and they were hurriedly shoving off, eager to get away from the junk, when Murray asked the rest if they were going to live on air, and reminded them that they would all be starved if they had not a supply of provisions.

"Very right, sare," observed Jos; "me go find food."

Accordingly he and the two midshipmen and Mr Hudson jumped on board again and hunted about for food. It was rather difficult to find in the dark, but they got some jars of water, and a bag of rice, and a collection of nameless things which they supposed were to be eaten. They got also a small stove, with fuel, and a saucepan. Altogether, considering that they seized whatever they could lay hands on, they had reason to be satisfied with the result of their search. Fortunately, just that particular spot was in comparative darkness, though on either side the pirates were firing away at each other as furiously as ever.

Captain Willock took the helm, and the two midshipmen, with Joe Hudson and the Malay, each seizing an oar, away they pulled at a pretty good speed from the scene of action. The shot, however, every now and then came whizzing over them, and made Madame Dubois shriek out rather too lustily. Her daughter, on the contrary, kept perfectly silent, or if she spoke, it was to entreat the old lady not to be alarmed.

"But, *ma chère fille*, if those horrid balls should hit us, how dreadful!" was the answer.

"Yes, *ma mère*, but crying out will not stop them," remarked Miss Cecile; an observation which Jack highly admired.

He and Alick and the rest pulled with all their might, as they had good reason for doing, with the prospect of liberty before them, and imprisonment or death if they were recaptured. As they drew out from the light thrown on them by the flashes of the guns, and away from the shot, they all breathed more freely, and Madame Dubois began to leave off screaming, giving way only at intervals to a short hysterical cry as the sound of a more than usual crashing broadside reached her ears. At last they were completely shrouded by the gloom of night, and they could only now and then hear a faint rattle in the distance.

Captain Willock steered north-west, the direction in which he supposed Canton to lie. On they pulled for several hours, till at last they grew very tired and hungry, so they stopped rowing and cried out for food. Joe Hudson had charge of the provisions. From the first bag he opened he produced some tough, dry lumps, on the nature of which no one could pronounce till they had reached the Malay. He bit away at one, and then remarked—

"Want boiling; crawl, crawl; berry good do."

"Slugs," cried Jack. "Hand something else out."

The next bag was full of some long, dried things, which might have been eels, but were very probably snakes. Frogs and snails in a dried or pickled state were not more tempting; but at last they came on a basket of shell-fish, which, with some unboiled rice, stopped the gnawings of hunger, but did not make a very satisfying meal. They were afraid then of lighting a fire, but they agreed that they would do so in the morning.

Once more they took to their oars. They now, however, could not make much progress, nor could they have done so had a breeze sprung up, as they possessed no sails. They hoped, therefore, that it would continue calm. In this, however, they were destined to be disappointed. Not long past midnight a gentle zephyr began to play over the surface of the water, and soon it turned into a light breeze, and that increased into a stiff one, and by degrees it grew stronger and stronger, and the sea got up and tossed the boat about, and that made Madame Dubois scream as loud as before, and now and then the spray washed over them, and then she screamed louder still; and next it was discovered that the boat leaked, and it was necessary to employ two men constantly in baling to keep her afloat. The more she tumbled about the more she leaked, and the louder poor Madame Dubois screamed. Her daughter proved herself a regular heroine, and made no noise, and only grasped the side of the boat tighter as it rose and fell on the seas. The morning approached, but matters did not improve; the wind blew stronger; the waves grew higher and seriously threatened to swamp the boat.

"I say, Alick, this is no fun," observed Jack. "What's to be done?"

"We must get under the lee of the land till the gale moderates," answered Murray.

The wind, it must be observed, was favourable; but the sea had now got up so much, that it was dangerous to run before it. Captain Willock agreed to Murray's proposal, and, watching their opportunity, they got the boat round head to the seas, and pulled in for the shore. This was very trying after all their labours; but they were not the only people in the world who have to toil in vain, or have to undo all the work they have done and begin again. They now shipped less water, but they made very little way in consequence of the heavy sea. Daylight at last came, but did not exhibit a pleasant prospect. The green seas tumbled and foamed about them; the dark clouds hurried along overhead, while about three miles off appeared the land with the harbour they had left a few miles along the shore on the port bow. The idea that they might get into some bay or inlet, and remain, there till the weather moderated, was a considerable consolation. Still, pull as hard as they could, they could not make their heavy boat go ahead, but rather found themselves drifting farther off the shore. The great thing, however, was to keep the boat afloat. Hour after hour thus passed away, till at last the wind began to fall and the sea quickly went down; and, instead of making for the shore, it was proposed putting the boat about and continuing their course. The captain was looking out for a lull to do this, when an exclamation from his lips made everybody turn their eyes in the direction towards which he pointed, the port they had left, where several large junks were seen rounding the headland which formed its side on the west. They all anxiously watched the junks; they were steering to the north-west.

"They are in pursuit of us," observed Jack.

"Little doubt about it, I guess," said Captain Willock.

"Can we not escape them?" said Murray.

"By lying quietly down at the bottom of the boat we might," said the captain. "We'll wait, though, till they come near."

The junks advanced, and from their appearance it seemed too probable that they were the very fleet of pirates which had entered the harbour the previous evening, and that, having been victorious, they were again sailing in search of fresh plunder.

"We had a narrow escape, then," observed Jack. "If we had remained, we should, long before this, have been food for the sharks in the bay."

"I guess that we shall be lucky if we are not down the throats of some of them before night," pleasantly observed Captain Willock.

Madame Dubois did not understand him, or it would have set her off screaming again. She willingly enough lay down in the bottom of the boat, and Jack in his choicest French begged she would keep quiet; her daughter followed her example; and as the sea had gone down, the oars were laid in, and the rest of the party placed themselves under the thwarts out of sight. As, however, the junks were steering almost directly for them, they had little expectation of escaping notice. Jack had great difficulty, he confessed, in refraining from jumping up every instant to watch the progress of the junks.

"What do you say, Alick?" he exclaimed, suddenly. "Suppose we arm ourselves with the boat's stretchers, and the moment a junk runs up to us jump on board and capture her? It's the best thing I can think of to do."

"We should probably be knocked on the head, and be sent overboard again," answered Alick. "We must stay quiet, and wait the course of events."

"I suppose it is the wisest thing, but I should like to have a fight for life," said Jack, with a sigh.

The boat kept slowly turning round and round, and just then, by lifting his head up a little, he saw the mast-heads and sails of two junks, which were bearing close down upon them. There seemed now an impossibility of their escaping detection.

"We are in for it," whispered Jack. "Let's have a fight."

"I guess it would be a short one," answered Captain Willock; "stay quiet, Mr Rogers, if you don't want all our throats cut."

Two minutes more elapsed, and the high sides of two large junks, crowned by big round shields and numberless hideous grinning faces looking down on them, appeared, one on either hand. A couple of grapnels were hove into the boat, which was nearly crushed between the two vessels, and a dozen or more pirates, armed to the teeth, looking more like demons than men, sprang into her. Before Jack, or Murray, or Captain Willock, or indeed any of the party, could offer any resistance, they had passed running nooses over their shoulders, by which those on deck hauled them up without power of resistance. Jack, Alick, the American skipper, and Jos were fished up on board one junk, and they saw, to their great regret, the Frenchwoman and her daughter hoisted up on the other, poor madame half dead with terror, shrieking out vain petitions to be set on her feet.

"Jos, Jos," cried Jack, when he saw this, "tell the pirates they must let the poor ladies remain with us. They will frighten them to death."

Jos shook his head. "No good, now," he answered, mournfully; "dey cut all our troats."

Just then, the junk which had caught the midshipmen separated from the boat, and they, with the captain and Jos, being dragged by the pirates into a cabin, were unable to discover what became of the rest of the party.

Chapter Thirty One
On Board the Junk

While the French lady and her daughter, with Mr Hudson, the American mate, one seaman, and Hoddidoddi were carried off by one junk, the two midshipmen, Captain Willock, and Jos, with the remaining seamen, found themselves stowed away on board another.

"I say, Alick, we must try and help those poor ladies somehow or other," observed Jack; "I hope the pirates will not hurt them."

"I hope not, though I am afraid they will frighten the poor mamma out of her wits," said Murray. "But without being selfish, we must first consider how we are to get free ourselves."

"Something may turn up in the wheel of Fortune," returned Jack. "We very nearly effected our escape; perhaps the next time we shall be more fortunate; at present I cannot say that I see any opening by which we may bring about that desirable event."

As he spoke he looked round the little cabin in which they were shut up with a disconsolate yet half-ludicrous air. The prisoners were sitting with their backs to the bulkheads, and their feet towards the centre of the chamber. The door was locked, and there was no lookout except through the chinks between the bamboos which formed the sides. They discovered by the motion of the vessel, that there was a stiff breeze, and that they were sailing along very rapidly. In vain they tried to ascertain in what direction they were sailing. They looked through the chinks, but all they could see were the figures of the crew as they moved about the deck, and the inner part of the bulwarks and the back of the shields which hung up above them. Hunger is a strong motive to exertion. It had the effect, when after a time the party began to feel its pangs, of making them somewhat less quiet than at first. Some of the men were for trying to break out of their prison, but Captain Willock assured them that the attempt would be useless, and suggested that Jos should try the power of his eloquence in softening the hearts of their captors. Jos expressed his approval of the proposed plan, and forthwith began a loud chaunt, which he informed his fellow-prisoners was descriptive of their present forlorn and famished condition, of the prowess of the warriors of Queen Victoria, and of the certainty that they would revenge any injury inflicted on any of their fellow-subjects, as also of their custom of rewarding those who treated them well.

"I say," observed Jos, "Queen Victoria knock on de head any one hurt us—give plenty money any one give us plenty food—make us fat."

"That's it," cried Jack, "sing away in that strain; they understand that sort of reasoning better than any other argument."

On went Jos again with his chaunt, the commencement of which sounded very like—

Hi fum diddle eye, ho fol lol,
Tittle-bats cats-call, tol de rol lol.

It is not necessary to give the whole of the song. Jos assured his companions that it was very pathetic, and that if it did not move the hearts of the pirates he would not believe that they had any hearts at all. Whether the pathos, or the threats of vengeance, or the hopes of reward held out had most effect is uncertain, but in a short time the door of the cabin was opened, and a Chinamen appeared with a big copper bowl or pot in his hands, full of a hot savoury mess. He looked at Jos and nodded, as much as to say, "We heard you," and then placed the bowl in the middle of the cabin. There were some chop-sticks in the bowl, but no spoons, or knives, or forks. Captain Willock looked at them with a puzzled air.

"If those are toothpicks they are whoppers, and I must say I would rather they were not there," he observed, as he tucked back the cuff of his coat. "However, I suppose we mustn't be particular, and as I guess we're all equal just now, here goes."

Saying this he plunged his fingers into the bowl, and drew forth a suspicious-looking mass. He gazed at it for a time, then shut his eyes, and plunged it into his mouth.

"A wise proceeding," observed Jack, as he and Alick, following his example, did the same.

The rest of the party were not so particular, and only opened their eyes rather wider than usual as odd-looking particles of food were fished out of the bowl. It was very soon emptied, for as everybody was hungry, they were all eager to get their due portions. Most of them at first fancied that they could have eaten twice as much; however, when Jack and Alick leaned back again against the bulkheads, they were soon convinced that they had had enough. In a little time, the door again opened, and another man, who looked from his richer clothes and manner like an officer, popped in his head and beckoned to Captain Willock and the two midshipmen to come out of the cabin. They, happy to have the opportunity of stretching their legs, jumped up with alacrity, and followed him on deck.

Jack's first impulse was to look out for the junk which had Miss Cecile and her mother on board, but she was nowhere to be seen. Their junk was, however, standing down towards a fleet of considerable size. As there was a stiffish breeze, they were soon among them, and from the hailing, and talking, and chattering, and the way in which they themselves were pointed at, the junks had pretty evidently not met for some time. Jos, who was shortly after this allowed to come out of the cabin, told them that they were right in their conclusions. The whole fleet now made sail together, and stood to the eastward. The night, when they were all shut up again in the same cabin, was not over pleasant. When daylight broke, the door was opened, and they were allowed to go out. It was a perfect calm, and the pirates were propelling their huge junks, so unwieldy in appearance, with long oars, or rather sculls, through the water at no inconsiderable rate. There was evidently an object in this speed, for the Chinamen are not given to exert themselves without a cause.

"Perhaps they are pursued by an enemy, and if so, we have a a chance of being rescued," observed Jack, as he first went on deck.

"No, I think not. See, the whole fleet are steering for the same point," answered Murray. "Ah! look ahead; what do you see there?"

"A brig, and I do believe a brig-of-war," exclaimed Rogers. "I shouldn't be surprised if she proves to be the *Blenny*. If she is, the pirates will find that they have caught a Tartar."

"She is not unlike your little brig, certainly, but at this distance it is impossible to say," remarked Murray. "But even a brig-of-war in a calm, surrounded by this host of junks, will have great odds against her; still, our fellows will do their best—of that I am very certain."

"That they will, there's no doubt about it," observed Captain Willock. "You Britishers fight well, I guess, and no wonder, when you've had us to practise with."

"I wonder, captain, that you do not declare that the Yankees taught us to fight," said Jack, laughing.

"And so we did, I guess," quickly answered the skipper. "We taught you a trick or two, at all events."

"What was that?" asked Jack.

"To keep awake," answered Captain Willock. "It is the first thing for a soldier or a sailor to do, you'll allow, and before that time you were apt to go to sleep now and then I calculate."

"Perhaps you are right, captain," said Murray; "but what was the other trick you taught us?"

"Not to despise your enemies, I guess," answered the skipper. "You despised us, and we beat you; you did not despise the French, who were ten times better soldiers than the Americans were, and had fifty times better generals than we had, and you beat them. There was the difference. Never think meanly of the people with whom you are fighting. Believe that you will drub them in the end—that's all right; but only fancy you can do so with a great deal of trouble and hard fighting, and always believe that they are about to play you some trick or other. That's my philosophy about fighting. I'd advise you to take up the same and stick to it. And this brings me to that brig of yours out there. You make sure that she'll drub the junks. Just take care that the junks don't drub her; not but that I know what your people are made of, and next to our people there ain't any people who fight better in the world when they're put to it, that I'll allow, but—"

"All right," exclaimed Jack, who did not wish to discuss the subject. "But see what these cunning rogues are about."

While the above discussion was going on, the fleet of junks had separated into four divisions. One led, keeping away so as to give a respectful berth to the brig, two others branched off on either side, and one, which was the junk which bore the midshipmen and their fortunes, gave up sculling and remained stationary. It was very evident that the intention of the pirates was completely to surround the brig. After a time, the last-named division began once more to creep slowly on, and, the circle being formed, the whole advanced, decreasing it by degrees, till they got within range of the brig's guns. So eager were the pirates that they paid little attention to their prisoners, who all, therefore, assembled on the deck to watch proceedings.

"She is the *Blenny*, there is no doubt about it," cried Jack. "Our fellows will not knock under as long as a man remains alive on the deck to fight her guns."

The Chinese knew that their shot would not fly across the brig so as to hit their friends on the other side of her, so as they closed in their circle became complete, with short distances only between each junk. The prisoners also watched proceedings with such intense interest, that they totally forgot the danger to which they themselves were exposed.

"I wish that the brig would open her fire, and give it these scoundrels well," cried Jack; "I wonder that they don't begin." He had scarcely spoken when there was a flash and a report from one of the brig's guns, and a shot struck the junk just astern of them. Several of the Chinese fired in return, but their shot scarcely reached the brig. The pirate admiral or commodore, on seeing this, threw out signals to close in still more, and as the junks began to move the *Blenny* let fly both her broadsides at the same moment, several of the shot striking the junks, and ripping open their sides.

This in no way daunted them. They seemed resolved on the destruction of the brig. The sculls were still more vigorously plied, and they advanced rapidly, till they had got her well within range of their guns. And now from every side they opened on her, while, she replied in the most spirited way, firing her guns as rapidly as they could be hauled in, loaded, and run out again. The shot from the pirate's junks told, however, with very considerable effect on her, and the midshipmen had too much reason to fear that many of their friends must have lost the number of their mess. The pirates all seemed to aim at the hull of the brig. They expected, apparently, that the calm would continue, and all they wanted was to kill as many of the Englishmen as they could before they attempted to board her.

"I say, I guess your friends aboard there will be getting the worst of it if this sort of fun lasts much longer," observed the Yankee captain to Murray.

"I am afraid so, indeed," answered Alick, with a deep sigh and a sinking of the heart; "I wish we were aboard to help them."

"I guess, now, we should have a better chance of helping them by being aboard here," answered the captain. Alick thought so likewise. He and Jack were glad that they were not compelled to fight against their countrymen.

The larger number of the junks had placed themselves ahead and astern of the brig, and kept pouring in a raking fire on her. To avoid this as much as she could, she got out her sweeps; but they continued to change their positions as often as she got her head round, so that the English had not a moment's respite. The pirates shouted with delight as they saw the success of their plan. They, of course, thought it would be a great thing to cut off an outer Barbarian man-of-war, and anticipated no small amount of valuable plunder as their reward. They, however, were all this time not escaping scot-free, for the brig's shot went through and through the hulls of their junks, and several of them were reduced to a sinking condition; while the musketry of the marines told with no little effect on their decks. Still they had the advantage of an immense superiority in numbers, and although they might lose twice as many men as the crew of the brig numbered, they might still come off victorious. Nearer and nearer crept the junks. For some time no people were killed on board the one which had captured the midshipmen. This made her captain and crew grow bold, and approach still nearer to the *Blenny*.

"They would be wiser if they kept at a distance," observed Rogers; "they'll catch it to a certainty."

"Perhaps they hope to bring the combat to a conclusion," remarked Murray.

"They'll not do that, let me tell them, in a hurry," exclaimed Jack; "they little think what sort of a fellow they have to deal with in Hemming. He'll give them more than they expect."

While Jack was speaking, several shots came crashing on board the junk, killing five men, wounding others, and knocking away part of the bulwarks. The wounded men set up the most terrific cries, and their shipmates, anxious to avoid a second edition of the same dose, put about, and sculled off to a more respectful distance. Another junk, the next in the line, was not so fortunate. The greater part of a broadside struck her. The midshipmen saw her reel with the shock, and immediately she began to sink lower and lower, till down she went, and the water washed over the spot where she had just before floated. Numbers of her crew went down with her or followed her to the bottom. Very few of the neighbouring junks took the trouble of lowering their boats to pick up the remainder, and numbers were drowned in sight of their countrymen, by whom, with a little exertion, they might have been saved.

The engagement had now lasted several hours, and neither side had gained any material advantage. Some junks had been sunk, and a good many Chinamen killed; but as a set-off against this, there could be no doubt that the brig had lost several men. Jack, too, observed that she now only fired when the junks pressed very close round her, and he could not but suspect that she was running short of ammunition. The evening was drawing on. It was a question whether darkness would favour the crew of the brig, or make her enemies bolder. She at length ceased firing, and manning all her sweeps, she began to move forward, very clearly with the intention of fighting her way out from among the pirates.

"She is coming towards us. Hurrah!" cried Jack. "Now if we could but knock the fellows aboard here on the head, we might render her some help."

"Don't be trying that on," said Captain Willock. "We shall only lose our lives if we make the attempt."

"But I must get on board her somehow or other," answered Jack, as he spoke, kicking off his shoes and throwing off his jacket. It had now grown very dark, though the constant flashes of the guns kept the scene well lighted up. The *Blenny* could be seen, though she had ceased firing, gliding on towards them. The pirates had been taking no notice of their prisoners for some time. The brig had got within a cable's length of them.

"Now or never," cried Jack. "Alick, in case I am drowned, you'll do all I have asked you." And without waiting for a reply, he sprang over the side of the junk, and catching hold of a rope, let himself down into the water without a splash, and struck off towards the brig. The pirates did not understand what he was doing till he had reached the water; at first they thought he was in despair going to drown himself, but when they saw him swimming away they began to fire at him with the jingalls. Favoured by the darkness, he was soon out of their sight. To avoid the sweeps, he had to make a wide circuit, and he was pretty well tired when he got under the stern of the brig.

"Brig ahoy. Heave a rope here, and help me aboard," he sang out.

"A man overboard!" exclaimed some one from the afterpart of the deck.

"Pass a rope here; be smart now. Heave!"

"Who is it? who is it?" cried several voices.

"It's I, Jack Rogers. Be quick, now, for I've had a long swim," cried Jack. He soon got hold of the rope which was heaved to him, and was hauled on board over the stern.

"What! Rogers, my dear fellow, is it you?" exclaimed Captain Hemming, as he grasped his hand. "Where have you come from?"

Jack told him, and urged that they should immediately board the junk he had left, and rescue the rest of the prisoners.

"My only doubt is, whether we can get alongside her," answered Captain Hemming. "However, we will try. I am glad to engage in any work with cold steel; but, Rogers, I am sorry to say that our ammunition is almost expended, and though we will not yield as long as a man remains alive to fight, I look with apprehension to what may occur." The brig was now approaching the junk, which fired away furiously at her, but this did not stop her progress, and before the pirates knew what was going to happen, she dashed alongside.

"Lash her to the junk. Boarders, follow me." Jack had seized a cutlass, and, dripping with wet, he sprang on board by the side of his commander. "Alick, Captain Willock, friends, all get on board the brig as fast as you can," he sang out.

Murray and the rest of the prisoners were ready enough to follow his advice. Seizing what weapons they could lay hands on, they cut down or knocked over all the pirates who opposed them, and soon gained the deck of the brig. The boarders in the meantime cleared the junk, the greater number of her crew who escaped their cutlasses jumping overboard and perishing in the sea. The seamen then hove overboard all the guns of the junk, and returned to the brig. They would have set her on fire, but had they done so, they would very likely have got burnt themselves.

"That's one enemy less, my lads," cried Captain Hemming in a cheerful tone, though he felt anything but cheerful. "We must treat the rest in the same way."

The pirates on board the other junks, discovering what had occurred, took very good care to keep out of the way of the brig.

Captain Hemming, therefore, spent the whole night in trying in vain to get alongside some more junks, and when morning dawned they appeared formed in a close circle round her as on the previous day. Those on board the *Blenny* had passed an anxious and harassing night; the prospect for the following day was gloomy indeed. The second lieutenant, a midshipman, and eight men had been killed, and twenty were wounded, many of them put out of fighting trim. Jack and his companions afforded, therefore, a very welcome addition to their strength. With daylight the pirates began to fire away as on the previous day.

Rogers and Murray, however, now felt very differently to what they had done on the previous day. Then all the shots they saw fired were against their friends; now the few Captain Hemming ventured to let fly were against their enemies. At length only three rounds remained on board. The brig ceased firing. The pirates thought that the time for boarding her simultaneously had arrived, and gliding up closed their circle round her.

In vain all on board looked out for the sign of a breeze. Not a cloud was in the sky—the sea was like glass. The sweeps were therefore again manned, and she advanced as fast as they could urge her towards the approaching line. The pirates came on, thinking that she would fall an easy prey into their hands.

"Reserve your fire, my lads, till we are close to them," cried the captain. "Now give it them." The broadsides of the brig were poured into the junks, which had ranged up on either beam, with terrible effect. One junk went down, and another was left without a scull to impel her, and with a third of her crew killed or wounded.

Still the pirates were undaunted. On they came, again to receive another broadside. But one now remained. The junks moved away to a short distance, to hold a consultation, it seemed. The result was to renew the attack on the brig.

"We'll give our last dose, lads, to that big fellow, who is, I suppose, their admiral," cried Jack, who had taken command of the guns on one side, in place of the lieutenant who was lolled.

With a cheer, the men obeyed, and the big junk reeled from the effect of their fire. The opposite broadside was discharged at the same time. And now the brig was unarmed; but she had still stout hearts and sharp cutlasses on board, and, grasping the latter, the crew prepared to defend her to the last.

Chapter Thirty Two
Fight to the Last!

The Chinese pirates now made sure that the brig was their own, though so severe was the lesson she had given them that they showed a considerable disposition to approach her with caution. Still, as they drew closer and closer round her, and she no longer continued to fire, they grew bolder in their proceedings. Hitherto the crew of the *Blenny* were not aware that their powder was exhausted. Captain Hemming thought it better to tell them. "My lads," he exclaimed, in as cheerful a tone as he could assume, "we have run short of powder, but as I take it, no one would dream of striking to these cut-throats; we'll show them that British seamen know how to use their cutlasses." The men gave a hearty cheer, to show that they responded to their commander's appeal. Still there were fearful odds against them. The pirate junks pressed on, and though the gallant tars would have despised the crews who manned them, still, from their very numbers, they might prove overwhelming.

"My dear Jack," said Alick, in a low voice, "I never thought it would come to this; but it seems that the enemy will get the better of us, after all. We'll render a good account of them, however, before that."

"We will," said Jack, drawing in his sword-belt a hole tighter, and clutching his cutlass with a firmer grasp. "That big fellow will be alongside us in half a minute. But, I say, what are those?" He pointed, as he spoke, through an opening between two of the junks. All eyes were turned in the same direction. Several dark objects were seen on the water. They were boats. The foam thrown up by their bows glittered brightly as the rays of the sun fell on it, showing the rate at which they were coming on. The British crew gave an involuntary cheer as they caught sight of them. They had no doubt they were friends. So intent had been the pirates on capturing their prey that they had not yet discovered the approach of the boats. The sight gave fresh energy to the British seamen. The big junk at length got alongside the brig, and from her lofty bulwarks down poured the pirates on the deck of the latter; but though they got there, they had reason to wish themselves back again, for the British cutlasses made very speedy work of them, and not one in ten escaped with their lives. Still, even the bravest of the English tars wished that the boats would arrive, for two more huge junks ranged up, one on the *Blenny* quarter and another on her bows, and they had to divide to repel the pirates who swarmed on their sides. Another and another junk came up, and soon joined outside of the others, so that the pirates had the power of throwing a continual stream of boarders on to the deck of the brig. Had they not known of the approaching boats, hope would certainly have forsaken the crew of the *Blenny*. A few musket cartridges remained, with which the marines kept up a fire on the denser masses of pirates. The smoke they produced, added to that of the guns from the pirates, threw so thick a veil over the scene that the expected boats were no longer visible. More than once Captain Hemming pulled out his watch to ascertain how time sped, and then again had to lead on his men to repel a fresh attack. Several times the British were almost overpowered, and the most resolute bravery alone could have saved them. Suddenly some sharp reports were heard close to them. The masts of several of the junks were observed to be receding, and then arose above the din of battle three hearty British cheers. The hard-pressed crew of the *Blenny* responded to it, but they had to exert every nerve and muscle to keep the enemy at bay. There were more shouts and shots, and then came shrieks and cries and the clashing of steel, and Terence Adair, with little Harry Bevan, was seen, followed by a party of seamen, cutting their way along the deck of the nearest junk, driving numbers of pirates before them, till they reached the point in contact with the brig, when, with a cry of joy, Terence and Harry leaped down on her deck. The meeting of the friends was brief indeed, but cordial, and then once more they separated, each with their followers, to attack in return the junks which pressed round them. At this juncture the brig's royals were seen to bulge out for an instant; there was an evident movement among the junks; the shouts and hurrahs of the British seamen were redoubled; the shrieks and cries of the Chinese increased. The mass of junks surrounding the brig began to break away. Those inside now seemed to be in the greatest hurry to escape. Mr Cherry's countenance, even in the heat of battle, looking jovial and rosy, was now seen, as he fought his way with his boat's crew from deck to deck of the junks, driving their crews into the sea. No quarter was asked by the desperadoes, and the British seamen were not much inclined to give any.

The roar of guns was heard. It was the frigate which was now coming up with a rattling breeze, firing at the flying junks. The pirates made the most desperate efforts to escape. They cut and slashed away with their axes in the most frantic manner at the grapnels which they themselves had thrown on board the brig, and at the ropes which secured them to each other, and, at length, those who could not free their junks began cutting their throats, blowing out their brains, jumping overboard, or disembowelling themselves, while others, in the madness of their desperation, fired into their magazines, or threw torches into the holds of their vessels, in the hopes of burning their foes with themselves. In this last amiable intention they did not succeed as well as they expected, for as the junks were by this time pretty well separated, though some blew up and some burned, a great number were captured by the boats. The frigate now got up to the scene of action, and her shot as she passed them sank several more of the junks which might have escaped, and crippled others, which the boats succeeded in capturing.

Jack and Alick had, meantime, with half a dozen followers, boarded a big junk, the crew of which made a most desperate resistance. While engaged in driving the enemy overboard, or otherwise disposing of them, the midshipmen perceived that the junk, which had all her sails set, had got free from the brig, and was driving rapidly away from her. They had very severe work, for when the pirates saw themselves free from the brig they made a stand, which nothing but the most determined courage could have overcome. Again and again the midshipmen and their followers charged them. At last the chief, with most of his officers, was killed, and the rest began to give way. The remainder finding this, and knowing that there was no chance of escape, began getting rid of their lives in the way which has been already described, the process being considerably aided by their conquerors, till the last gang of them, with terrific shrieks, went overboard together. As to the English seamen attempting to save the lives of any of them, that was impossible, for they themselves even would not allow it.

"Hillo!" cried Jack, as the last party of them disappeared, and left the deck clear of all but the dead or dying, "where are we?" Well might he ask the question, for the junk had been driving away before the wind, and had by this time got nearly a couple of miles away from the brig. "At all events, we have got an independent command," he continued, when he had ascertained the state of affairs; "and, Alick, I vote we take a cruise by ourselves, and capture some more of the enemy. You and I look like Chinamen already, and we can easily rig out our men in some of the clothes of these fellows, and so I have no doubt we shall be able to get alongside without their suspecting us."

Murray thought the notion not a bad one, and the men were delighted with it, very soon transforming themselves into fierce-looking pirates, pigtails and all, for they very rapidly cut off the latter appendages from their conquered foes.

Their next business was to throw the dead men overboard, and to bind up the wounds of those who still lived; but those who had strength tore off the bandages as fast as they were put on, and were evidently intent on quitting the world. The midshipmen did all they could to prevent them by keeping all weapons out of their reach; but one fellow got hold of a knife and stabbed himself to the heart, another blew out his brains with the pistol which he drew out of his comrade's pocket, and a third, after his wounds had been bound up, and he had a little recovered his strength, took the opportunity of scrambling overboard. If Jack and Alick would have allowed it, the seamen, on observing this, would have thrown the rest of the prisoners after them.

"What's the use of coopering up these chaps, if that's the way they goes for to behave to themselves?" exclaimed Dick Snatchblock, the boatswain's mate, as he caught another fellow by the leg who was attempting to do the same. "Keep quiet you, I say," and he dealt him a box on the ears which knocked him flat on the deck. They now made sail after three junks nearest to them. The whole fleet were scattered far and wide to every part of the compass.

"I wish that Hemming and the other fellows on board the brig knew where we were," observed Jack; "we shall be reported dead or missing."

"They will value us so much the more when we make our appearance," answered Murray. "But, Jack, look at that junk! Her crew seem to have more spirit than the rest of the scoundrels. They do not seem to be in such a hurry to run away."

"They take us for friends," observed Jack. "Perhaps we have got hold of the admiral's ship, and they probably are bound to wait for him. We shall undeceive them, I guess, pretty soon. See all the guns ready therefore and aft. We'll astonish them when they get near us."

The two junks drew closer and closer. They were well within range of each other's guns. Jack was on the point of giving the order to fire, when who should jump up on the bulwarks of the stranger but Paddy Adair. Jack jumped up also and waved his hat. He forgot that he looked like a Chinaman, and that all his crew were similarly disguised. A broadside from Paddy's junk, and a rattling fire of musketry reminded him of the fact. Happily the shot flew high, but he got the upper tip of his ear taken off. He jumped down again on the deck. "What shall we do? We've no ensign with us. How shall we let Paddy know who we are?" he exclaimed. "If he were an enemy, I shouldn't care, but to be shot by one's friends is too bad."

"Perhaps we may find a tablecloth, or some sheets, or something of that sort," suggested Murray.

Nothing of the sort was to be found; and they were expecting every moment that Adair would send another broadside into them, when Jack bethought him that perhaps a pair of white trousers would answer the purpose of a flag of truce. A pair which had been exchanged for a Chinaman's nether garments was run up at the peak, and every other flag was hauled down. This had the desired effect, for Adair did not again fire. As soon as the two junks got within hail, Jack shouted out, "Paddy, ahoy! Paddy, my boy! don't be after blowing up your friends, if you love them."

Terence jumped up again on the bulwarks, and peered eagerly at the big junk.

Jack and Alick then showed themselves, and the two vessels were soon alongside of each other. Very little time was lost in greetings, and it was quickly arranged that they would again start off to secure two or three more junks before they returned. As, however, during the time they had been approaching each other the enemy had got considerably in advance, and as the frigate at the same moment began to fire guns to recall her boats, they agreed that they ought to return. Another reason which had still more weight with them was, that they had several of their men wounded, for whom they wished to get assistance.

They at once, therefore, hauled their wind, but they had considerable difficulty in beating up toward the frigate, till they bethought them of lowering the junks' leeboard, when they found them sail wonderfully well to windward. Before dark the captured junks were assembled under the guns of the frigate and brig. The reception the midshipmen met with on board the frigate was cordial in the extreme. All rejoiced, fore and aft, that Rogers and Murray had once more turned up.

"Well, it's a mighty satisfaction to be lost, for the sake of the pleasure it affords one's friends to see one back again," observed Terence; "and, old fellows, I knew you would come back, somehow or other; I always said so; astride of a dolphin if in no other way, though Harry here and some of our friends would not believe me."

"I am very glad you were right, Paddy," said Jack. "But we haven't done with the pirate yet. The villains have carried off two ladies, and some seamen, and we must be after them."

"We shouldn't lose time either," observed Murray. "We should tell the captain, and get him to send off an expedition at once to search for them."

All agreed to this; so Jack and Alick instantly went to the captain's cabin and made their report. On hearing it, Captain Grant, without loss of time, organised an expedition, which was placed, as had been the former one, under the command of the indefatigable Lieutenant Cherry. Captain Willock volunteered his services, as did his men, and Terence got leave to accompany it with Jack and Alick.

The wounded men were in the meantime removed from the brig; she was furnished with a supply of powder, and fresh hands were sent to her from the frigate. Captain Hemming was then ordered to cruise in whatever direction the boats might go, to render assistance if necessary. He and his officers were glad of the opportunity, that they might inflict a further punishment on the pirates, should they fall in with them. The question now arose as to the direction in which they should proceed. Captain Willock suggested that they were not likely to be very far off, and, as he knew the haunts of the pirates, he undertook to act as pilot.

In spite of the attempts of the pirates to destroy themselves, several had been secured alive and unwounded. Two of the most intelligent, and who seemed most willing to be communicative, were selected to accompany the expedition, and they were made to understand by signs that if they assisted in discovering the prisoners, they should be handsomely rewarded. Their little pig-eyes glittered when they saw the gold held out to them, and there appeared to be little doubt that they would try to earn it. One fellow, however, made a clutch at it at once, and intimated that he should like to receive the reward first and do the work afterwards.

"Catch a weasel asleep, old fellow," said Paddy, who stood by, making a significant gesture, which the Chinaman seemed to understand fully, for his eyes twinkled more than ever, and he laughed heartily, as if he thought his proposal a very good joke.

Jack and Alick, having washed off the stains of gunpowder and blood with which they were pretty well covered, and reassumed their proper uniforms, declared themselves ready to proceed. They laughed at the notion of wanting rest.

"Let us get back the old lady, and the young lady, and the other prisoners, and then we will turn in and take a spell of twenty-four hours at least," exclaimed Jack as he jumped into his boat.

The American master went with Mr Cherry, as did also the interpreter belonging to the frigate, as without him they could not hope to do much. The three midshipmen had each the command of a boat. They all kept close together, steering to the south-east, for which point the wind was favourable. Light hazy blue hillocks, indicating islands, lay away to the south-east. The brig, having caught up the boats, took them in tow and stood towards the islands, till she got close enough in to be visible from the shore. She then cast them off, and they stood in alone. It was quite dark before the boats reached the land. They pulled noiselessly along till they reached a sheltered bay, into which they ran, and brought up under a high, rocky point, where they might lay concealed till the return of daylight should enable them to proceed on their expedition. They had passed several such nights, since they had come into the China seas, and many more on the coast of Africa, so that there was nothing very particular to interest them. One officer at a time and two men in each boat were directed to keep watch while the rest went to sleep. It was Jack's middle watch. It is not surprising, considering all the fatigues he had gone through, that he should be very drowsy. Still, he did his utmost to keep awake. He kept pinching himself and rubbing his nose, and then he lit a cigar and tried to smoke; but, in spite of it, he was conscious that more than once he indulged in a loud snore. His head nodded, too, just like that of a person who unfortunately falls asleep in church. He had kept the prisoner who had been committed to his side. The man appeared to be fast asleep. Jack, in spite of his drowsiness, became conscious that something was moving close to them. There was a splash. He started up. The prisoner was not in his place. At a little distance off a round object popped out of the water. In an instant Jack, giving a loud shout, was overboard and darting away in chase of the man. The shout he gave and the noise of his plunge woke up the people in the other boats, only in time, though, to see the other Chinaman swimming away in the direction taken by his countryman. On this all the boats slipped their cables and made chase, though there appeared a great probability that in the darkness the pirates would effect their escape.

Chapter Thirty Three
An old Acquaintance

A swim in the dark through waters where sharks abound, and in chase of an enemy who may very likely be armed with a sharp creese, is far from an agreeable amusement.

Away swam the pirate, and after him swam Jack. "If he has a knife, it won't be pleasant," he said to himself. "However, I must be cautious as I get up to him. Ah! there he is. Now, old fellow, what have you got to say for yourself?"

Jack was within about a couple of yards of the Chinese. The man turned his head to look over his shoulder. Jack darted on. At that moment Jack saw an object in the pirate's hand, gleaming from the bright light of a star hitherto obscured. It was a creese. The man turned round to meet him and plunge it into his body; but at the moment he did so Jack dived down, and coming up on the other side of him, caught him by the legs with one hand, while with the other he grasped the arm which held the weapon. His great difficulty was to prevent the pirate from changing the creese from his right-hand to his left. While thus desperately struggling, Jack observed two dark heads close to him, with the most fierce and malignant countenances. The men were probably armed with creeses. Jack expected every moment to feel the sharp blades running into him, when the shouts of his friends alarmed his foes, and they darted away in the hopes of securing their own safety.

Terence and Alick, meantime, naturally felt very anxious for Jack's safety. They shouted loudly his name.

"All right," he sang out; "I have got a fellow, but he is as slippery as an eel, and very hard to hold. Lend a hand here, do."

The tone of his voice showed that he was struggling hard with his prisoner. His friends dashed after him with their boats, but his own boat, of which Needham was coxswain, had already got up to him, and were hauling him and the Chinese on board.

"Look after the other two fellows. They are away there," he shouted, never for a moment losing his presence of mind.

Alick's boat darted after one, Terence's after the other. It was not likely that the men could have got very far; but a black head at midnight on the world of waters is not very discernible. Murray, as his boat pulled on, kept his eyes about him on either side. He caught sight of a head. "There he is," he cried, leaning forward and making a clutch at the pirate. A creese flashed up as he did so, and he got a cut in his arm which was intended for a more vital part. The next instant the man had disappeared; but as his object was to escape, and not to get drowned, he had to come up again to breathe. As he did so, he got his creese ready to give another plunge with it; but the seamen were not quite so green as he supposed, and this time they were ready with the boat's stretchers, and, as he lifted up his arm, he got a blow which sent his formidable weapon to the bottom, and wellnigh broke his arm. This prevented him from diving, and the next instant he was, in spite of his struggles, hauled into the boat, and he found himself lashed with his hands behind him to the after-thwart. There was another prisoner to be accounted for. Terence told his crew not to make a noise as they went in chase. The man was the strongest of the three prisoners. He had taken a circuit, hoping thus to escape unobserved to the shore. It occurred to Terence that this was what very likely one of them would do, and thus before long he caught sight of the man's head, as he swam rapidly through the water. "The fellow swims beautifully," thought Terence, "I'll let him enjoy himself a little longer." The noise made on board the other boats deceived the Chinaman. He fancied that he was not pursued. "We must catch him now," thought Terence, after an interval, and he made a sign to his men to give way, when a loud shriek was heard, the pirate's arms were seen to rise up above his head, and then down he went, like a shot, beneath the waves. Terence shuddered. "Jack shark has caught him," observed one of the crew, and as they pulled over the spot they could see the water still bubbling and agitated, as if some violent struggle was going on beneath its surface. Then all was quiet. The monster had dragged off his prey to be devoured at his leisure.

"I'm heartily glad it was not Jack Rogers," said Terence, as on pulling back he recounted what had occurred.

"Thank you," answered Jack. "It was certainly a terrific risk I ran; but as the fellow had escaped through my negligence, I was determined to catch him at all costs."

How the pirates had managed to conceal their creeses was a wonder which no one could solve, though the seamen declared that they believed they had kept them hid away inside their throats, for they could not have had them anywhere else. After all the noise that had been made there was little hope of concealment, so Mr Cherry ordered the squadron of boats to pull out of the bay and to proceed farther along the shore to the eastward.

Scarcely had they got round the rocky point which had concealed them than they saw right before them a dozen or more dark objects, which, after watching for some time, they made out to be as many large row-boats. They hoped that they were not perceived; so Mr Cherry ordered them to pull back under the shadow of the cliff. On came the boats. It was pretty certain that they were pirates, and that by some means having discovered they were there, their purpose was to surprise them. The guns in the bows of the boats were loaded, as were the muskets which each man had by his side, and the oars were kept out, so that at a moment's notice they might give way after the enemy. As Paddy remarked, "They looked like four huge centipedes ready to dart out on their prey."

The row-boats must have been too far off at the time of the chase of the three prisoners to have heard the shouting, so they probably hoped to catch the British asleep. Mr Cherry was in doubt whether he should attack them unless they were aggressors. They might, after all, be only harmless traders. They glided on pretty rapidly. Soon they had rounded the point, and were making for the spot where the boats had been, when those on board them discovered the Englishmen. They stopped, and then came dashing on towards the point.

"They are enemies," cried Mr Cherry; "give it to them, my lads." A sharp fire of grape, accompanied by musketry from the four boats, right into the bows of the junks, had the effect of arresting their progress. They could not tell how many more boats there might be behind those they saw.

"Reload your pieces, my lads, as fast as you can—quick!" shouted Mr Cherry. It was done before the pirates had recovered from their confusion, and when they once more advanced, a second dose was ready for them. This was given with such good effect that they pulled round to escape. The commanding officer, observing this, ordered his boats to advance. On they dashed, the men loading and firing as they could, till they reached the junks. Then, each boat selecting an antagonist, the seamen leaped on board, and with their cutlasses very soon drove the crew overboard. None of the pirates would yield, and not a prisoner was taken. As some time was expended in this engagement, the remainder of the junks escaped. Where they had gone it was difficult to say in the darkness; but Jack Rogers told Mr Cherry that he thought he had seen them steering for the bay.

Into the bay, therefore, the boats proceeded, and pulled round and round it. In vain they searched, however, and at last Mr Cherry ordered them to bring up and wait till daylight. As soon as it was dawn it was "Up anchor and out oars," and away they pulled again. They had not gone far before they discovered the boats run up on the beach deserted by the crews.

Paddy Adair and Jack were for dashing in at once; but the more prudent lieutenant called them back. He first ordered that all the guns should be loaded and pointed towards some suspicious-looking bushes on a height above the beach, and then directed Terence to pull rapidly in towards the boats, and to set them on fire. The other boats advanced more slowly, two at a short distance to the right and two to the left of him.

Paddy was very much inclined to think all this precaution superfluous. "What's the use of it, when we have only a set of ignorant niggers to deal with?" he observed to Jack, as he pulled on. "Give way, lads." He reached the beach—a light was struck. There was an abundance of dry driftwood thrown up by gales on the shore. Some of it was speedily collected, and they had succeeded in setting one boat in a blaze when, from the suspicious bushes, there came a rattling shower of bullets, and directly afterwards some fifty savages, with creeses in their hands, dashed out towards them.

Two of the Englishmen had fallen, and Terence and the rest rushed to their arms to defend themselves as best they could, though they could not help looking round to see if the other boats were coming to their assistance, when from either side so hot a fire was opened, with grape and bullets, on the pirates, that before they reached the boats they wished to defend, numbers were tumbled over, and the rest turned and fled back into the cover. Before he could allow the boats to advance, Mr Cherry had all the firearms again loaded. Meantime Terence continued to set the boats on fire, and performed the work without molestation.

The lieutenant then led the flotilla to a spot where there were no trees or rocks to shelter an enemy, and leaving three men in each boat, he landed with the rest and advanced to the top of a neighbouring hill. There were no habitations in sight, and as it was agreed that it would be worse than useless to follow the pirates, the party again embarked.

The wounds of the poor fellows who had been hit were bound up, and all possible attention was paid to them. Notwithstanding this, soon after the boats again shoved off, one of them died. It was impossible to keep the body on board, and as landing was dangerous, a shot was fastened to the feet, and with scant ceremony it was launched into the sea.

"Has Bill gone?" asked the other wounded man, with a faint voice, "I wish as how he'd waited a bit before he slipped his cable, so that we could have borne each other company; maybe, if I clap on more canvas, I shall get up with him. Howsomdever, I shan't be long after him, and that's a comfort."

For several hours the boats proceeded on, looking into every bay and creek for signs of inhabitants, from whom they might obtain information.

At last some huts were seen, and the expedition pulled on for the shore. Mr Cherry and about five-and-twenty men landed, and, the ground being open, marched up towards the huts, carrying the two prisoners with them. One of them was then made to understand that he must go and make inquiries as to whether they knew what had become of the two ladies and the other people the pirates had carried off. The man nodded his head and showed that he fully comprehended what he was to do. While they were speaking, some thirty or forty natives appeared at a short distance off. "Understand," added the interpreter, "you may go as far as that tree, so that you may talk to those people, but if you go a foot farther, you will be shot. Remember that we are not joking." The pirate went on, first very slowly, then rather quicker, then faster and faster. The natives shouted, and he cried out something in return. He evidently had friends among them. He reached the tree, he stopped a moment, then he looked back; the marines, looking very grim with their muskets presented, stood ready to fire. He talked on, then he looked again; the desire to escape overcame all his fears. He sprang forward, but, as he did so, half a dozen bullets were lodged in his body. No sooner did he fall, than numbers of natives rushed out from all directions, and began to fire on the English. Giving the marines time to reload, Mr Cherry called his men to charge, and dashing forward with bayonets and cutlasses, they speedily put the enemy to flight. A considerable quantity of European goods of various descriptions was found in the houses; as this proved without doubt that the inhabitants were either pirates or in league with them, the habitations, and such goods as could not be carried off, were committed to the flames. The fields, gardens, and plantations of every description were likewise ruthlessly destroyed.

"It is a cruel necessity," observed Mr Cherry to his subordinates, "but it must be done. The only way that I can see of putting a stop to piracy is to teach the pirates that their trade will not longer answer." Murray was the only one of the party who was not entirely of the lieutenant's opinion. That evening, when they had returned to the boats, he addressed Jack Rogers. "I wonder now, whether it might not answer to catch some of these wild fellows, to show them the beauties and advantages of Christianity and civilisation, and then send them back among their countrymen as a sort of missionaries. Offer to trade with them, and prove to them that honest commerce will be more profitable to them than dishonest piracy. I think this plan would answer our purpose better than burning down their houses and cornfields." Jack was not quite certain which plan he thought the best.

"Ours is the shortest and most simple, at all events," he observed.

"I think not, because our present work can never end," answered Alick. "As soon as we disappear, piracy will again appear; whereas if we teach the people the advantages of commerce, they will not only no longer rob themselves, but it will be their interest to aid in putting down piracy everywhere else."

"Well, Alick, I do believe you are right, as you always are," said Jack. "But, I say, I hope we shall find poor Madame Dubois and Mademoiselle Cecile before long. What a state of fright the poor old lady will be in all this time!" While they were talking, their boats being close alongside each other, Terence was attending to the wounded man in his boat. The poor man grew weaker and weaker.

"I shall not see another sunrise," he remarked. "Bill won't have a day's start of me; so, maybe, after all, he and I will steer the same course alongside each other." He continued talking in the same style to the last, showing clearly that he had his senses perfectly, but that he was painfully ignorant of the truths of religion. Adair thought that he ought to set him right, but did not know how to begin, and, if he had begun, he felt that he should not know how to go on. The seaman's voice grew fainter and fainter, the pale light of of dawn began to appear. Suddenly he lifted himself up, exclaiming with a strong voice, "Yes, Bill, all right; I'm casting off the turns. Good-bye, shipmates. I'm after you, Bill." Then he fell back, and was dead. Scarcely was the body cold before it, too, was lowered into the water, and as the sun rose Mr Cherry gave the order to weigh and continue the voyage. A pleasant breeze sprang up off the land, which carried them along at a good speed. At noon they turned to dine, still continuing under weigh. A lofty headland was before them. No sooner did they round it, than a deep and beautiful bay opened on them, with rocks and high but not precipitous banks. In the very head of it there appeared a large junk anchored close in with the shore.

"That's her!" exclaimed Jack, and Alick, and Captain Willock in the same voice. "It's the very junk which carried off the ladies."

"If it's not her, it's as like as one pea is to another," observed the American skipper. She appeared to be full of men, and numbers came scrambling up from below. It was evident that the boats were unexpected visitors. A few shots were fired at the boats. On this Mr Cherry ordered the sails to be lowered, and the oars being got out, away they dashed towards the junk, getting ready to fire as they approached. Scarcely had one discharge been given, than the pirates were seen to be making their escape from the junk. Some were lowering themselves into the boats which hung alongside, and others were leaping into the water to swim on shore. The nearer the British drew, the more violent were the attempts the pirates made to escape. By the time the boats had got within fifty yards or so of the junk, the greater number had made their escape, and most of them were seen climbing up the hill, or hiding themselves among the rocks. At that moment half a dozen people were seen on the deck, and it appeared to Mr Cherry that they were about to discharge some of their guns before they made their escape. He was just giving the order to fire, when Jack shouted out, "Stop in, stop! They are not pirates. They are Madame Dubois and Miss Cecile, though they are dressed up like Chinamen; and Hudson and Hoddidoddi, and the rest."

The crews of Adair's and Murray's boats were, however, in so great a hurry that they fired before Mr Cherry could countermand his order, and then on they dashed. Jack was dreadfully afraid that the ladies might be hurt, and this made him also eager to get alongside to ascertain. This anxiety was, however, speedily relieved, by the appearance of Miss Cecile on the upper deck of the junk, waving a petticoat, which she had made do duty as a flag of truce. The whole party were soon alongside. Jack was the first on deck. He very nearly burst out laughing when he caught sight of poor Madame Dubois rigged out in a Chinaman's costume, with her hair twisted into a pigtail, and a little round Chinese hat on her head. Miss Cecile had on the same sort of dress, which Jack did not think particularly became her; indeed, she appeared to him to be very different to what she had before seemed when she was instructing him in French. All this time the pirates were scrambling away up the rocks as fast as they could go. So great had been the panic that they had not even taken their arms with them, so that they could not interfere with the proceedings of the conquerors. Mr Cherry did not think it worth while to follow them; indeed, as they appeared to have treated the prisoners well he did not think that he should do right to inflict on them any further punishment than the loss of their vessel and booty. The junk's huge wooden anchor was therefore hove up to her bows, and the boats, taking her in tow, carried her off in triumph out of the bay. Before leaving, however, Mr Cherry told the interpreter to impress on the minds of the two pirate prisoners that, if they returned to their old habits, they would be caught, and if caught they would be hung, but that if they took to any honest calling they would be protected and favoured by the British.

"Go and tell your countrymen this, and don't forget it yourselves," added the interpreter. The men were then landed, and off they scampered to join their friends; but whether or not they benefited by the advice given them, it is impossible to say. Jack, with Mr Cherry and a few of the men, went on board the junk, when Jack inquired of Miss Cecile how it was she and her mamma had come to assume the attire in which he found them clothed.

"Oh, it was all Mr Hudson," answered the young lady. "He say we must, to run away. But poor mamma, she does look very funny, ha! ha! ha!"

"Your respectable relation has certainly a very curious appearance," answered Jack, not particularly well pleased with Miss Cecile's tone. "It strikes me indeed, young lady, that the sooner she changes her dress, the less ridiculous she will appear."

Miss Cecile, however, did not seem to care much about this point, and continued laughing as heartily as before. Hudson afterwards explained that, having found a chest of Chinese clothes in the cabin in which they were shut up, they had dressed themselves in them, in the hopes that thus disguised they should be the better able to make their escape.

Before night the *Blenny* hove in sight, and taking the boats on board and the junk in tow, the expedition returned to Hong Kong, where they found the frigate at anchor. Jack and Alick here bade the companions of their late adventure good-bye. Jack was a little sentimental when parting with Miss Cecile, but he very speedily recovered his usual state of feeling when he heard that she was about to be married to Mr Joe Hudson, the mate of the American brig.

While the *Dugong* and *Blenny* lay at Hong Kong, Captain Hemming was asked to take a poor young gentleman on board, who had suffered from the climate, and was very ill. A trip to sea might give him some chance of recovery. Hemming, in the kindness of his heart, at once consented, without asking who he was, and promised him a berth in his cabin. Scarcely had the stranger been lifted up on deck, than Jack recognised in his features, though pale and sunken, those of his old schoolfellow, Bully Pigeon. He was placed in the shade under an awning on deck. He had not been there long before he sent a boy to call Jack.

"Ah! Rogers," he said, in a faint voice, "I dare say you scarcely like to speak to me; but I am not as bad as I was. I have been thinking a good deal lately, and a friend has talked to me and read to me, and I have seen my folly. I believe in the religion I once laughed at, and I see that, had I before believed in it, I should have been a thousandfold more happy than I was. I have thrown life away, for I shall soon die; but I am not miserable as I was lately, for I know that I shall be forgiven."

The next day the frigate and brig sailed for the north. They had cruised for about a fortnight, when a steamer overtook them, and gave them notice that war had broken out once more between England and China, and that there would be plenty of work cut out for them before long.

Chapter Thirty Four
Promoted

The frigate and the brig which had the honour of conveying the three midshipmen between them, with the south-west monsoon blowing gently aft, proceeded northward among the numberless islands which stud the China seas, looking for the admiral and the rest of the fleet. They were surprised, as they sailed along the mainland, to observe the great number of towns and villages on the shores and vast tracts of country under cultivation. Several times they fell in with small squadrons of large government war-junks, with heavy guns, gaudy flags, flaunting vainly like peacocks' tails, and stout mandarins sitting on their decks. Some tried to escape, and succeeded, but others were caught, and the stout mandarins either were or pretended to be very much astonished that their vessels were lawful prizes to the squadron of Her Britannic Majesty. They received very little commiseration, for it was well-known that they were in league with the pirates who infested those seas, and that when any grand piratical expedition was about to take place, they invariably kept out of the way. Sometimes they passed among whole fleets of tiny fishing-boats, to be counted by thousands, like shoals of fishes, themselves engaged in procuring food for the teeming multitudes on shore, and giving an idea of the vast numbers of the finny tribes which inhabit those seas. Frequently, too, there glided by one of those roguish, rakish, wicked-looking craft—an opium clipper, fleet as the sporting dolphin, and armed to the teeth, for she has foes on every side; the pirates long to make her their prey, and the mandarin junks ought to do so, but dare not.

For several hours the frigate and the brig lay becalmed close together. Alick and Terence went to pay Jack a visit. While they were on board the surgeon sent to tell Jack that Pigeon was very much worse, and desired to see him. Jack hurried into the cabin where he lay; when he heard that his other two old schoolfellows were on board, he begged to see them also. They saw that the stamp of death was already on his countenance.

"I am glad you are come," he said in a very faint voice, trying to lift himself up. "I wish to tell you that I have at last discovered that I have lived a life of folly. I thought myself very clever and very wise, but I now know that I was an arrant fool. I have often said things which might have done you a great deal of harm, but my earnest prayer is that you did not listen to them. What I wish you to do is to point to me, and to guide all your friends or acquaintances against the horrible doctrines which I took up. They only brought me pain and suffering from the first, and wellnigh destroyed my soul at the last; indeed, I feel that it is only through God's grace and mercy that I have been preserved."

The three friends endeavoured to assure the poor dying man that his pernicious doctrines had in no way made any permanent impression on them, though Terence owned that he had often thought over what he had said, and that it had for some time raised all sorts of painful doubts in his mind which he could not get rid of. Their assurance seemed alone to bring him any satisfaction. The interview was short, for he was very weak, and that evening he died. His schoolfellows felt somewhat graver than usual for a short time; but as he had never gained their love they could not pretend to regret him.

Shortly after this they fell in with the admiral, and the whole fleet sailed to the southward. Once more they were off Hong Kong. It was ascertained that large numbers of Chinese war-junks were collected, keeping out of the way, as they fancied, of the outer barbarians, in the various creeks and channels which run into the Canton river. These channels were narrow and shallow in some places, and guarded with forts and booms, and natural as well as artificial bars. Nevertheless the admiral determined to proceed up them with such part of his force most fitted for the work.

The ships of war had congregated in the Blenheim passage of the Canton river. The steamers, which had gone up to explore, had reported that there was a high hill with a strong fort on the top of it on the left of the channel, and other forts on the opposite side, and that above these forts there were no less than seventy large war-junks. The Chinese evidently believed that their hill fort could not be taken. Had they read the history of the battles of the English, they might have had some unpleasant misgivings on the subject.

It was pitch dark as the various boats of the flotilla collected round the steamer on board which the admiral had hoisted his flag. The screw steamers towed up the boats. The three midshipmen managed to keep close to each other. In silence they glided over the smooth water, some small lights on buoys showing the passage up. It was hoped that they might surprise the enemy, but first a rocket on one side and then one on the other, answered by the fleet behind, showed that they were wide awake.

"The dawn is breaking, we shall soon be in the thick of it," observed Jack. Soon after this, just through the grey twilight, a bright flash burst forth high up the hill, followed by a report, and a shot pitched into the water right ahead of the steamer, and sent its spray flying over her. With unabated speed on she went, and now flash after flash burst forth from the hill, and the shot came hissing and bounding on every side round the steamer: still no one was hit. The steamer was making directly for the fort; suddenly she came to a full stop; she had run on a bar formed by the Chinese for the defence of the positions. The boats ran in one upon another; but the oars were got out, and they were soon clear. The order was then given to land, and storm the fort. A steep side of the hill was left unprotected. The simple Chinese were under the impression that no human being could clamber up it. On went the marines and bluejackets in beautiful style, about to show the Chinamen a thing or two. They reached the foot of the hill. Up they climbed, as if it was no impediment whatever; but the Chinamen did their best to stop them. It was no child's work; jingall balls and round shot came crashing down on the assailants, and stink-pots and three-pronged spears; and heads and arms and legs were shot off, and many a tall fellow bit the dust. Post-captains and commanders and lieutenants went ahead of their men, and the midshipmen followed quickly after.

"This puts me in mind of old days on the coast of Syria," observed Murray to Rogers as he thought; but getting no answer, he looked round, and to his dismay discovered that Jack was not by his side.

"He is hit," thought Alick, and it went to his heart that he could not go back to help him; but duty pointed the way to the top of the hill, while the glance over his shoulder had shown him his old schoolfellow rolling down it. Terence, who was a little to the right, also saw what had occurred.

"Oh, we must go and help him," he cried out; but at that instant up jumped Jack again, and began to scramble up the hill with such energy that he was very soon abreast of his friends.

"I am all to rights," he shouted out. "I put my foot on a rolling stone, and over I went."

Terrific was the noise, the shouting and shrieking, loud above all which arose the British hurrahs, as they clashed up the steep ascent. The Chinese happily could not sufficiently depress their guns, or a shower of grape would have made sad havoc in the ranks of the assailants. Now the marines and bluejackets were near the top. A huge Chinaman stood there, pointing his matchlock at Jack. Murray fired his pistol at him, but missed him. The matchlock hung fire, so he dashed it at Alick's head, and then hurled at them a couple of heavy shot. Terence was springing on, when the Chinaman seized a long spear, and was hurling it at him with an accuracy which might have been fatal, when Jack leaped to his friend's aid, and with his pistol shot their enemy dead. The rest of the defenders of the fort, seeing the death of their brave, grinned horribly, and, whisking round their tails, walked leisurely down the opposite side of the hill. More than one volley from the marines was required to make them run. They were braves selected for this post of honour and of danger. Perhaps they had suspicions that their heads might be cut off when they got back to their friends. The English flag was hoisted on the fort, and some of the guns turned down on the fleet of junks below, with whom not very injurious shots were exchanged. The marines occupied it, while the greater part of the bluejackets descended to their boats, the three midshipmen being among the number.

On screwed the steamers, and on dashed the boats. They were soon up with the seventy junks, which began firing away, most furiously, round shot and grape and langrage; the latter, scraps of old iron, they were fond of using, and terrible are the wounds caused by it. The steamers and the boats returned the compliment. Faster and more furious grew the fire from the twelve guns on board each of those seventy big junks; but one, larger than the rest, lay across the channel: the midshipmen dashed at her; a terrific fire of grape saluted them, but they were already close under the guns when they went off, and the shower of missiles passed over their heads. As the Chinamen were looking out, expecting to see their mangled limbs and the fragments of their boats scattered far and wide, the jolly tars, unharmed, were climbing up the side of the junk, and a few pokes with their cutlasses soon sent every mandarin and seaman leaping overboard. Scarcely had the victors time to look about them, than the prize was found to be on fire, fore and aft. "To the boats! to the boats!" was the cry. The seamen had barely time to obey the order and to shove off than up went the junk into the air with a loud roar, and very soon afterwards down came her fragments rattling around the boats, very nearly swamping them, and wounding several poor fellows among their crews. As the boats emerged from the smoke, the rest of the junks were seen in full flight in different directions, but a great number were overtaken, and as the British got alongside the crews deserted them. In many of them the flames immediately burst forth, and one after the other as they drifted on the shore, they blew up. Some were deserted by their crews before they had time to set them on fire. Several, however, escaped, and vanished up some of the unknown creeks to the left. Meantime, the steamers grounded, and at length the boats alone, with the gallant commodore leading, dashed away up the river in hot chase of the fugitives.

Numbers of junks were passed, deserted or stranded. For four miles they pulled on till they reached a fort on an island in the middle of the stream. There was a passage on each side, but so narrow that two boats could not pass abreast. Above it appeared a fleet of junks. Again the shot came rattling furiously among them. Several boats were struck. Many fine fellows, officers and men, were killed. The commodore's boat sank under him, and barely had he time with his crew to leap out of her, than away she drifted with the body of his coxswain, who had been killed, and a favourite dog who would come with him towards the enemy. Several times was the passage attempted, till at length the boats retreated. Their gongs began to sound, and trumpets to bray forth notes of victory; but the Chinese braves were rather premature in their rejoicings. The boats' crews went to dinner, and while thus pleasantly engaged, notice was given that the enemy's junks were getting afloat. The crews sprang to their oars. "On, lads, on!" shouted their gallant leader. Fierce was the fire they had to pass through, more men were killed, and another boat sank. Still enough remained with which to follow the enemy. The narrow passage was passed, and away in hot pursuit after the still flying junks, manned by a hundred rowers, they go. The junks move swiftly, but the shot and shell go faster. One after the other the junks were deserted, but five were still seen ahead. "We must have them all, lads," shouted the commodore. On they went. Suddenly they found themselves with the junks ahead in the centre of a large town with a vast population. "We must get the junks," again shouted the commodore. The crews cheered in response to his appeal. Their shot find out the junks, and they follow. The wise Chinamen leap overboard and swim on to shore. There were plenty of spectators, many thousands looking out of windows, and doors, and balconies, and thinking that those outer barbarians had become rather bold and impudent. But there was a general in the city, and for his military credit he turned out his army to annihilate the invaders. Seeing this, the commodore landed his marines, whose steady fire on the braves sent them to the right about, and made them march back again in double-quick time. The five junks were then taken in tow, and, very much to the enlightenment of the minds of the citizens, were carried away in triumph down the river. Altogether, upwards of eighty war-junks were destroyed or captured, though for each junk thus disposed of the British lost a man killed or wounded.

The three friends met again in the evening. Greatly to their mutual satisfaction none of them had been hit.

"We have had a pretty sharp day's work," exclaimed Jack; "but there's one thing I hope we shall get for it—our promotions."

"And good luck to the wish," cried Adair, who had just filled a glass with wine. "It's little else I have got to look to to keep me in food and clothing. The last letter I got from my dear friends at home gave me the pleasant information that all the family estates have been knocked down, and that it would be rather worse than useless for me to draw any bills in future on my agents. What the knocking down means, I don't quite know; but the matter of the not drawing bills sufficiently elucidates the subject to my mind."

"Oh, that is a trifle," answered Rogers and Murray in a breath. "We are over well supplied, and so you can't want, you know; and then the chances are that, before long, we pick up a good store of prize-money."

"I know, I know, my dear fellows; I never should doubt you," said Adair, warmly; "but— Well, I'll come on you when I am hard up. But perhaps I shall be settled for some other way."

"If it is a pleasant and satisfactory way, I hope so," observed Murray, pretending not to understand him.

The conversation very soon came to an end by Paddy himself falling asleep, an example which the rest of the party, looking out for a soft plank, were not slow in following. After this the three midshipmen and their men returned to their ships, which sailed away on a cruise to the northward.

The *Dugong* one day had sent two of her boats, under charge of Murray and Adair, up a river to obtain fresh provisions. Their comprador, or Chinese purchaser, who acted also as interpreter, having landed to make arrangements, the boats proceeded higher up the river on an exploring expedition. At length they reached a pretty, peaceful-looking village, and were induced by its tempting appearance to go on shore. They strolled about for some time, looking into the houses, the natives treating them with perfect civility. At last Murray suggested that it was time to return.

"A few minutes more. See, there is a curious pagoda, let us go and visit it."

The pagoda was explored; and the priests of Buddha were seen burning paper matches before the altar.

"We have had a pleasant trip. These Chinamen are really good sort of fellows," observed Terence; but scarcely had he spoken, than they discovered a strong body of soldiers drawn up between them and their boats. Not a word was said; but as they advanced the troops opened fire with their jingalls and darted their pronged spears at them.

"We must cut our way through the villains," cried Murray. "If we let them press on us we are done for."

"I'm with you," exclaimed Adair. "Charge, lads."

With loud shouts the British seamen dashed on; but the Chinese outnumbered them as twenty to one, besides being all armed with jingalls, matchlocks, or spears. Even Murray more than once thought that it was all up with them. He was slightly wounded, a ball had gone through both of Adair's legs, and he was bleeding much, while four of their men were killed, and two others so desperately hurt that they were unable to walk without the aid of their companions. Every moment they were growing weaker and weaker. Adair, too, was suffering dreadfully from his wounds. "I can stand it no longer," he exclaimed, at last sinking on the ground. "Go on, Alick. Leave me to my fate. If you attempt to stop you will be cut to pieces. See, there are more of the fellows gathering round us."

"Leave you, Terence? I hope not," cried Murray. "Come on, lads; we'll soon put the villains to flight."

Lifting up their wounded companions, the seamen made another dash at the enemy. The treatment which the dead bodies of their comrades met with showed them that they had death alone to expect, unless they gained the victory. The moment the bodies were left the Chinese rushed forward, and cutting off their heads, stuck them on the ends of their spears, shouting in triumph.

There is something particularly dreadful in seeing the head of a comrade, who but a few short moments before was full of life, thus exposed. Poor Adair looked up. "Will my head be soon thus placed?" he said to himself. There seemed too much probability of it. Another man was so desperately wounded that he could not walk. The party, thus reduced in strength, could no longer push on towards the boats. When they halted, the Chinamen became more daring. Back to back they stood, forming a hollow square, like brave men, with their wounded comrades in the centre, resolved to sell their lives dearly if they could not drive back their assailants. Murray was again wounded. He felt himself fainting through the loss of blood. Another man sank to the ground, and several more were hit. Still, loading and firing as fast as they could, they kept the enemy at bay. Yet even Murray believed that it was only a matter of time, and that every one of them would soon be numbered among the dead. Still, by voice and example, he endeavoured to keep up the courage of the men with him. At last he had to tell one of them to hold him up, for he could scarcely see the enemy crowding round them. It was a bad sign, the courage of some of the seamen began to waver, and they looked wistfully towards the boats, as if they would make a rush at them. Great was their dismay to see a body of Chinese hurry down to the bank and begin to fire at the men in them. Their only chance of escape appeared destroyed. At that moment a shout was heard, followed by a rapid fire of musketry; and then came the sound of a big gun, and the peculiar rattle and crash of grape. The Chinese attacking the boats wavered and fled, followed by those between the English and the river; and a party of bluejackets and marines, headed by Jack Rogers, was seen hurrying up from the water. There was no time to be lost. The Chinese might recover from their panic; so lifting Adair and Murray on their shoulders, with the other wounded people, his men carried them to the boats. The Chinamen looked with astonishment at what had occurred, and then, recovering their senses, rushed down again towards the boats; but, though they were too late to get back their prey, they got more than they expected; for Jack Rogers, ordering the boats once more to pull round so as to present their bows to the enemy, a rattling fire of grape was thrown among them, which once more very rapidly sent them to the rightabout.

Considering the number of wounded, Jack very wisely pulled down the river as fast as he could go. He meantime had the hurts of the wounded men bound up. Murray soon recovered, but Adair continued so weak that his friends became very anxious for his safety. Jack told Murray that the *Blenny* had come in directly after the expedition had started—that he had been sent up to obtain provisions at the village where they had landed the comprador, and that from that personage he had received so alarming an account of the disposition of the natives higher up, that he had hurried on in case they might be attacked. Jack was heartily glad when he got his wounded friends on board the frigate. The doctor looked grave when he saw Adair. Murray, he said, was in no danger. No one could have been better nursed than was poor Terence, and he at length gave signs that he was recovering his strength, and the doctor looked brighter when he spoke of him.

Some weeks had passed, when the frigate and brigs were standing in for the land, a steamer hove in sight, and a signal was made that she had the mail-bags on board. It was the first day Terence had been able to sit up in the midshipmen's berth. Jack had come on board to see him. A long, official-looking letter was handed to each of them, "On Her Majesty's Service." One was addressed to Lieutenant Jack Rogers, another to Lieutenant Alick Murray, and a third to Lieutenant Terence Adair. There was a general shout, and warm congratulations were showered on them. I ought to have said that, when last in England, they had all passed their examination for navigation, having before that passed for seamanship. They were in reality, what were then called master's mates, a rank to which the more satisfactory title of sub-lieutenants has been given. They were appointed to different ships on the station; when in their new rank they performed a number of very gallant acts, which may some day be chronicled for the benefit of my friends. However, as they now belong to a higher rank, I must bring to a termination the adventures of my old schoolfellows, the Three Midshipmen.